---

about the author

---

chad kultgen graduated from the University of Southern California School of Film and Television. He lives in California. This is his first book.

the average american male

the **average** american **male**

a novel

chad kultgen

HARPER

Harper
An imprint of HarperCollins*Publishers*
77–85 Fulham Palace Road,
Hammersmith, London W6 8JB

www.harpercollins.co.uk

A Paperback Original 2007
1

A catalogue record for this book
is available from the British Library

978 0 00 726398 1

Printed and bound in Great Britain by
Clays Ltd, St Ives plc

the average american male

Christmas with Mom and Dad

Same old bullshit.

The Flight Back to L.A.

It's two days after Christmas. I'm in Denver International Airport watching this old fat bitch eat a cup of yogurt. My blood is boiling.

She has this weird little baby spoon, and these leathery fucking jowls, and this twitchy mouth, and her little tongue keeps jerking around to lick this shit off her lips — it's really fucking disgusting me. But even more disgusting to me is the fact that her mouth has had cocks in it. I wonder what it is, other than age, that turns a mouth a man would want to put his cock in into a twitching hole getting yogurt shoveled into it with a baby spoon.

At some point in this old cunt's life some guy was paying for her dinner, buying her presents, and being as nice and romantic as possible just so he could put his cock in that disgusting fucking hole.

On the plane —

There's a girl sitting next to me with red hair and perfect rock-hard C cups. She can't be more than nineteen and I'd love to know her name so I could see if it fits. I don't ask her even though she'd probably tell me, and it might even lead to a full-on conversation, which might lead to something else, like getting her number or taking her out to dinner. Instead, I just lean back, get a big whiff of her shampoo, and wonder if she could ever possibly know that I'll think about her for the next few weeks every time I jerk off. Probably not.

And I'm out like a light.

I'm still in a weird kind of dream when I get off the plane at LAX so I'm not sure if Trent Reznor walks past me at the Delta baggage claim. I am sure that the redhead is standing by me, and even though I don't have any bags to wait for, she does, so I pretend to.

I look at her luggage tag when she picks up her suitcase. Alyna Janson. It fits.

Satisfied, I go wait for twenty minutes to pay twenty dollars to ride a SuperShuttle back to my apartment in Westwood. Coincidentally enough, Alyna gets on the same SuperShuttle and tells the driver she's going to UCLA, two blocks from my house.

I stare at her without her knowing or caring until we get to her stop. When she gets out I don't make any effort to move out of her way, so she has to brush me with her ass, and she has a nice fucking ass.

When I get off the bus at my own stop I'm glad I never talked to Alyna. When I walk through my front door I wish I had. When I hit my bed, I'm glad I have a girlfriend I can fuck on a regular basis. When I wake up the next morning to a phone call begging me to spend my last days off going to the gym and shopping at Century City with her, I wish I didn't.

Casey at the Gym

Casey has a fat ass. She's a pretty cute brunette with a completely normal upper body, just with a big fat ass attached. She knows it's fat and got a membership to my gym so she could go with me and "get cute tight buns." She even toyed with the idea of getting a personal trainer and she bought an exercise book called *The Daily Butt Regimen*.

So I'm sitting on the calf machine ready to put my head through the fucking mirror. Casey's across the gym, smiling at me, doing curls. For the past six months, since she started her ass-slimming campaign, all she's done is fucking curls and bench presses—and her ass shows it.

I've tried to get her to do squats with me, leg presses, quad extensions, hamstring machine, any fucking thing having even the most remote influence on the movement of muscles in her lower body, and she always says, "I think I'll just do some curls."

I finish my set and move to another part of the gym so I can't see her.

That night, after suffering through a TiVoed three-episode *Real World* marathon, I'm rewarded by her letting me fuck her doggie style. As I look down at her fat ass, I wonder if fucking her hard enough will have any kind of slimming or toning effect. Couldn't hurt.

chapter three

Century Fucking City

The one good thing you can always count on at Century City, and any place in this fucking city for that matter, is that there will always be a shitload of hot bitches with perfect bodies walking around. As chance would have it, I'm staring at one when my girlfriend says, "Do you wish I looked like that?"

I wonder if the three hours I've spent looking at shoes and other gay shit could possibly earn me one second of honesty with Casey. Probably not. Instead of answering her, I just look up at nothing in particular and say, "Do you smell pizza? I'm hungry."

On our way to the food court we pass a bookstore with a big line of middle-aged women, housewives mostly, some with kids, snaking out the front door. None of them are hot. They all seem like they're from the Valley or maybe Pasadena. I hate myself for being able to make the distinction. The window advertises that Marie Osmond is inside signing copies of her book *Behind the Smile: My Journey Out of Postpartum Depression*. I turn my head to ask Casey if she wants pizza, too, but she's already in line behind a woman who has a fat ass similar to her own and could easily be Casey's future self.

I'm pretty sure Casey knew about this and actually wanted to come to Century City just to see Marie Osmond, which means the fucking hours of looking at stupid shit were just insult to injury. Because of this, I kind of want to disappear into the food court and spend the rest of the day changing my phone number, but I decide it's not worth the effort of finding someone else to have regular sex with and get in line with my girlfriend.

Future Casey turns around and begins the following unsolicited conversation:

"Are you fans of Marie?"

Casey says, "I love her. I think it took so much courage to write about what she went through."

Future Casey says, "You know, a lot of women go through postpartum depression." She holds up her right hand like she's swearing on a Bible before she testifics, then she testifies, "Speaking from experience here. And I think this book is really going to help a lot of us. I mean it just makes me feel better to know that even somebody as important as Marie Osmond has felt what I felt."

I then end the conversation with this: "Maybe that woman in Houston who drowned all five of her kids should have read it."

Future Casey turns around and buries her nose in the latest issue of *Women's Health* magazine. Casey gives me an accusatory stare. I respond by saying, "I guess Marie can't help everyone." Casey responds by rolling her eyes and picking up the most recent issue of *O* from the magazine rack, which the bookstore has conveniently moved outside and stocked only with *O* and *Us Weekly*.

She reads it for the next fifteen minutes while we wait. I read it over her shoulder and these are the results:

Pictures of Oprah: Twenty-two (including her standard cover appearance).

"Articles" "written" by Oprah: Six (including the O magazine staple "What I Know for Sure," in which Oprah lies about how hard her life is and hammers home how much more spiritual she is than the average person).

Uses of the phrase "Self-realization": Ninety-four (in thirteen different "articles").

Ads for Oprah-related products: Seven (including one for Dr. Phil's show).

Paragraphs containing poorly veiled condescension: Four hundred sixty-three.

Impulses to ram the magazine up Oprah's cunt: One (that lasts for the entire fifteen minutes I stare at O).

The other conversations around us might as well be the same as the one Future Casey started with Casey, the main difference being that I can't stop any of the others with the uneasiness of honesty. I try to keep myself entertained by explaining to Casey the importance of the Nintendo Wii as a next-gen console actually being able to compete in the marketplace against the vastly more powerful Xbox 360 and PS3. She reopens O. So I decide to just stand there and not listen to the cackling around me.

This is what I hear: "Marie Osmond has amazing courage. . . . Marie Osmond is a genius writer. . . . This book should win an Oscar, or whatever the writing Oscar is. . . . The writing Oscar is the Nobel Prize. . . . She's a hero. . . . Yesterday Dr. Phil was giving women the courage to leave abusive relationships and lose weight at the same time. . . . Today I think the Dr. Phil show is about teaching women how to be independent. . . . Dr. Phil is probably a great husband. . . . Cloning and stem cell research is evil because they have to murder babies to do it. . . . If Oprah was sick or dying, it would be worth sacrificing one child to save her, though. . . . Carney Wilson wrote a courageous book about her lifelong battle with weight. . . . It took amazing courage to have her stomach surgically reduced to the size of a thumb."

The uneasy rage all of this creates in me starts out as something general, shapeless. But as it continues and we move up in line, Marie Osmond becomes the focus of everything I feel and the reason I feel it. I leer at her.

She smiles the same smile every few minutes. She sips from the same lipstick-smeared Diet Coke can every few minutes. She gives the same genuinely concerned expression every few minutes. She checks the same clock on the back wall every few minutes. She makes the same $150 every few minutes.

I try to calm myself by thinking about the fact that someday this woman will die, when she says, "Who should I make this out to?" and we're standing a foot away from the courageous Marie Osmond.

Casey says, "Casey Childress, please," and continues with, "I really love your work and I'm a huge fan."

Osmond follows up with a concerned face and, "Well, I just hope this book has helped at least a few women out there."

I want to say something mean, something wrong, something that will make me feel like this entire day isn't a complete waste, but I know if I do Casey won't suck my dick until tomorrow at least, maybe even the next day. So I shut up and steal a quick peek down Osmond's shirt while she's signing the book. Not bad for an older bitch.

She looks back up at Casey, smiles, and says, "There you go, thanks." I picture myself behind her, pushing her head down on the table right in the middle of all her books and fucking her until she goes catatonic. I smile and say, "Thank you, Ms. Osmond." Then we leave.

Back at Casey's place, I kiss her and take off her shirt. "Aren't we frisky?" she says.

"No, I'm fucking horny and I want to fuck you right now," I whisper, knowing after a year of being in this relationship that whispering "fuck" in her ear makes her feel naughty enough to let me do anything I want to her. She unzips my pants as I sit down on her couch. She jerks me off a little before I push on her head and she gets the hint to stop fucking around and suck my cock. While she does, I look over at

Marie Osmond's smiling face on the cover of Casey's new book. I pretend Casey's mouth is Osmond's cunt and I try to hear Casey slurping as Osmond sobbing. Aside from Casey spitting my semen all over my stomach, which she always fucking does, it ends up ranking in my top five blow jobs of all time.

chapter four

Brunch

Casey's telling me that she doesn't like it when I come to her house drunk. She says, "Last night was like having sex with a different person."

I want to ask her if that's good or bad, but by the time the question gets to my mouth I'm thinking about the dream I had last night and Casey still has a lot more to say, so I never do.

The dream:

I'm walking around the halls of my old junior high trying to find my locker. I think it's on the second floor, but the school doesn't have a second floor. So I go to the principal's office to get a map and a piece of bubble gum, which for some reason I'm sure will help me. Once I get there, though, the office is really this comic book store I used to hang out in when I was a kid, and Alyna, the girl that sat next to me on the plane, is leaning up against a magazine rack reading an old issue of The New Mutants.

I say, "What's the deal? Where's my locker?"

She says, "I don't know." Then she kisses me with one of those dream kisses that make you think when you wake up you'll have been married to the person who kissed you for twenty of the happiest years of your life.

I get tipped off that this probably isn't real when my old family dog who died when I was ten walks in and says, "Do you guys have change for a five?"

At that point I was just a little too conscious to hold on to it and I woke up with that awful empty feeling you get when you realize the person who can make you happier than anything is a fucking dream.

Casey's chewing off the corner of a grilled cheese sandwich and I'm so sick of the fucking cows on the walls in this place and the bitchy waitress. I think I smell dirt but it's just the hippie-type girl next to me with blonde dreadlocks and a bent-up straw cowboy hat.

Casey says, "You don't like the cows? I think they're the cutest."

And I guess I must've said that last bit out loud. I wonder if the hippie cowgirl heard me, but she's not looking at me so fuck it.

I think very briefly about asking Casey what she thinks about all day. Instead I stare at our waitress's ass as she refills a butter tub and wonder if Oprah Winfrey sucks cock, or ever has for that matter.

An Average Sunday

9:20 A.M. Wake up with a hard-on.

9:21 A.M. Start jerking off to the bonus gangbang on *Cum Guzzlers* DVD left in DVD player from last night.

9:24 A.M. About to shoot my wad, flip the TV to a TiVoed episode of *The View* I keep for just this purpose and get supreme satisfaction in imagining what any of the bitches from this show would think if they knew I just blew a load into a dirty pair of underwear while watching their program.

9:25 A.M. Watch MTV for an hour even though I've already seen everything aired in that hour.

10:25 A.M. Try in vain to crack the top ten online scores for Mutant Storm Reloaded in the Xbox 360 Arcade.

11:16 A.M. Take good shit.

11:22 A.M. Try Mutant Storm Reloaded again. Quit after getting blown up on level sixty-four.

12:36 P.M. Check e-mail. Take opportunity while online to download some porn. Best of seventeen downloads is a 1:15 clip with sound called pussstretch.mpg in which a woman inserts a vibrating dildo into her cunt while a guy fucks her from behind at the same time. Loop it on my Windows Media Player and jerk off.

12:50 P.M. Put on clothes and walk to the LA Fitness in Westwood. Think about the first time I fucked a mulatto girl named Mary Cook as I walk.

1:04 P.M. Flirt with hot bitch behind the desk at the gym. Imagine fucking her in the whirlpool next to the women's dressing room.

1:06 P.M. Hate lifting weights.

2:18 P.M. Walk to Quiznos. Flirt with hot college bitch while she makes my foot-long Italian on white. Imagine fucking her with her ass in the lettuce bin. Smile at three hot sorority bitches sitting at a table in the back while I eat.

2:33 P.M. Pass another hot college bitch on my walk back home. Say hi to her. Think about what it would be like to fuck her in my shower. Consider asking her if she'd like to fuck—no strings.

2:46 P.M. Take off clothes in preparation for shower. Jerk off standing up over the crapper thinking about fucking Alyna, the girl on the plane, doggie style. Blow load in toilet.

2:52 P.M. Take shower. Wonder what Casey's doing. Think about Casey fingering herself. Want a blow job. Wish I was still in college. Regret missed opportunities.

3:02 P.M. Think about getting a haircut. Wonder who will be the next Nirvana. Remind myself that one day the sun will destroy this planet so nothing really matters.

3:03 P.M. Lie in bed. Catch a faint whiff of Casey's pussy in my sheets. Realize the cunt smell is actually on my face. Take a deep breath.

3:05 P.M. Check empty mailbox.

3:06 P.M. Watch an old episode of *Martin* in which Snoop Dogg guest stars as himself and throws a house party in Pam's apartment. Martin and Gina are too busy arguing to make it to the party on time. When they finally get there, all they find is a note left by Pam, Tommy, and Cole explaining that they all went with Snoop to an after-party on his pimp jet.

3:31 P.M. Feel balls for lumps.

3:32 P.M. Get a hard-on. Jerk off to a disintegrated VHS copy of *Beautiful Black Fuckers*. Blow load to memory of Mary Cook in the sixty-nine.

3:38 P.M. Hook up the 8-bit Nintendo. Start to play Contra. Get bored. Really want to play Super Mario Bros. but can't find the cartridge. Turn my room upside down looking for it.

3:47 P.M. Find *Footloose* cassette I received from Lisa Franklin for fifth-grade birthday. Wonder what happened to Lisa. Imagine what she looks like now. Imagine titty-fucking her adult version. Think better of it. Imagine fucking her doggie style.

3:48 P.M. Play *Footloose* cassette. Imagine being back in the fifth grade. Wonder if anybody was fucking in the fifth grade. Wonder if I could have even gotten a hard-on in fifth grade. Try to remember the first time I got a hard-on. Can't.

3:50 P.M. Think about the girls I could have fucked in junior high.

3:53 P.M. Think about the girls I could have fucked in high school.

3:57 P.M. Think of all the hot bitches from high school that I never fucked who are now married. Wonder if I'll ever fuck a bitch who's unbelievably hot.

3:59 P.M. Wish I was famous.

4:00 P.M. Wish I was rich.

4:01 P.M. Decide not to make bed again. Check eBay for Street Fighter II arcade game. Bid $10.00 on 1983 child's-size medium Skeletor Halloween costume. Bid $12.50 on Hypercolor "like new" size large T-shirt. Bid $2.00 on naked lady lighter.

4:17 P.M. Log on to World of Warcraft Proudmoore server and play my Tauren Hunter. Farm gold in Burning Steppes because there's nothing else to do.

8:34 P.M. Lose connection to server. Get call from Casey. Receive command to go to her house.

9:06 P.M. Get to Casey's house. Force her to watch *UFC Unleashed* with me. Want to fuck the round card bitch.

10:01 P.M. Watch the news. Want to fuck the news bitch. Look at Casey. Wish she had tits like the news bitch.

10:37 P.M. Wonder if any bitch actually really likes to be titty-fucked. Probably.

10:40 P.M. Take off my clothes and go into Casey's bedroom.

10:42 P.M. Lie in Casey's bed naked. Watch MTV. Seen it all this morning. Watch it anyway.

11:00 P.M. Watch Leno/Letterman.

12:30 A.M. Watch Conan/Kimmel.

1:07 A.M. Get head.

1:16 A.M. Wish Casey was the round card bitch from UFC while I fuck her.

1:32 A.M. Bullshit way through overly emotional postsex conversation about future of relationship while trying to stay awake. Hope for memory of conversation to stick in case she ever references it again.

1:48 A.M. Hear I love you, say I love you.

1:52 A.M. Welcome dreamless sleep.

chapter five

Groundlings Party

After a phone conversation with my friend Todd in which he tells me to rent *The Gift* because Katie Holmes is nineteen in it and she shows her tits, which are slightly hangy but still great C cups, Casey calls me. She says, "My improv class is having a party tonight and it's on the west side so you have to drive."

I pick Casey up and realize that she looks better for this party than she did on our first date. I wonder if there's a guy in her Groundlings class she wants to fuck, or maybe has fucked already. I don't ask her.

At the party—

The place is nice, the booze is free, and to my surprise there are actually some pretty hot bitches roaming around. It seems tolerable. I see Casey talking to some people in the living room so I head to the opposite end of the house, where I approach the hottest bitch I can find and instigate the following train wreck:

"How's it going?"

"I'm Julie." She puts out her hand.

I shake it, say, "Nice to meet you," and notice she smells fucking great—clean.

"I haven't seen you in class. Are you in intermediate?"

"I'm actually not in Groundlings."

"Well, what do you do?"

"Nothing interesting or important."

She laughs one of those laughs that says *Will & Grace* is her favorite show. Then she says, "Oh, that's so funny. You must be in class . . . or maybe . . . are you a Groundling trying to come to this party on the DL? Coming here to scout? You know, I've gone through intro and basic and now I'm in intermediate and I didn't even have to repeat once. My teacher, Tim, said Phil Hartman is the only Groundling who never had to repeat a class. But I'm keeping my fingers crossed. Tim told me I'm kind of a cross between Victoria Jackson, Molly Shannon, and Ellen Cleghorne. What do you think? Here, I'll do one of my characters."

She puts on a bad Russian accent and says, "I try to git vith ze man from Amerika, but all he vants ees ze sex vith eighteen-yer-uld."

She bows. "What do you think? It's like a Russian mail-order bride who's too old and ugly to get an American guy interested in her."

"Ouch!" I grab my head and act like I got hit by something. I walk away from Julie and wind up in the kitchen with two other hot bitches who are having the following conversation:

Hot Bitch #1 says, "I think *MADtv* is having auditions."

Hot Bitch #2 says, "My character work isn't strong enough for that yet."

"Mine either. I'm thinking about taking some WOW classes."

"I heard those really help keep you sharp."

I decide it's time to insert myself with, "What's going on?"

I get the "fuck off" eyes from both of them.

Hot Bitch #2 says, "Who are you? Are you even in class?"

"No, I'm here with some friends."

Hot Bitch #1 says, "Who?"

I remember the teacher's name. "Tim."

Hot Bitch #2 changes her tune pretty fucking quick. "You know Tim?"

"Yeah. We're good friends."

Hot Bitch #1 says, "I'm Jenny. Jenny Gilmer."

Hot Bitch #2 says, "Sharon."

They take turns saying, "Has Tim said anything about me? Does he think I'm funny? Has he said who he's passing on to the next level?" Plus at least five more minutes of explaining why they're the funniest girls in their class and how they're going to join Phil Hartman as the only Groundlings who never had to repeat.

I want to get the fuck out and I can't think of anything better, so this is what they get: "I have to take a shit."

I walk away hoping Casey will talk to whoever the fuck she has to talk to so I can get out of here, go back to her house, and pretend to accidentally finger her asshole before I fuck her. I also decide to get completely drunk immediately and not talk to anyone else for the rest of the night.

Once I'm finally drinking scotch straight from the bottle and telling any girl who tries to start up a conversation with me that she's too fat to talk to, I find myself standing in front of a TV watching Conan O'Brien.

Some complete asshole says, "Conan is so passé. I mean really, he's like the Jim Carrey of late night."

Some other fuckhead says, "You're so right. I mean, the Triumph bit is played out." I break my rule about not talking to anybody with, "Hey, ass-eyes, all that money you're spending on Groundlings classes is really paying off, 'cause it sure is funny that you're criticizing Conan fucking O'Brien when you're just standing here in a fucking jacket like a turd."

Even as I'm saying this shit, I know it only makes vague sense at best and people are looking, so I tack on, "P.S. You're gay."

I don't know why I say the last part, but it gets some laughs, which are hushed pretty quickly, and all of a sudden I'm the drunk guy at the party who nobody knows. Where the fuck is Casey?

I turn to get the fuck out and stumble a little bit. I don't fall or anything, just a little drunken stumble, and Fucknose says, "Hey, why don't you try some walking lessons," which is retarded but of course gets big laughs from all his cronies. I fight the urge to piss all over the floor and I really want to say, "P.P.S. You're a fucking idiot," but I'm pretty sure I need to lie down. So I stagger off down some hallway, wondering how Casey can associate with these fucks and genuinely wishing she would take me back to her place and just hold me for a while, which makes me realize this is the most drunk I've been since college.

I find a room that's not a bedroom, but it's dark and it has a door I can close so I go in. There's a washer, a dryer, an ironing board, a shitload of unpacked boxes, and a girl that might as well be one of the bitches I talked to earlier passed out on the floor in the corner.

I lock the door behind me, leave the lights off, and hit the floor hard enough to wake the bitch up from her booze coma.

She says, "What took you so long? I thought you just had to go to the bathroom."

The five words she doesn't actually slur sound like mush by the time they get to my booze-soaked brain so I have no fucking clue what she just said. But when she starts unbuttoning my pants and licking my belly button, I'm pretty sure she thinks I'm somebody else. Even though the room's pitch black, I can tell it's spinning just before I pass out.

I come to and I'm kind of surprised by somebody licking my balls and jerking me off. I'm even more surprised by the fact that I'm wearing a rubber. For some reason I become horrified at the possibility that the tongue on my nuts belongs to a guy. I reach down and squeeze two very well-made tits unencumbered by any clothing and my mind's at ease. The room's spinning a little but it's kind of nice in conjunction with the blow job from a complete stranger.

I realize that I'm actually cheating on Casey by letting this bitch suck my cock. At first I think the complete absence of guilt is directly related to the amount of booze I've been drinking. But somewhere through the spinning haze a bright and strange ray of truth emerges. It's not the booze, it's the ease. I would probably cheat on Casey all the time if I had to put out as little effort to do it as I am right now, drunk or sober.

From my crotch I hear, "So you're going to move me to advanced, right?"

I am fucking clueless. I don't answer.

She stops. "Tim, you're gonna move me up if I do this, right?"

I've never met Tim but I bet his voice sounds something like this: "Yeah, keep going."

I'm pretty hammered and it takes what I estimate to be fifteen minutes to get anywhere near shooting a load. It's when I'm squeezing her tit with one hand and controlling the pace of her head bobs with the other that I feel her start to finger my asshole. It's a first for me and it doesn't feel good per se, but it's not as bizarre as I might once have thought. More than anything, it gives me an idea.

"You know I can pull some strings for you even after the next level if you're willing to do a little extra."

"Are you saying you can get me in Sunday Company?"

"What do you think?"

"Well, I guess you are one of the people who votes on it . . . what do you want me to do?"

Thirty seconds later I'm balls-deep in her asshole and she seems to like it, corroborating my suspicion that all women secretly like being ass-fucked. I tell her to talk dirty, so she says, "Oh yeah, fuck my ass. Fuck it harder." So I do for another few minutes, then I pull out, peeling the rubber off as I do so it's still hanging out of her asshole when I turn her around and shoot a load all over her face and in her mouth.

I lie back in the dark and start pulling my pants back up. She's wiping my semen out of her eyes with a towel she found in the dryer. Wanting to be faithful to Tim, who I can only imagine is a complete fucking asshole, I say, "Welcome to Hollywood."

She's working on a glob of cum stuck in her hair, wondering if Phil Hartman ever had to do this, when I go back to the party, which has started to die down. I'm getting some weird looks from people who all look semi-familiar to me. One guy looks at me and says, "Get lost in the toilet?" Then they all start laughing and I'm trying to piece together what happened before I fucked that girl in the ass, but I get nothing. So I decide it's probably some stupid fucking Groundlings inside joke and head out back.

I make it outside and find Casey without incident. She's talking to some guy, and when I come walking up she says, "Tim, this is my boyfriend."

I've got a huge smile on my face when I say, "It's great to finally meet you. I've heard so much about you, I feel like I already know you," and I shake his hand with the one I used to prime that girl's asshole before I fucked it.

All guys know the look of knowing you're about to get some pussy, and that's the one that's on Tim's face when he checks his watch and says, "Great, great to meet you. I was just telling Casey here that I was supposed to meet up with another student of mine a few minutes ago." He leaves.

I look over at Casey and she might as well be in junior high dreaming about marrying her fucking history teacher. I want to puke. Instead, I know the shit's going to hit the fan pretty soon, so I say, "Let's get outta here, go someplace where it's just us." I flash my best "I love you" smile and it drills through her adolescent fantasy about Tim.

"Okay, that sounds good. Let's go."

Casey's cats are watching us fuck and I can't help but wonder if that girl realized I wasn't Tim after the fact, but kept it to herself and sucked the real Tim's cock when he went in that room anyway.

Casey cums. I'm not even close and I'm incredibly bored so I fake it, look her in the eyes, say, "I love you," kiss her forehead, wait until she falls asleep, go in the bathroom, and jerk off to memories of the girl I butt-fucked a few hours earlier.

chapter six

My Gay Buddy

I have one gay friend. His name's Carlos and I've known him since college. We eat lunch every Saturday at the California Pizza Kitchen in the Beverly Center.

It's just such a Saturday and I'm sitting on a bench outside CPK flipping through an *LA Weekly* waiting for Carlos to show up. This girl sits down next to me and I notice she's hot as fuck. I further notice that she's more than just hot as fuck. She has some quality that makes me think I could live with her. She smiles at me.

I say, "How're you doing?"

"Fine."

I almost get in another sentence when Carlos shows up and says, "So you ready to have lunch with your favorite cocksucker?"

I want to explain to this girl that I'm not gay, that Carlos is just my gay friend, but she's already laughing and I notice that her tits are a little saggy. So I just get up and follow Carlos into CPK.

We sit down, order the same shit we always do, and Carlos starts up a conversation that's pretty much identical to a million we've had before. He wants to be an agent, but not at Paradigm, where he's currently an assistant. He always gets crushes on straight masculine guys. He's never going to find a fag who's masculine enough to satisfy him. And he rounds it out with some other shit about life not going the way he wants it to.

As the waiter walks away from the table after setting down our drinks, the following conversation takes place:

Carlos says, "I'd like him to plow my ass like a cabbage field."

"Tell him that the next time he comes over and see if it works."

"Hell, it wouldn't be the first time."

"What? You've just come out and told some guy that you want him to 'plow your ass' and then you go do it?"

"Yep."

"I don't fucking believe that."

"It's not the same as how you poor cunt-lickers have to deal with women. Think about it. If a woman came up to you and said she wanted to fuck your cock till it broke, you'd go home with her in a heartbeat, right?"

"Yeah."

"But a woman would never be that honest and no guy can say anything even close to honest to a woman if he ever wants to get laid. But if you just get rid of all that woman shit, all you've got left is two guys who want to fuck and have no problem telling each other as much."

"So in a bar you just go up to a guy and say, 'Let's fuck,' and within fifteen minutes you're back at one of your places fucking?"

"Not exactly. This is where the whole woman thing has its benefits. Once you straight assholes know there's going to be fucking, there's never any question about who's fucking and who's getting fucked. With two faggots, that's the only question. Usually before you even bring up the possibility of fucking, you ask, 'Are you a top or a bottom?'"

"What're you?"

"I'm a bottom all the way."

"So you let guys fuck you in the ass?"

"I beg them to. It's the only way I can cum."

"So you don't ever actually put your dick in anything? You don't even like getting your dick sucked?"

"I tried it once, but couldn't finish. I suck dick and take it up the ass and that's all I do."

"You must be pretty popular."

"Please, ninety percent of the faggots on this planet are bottom boys and most of 'em are far better looking than me."

"So most gay guys don't like to fuck, they want to be fucked?"

"Think about it, if we wanted to put our dicks in a hole, we could just get a girl. Speaking of, how're you and Casey doing?"

"Same old bullshit."

"Is that good or bad?"

"It's just . . . the same."

"I guess that's better than bad. Is she still doing Groundlings?"

"Yeah."

"You know, I met some guy at a party last week who said he was in Groundlings. I offered to suck his cock, but he was a complete bottom, too. That's usually how it works."

"So what happens with two bottoms?"

"The same thing that would happen if you met a girl who told you the only way she could get off was to strap on a dildo and fuck you in the ass and she would never suck your cock or let you fuck her . . . you never talk to each other again. Unless, of course, you're both drunk and horny and no other prospects are shaping up. Then you go home together, try to fuck each other with limp dicks, and then get out the dildos."

"So you use dildos on other guys instead of your own dicks?"

"I'm a fucking bottom, that's what I've been trying to tell you."

The waiter hears that last bit before he sets down our lunch. I think I see him flash Carlos a smile before leaving.

The rest of the lunch conversation is less interesting, mostly about

Reese Witherspoon's movies and mostly coming from Carlos. When we get the check there's another piece of paper with it that Carlos picks up, reads, and then shows me.

It reads, "I would love to plow your tight ass," followed by a number.

Closure

I get an e-mail from Jenna.

It reads, "I don't know exactly how to tell you this, so I guess I'll just do it. I'm getting married to Mitch on Saturday. — Me."

Jenna was my longest relationship — four years. I'm pretty sure she was the only girl I ever really loved. She was going to move out to California with me after she graduated from college in Colorado so we could get married. Instead, the week of her graduation, she got arrested for stealing from Forever 21, where she was an assistant manager and apparently the ringleader of a scam in which she and fellow employees would take clothes that customers returned instead of noting the return and putting the merchandise back on the shelves as dictated by the Forever 21 employee handbook. The same week she told me she couldn't afford a place of her own so she moved in with her "friend" Mitch, who was the manager of a NASCAR Superstore in the mall. She dumped me a few weeks later. We haven't talked since.

I remember meeting Mitch and the only things that stand out are that he had fucked-up teeth and that he's a born-again Christian.

Strangely the e-mail doesn't surprise me that much. It doesn't bother me at first, but then I realize the concrete reality of the situation is that I will never fuck her again. I immediately turn off my computer and jerk off to memories of fucking Jenna in the ass in her parents' bed, her jerking me off as I shoot a load on her face, fucking her in her parents' swimming pool while they were inside with a prayer group, every load I ever shot down her throat, and the night I took her virginity. I try to convince myself that this is the last time I will ever think of Jenna. I immediately know I'll think about her again if for no other reason than she was the first girl I ever fucked in the ass, and that is one of my favorite memories.

chapter seven

I Don't Believe in Destiny

I'm walking back to my apartment through Westwood after having just come from the gym. As I pass a record store a Tori Amos poster catches my eye. I remember a girl in college who fucked me a few times because she saw my roommate's copy of a Tori Amos album lying on the floor and thought it was mine. She thought I was a sensitive guy who listened to that type of shit and to my surprise gave some of the best head I've ever had. I always kind of felt guilty for never paying Tori back.

Past the poster, through the window, I see something and almost shit my pants. Alyna the plane girl is working behind one of the registers. I decide to buy a fucking Tori Amos album.

As I walk in, I'm immediately hit with a wave of panic. I don't know if I should act like I remember her from the plane or if I shouldn't. What should I do if she remembers me? I busy myself by walking over to a listening station, but it's broken.

I browse the DVD section.

Fuck it, I walk up to the counter, straight to her.

"Do you guys have a new release section or something?"

"Yeah, it's over there."

I walk over in the direction she pointed without a doubt in my mind that she remembers me. I wander around for a few minutes, away from the new releases, until I find some Tori Amos CDs. I take one, pretend to look around at some other shit and see if I can catch her checking me out. I can't.

I go back up to the register and toss the disc on the counter. She picks it up and looks at it, then looks at me.

"Are you really into this?"

I don't know what the fuck to say. "Uh, yeah, I like her stuff, why?"

"All of her music sounds the same."

"Whose doesn't?"

"Good point."

She rings me up and that's our first conversation.

That night Casey comes over and sees the unopened CD lying on my couch.

"I never knew you liked Tori."

She unwraps the CD and starts playing it. I wonder if she ever fucked a guy based on his musical preference.

Later that night she tells me that she's just not in the mood for sex. For the first time since we've started fucking, this doesn't bother me. Casey curls up next to me and falls asleep in my arms without touching my dick at all and it doesn't bother me. I wonder what Alyna's ass looks like when you fuck her doggie style and spread it apart a little bit, and I fall asleep.

chapter eight

Casey's New Diet

We're at Johnnies New York Pizzeria on Sunset because it's one of Casey's favorite places to eat. To be fair, the rolls are fucking amazing, and we did see Lara Flynn Boyle there once. So I'm content.

Casey's retelling me a joke she says she got forwarded to her by her Groundlings teacher. The same joke was sent to me by Casey herself a few days ago in an e-mail that explained she had come up with the joke herself, which I knew to be untrue even then because it had already been forwarded to me by my mom.

Nonetheless, Casey is butchering the joke, and even though I already know what's coming, I let her continue, and when she retells me the punch line, slightly botched, I laugh convincingly enough to assure a decent prefuck blow job tonight.

After what seems like a fucking eternity of her telling a drawn-out story about losing her dad's credit card in the Beverly Center Gap, Casey finally gets up to go to the bathroom. Just as she leaves, the waiter puts our plates down, giving me the perfect opportunity to make my move.

About a month and a half ago I was watching some late-night TV after having jerked off twice in a row to a videotape I found in my closet of me fucking my high school girlfriend, Katy. Flipping through the channels, I was blessed with an infomercial for a product called Bloussant.

Bloussant is a pill taken daily that is guaranteed to enlarge tits by at least one cup size. Seventy-four dollars and fourteen business days later my own two-month supply of Bloussant arrived in the mail. I crushed up all the pills into a powder that I've been mixing into as many of Casey's meals as I can. I've been doing this for about a month and so far the results could be better.

I decide to increase her dosage and spoon out two heaping mounds of the stuff from the Ziploc Baggie I have in my right back pocket. An old guy sitting next to me notices but doesn't give any reaction. I mix it in the best I can and decide it would be a good move to put a third spoonful in her Diet Coke.

I'm concentrating too hard on making sure the Bloussant is completely dissolved to notice that Casey's come back from the bathroom and is standing at the table watching me stir her drink.

She says, "What're you doing?"

Something quick, nonchalant, believable: "I thought I saw a fly or something in your drink."

"Then I'll just get the waiter to bring me a new one when he comes back."

"No, no. You don't need to do that. There wasn't really a fly. I just thought there was. It must have been the ice. C'mon, sit down, let's dig in."

She looks at me like I'm semi-insane and for a split second I wish I was so I could be honest enough with her to tell her that I've been slipping an unproven breast-enhancing drug into her food and drink because I think her tits are too small and I was stirring her Diet Coke to make sure it had completely dissolved. But her look fades as she sits down, spreads her napkin across her lap, and takes a huge bite of fettuccine Alfredo–Bloussant. Her reaction to a strange taste is nonexistent.

I grab her tits much more than I normally would that night as we fuck in an attempt to feel any kind of progress at all. She says, "Hey, calm down, they'll last longer if you don't rip them off." I'm surprised at how genuinely funny I think this is while my dick's buried in her pussy. But the distraction's not enough to keep me from thinking that at her current increased dosage, I only have enough Bloussant left for about a week and a half. If I don't see better results by then, I'll have to buy two more shipments and further increase her intake. This may mean I'll be forced to take up cooking to learn how to mask the taste.

Communication Is the Foundation of Any Good Relationship

In Casey's car on the way to the beach I'm staring out the window wondering if Alyna knows how to suck cock when Casey starts the following conversation with me:

Casey says, "Yesterday I get this e-mail from Lem. He asks me if I was invited to Eliza's party. And, of course, I was, but he wasn't. So I e-mail him back that I was. Then he e-mails me back and asks if I can forward him the invitation just so he can see who was invited. I mean, what is he thinking? So I e-mail back that I'd forward it to him, but I told him if he doesn't get invited he can't go. You know, like don't use this e-mail that I'm about to forward you as an invitation if you don't get one yourself. Then he e-mails me back that he's all pissed off at me because how dare I think that he would try to come to a party that he wasn't invited to and blah, blah, blah — and I'm trying to IM with Nancy at the same time to see what she's wearing to the party, but his e-mails keep popping up. I was so afraid I was accidentally going to send him an e-mail about what he's wearing to the party after I pretty much already told him not to come. I couldn't believe he got so mad when I told him not to show up unless he got his own invitation. Who does that? Who comes to a party without an invitation? I mean, he shouldn't be surprised that he doesn't get invited to things. He just doesn't know what it's all about, you know? I mean, can you believe that?"

I say, "Huh-uh."

She says, "Then he sends me another e-mail where he's mad because Joan got invited and he didn't. I mean, of course Joan's going to get invited. That doesn't mean he is. You know, it's like he thinks Greg still owes him something or something. If he wasn't so socially retarded he might get invited to more parties. And plenty of people think that, but it's like, who's going to be the one to tell him? So anyway, the last e-mail he sends me is all like crazy and pissed off about the fact that he hasn't been invited to the last two parties and he asked me to e-mail Eliza and ask her to e-mail him an invitation. Can you believe that?"

I say, "Huh-uh."

She says, "I didn't even write him one back. If he's that desperate to go to her party, then he can ask her himself. Can you imagine me e-mailing her to ask if she'll invite Lem to her party? Oh, yeah, and he asks me if I have Shawna's phone number. Hello, Shawna moved to New York like four months ago. If you don't have her number, it's because she doesn't want you to have it. I mean, seriously, learn to take a hint. And he sends me this thing that he sent to like thirty other people about his stupid jazz trio playing somewhere in North Holly- wood. North Hollywood, can you believe that?"

I say, "Huh-uh."

She says, "Who plays in North Hollywood? Nobody good. I'm sure nobody'll go. I kind of feel sorry for him. But it's like it's his own fault, you know. He just doesn't get the whole thing. So then I send Eliza an e-mail saying basically watch out for an e-mail from Lem inviting himself to her party. He's been asking around about why he wasn't invited. Then she e-mails me back saying that Lem already called her at work and wanted to know what the deal was—if Eliza had lost his e-mail address or something. She told him that she was sorry and she must have lost his e-mail otherwise he would have been invited, but the party was only open to the first fifty people who RSVPed because her place is kind of small. Then she told him that she'd definitely make sure he was on the list for her next party, but there's no way. Now he'll never get invited to anything again because everybody knows that he tried to invite himself to this party. I just—I mean, can you imagine being like that?"

I say, "Huh-uh."

An old No Doubt song comes on the radio. She doesn't say anything while it plays. I think about Alyna's ass and what she's like after sex. When the song's over Casey says, "Oh, yeah, my sister had her baby yesterday and my parents bought me a ticket to go home and see her. So I'll be gone for a few days next week."

I say, "That's great."

chapter nine

Burbank Strip Club

I'm at Todd's house in Toluca Lake. We've been playing Madden for a few hours and drinking heavily. After his fourth defeat he says, "Dude, let's go see some titties."

Twenty minutes later we're driving over some train tracks at a non-descript location in Burbank and pulling into the parking lot of a strip club I never knew existed.

We sit down, order the first of our two-drink minimum and look to stage one, where a moderately attractive girl with no ass grinds her crotch in the air to the beat of a far-past-its-prime Limp Bizkit song.

I say, "I think I'm going to ask that girl out."

"That girl from the record store?"

"Yeah."

"Like on a date?"

"Yeah."

"Why?"

"I think about her constantly."

"Do what you gotta do."

Two strippers, both far below par as strippers go, approach us about some lap dances. I'm hesitant, but then they explain their rates.

This pudgy Asian stripper says, "You get three songs for twenty dollars." I say, "Why so cheap?"

Her partner, a pock-faced white girl with some kind of Scandinavian accent, says, "It's three-for-one night." Then she leans in and licks my ear. I'm almost repulsed by the idea of a three-for-one rate on lap dances, but the bitch is already sitting in my lap. Fuck it.

The pock-faced white girl has her ass in my face while the chubby Asian girl rubs her tits on Todd's head.

Todd comes out from under her tits, looks at me, and says, "Dude, what about Casey?"

I stop staring at this stripper's asshole long enough to look at Todd and say, "What about Casey?"

"How're you gonna take that record store girl on a date without Casey finding out?"

My stripper flips around and mashes her little hard tits in my face. I say, "Casey's leaving town for a few days."

The Asian bitch rolls her head around in Todd's crotch. He says, "Lucky."

The pock-faced bitch breathes on my cock through my pants. I say, "Yeah, I know. But I don't even know this girl's phone number or anything."

The Asian bitch takes Todd's hands and puts them on her slightly dimpled ass. He says, "Dude, you know where she works."

The pock-faced bitch starts semi–jerking me off through my pants. I say, "But I don't know when she works. I can't just hang out in the store all day."

The Asian bitch does this crab-type maneuver that has her crotch gyrating right under Todd's nose. He says, "Dude, just ask somebody who works there when she works."

The pock-faced bitch matches her partner. I try to sniff her cunt, but it's masked by the stripper smell. I say, "Good idea."

The Asian bitch puts her hands under Todd's shirt and presses her face into his cock. He says, "No shit."

Our conversation ends and our drinks come. The strippers get off us for a few seconds so we can dig our money out of the pockets they've been rubbing their asses all over. I feel a little ripped off by the convenient hiatus created by the waitress's arrival. The waitress leaves and the bitches get back to work.

Some Tool song and a Linkin Park song finish out my three-for-the-price-of-one session. The highlight is when the pock-faced stripper accidentally slips off the side of the chair, hits the ground, and says, "Fuck, I hate these fucking shoes," with no trace of the Scandinavian accent.

chapter ten

Stevie

I'm at the Gap in Westwood with Casey watching her look at clothes.

She says, "Do you think I should get a Gap credit card?"

"Sure."

"I mean, I think you get ten percent off and you can use it like a normal credit card. Should I get one?"

"Yes."

"I don't know if I should though. Should I?"

"Do it."

"I'll think about it. I need to look around some more. If I find something that I like, I might get the card, too. I'm going to try some things on."

I wait until she takes an armload of clothes into the dressing room and then walk across the street to the record store where Alyna works.

She's not in the store, but a kind of overweight middle-aged guy with glasses and a crew cut is. His name tag reads STEVIE — MANAGER.

I say, "Excuse me."

"How can I help you?"

"Do you know Alyna?"

"Yes, I do."

"Do you know when she works next?"

"Yes, I do." He points at his name badge. "I *am* the manager." He laughs.

"Right. So when is she supposed to work next?"

"Are you a family member?"

"No, I'm—a friend."

"Then I'm afraid I can't tell you."

"Why not?"

He points to his name badge again. "Like I said, I *am* the manager, and as the manager I have a duty to my employees. I can't just go around giving out their personal information to every stranger who asks for it, now can I?" He laughs again.

"It's not personal information."

"I'm sorry, I can't help you."

"Well, can I leave a message for her?"

He thinks about it. "I suppose that would be all right."

"Do you have a piece of paper?"

He gives me a promotional flyer for Justin Timberlake's new record.

"And a pen?"

He gives me one.

I write down something short, and put my phone number next to it. I fold it up, write Alyna's name on the outside, and hand it back to Stevie.

He unfolds it and starts reading it out loud. "Alyna, I bought the Tori Amos record from you a few days ago. We kind of had a conversation about it. I was wondering if you might want to get dinner sometime. Call me."

Stevie looks at me, then rips the paper in half and tosses it in the trash.

"What're you doing?"

"You said you were her friend, which is clearly not the case. I try to create a safe and comfortable work environment here and I will not have my employees harassed during the course of their workday."

"Are you kidding?"

"Sir, if you do not wish to make a purchase, I'm afraid I'm going to have to ask you to leave my store."

"It's not your store, Stevie."

I leave without incident, pissed.

I slip back into the Gap just in time to wait for another thirty minutes before Casey comes out of the dressing room and buys a sweater with her new Gap card.

As we walk out of the Gap, Casey says, "Hey, let's go in that music store. My No Doubt CD got stuck in Jen's CD player and she scratched it trying to get it out. I need a new one."

"You go ahead. I'll be next door looking at video games."

I browse the used section while I'm positive Stevie is next door drooling over my girlfriend's tits and taking way too long to help her find her No Doubt CD.

That night as Casey and I are in the sixty-nine and I'm staring into her asshole, I wonder if Alyna will be working at the record store tomorrow. I wonder if my ripped-up note will still be in the trash can by the front desk. I wonder if she might see her name on it and pull it out. I wonder if she'd even remember who I was anyway.

Scarface Part 1

I'm sitting in a bar called Goldfinger after getting a phone call from Todd promising me that at least three hot bitches he knows from college who are all horny and drunk will be there. After my third beer and Todd's sixth assurance that they must be on their way, I'm pretty sure there might never have been any hot bitches, and I'm positive if they do exist they're not showing up here tonight.

I get up to go get another drink, and when I come back Todd has somehow managed to fill our booth with not the promised three hot bitches, but four average-looking bitches. I conclude that these are not the girls he was originally talking about, but I don't really care. I sit down and learn the following:

The taller bitch with reddish hair is named Leslie Leonard and she's visiting from Virginia. Two of the brunettes' names make no impression on me and I don't remember them even as they tell me, but I do latch on to the fact that they're sisters and Leslie is their cousin. The third brunette is Asian and semi-hot from what I can see, until the candle flicker at our table bounces off a nasty fucking hairlip. I think she gives her name as Amy, but I immediately give her the name Scarface in my head.

After they're done telling us whatever their stories are, Scarface says with a lisp that isn't altogether unattractive, "Do you guys have girlfriends?"

It's a weird question. Todd says, "No." I don't say anything. Scarface says, "Cool."

I'm strangely attracted to her weird lip. I wonder if she's had to develop some super cocksucking technique to compensate for her deformity. I wonder if she can even suck cock at all. Maybe she can't suck cock so she's had to expand her sexual repertoire to keep men interested. I picture myself fucking her in the ass and her genuinely enjoying it because she has to, because she knows that her openness to things other women aren't is the most and only attractive quality she has.

Leslie Leonard says, "So have you guys seen any good movies lately?"

Todd says, "Movies are pretty gay right now. I saw the last UFC though."

One of the sisters says, "What's UFC?"

Todd says, "Ultimate Fighting Championship."

The conversation is dead until Scarface says, "Is that like boxing?"

I wish the beer I'm drinking was Scotch.

Scarface keeps on talking, "Boxing is pretty cool. I don't mind watching that."

Scarface keeps going on about how much she can tolerate boxing, even more than watching football, and I keep watching her mouth move and wondering if there's any way I could actually get her to suck my cock tonight. She seems kind of stupid but that doesn't give me enough of a read to devise a game plan. I decide to wait it out, let her talk, let her get comfortable with me, and see where it goes.

Two hours later I'm more drunk than I wanted to be and Scarface's lip doesn't look abnormal to me at all. I don't know if it's because I'm drunk or because I've stared at it for so long that it just seems normal. They shut down the bar and our whole group goes outside.

I look over and see Todd kissing Leslie Leonard, which makes me realize there must have been an entire part of the night that I somehow missed while I was staring at Scarface's lip, which I'm still doing when it moves and she says, "So are you gonna give me your number or what?"

The alcohol and the hypnotic spell her lip has cast on me slow my mind to the point of not being able to produce a fake number. I give her my real one, not remembering even as I say it to find the strength to change a single digit.

Scarface gives me a hug and for the first time all night I notice her body, which is nice. Hard little tits and a flat stomach. I wonder if she works out at home or if she braves a public gym with her lip. I wonder if she gets a Jamba Juice after she works out like I do sometimes and I also wonder if she uses a straw or if she even has the ability to use a straw.

She hops in a car driven by one of the two sisters, as does Leslie Leonard, leaving Todd and me standing on the sidewalk. Todd says, "Dude, that bitch gave me her number. She's only in town for another four days and she gave me her number. It's fucking on."

I didn't know at the time I decided to recognize her as Scarface if Todd did the same, but when he says, "So what happened with you and Scarface?" I realize he did. This also makes me realize that most guys' default nickname for a bitch with any facial deformity is probably Scarface.

I say, "I think I gave her my number."

"Holy shit. Your real number?"

"Yeah."

"Why?"

"I don't know."

"Dude, her face is fucked up."

"I know."

"You think she'll call you?"
"I don't know."
"Holy shit."
"I know."

chapter eleven

I'm Starting to Believe in Destiny

I'm in the Beverly Center pet store with my gay buddy, Carlos. We just finished our weekly lunch and he's thinking about buying a dog. There are two thirty-something flaming fags next to us also thinking about buying a dog. One of them is holding a baby pug.

Fag 1 says, "I just don't know if I should get him. I mean, I'm leaving town for two months. What would I do?"

Fag 2 says, "I'll watch him for you."

Fag 1 says, "You would?"

Fag 2 says, "Of course. But he's so expensive, are you sure you want to get him?"

Fag 1 looks at the price on his cage. He says, "Thirteen hundred. That's not too expensive for me."

Fag 2 says, "Ooh, you're so naughty."

Then Fag 1 slaps Fag 2 on the ass and says, "You know it."

Carlos nudges me and says, "Let's get the fuck out of here."

As we leave the pet store and head to EB Games, Carlos says, "I fucking hate fags who're like that."

"Like what?"

"You know, all flaunting their money and their asses in public. I mean, please, who wants to hear that you can waste thirteen hundred dollars on a fucking dog? And who doesn't know that all homos have money because we have no women or children to suck us dry? And once you get out of college, who still slaps another guy on the ass? I need a fucking straight man who's willing to just let me suck his dick and who'll fuck me in the ass every once in a while without all the bullshit."

He bats his eyelashes at me.

"As much as I like blow jobs, I only like 'em when they come with tits."

"I'm not against implants."

He laughs at his own joke as we walk into EB Games.

I walk to the back of the store and look through their rummage bin, which is usually filled with old Sega Genesis and Super Nintendo games.

I've been looking for a game called Super Populous since the eighth grade. In the game you play a god who controls a population of people. The computer plays a rival god controlling its own population. The object of each level is to raise your population to such a large number that it completely destroys the opposing god's population. Each level takes roughly forty-five minutes to an hour to beat. There are 999 levels. After its release in 1990, it was rated the worst game of the year by several gaming magazines. One even rated it the worst game ever made. As a result, no store carried it for more than a month after it was released. So I had resigned myself to renting it from the only video store in town that carried it in the hopes of one day beating it.

Over the course of several rentals, I had progressed to the eighty-seventh level. One weekend while trying to rent it again, I was notified that it had not been returned and was thought to be stolen.

Since that day I've looked in any and every used game section I've come across. I've looked on eBay, I've looked at garage sales, I've even flipped through the classified ads every once in a while in the hopes of finding a video game collection for sale. Now, in the upper left part of the bin, right on top of the pile in this particular EB Games, is Super Populous for $2.99.

I'm almost catatonic with disbelief. A quest that has consumed multiple years of my life has finally and unexpectedly ended.

"How's that Tori Amos CD?"

Alyna Janson is standing in front of me holding a DS Lite.

"I actually haven't listened to it yet."

"I thought you were a big Tori fan."

"Not that big."

She looks at Super Populous in my hand. She says, "What's that?"

"Super Populous."

She doesn't know what it is or that my holding it means the end of a fifteen-year search.

I say, "Do you want to get dinner with me sometime?"

"Sure."

She takes a pen and paper out of her purse, writes down her number, and hands it to me. She says, "Here's my number, give me a call and we can hash out the details."

I take her number, put it in my back pocket, and say, "Okay."

She walks up to the counter to buy the DS Lite. I assume she's buying it for a brother or friend. She's wearing a pair of tight jeans that make her ass look slightly better than I remembered it. I pretend to look through the used game bin some more so I don't have to make eye contact with her again and possibly start up a clumsy and unnecessary conversation after just having successfully asked her on a date.

Carlos comes over to me and says, "Did you just ask that girl on a date?"

"Yeah."

"You little fucker. Are you and Casey still together?"

"Yeah."

"Then what the fuck are you doing?"

"I don't really know."

"You just saw some girl you wanted to fuck and asked her out or what?"

"No. I've seen her before. I saw her on a plane, and then I saw her in a record store. She sold me a CD. I constantly think about her."

"I guess I'm not the one to be giving you a lecture on fidelity. God knows I've fucked around on half of West Hollywood. But you better be fucking careful. Shit like this always blows up in your face."

I pay for Super Populous and we leave the Beverly Center.

When I get home I jerk off thinking about the possibility of fucking Alyna on our first date. I wonder if she's ever fingered herself while thinking about me.

Scarface Part 2

I've been playing Halo 2 campaign mode for the past four hours on Legendary difficulty. I'm having trouble with the part where you have to pilot a Ghost around while a giant Covenant walker robot is decimating the city. The Covenant Ghosts do too much damage and there are too many of them. The phone rings. I answer it without stopping my game and hear a vaguely familiar lisp. It's fucking Scarface, who begins the following conversation:

"I had a really good time meeting you and your friend Todd when we were all out the other night."

"Uh-huh . . ."

"Did you?"

"Uh . . . sure."

"Cool. So what are you up to right now?"

"Uh . . . I'm playing Halo."

"Cool. What's that?"

"A video game."

"Cool. I love video games. I'm awesome at Tetris. You ever play Tetris?"

"Not really."

I have a bead on an enemy Ghost and my plasma cannon is fully charged. Before I pull the trigger I pretend Scarface is piloting the Covenant ship. As I blow him out of the air, I see his body falling down to the ground below.

Scarface keeps talking, "Hey, what kind of music are you into?"

"Uh . . . all kinds, I guess."

"Cool. Me too. I listen to pretty much everything."

What must be forty-five seconds pass and all I hear on the other end of the phone is air blowing in and out through Scarface's deformed lip. I try to ignore it as I mop up some more Covenant ships.

Then she says, "So do you date much?"

"Not too much."

"Yeah, same here. But when you do go on dates, what kind of stuff do you like to do?"

"Eat, I guess."

"Yeah, that's a really good thing to do on a date. Where do you like to eat?"

"I don't know, depends on what I'm in the mood for that day."

"Yeah, it totally does depend on that. Do you ever get in the mood for Italian food?"

"Uh . . . yeah, sure."

"I love Italian food."

There's another long pause during which I've managed to land my severely damaged Ghost and pick up an entirely new one to continue fighting.

She says, "Maybe we could go get something to eat at that Italian place in the Grove sometime soon if you're not busy."

I do a dive roll to avoid a salvo of glowing plasma rounds from an enemy ship and then say, "Uh . . . I'm not sure that's the best idea."

"Oh, oh, okay . . . cool. Well, I've got your number. Maybe I'll give you a call some other time."

Before I can say anything she hangs up and I find myself feeling genuinely bad for Scarface, bad enough to pause my game. I think for a few seconds about Scarface and how she must have similar conversations with guys all the time. I think about star-sixty-nining her and taking her up on the offer. She might be happy enough to have a date that she'd suck my dick or let me fuck her in the ass. I jerk off as I imagine her sucking my cock and I cum as I imagine blowing my load all over her deformed lip.

I use a paper towel from the kitchen to clean myself off and then unpause my game.

chapter twelve

Plans

I make specific plans not to go to Casey's house so I can call Alyna to set up our date. I've tried to prepare myself so I don't sound like a retard on the phone, but when I dial the number she gave me at EB Games and Stevie answers, all my preparation dissolves. I immediately wonder why she gave me her work number instead of her home number.

I say, "Is Alyna there?"

Stevie asks, "Who's calling?"

"A friend."

Surprisingly, Stevie gives me no shit and gets Alyna. When she gets on the phone I want to ask her why she gave me her work number, but I decide not to push the issue. It's not that relevant.

She says, "Hey, how've you been?"

I say, "Fine."

"So where are you taking me?"

My call waiting beeps. I don't want to answer it, but I can't help myself. I say, "Can you hang on one second?"

"Okay."

I switch over. It's Casey. She wants me to come over despite the fact that we've already decided to not see each other tonight. I'm very quickly faced with the fact that to get her off the line with any expedience, I have to promise to see her tonight. So I do. She says she loves me and I tell her I'll see her tonight before hanging up on her and switching back over to Alyna.

I say, "Sorry about that. So what kind of food do you like?"

"All kinds. Why don't you surprise me."

"Okay."

"And you can pick me up at eight-thirty on Friday night. That's my night off."

"Okay."

Then she gives me her address.

"See you then."

"Okay. See you then."

"Bye."

She hangs up before I can return the good-bye.

That night at Casey's house, I purposely cum in her mouth while she's giving me a standard foreplay blow job that should have led to sex. I don't apologize.

chapter thirteen

A Call from Casey's Mom

A few nights later I'm at Casey's house. She promised me she was horny and if I got to her house as fast as I could, she'd be waiting for me naked on her bed. We haven't fucked in a few days and she's leaving town tomorrow, so I accepted her offer.

Casey's lying on her bed, as she promised, but she's fully clothed and talking to her mom on the phone. Occasionally I can hear Casey say one of the following things: "I don't know. How am I supposed to know? I guess. No, you're right. I never thought about it like that. I will."

I'm sitting on her couch watching an old episode of *Who's the Boss* in which Tony Danza gets pursued by his overly aggressive high school girlfriend who just wants to have a fling for old time's sake. And although Tony really wants to fuck her, he can't stop thinking about Angela.

Who's the Boss ends and Casey's still on the phone. I find nothing to eat in her refrigerator, then go to the bathroom to piss.

When I lift up the toilet lid there's already piss in the bowl, and I'm reminded that in an effort to conserve water Casey never flushes after she pisses. There's something slightly unsettling about my piss mixing with her piss. When I flush I hear Casey say, "Only if it's brown."

I ignore her and go back to the living room, where I settle in for an episode of *Family Ties* in which Michael J. Fox takes amphetamines so he can study for a test without knowing the serious harm he could be doing to himself. It's just getting to the part that they use in the opening credits where a speed-wired Michael J. Fox slides across the floor in a rolling chair, when Casey steps right in front of the TV.

I try to look around her, but Michael J. Fox has already rolled across the floor. I missed it.

I notice she's not talking on the phone anymore when she says, "Sorry. She called right after I called you."

"That's okay."

I get up and start kissing her neck as I unzip her pants.

"Hang on."

"What?"

"I want to talk about something first."

"I thought you said you were horny."

"I was."

"But not now?"

"I just got off the phone with my mom."

"So?"

"She was asking me if we were ever going to get married."

"So?"

"So are we?"

I wish I would have left work ten minutes earlier so I wouldn't have been there when Casey called, or that I had just jerked off in the first-floor bathroom so the lure of fucking her wouldn't have been so strong. I wish a pot of scalding water was on the stove so I could dunk my head in it.

I can't talk. I just stand there.

She says, "Well . . . have you ever even thought about it?"

I can't think. I just open my mouth. "No."

"You've never even thought about us getting married?"

"No."

"We've been dating for like over a year."

"Right."

"And you haven't ever even given it the slightest thought? Like what I'd look like in a wedding dress?"

For the first time in my life, I imagine Casey in a wedding dress. She actually probably would look good from the front.

"No. Have you?"

"Of course. I love you."

My involuntary reactions come back to me. "I love you, too" crawls out of my mouth.

"Then why wouldn't you think about us getting married?"

"Why are you bringing this up now? What did your mom say to you?"

"She wanted to know if we were thinking about getting married yet or like thinking about having kids."

"Kids?" Is this a fucking joke?

"She had me when she was twenty."

"Kids?" It's not a fucking joke.

"My sister just had a baby and my mom wants me to give her grandchildren, too. I don't think that's so bad."

Her cats are sitting on the coffee table watching us argue. I wish they were watching us fuck.

I have to get out of this. I say, "Do you want to go get a sandwich?"

"What?"

"I didn't eat before I came over here. Do you want to go get a sandwich?"

"What are you talking about?"

"I want to get a sandwich."

"Are you like trying to change the subject or something?"

"No, I just, I'm just hungry."

She gets really pissed. She stomps off into her bedroom and slams the door shut. Her cats are still sitting on the coffee table just staring at me.

I'm afraid to knock on her door because I know the marriage conversation will have to be resolved. So I sit back down on the couch and finish watching *Family Ties*. I wonder how many eighteen-year-old hardbodies Michael J. Fox fucked in his prime—before Parkinson's, before marriage.

I watch TV for the next few minutes, during which I formulate my apology and the quickest route of conversation that will lead me to fucking. I watch a little bit of a soft core porno on Cinemax called *A Rock and a Hard Place*. I contemplate jerking off in Casey's living room and then going home, but I ultimately decide against it. It turns out to be a good decision, as Casey comes out of her room ready to start up the conversation again.

She says, "So are you ever going to apologize?"

I don't think I've done anything wrong. I say, "Of course. I just thought you needed some time to yourself. I didn't want to interrupt you before you were ready to fully talk about this whole thing."

"Well, now I'm ready."

I take a deep breath and try to look like I care. I say, "What you said earlier just caught me by surprise. I came over here thinking about one thing and then your mom called and I ended up getting another. You know how us guys think."

"Yeah, like rocks."

"I know. I'm sorry."

"So then what do you think about the whole us getting married thing?"

This question inspires me to create the following masterwork: "Of course I've thought about us getting married. It's not like I don't see us together in the future. I guess what I meant was that I never even questioned whether or not we'd be married so I never really gave it much thought. It's just something that I kind of take as a given."

That one got her. She smiles and says, "So you think we'll get married?"

"Someday . . . in the future."

She sits down next to me and puts her arms around my neck. She says, "I knew you'd thought about it. You must have just been confused. Like you said."

"Right."

"And now that you've had some time to clear your thoughts, you realize that we should get married."

"Sure . . . at some point."

She squeezes me and kisses my cheek. She says, "I love you."

"I love you, too."

She pulls away a little bit and looks me in the eyes. She says, "So then we're basically engaged, right?"

"Uhh . . ." The only sound I can hear is the blood pounding against the back of my eyes. I'm dazed. She must take my slack-jawed stupor to mean yes because she hugs me tight and says, "I love the feeling of being engaged."

Dazed becomes paralyzed. I wish a plane would crash into Casey's living room.

She pulls back again and stares at me, this time with a look in her eye that I haven't seen since we first started dating, and she says, "You know what we should do to celebrate our engagement?"

I want to get the fuck out of her house and celebrate by wrapping my car around a telephone pole.

She says, "We should make love."

She insists on fucking missionary style so we can look into each other's eyes. She keeps holding my face and saying she loves me as I'm trying to fuck her hard enough to erase the memory of this entire night. She's nowhere close to cumming and I don't care because she keeps trying to hug me as we're fucking and she won't stop telling me how much she loves me.

I'm about to blow my load so I pull out and shoot it all over her stomach and tits, knowing that I'll get at least a little break from her "I love you" barrage while she goes to the bathroom to clean up.

I'm almost asleep when she comes back from toweling down. She snuggles up beside me and forces me into the spoon position.

Again she says, "I love you," and I almost lose it. I almost get up, get dressed, and walk out, but I'm tired. Maybe I can just ignore this whole night. Maybe we'll never talk about getting married again.

I'm almost asleep when she says, "You're still taking me to the airport tomorrow, right?"

"Yeah."

"I can't wait to tell my parents I'm engaged."

chapter fourteen

First Date

I drop Casey off at the airport at 5:30 P.M. I have to pick up Alyna for our date at 8:30. Casey kisses me on the cheek and says, "See you in a few days, fiancé."

"Right."

As I drive back to my apartment I hope her plane goes down or gets hijacked before she has a chance to tell her parents that we're engaged.

Back at home I prepare for my date by jerking off while watching a rerun of 90210. I brush my teeth twice, take a dump, and then jerk off one more time in the shower just to make sure. I put on some clothes that I think are nice but not too nice, and wonder if Alyna will be wearing any underwear tonight. I wonder if she wears thong underwear. I imagine her ass in thong underwear. I jerk off again, then take a half shower in which I only scrub my dick and balls.

Alyna lives about three minutes away from my apartment in a university-owned off-campus apartment complex. I park my car and ring her apartment number on the call box of her building.

A girl says, "Hello."

"Hi, I'm here to pick Alyna up."

"She's still getting ready, but I'll buzz you in."

When I get to Alyna's door, I meet her roommate, Simone.

Simone is a hippie-type bitch who doesn't shave her armpits or wear shoes. Despite the fact that she's kind of fat, I wonder if there's any chance of getting both her and Alyna drunk and coaxing them into a threesome. I wonder if she would lick my balls while I fucked Alyna.

Simone says, "So what's your deal?"

"How's that?"

"What's your deal, man? What're you up to?"

"I'm just here to take Alyna out."

"Yeah, I know."

I sit down on their couch.

She says, "So where are you from?"

"Originally?"

"Yeah."

"I'm from Colorado. How about you?"

"Northern California. Santa Cruz."

"And you go to UCLA with Alyna?"

"Yeah."

"Have you known her long?"

"A year. You?"

"We actually just kind of met a week or so ago."

I'm suddenly repulsed at myself for trying to get this hippie bitch to like me, but the thought of her eating Alyna's pussy while I fuck her is enough for me to remain cordial.

She says, "Yeah, well, everybody meets everybody at one point in their relationship, you know, man?"

"Right."

Alyna comes out of some back room—maybe a bathroom, maybe a bedroom. She says, "Sorry. You ready to go?"

"Yeah. Nice to meet you, Simone."

I put my hand out to shake hers and she hugs me. She has mild body odor, but as her tits press against me I learn that they're full and kind of sloppy, which, surprisingly, doesn't repulse me.

Simone says, "You, too."

As we're walking out the door and I'm looking for a panty line on Alyna's ass in a pair of tight slack-type pants, she says, "Bye, Simone. Don't wait up." I can't see a panty line.

The ride to the restaurant is uneventful. She looks through the CDs I have in my car and we talk about our musical interests. As we pull into the restaurant parking lot she semi-leans over me to put a CD back in my sun visor CD carrying case and brushes me with her tit. It's a little smaller than I originally thought, but a rock-hard B cup nonetheless. I think about her straddling me as I lick and bite at her tits.

The restaurant is a French place called Le Petit Chateau in North Hollywood.

When we get inside, we start drinking wine and the conversation comes a little easier. We cover the basics—ages, interests, hometowns, and we skirt around the issue of previous relationships. I don't mention Casey.

A couple comes in and sits a few tables away from us. Alyna and I both notice them. The girl has a fucking amazing body, but her facial features are disproportionate in a way that makes me wonder if she has some kind of mild medical deformity.

She says, "Do you think they're on a first date, too?"

"I don't know."

"I bet they are."

"How can you tell?"

"It's all in the way the guy is treating her."

"And how's he treating her?"

"The same way you're treating me. He's trying to impress her. He's pulling her chair out, he's being really nice, and he's acting like he's really interested in whatever it is she's saying. He even unfolded the napkin and put it in his lap, just like you did when we sat down."

"What does the napkin have to do with it?"

"I bet you never do that when you just go out to eat with your guy friends or with somebody you're not trying to impress."

I think about the last several times I've gone out to eat with Casey. Alyna's right. She becomes immediately more attractive to me based on the fact that she seems smarter than Casey even though she's younger.

I say, "Maybe it is their first date."

She says, "Who do you think is having a better first date, us or them?"

"Definitely us."

"And why's that?"

"Because they're not looking at us wondering if it's our first date."

She smiles.

The guy from the couple gets up from the table and excuses himself.

Alyna says, "Where do you think he's going?"

"To the bathroom."

"What if he's going to call one of his friends to tell him how horrible the date is going and how he needs the friend to call him in the next ten minutes with some urgent emergency so he can get out of the date?"

"Do you have something like that planned to get out of this date?"

She laughs. "I might."

We get our food and start eating. She eats like a girl—taking small bites and covering her mouth with her hand. But the pasta she ordered makes her lips wet and all I can think about is her sucking my cock. I make it my goal to shoot a load down her throat before the night's over.

As we eat and talk some more we notice that the guy who left his first date earlier still hasn't come back. The hot-bodied bitch is sitting at the table by herself, getting visibly worried.

Alyna says, "I bet he snuck out the window or something. I feel so bad for that poor girl."

If the guy did sneak out the window, I admire him.

The front door opens and a guy in full knight armor walks in. Everybody in the place stops eating and watches the following first-date nightmare unfold.

The knight walks over to the table where the hot-bodied bitch is sitting alone and gets down on one knee. He flips up his visor and it's the guy who went to the bathroom twenty minutes ago. He proposes. She accepts. The whole place goes crazy. As Alyna stares in silence at the unfolding events, I can't tell if she's disgusted or on the verge of tears because this moment is so magical.

I want to know what's running through Alyna's head. It's probably something attaching far more meaning to this event than it deserves, especially since it happened on our first date. Casey would have thought the whole thing was a sign from God that we should get married.

To diffuse the situation I try to make a joke. "I guess they're having the better first date now."

She says, "That is so fucking stupid."

I can't tell if she's talking about the knight or about my joke.

She says, "Does that guy think he's being romantic?"

She's talking about the knight.

"It worked."

"I just think marriage is so stupid. Seriously, what we just saw basically defines all marriages—some guy makes an ass out of himself and the girl is too overwhelmed by it to think straight enough to say no."

I'm impressed. I say, "So you don't want to get married?"

"Look, I know this is kind of a big subject for a first date and everything, but no, I don't want to. I don't want to have kids either. What about you?"

"Same pretty much."

She smiles again.

As we finish eating, the newly engaged couple is visited by practically every woman in the place. They all tell the guy in the knight suit that it's the most romantic thing they've ever seen. Alyna just eats her pasta.

When we're done, I pay the tab and we leave.

Once we're in my car she says, "So what're we going to do now?"

"Whatever you want."

"I want to see where you live."

I wonder if I should fuck her doggie style on the first date.

As we walk through the front door of my apartment, I can feel my cell phone vibrating in my pocket. I know it's Casey, so I don't answer it.

I say, "Do you want something to drink?"

"No. I'm fine. How long have you lived here?"

She walks in and sits on my couch.

"A year or so."

I pour myself something to drink and then join her on the couch. Her pants are riding down in the back a little bit to give me a small shot of the top of her ass. She's wearing a thong, which contradicts my earlier assessment of no underwear at all.

I say, "So . . ."

She takes the cue, leans in, and kisses me. Her mouth is warm and wet and I can already feel it on my cock. I get a hard-on instantly.

She pulls back and looks at me.

She says, "I better get back home. I have some tests to study for this weekend."

I feel like I just hit a fucking brick wall going sixty and I'm flying through the windshield as I say, "What?"

"Yeah, I just have some things to do and I should really go home."

I'm too confused to be pissed off and I say, "Okay, if you have to go I'll give you a ride."

"That's okay, I can walk."

"It's late. I can drive you."

"No, really, it's fine."

She gets up off the couch and says, "I had a really good time tonight."

"Me too, so why are you leaving?"

"We just probably shouldn't see each other again."

"Why?"

"Listen, I should have never gone on a date with you in the first place. I have a boyfriend. We're having some problems right now, but he's still my boyfriend."

Holy shit. I want to tell her that I have a girlfriend, that it doesn't matter, that they don't have to know. Instead I say, "Oh . . ."

She kisses me on the cheek and says, "Seriously, thanks, I had a really good time and you're a really nice guy."

She turns to leave and I say, "Why did you go out with me in the first place?"

"I don't know. I'm sorry."

And she leaves. As she walks out the door, I wish I would have fucked her or at least felt one of her tits. I lie down on my couch and smell the spot she was sitting on. I jerk off to the thought of her sucking my cock. I shoot my load into a napkin that's been on my coffee table for a few days. I stare at the ceiling wondering if I could've fucked her if I had tried a little harder. I wonder if she'll fuck her boyfriend tonight. I wonder if he'll fuck her doggie style. I wonder if she'll think about me while he does.

I experience a surprising moment of genuine sadness as I realize that I might never see Alyna again, when my cell phone vibrates again and it's Casey calling from her parents' house in Nebraska. She asks me what I did tonight but doesn't let me answer before she tells me the good news that her parents were so excited when she announced our engagement that they're coming out to visit their future son-in-law in a few weeks.

She's still talking about something when I put the phone next to my head and fall asleep.

chapter fifteen

The Morning After

I wake up, take a shower, and realize I'm supposed to be eating lunch with my gay buddy Carlos in thirty minutes.

Forty-five minutes later, I walk into the Beverly Center California Pizza Kitchen to see Carlos sitting by himself and pissed off.

He says, "Where the fuck have you been, you little asshole?"

"I was tired. I forgot."

"You fucking forgot. You ungrateful piece of shit."

"Sorry."

"Well, now you have to buy my lunch because you're a fucker."

"Sure."

We get seated and look at the menus for no reason.

"Hey, see those two guys over there?" He looks in the direction of two guys in their late thirties sitting at a small table in the back. One of them is wearing a shirt with pink letters that read NAUGHTY BOY.

I say, "Yeah."

"The one with the brown hair has the smallest dick I've ever sucked. So what in the hell have you been up to besides making me wait to eat lunch when I'm fucking starving?"

"I had that date last night."

"Oh, right, that bitch you met in the video game store. And Casey doesn't know a thing?"

"Right."

"Well, how did it go? Did you at least get blown?"

"I thought it went pretty well until the end. She invited herself back to my house—"

"Wow, so you definitely got blown. You probably fucked her."

"I didn't get blown or fuck her. She kissed me and then said she had a boyfriend and had to leave."

"That little bitch. But seriously, that doesn't sound too bad. At least all she did was kiss you and at least all she had was a fucking boyfriend. I've been on my knees with cum dribbling out of my ass and down my chin and had some son of a bitch tell me he was married with kids. Try that one on for size."

"I just don't get why she even went out with me in the first place."

"Who the fuck knows? Women can be complete cunts. At least with guys you know they always go out with you to fuck you, plain and simple. That's why you went out with her, right?"

"Yeah. For the most part."

"What other part is there?"

"I don't know. None, I guess."

"Listen. It's better it ended up this way. I mean, Casey would've eventually found out about this thing if it had gone on for very long."

"I know."

"So count your blessings. You got to go on a date with a hot piece of ass and you still get to keep your girlfriend."

I almost wish I had answered the phone when Casey called the first time. I almost wish I had let her hear Alyna in the background. I wish I had the balls to call Casey right now and tell her I fucked some drunk bitch in the ass at her Groundlings party while posing as her teacher. I almost wish she wasn't my girlfriend.

The waiter comes to our table and we order the same things we always order and strike up the same conversations about the same things we always talk about for the rest of lunch. After an hour we leave.

When I get home, I put in the Tori Amos CD that I bought from Alyna and jerk off.

Hobo

I'm walking out of Jerry's Famous Deli in Westwood when a semi-insane-looking hobo says, "Could you spare some change, brother?"

I have thirty-five cents in my pocket and I'm fully prepared to give it to him. I reach in my pocket, get the coins out, and begin the process of handing the money to the hobo when the following occurs.

Somebody says, "Don't do it."

I look over, and walking toward the hobo and myself is an Asian girl with fucking full-blown Down syndrome. She's wearing glasses and her tongue's kind of hanging out and she's waving her arms around like a maniac as she keeps saying, "Don't do it. Don't do it."

I pull the money back from the hobo, waiting for things to develop.

The retard says, "Mister, don't give him any money."

I say, "Okay."

She points her retarded finger at the hobo and says, "What's wrong with you? I make six dollars an hour. Why can't you get a job?"

The hobo is speechless. So am I. The retard's not.

She says, "You could get a job if you really wanted to, but you don't. You're lazy and I hate lazy people. You should not ask people for money that they've worked for. I would never give you money. I make six dollars an hour. I have a job. Why should I give you my money?"

I can't tell if the hobo is genuinely moved by the retard's rhetoric or by the poetic justice of this whole thing or what, but he stands up, says, "Shut your trap, I'm leaving," and takes off down the street. All the while the retard keeps yelling after him, "Get a job! I have a job!"

Once he's finally out of earshot the retard turns to me and says, "You should never give them your money. They are lazy. I hate them." Then she turns around and trudges off down the street. I hope she's on her way to deliver some more motivational speeches to hobos.

When I get home I wonder what retards are like when they fuck—if they're crazy, or if they go limp. I wonder if they're any good at sucking dick and I decide I would fuck a retard if given the opportunity so I could answer these questions.

chapter sixteen

Casey's Homecoming

I'm at the airport to pick up Casey. As I'm waiting by the baggage claim I see a guy in a brown jacket holding some flowers that he probably bought at the airport for his girlfriend. I know Casey would like me to be waiting for her with flowers. I see the little guy selling the flowers. I also see an average-looking bitch standing across from me. We exchange a glance. Casey's plane lands in ten minutes. I wonder if the average-looking bitch would accept a no-strings-attached offer to fuck in the bathroom. I wonder who she's here to pick up. Probably her boyfriend, who probably bought flowers for her at whatever airport he's coming from. Casey's been gone for two days, in which time I haven't fucked. I decide to buy her flowers.

Fifteen minutes later Casey wanders out into the baggage claim area like a lost little kid along with all the other people who were on her flight. The guy in the brown jacket gives his flowers to a girl who doesn't look that much different from the average-looking bitch. She kisses him. The average-looking bitch gets flowers from a guy who doesn't look that much different from the guy in the brown jacket. She kisses him. I give my flowers to Casey. She hugs me and kisses me and says, "Oh, thank you. You're so sweet."

As she's hugging me I feel her tits through her shirt. I whisper in her ear, "Let's get your bags and go straight to your house and fuck."

She says, "I can't believe we're engaged. Can you?"

I don't know if I had convinced myself that it was all a bad dream or if I had forced the memory of three nights ago so far down that I couldn't remember it, but we're engaged. Casey thinks we're engaged and she told her parents that we're engaged and now I'm giving her flowers in an airport. We're fucking engaged.

She says, "When I told my mom she started crying."

I can't say anything. I let go of her and start walking over to the baggage carousel. She follows me, still talking.

"My dad was like, 'Well, I guess we can expect another grandchild pretty soon.'"

I look around the baggage claim, kind of frantic. I need to find something that makes me think I shouldn't run out and throw myself in front of the first SuperShuttle I see. I see a semi-hot bitch with a great ass and a pretty good cocksucking mouth. I tell myself that I may have a very slim chance of ever fucking a girl like that, but if I'm dead I'll have no chance. I keep walking toward the baggage carousel. Casey keeps talking.

"At first I thought my dad was nuts, but I guess he's kind of right, you know? I mean, after you get married, it's like kids usually come pretty soon after. Do you want to have a boy or a girl first?"

I can feel the cold sweat dripping down the middle of my back into my ass crack. I wonder if Casey stopped taking the pill after the conversation with her dad. Maybe I should insist that we start using rubbers. Maybe I should only let her suck my dick. Casey keeps talking.

The first few bags come out of the baggage chute. They hit the carousel and start their crawl around it. The bitch who saved me from committing suicide comes over and stands right next to me. I stare at her ass. Casey keeps talking.

"You know, I think we should move in together before we get married. Maybe we could get a little dog, too. I don't know, though. The cats might not like having a dog. I guess the dog could be a strictly outside dog if we could get a place with a yard—somewhere in the Valley." I fucking despise the Valley.

As I'm staring at this girl's ass I notice she's trying to get a bag that slid past her and is now right in front of me. I reach down and get it. She brushes my arm with her hand as I lift it off the carousel. She looks up at me and smiles. She says, "Thanks," pops out the little handle, and shakes her ass out the door toward the waiting taxis. Casey keeps talking.

The rest of what she says is inaudible to me. Whatever she says becomes a high-pitched ringing in my ears. I grab her bag when I see it and we leave.

That night she says she loves me a few dozen times, she coaxes me into taking a bubble bath with her, she wears some lingerie she hasn't worn since Valentine's Day when I bought it for her, she snuggles up next to me, we don't fuck, and I fall asleep wondering if our daughters would be cursed with Casey's fat ass.

chapter seventeen

Chance Encounter

Casey and I have been engaged for a few weeks now. I haven't told any of my friends or family members. Casey has told all of hers multiple times. I'm listening to one of them congratulate Casey in the food court of the Beverly Center.

Her friend says, "Oh, I'm so happy for you guys."

Casey says, "Thanks. We're really excited. We're thinking about getting a place together."

Her friend says, "Oh my god, that is so fun. When Ronny and I got our place it was like the best day of my life, except for the wedding, of course." Then she pukes out a laugh.

Casey says, "Yeah. I can't wait."

Her friend says, "When's the big date?"

Casey says, "We really haven't picked one out yet. Probably sometime in the summer."

Her friend says, "You still have my address and everything to send an invite, right?"

Casey says, "Of course."

Her friend says, "Great," then she fake-whispers this next bit to Casey: "And don't forget to let me know about the bachelorette party."

Casey fake-whispers back, "I won't."

They hug and Casey says, "And don't be a stranger, let's get lunch sometime."

Her friend says, "Okay, I'll give you a call. You kids behave." Then she heads toward the escalators.

Casey says, "Have we ever come to the Beverly Center and not run into someone we know? Seriously, it's like everyone in town comes here on the weekends."

I start walking toward the Orange Julius/Dairy Queen without hearing what she just said. I remember in seventh grade home-ec class, Mrs. Baker taught us how to make Orange Julius with vanilla extract, orange juice, sugar, and ice. Mrs. Baker wasn't particularly attractive but I would have fucked her.

I buy a chocolate-dipped cone and Casey gets a small Julius. As we leave the counter I literally bump into Alyna, who is walking by with her arm around some asshole. A conversation is unavoidable and I'm sure it's going to lead to the discovery of our date by both of our significant others. But I'm more worried about Alyna finding out I have a girlfriend.

Alyna says, "Oh, hey. How are you?"

"I'm fine, you?"

"Pretty good."

"This is my boyfriend, Duane."

I fucking shake his hand. Casey gets tired of not being introduced and says, "I'm his fiancée, Casey. Nice to meet you guys."

Alyna shakes Casey's hand and says, "Hi, I'm Alyna." I can tell Alyna's surprised. I feel worse than I should for never telling her about Casey. Even though I have no chance with her, for some reason I still don't want her to be mad at me.

Casey is jealous immediately. She says, "So how do you two know each other?"

I kind of want to let it all out, expose the truth, see what happens. Alyna answers before I can say anything. She says, "I had a flat tire over in Westwood and your husband-to-be here helped me change it."

Holy shit. This is the most insane lie I've ever heard in my life. There's no way either of our respective counterparts will swallow it.

Casey says, "I didn't know you knew how to change a tire."

I say, "Well, I do."

Casey says, "Huh. I'll have to remember that," then she laughs.

Duane also laughs for some reason.

Alyna says, "Well, you guys take it easy. We have some shopping to get to."

I say, "Yeah. You, too."

As they walk away, Alyna says, "It was good to see you again."

I say, "Yeah. You, too."

I try to convince myself that this was just a strange coincidence, that there was no greater purpose behind running into Alyna, that she isn't thinking about me as she walks through the Beverly Center with Duane.

Casey says, "You never told me you helped somebody change their tire. That's a good story, why didn't you tell me about that?"

"I don't know."

"Do you want to go look at invitations or rings?"

I want to turn around, chase after Alyna, and never have to hear Casey's voice again. I say, "You pick."

Internet Personals

After downloading some double-dong lesbian pornography I check my e-mail. In my inbox is a message from Caligurrl669 with the following as a subject heading: "Saw you on match.com and thought you looked cute."

Despite having numerous profiles on different Internet personals sites for almost a year, this is the first e-mail response I've ever received. I open it.

Caligurrl669 tells me that she thinks I look like Eric Stoltz, who is one of her favorite actors. She recently moved to Los Angeles from Ohio to become an actress. She loves the Cure and the Smiths. She doesn't consider herself religious, but she is very spiritual. She has a dog and wants to know if I like animals. The last guy she dated was really into pro wrestling. She wasn't. She wants to know if I'm really into pro wrestling. She signs the e-mail with a smiley face and a link to her profile. I check the link.

Caligurrl669 is a little chubbier than I imagined from her e-mail, but not fat. Her tits are a little smaller than I imagined, but not bad. Her face is acceptable.

I wonder if Caligurrl669 sucks dick on the first date. I wonder if shes likes anal sex. I wonder if Caligurrl669 is actually a guy trying to lure me into showing up somewhere so he can beat the shit out of me and take whatever cash I brought.

I respond with the following message:

Caligurrl669—
I only set up dates with girls who send me nude photos of themselves accompanied by detailed descriptions of how they perform fellatio. To further pique my interest you might want to do something in the photos that lets me know you have a unique talent, you know, something to separate you from the crowd. I look forward to your response.

Caligurrl669 probably won't ever write me again and that doesn't bother me. But then again, she might.

chapter eighteen

Casey's Parents

Over the course of our relationship, Casey's parents have come to Los Angeles to visit her several times. I've eaten dinner with them more than once and have been forced to endure multiple trips to the mall with them and Casey to look for clothes. As much as I hated all of that, the prospect of spending the next two days with them as their future son-in-law is on a different level of agony. But somehow the impending doom of my life ending in marriage to Casey is less threatening than the more immediate disaster that would result from breaking up with her now.

We're in my car on the way to LAX to pick her parents up. Casey says, "Remember, you can't curse around my mom. She'll think you're a bad influence and that our marriage will be bad. And offer to pay for things. You'll never have to, but if you offer to pay for things my dad will think you're a provider and that's good. And don't bring up France with my dad. He'll go crazy and won't stop talking for an hour. And if my mom asks you where you think we're going to live, just tell her that it's still up in the air and it really depends on where we can find the best place. And if they ask you about a wedding date, tell them a.s.a.p. And if either of them ask you about when we're going to have kids, just say as soon as we get settled we're going to start trying. Wait, maybe don't say anything about trying because they'll think about us having sex and I don't want my parents thinking about that. Just say as soon as we're settled."

When we exit the 405, there's a hobo with a sign that reads HOME-LESS, HUNGRY, AND HANDSOME — ANYTHING WILL HELP at the first stop-light. I like his sign so I roll down my window. He walks in between a few cars also stopped at the red light and holds out his hand. I reach in my pocket and realize I only have a five-dollar bill. I don't really want to give him five dollars, but I already rolled down my window and now he's standing at it. I give him the five-dollar bill. He thanks me, the light turns green, and we keep driving. Despite the satisfaction I genu-inely get from giving hobos money, I gave this guy money specifically to get the following reaction from Casey:

"Why do you give them money? It's so stupid. They just spend it on drugs and booze."

There's something about her hating the fact that I give hobos money that makes me happy.

We park at LAX and go into the baggage claim area to wait for Casey's mom and dad to come out. She says, "God, isn't this exciting. I mean, I know you've met them before and everything, but you've never actually met them as your future in-laws. Seriously, aren't you excited?"

I think she's asking a rhetorical question so I don't answer.

She says, "Well, aren't you?"

"Yeah."

Some people start coming out of a door toward the baggage claim.

Casey says, "Do you think that's their flight?"

I think I want to walk back to my car and drive back to my apart-ment and play World of Warcraft. I think I don't want to spend the next two days being dragged around L.A. looking at clothes I couldn't care less about and eating food when I'm not hungry. I think I don't want to do this anymore.

Her mom and dad walk through the door and spot us. Her mom half jogs over to Casey with a big smile on her face, while her dad is left to drag both of their carry-on bags behind him.

Her mom says, "Oh, congratulations, you two. I just knew Casey would get married one day. I just knew it. My little girl. And you," she says to me, "come here."

She gives me a big hug and says, "It's about time, huh? We were starting to wonder about you."

For an older woman Casey's mom has a noticeably nice ass. I wonder if Casey's will slim down if I stay with her until she's in her fifties.

Casey's dad finally manages to make it over to the group. He says, "So, my little girl's getting hitched?" He gives her a hug, then turns to me and says, "And I'm going to have a new son." He shakes my hand in a weird kind of overexcited way.

Casey's mom says, "So we thought we could go eat a little lunch when we get out of here and then you guys can drop us off at our hotel for a few hours so we can rest for a bit, and then you can come back and pick us up and we can go shopping, or I figured that you guys would probably start looking for a place to live together . . . we could come with you. That would be so much fun. How does that sound?"

Casey says, "That's exactly the way I had it planned, too."

If I had a cyanide pill I would probably eat it.

Casey's dad says, "Great. We just have a few bags."

We wait at the baggage carousel for a few bags, which turns out to be five.

When we get in my car and I start it, I become immediately aware that Casey forgot to take my Snoop Dogg CD out and Casey's parents are treated to the following pro-marriage rhetoric:

You talk too much
Ho get up out my face unless you tryin' to fuck
'Cause on the real a nigga kinda drunk

Casey turns the music off before Snoop can say anything else. Everyone in the car heard it and no one's saying anything. I put the car in reverse and pull out of my parking spot. No one's saying anything. I start driving to the parking structure exit. No one's saying anything. I pull up to the booth, grab my ticket off the dashboard, and roll down my window. Casey's dad says, "I just can't get over how nice the weather here is."

We pull up to the booth and I give my ticket to a little Asian guy. The meter flashes $3.00. The little Asian guy hammers it home by saying, "Three dollars, please."

I realize I gave my last five dollars to the hobo on the way into the airport. Casey said her parents would never let me pay for anything, I just had to make the offer. I say, "I got it." I reach in my pocket to make the offer seem real. I'm feeling around inside my empty pocket when I hear Casey's parents say nothing.

I don't know if they're pissed at me for Snoop Dogg or if this is the one time they're actually making me pay for something as some kind of test. In either case I have no way of paying the three dollars. The little Asian guy says again with exactly the same inflection, "Three dollars, please."

Casey's getting nervous next to me. She turns back and smiles to her parents. She says, "How was your flight?" She's trying to stall them, but it's not working. I can see her mom's face in my rearview mirror. She's getting anxious. Her dad looks disappointed. Deep down I don't really care about any of it. And I'm kind of happy when I say, "That's funny, I don't seem to have any money on me. I guess I just gave my last five dollars to that homeless guy."

Casey's mom reaches for her purse and says, "Why do you give them money? They only spend it on drugs and drink." Then she adds,

"I think I have three dollars." She's almost disgusted when she hands me the bills.

I say, "Thanks, sorry about that. Dinner's on me tonight."

Casey's dad says, "Don't be silly. It's only three dollars." But I can tell he's pissed, too. It's more than just three dollars to him. It's the guy who's about to marry his little girl not being able to get out of a parking lot. I hope it keeps him awake at night. I hope I'm the secretly hated fiancé, the one they complain about to their friends at the country club, the one who always gets shitty presents at family Christmas parties, the one who ruins their perfect family.

As we pull out of the parking structure, Casey says, "So where do you guys want to eat?"

I know her dad is thinking that now I can't even offer to pay for lunch because everyone knows I have no money. I think I might offer anyway. Her dad says, "Somewhere with steak."

Her mom says, "You already had your steak for the week."

He says, "We're on vacation."

She says, "That doesn't matter. You're not having another steak. Casey, you pick."

Casey says, "Okay, I know a good place. Daddy, there's no steak but I think you'll like it."

He says, "Do they have beer?"

Casey's mom says, "You can't have any more beer this week either. Are you just trying to kill yourself right before your daughter's wedding? Is that what you want?"

He says, "It's my vacation."

She says, "That doesn't matter. Your heart doesn't go on vacation and neither does your high blood pressure."

They keep arguing as we drive down the road to one of Casey's favorite lunch places, the Daily Grill. I wonder if they still fuck or when the last time was that she sucked his cock.

chapter nineteen

Apartment Hunting

We've been in the Valley, Toluca Lake, for four hours looking at apartments with Casey's parents and a woman from a rental agency that Casey called, who seems to be in her mid-thirties with great tits. I fucking despise the Valley. I'm standing in the living room of the third place we've looked at today. Casey, her mom, and the rental agency lady are in the bedroom. Her dad's standing with me.

He says, "So how'd you propose to my little girl?"

I try to remember exactly how we became engaged. I can't. I only vaguely think Casey invited me over to fuck and then somehow we were engaged without fucking.

I say, "I got down on one knee."

He says, "I figured you for a one-knee man. That's how I popped the question to her mother, too. One knee's the best way to go. It's not too creative, but it gets the job done and it's classy. Things like that are important moments in a woman's life and they should be classy." He pats me on the back, then says, "You know, Casey's sister just had a baby. Do you think you guys'll have kids pretty soon after you're married?"

I can't remember what Casey told me I was supposed to say but I think it was something like, "Yeah."

He says, "That's great. That's really the only way to do it. Start your family early, then when you get to be my age you have some time for yourself. Not that raising kids is all bad or anything, but trust me, when you hit forty-five you can barely stand your wife, let alone kids running around the house. But don't get me wrong, marriage is a wonderful thing."

Casey, her mom, and the rental agency woman walk in from the other room. Casey's mom is pointing at the walls, saying, "You could do some amazing things in here. There's so much light. Really, this would make a great family area. And that little half bedroom would be perfect for the baby. This place is absolutely perfect."

The realtor says, "It really is perfect for married couples just starting out. The last tenants were a married couple and they were here for two and a half years, and now that they have their third baby on the way and a little more money in their pockets, they're going to buy their first house."

Casey says, "I can't wait till we can buy our first house together." Then she hugs me. I wonder if the rental agency woman would do a three-way with me and Casey, or if she'd just suck my cock if I stopped by her office one day.

Casey's dad says, "Well, do you guys think this is the one?"

Casey says, "I really like it."

Her dad says, "Then you guys should get the ball rolling—no time like the present."

Casey says, "I guess you're right. What do we need to fill out?"

The rental agency woman says, "Well, we can start getting the paperwork in order, but it really depends on when you'd want to move in. The current tenants officially move out in a couple of months. I don't know when the big wedding date is for you guys and how that fits into your plans, but that's the soonest they could be out."

Casey's mom says, "I can't believe we never even asked when you're getting married."

Casey says, "Well, we wanted to have some time to plan it out and everything, but if we need to be ready to move, I guess we could move things up."

Casey's mom says, "I'll help you plan everything. It'll go like clockwork. You can still have a beautiful wedding even in a few months."

Casey says, "Would you really help me plan it, Mom?"

Her mom says, "Of course. I know exactly how everything should be."

Everything else either one of them says becomes a high-pitched ringing in my ears. I think about Alyna and wonder what would have happened if I hadn't gone over to Casey's house that night to fuck.

Later as we're eating dinner to celebrate the paperwork being started on our new apartment, I look at Casey's dad and try to picture myself at his age, visiting my daughter who's forced some guy into a marriage he doesn't want. I wonder if Casey's dad really wanted to marry her mom. I wonder if there was a girl like Alyna for him. I wonder how many times a day he jerks off. I wonder if I'll still jerk off when I'm his age.

When we're finished with dinner I offer to pay and her parents let me.

Blood Cock

When Casey has her period she refuses to suck my dick and she's very uncomfortable with fucking. I usually have to coax her into it by promising to buy her dinner at one of her favorite restaurants. As I'm fucking her on this particular occasion I've only had to promise to take her for ice cream.

She's lying on a towel so the blood that runs down her ass crack doesn't get on the sheets. As I fuck her I look down at her face and she's completely uninterested. I decide to make sure she gets off just to prove to myself I can do it at will. I slow down my pace a little and reach down with one hand to play with her clit. This seems to be working at least on a rudimentary level.

I lean down and whisper in her ear, "I love you so much. I can't wait until we can make love in our own house."

She starts moaning.

I kiss her slowly on the lips and take the hand I was using on her clit and touch her face. After the kiss I pull back and look into her eyes, ignoring the bloody smear I left on her cheek. I say, "I can't wait to spend the rest of my life with you."

She moans louder. She reaches around and grabs me by the ass, pulling me toward her.

I go back to stroking her clit and say, "I love you more than anything."

She cums like a ton of bricks so I stop holding back and blow my load with three deep, hard thrusts.

When I pull out I make sure to hang my cock over her stomach to let some of the blood and semen drip off my dick onto her stomach, knowing this will disgust her.

As I'm getting up to go to the bathroom, she says, "That was better than I thought it was going to be."

We take a shower together to clean up. I watch the blood and semen run down her legs and into the shower drain. She cleans her cunt but doesn't wash her face, leaving the smudge of blood so it's still there when we leave a few minutes later to get her ice cream.

chapter twenty

Bon Voyage

I'm at the airport with Casey and her parents eating chicken strips in a Chili's Too. I've had to shit since I woke up, but Casey told me there wasn't enough time to drop a deuce because her parents had to be at the airport. Casey's mom says, "I'll be out here again next weekend to help you start planning for the big day."

I wish I would have taken that shit.

Casey says, "Are you coming back, Daddy?"

He says, "Not if you want me to pay for it. I have to work."

Casey's mom says, "So it'll just be me. And I'll stay as long as it takes to get everything together."

I don't particularly dislike Casey's mom, but the prospect of her staying "as long as it takes to get everything together" makes the impending shit lurch in my intestines and want to come out.

Casey tries to coax the turd out a little more by saying, "Mom, if you don't want to hassle with a hotel while you're out here, you can always just stay with me."

I immediately picture Casey refusing to suck my cock or fuck me because her mom's in her apartment. I chew my chicken strip hard enough to grind my teeth down to nubs.

Casey's dad says, "That wouldn't be a bad idea except for your mom's back. You know she wouldn't be able to sleep on your futon."

Casey saves the day with, "Well, I could sleep on it while you're out here and you could have the bed."

My intestines are at full boil. I say, "Excuse me, I have to go to the bathroom."

As I leave the table kind of abruptly I can tell Casey's mom is somehow offended that I'm exiting while they talk about obviously important matters. When I stand up a silent fart leaks out and I try to point my ass slightly in the direction of Casey's mom so there's a possibility that she'll be blamed for it.

After I clean off the toilet seat in the Chili's Too bathroom and apply three toilet seat covers, I rip my pants down and open the floodgates as a torrent of liquid shit flies out of my ass in a way that makes me think I might have possibly shit some vital organ into the water below. And then I feel fine.

I sit on the crapper for another five or six minutes before wiping, just feeling lighter, better. When I come back out, all of our food has already been cleared away and Casey's dad is signing his credit card bill. I thank him for lunch in a mandatory attempt at politeness.

We walk with her parents to the security check. Her mom hugs me and her dad shakes my hand just before they walk through the metal detectors and disappear around a corner to go to their flight.

As I drive back to Casey's place with her in the passenger seat, I reach over and start unbuttoning her pants with one hand, trying to get her in the mood so once we do get to her apartment we can get right to fucking. As I get to the second button she stops me and holds my hand.

We drive down the road in complete silence for a few miles listening to 50 Cent. As soon as he tells us that he's into having sex, he ain't into making love, Casey turns the volume down and begins telling me the following information: "I love you so much. We're going to have the best life together. I can't wait." Every word she says makes me feel a little more like faking a stroke and pretending to lose all memory of who I was, but it's not until she looks me in the eye and says in all seriousness, "You're my soul mate," that I realize I am not going to marry her.

chapter twenty-one

Be the King

Todd and I are at a bar in Westwood. Next to us is a table full of seven Asian bitches playing some kind of card game. Three of them are extremely hot and the rest are definitely worth fucking or at least getting head from.

Todd says, "So what's the deal now, you're getting married to Casey?"

"No. I'm not."

"But you just said her mom is coming back here to start planning the wedding in a few days, dude."

"Right."

"So when are you planning on not marrying her?"

"I don't know."

"Dude, do you think those Asian sluts would let us play with them?"

"I don't know."

"Dude, I'm gonna ask 'em."

And he does. The hottest one of them all appears to be the only one who speaks English and answers for the whole group when she says, "If you want play with, you and friend can play with."

Todd and I sit down at their table and listen to the following explanation of a new card game we've never heard of. "Okay, we play Be the King. It go like this. We have nine person to play so there will be cards one, two, three, four, five, six, seven, eight, and then king."

She starts pulling out the ace through eight of clubs and a king.

"Okay, now I deal."

She gives everybody at the table a card.

"Okay, now you look at card, but no show to us."

Todd and I look at our cards. I have the three of clubs.

"Okay, now who has king?"

One of the Asian girls sitting next to Todd goes fucking crazy, tosses her king into the middle of the table, and starts screaming, "I king, I king!"

The one who speaks English calms her down, "Okay, okay, okay. Now that she king, she tell us what to do."

I'm semi-drunk by this point and completely confused until the "king" says something of which I understand the following, "Okay, four—seven—"

The girl who speaks English explains to us that her friend, the king, has told whoever has the four and whoever has the seven to kiss for thirty seconds. And the game has just become infinitely more interesting and corroborates a long-held theory of mine that there are only two kinds of Asian girls—nymphomaniacs and corpses.

We all reveal our cards and it turns out that two of the really hot girls are four and seven. They kiss each other in this innocent giddy way that gives me a hard-on immediately. Todd and I agree to somehow let each other know which cards we pull.

In the next round I pull the king and Todd tips the corner of his card my way to show me he has the five. I say, "Okay, everyone except the king, kiss number five." Our friend, whose American name we've learned is Danni, translates it to her pals. They do a gang kiss on Todd, sometimes kissing each other.

The next round I pull a four and Todd shows me via a less stealthy and progressively drunker upturn of the corner of his card that he's drawn the eight. One of the semi-attractive Asian girls has drawn the king. She commands one of the girls to take another girl's head and pretend to smash it into a wall. Then the girl whose head was pretend-smashed into the wall has to scream and pretend her head really was smashed into the wall. Despite the fact that this act is in no way sexual, it is highly entertaining.

The longer we play, the more Todd and I try to turn Be the King into an orgy of Asian bitches to which we've somehow become privy, but there's something about these girls that won't allow us to succeed. They're naive and it seems like they're probably virgins and all of them find just as much excitement in pretending to beat each other up as they do in kissing each other.

The next time I get the king, I decide to see how far I can take it. I know Todd has a three, so I say, "Number four and number five have to suck the king's dick."

Danni says, "What is dick?"

I say, "Penis."

She says, "What is penis?"

I point to my crotch.

She says, "Oh," and giggles, then translates it for all of her buddies. They all giggle and start looking down at the ground. Four and Five start talking to Danni.

She says, "They say they no want to do that."

"But I'm the king."

"If they no want to, they no have to."

"Then what's the point of being the king?"

"To have fun and do funny thing."

"A blow job is a funny thing, Danni."

They all start talking to each other for about a minute. Todd and I just drink our beers. I look around the bar and notice that a group of people has kind of surrounded our table and has been watching us play this game for a while. Finally the Asian bitches come to a consensus.

Danni says, "We all go now."

Todd says, "No, you don't have to go, dude. We can let you be the king and slap each other around or whatever you guys want to do. Don't go."

Danni says, "We need to sleep for tests. It nice meeting you."

With that, Danni and her gang of Asian girls leave the table and the bar, leaving Todd to dispense the following accusation, "You made them leave, you fucker. If you hadn't scared them off by commanding them to give you a blow job, we could have—"

I say, "What, gotten blow jobs?"

Todd laughs. We discuss the nature of the game and how bizarre the Asian girls were before the conversation returns to Casey.

Todd says, "Seriously, dude, what's so bad about marrying her? Free house, she has rich parents—all that shit sounds good to me."

"Yeah, I guess."

"Then you should do it. I mean, fuck, dude, free fucking house. She ain't bad lookin'—that's pretty sweet."

"Yeah." No.

Later that night, after I've gone home, I lie awake staring at the ceiling and jerking off to thoughts of fucking the Asian girls we played Be the King with, which somehow reminds me of the first time I fucked my high school girlfriend, Katy. I remember the first time I shot a load down her throat when I shoot a load all over my own hand and the postejaculatory calm washes over me. For the first time in a while, Casey and my life's ruin is the furthest thing from my mind.

I wipe the semen off my hand and my dick with a towel that was lying on my floor and stay awake for a few more minutes wondering if I should have asked the Asian bitches to have anal sex with me, if somehow that would have offended them less. I also wonder if some of them were willing to suck my dick and Danni or one of the other bitches convinced them to leave. I wish Casey was Asian. I wish I hadn't thought about Casey.

Little Kids

I'm eating a cheeseburger at Topz on Melrose. This semi-old-looking bitch is sitting a few tables away from me with a little girl who's probably about two or three years old. Across the room there's another bitch with a little boy who's probably about the same age.

The little boy keeps staring at the little girl and touching his cock. I wonder if he's actually thinking about fucking her or if he's getting a boner and doesn't know what it is or if he's just pawing at his dick because that's what little kids do. I myself don't think I ever thought about fucking when I was two, but I don't really remember.

As I keep looking at these little kids and wondering if they're thinking about fucking each other, I can't help thinking that at some point in each of these two-year-old kids' lives, they're going to be fucking somebody. That two-year-old girl whose mom dressed her up in a little pink dress to take her to Topz after Sunday church is going to suck cock, take it up the ass, have load after load of semen shot in her face, and eventually have another little girl who's eventually going to do all the same shit. And that little two-year-old boy whose mom dressed him in his Spider-Man T-shirt to take him to eat lunch after his favorite morning cartoons is going to fuck a girl, eat pussy, get twat hairs stuck in his throat, get his dick sucked, and someday have kids who will do all the same shit.

I wonder if either of the kids' parents have thought about any of this. I wonder if I'll have kids. If I do have kids I wonder if I'll look at them and think about them eventually fucking. I wonder if my parents ever thought about me fucking. I wonder if my parents are still fucking.

chapter twenty-two

Hi, Mom

I spend the night at Casey's apartment because we have to meet her mom at the airport the following morning and Casey wants me to drive. I assume that we'll fuck because this is the last night we have before her mom is in town and possibly in Casey's house for an indefinite amount of time. At 11:43 P.M. Casey's snoring makes me realize I shouldn't have assumed anything.

I'm unable to sleep, and my restless libido starts turning into rage. I lay awake staring at the ceiling listening to the sound of Casey's nose whistling in between her snorting gasps for air. I have to fuck. I nudge her a couple of times.

"Casey, Casey."

She wakes up. "What? I was asleep."

"Let's make love."

"My mom's coming tomorrow morning. We have to get to sleep."

"But don't you want to make love one more time before your mom gets here?"

"Why?"

She doesn't understand, or maybe she just doesn't care that once her mom is in town the frequency with which we have sex will be cut in half, or probably even worse. I say, "Because I love you."

"I love you, too. But I'm tired and I don't want to be even more tired when my mom gets here."

She kisses me on the cheek and rolls over, turning her fat ass toward me. She says, "Good night."

I can't take it. I get out of her bed.

She says, "Where are you going?"

"I have to go to the bathroom."

She goes back to sleep never knowing that I walk into the bathroom and jerk off into a bottle of special color treatment shampoo that she bought because it was featured on an Oprah show as one of Oprah's favorite things. As I jerk off, I think about kissing Alyna and fantasize about fucking her. For a split second, just before I cum, I entertain the thought of leaving Casey's apartment and driving to Alyna's to see if she'd be up for going to get coffee, but then I blow my load and I calm down enough to wipe off the top of the bottle, screw the lid back on, put it back in Casey's shower, and crawl back into bed with her.

I dream about nothing.

I wake up the next morning to an already awake and chipper Casey saying, "Come on, sleepyhead, it's time to take a shower and get ready to go pick up my mom."

We take a shower together. She uses her special color treatment shampoo. I use the Pert that's been in her shower as long as I've known her—probably left there by a previous boyfriend. Seeing her massage nine parts shampoo and one part semen into a thick lather on her head is more satisfying than any sex the night before could have been.

In the car on the way to the airport Casey turns off the volume on my stereo, which was playing "Xxplosive" from Dr. Dre's *Chronic 2001*. She says, "You know you can't listen to that when my mom gets in the car. She'd be completely offended. I mean, I'm actually kind of offended, too. But I guess because I'm younger and like I've grown up with rap music, I can at least deal with the way they talk about women. But my mom would not be okay with it."

I let her turn off my music without any rebuttal.

Then she says, "I'm sorry about last night, you know, not wanting to make love, but I think that other things are just a little more important right now. I mean we're about to start planning our wedding. That's like a day that we'll remember for the rest of our lives."

She keeps talking about things as I stare down the road trying to imagine what the couple in the car in front of us is talking about. I can see the silhouette of the woman in the passenger's seat. She's kind of flailing her arms around and every once in a while pointing at the guy driving, who's completely motionless, staring straight ahead and probably looking at the car in front of him wondering what the woman in that car's passenger seat is saying to the guy driving.

As I pull into a parking space in structure #4 at LAX I realize Casey is still talking about something. I hear, ". . . take us to breakfast at the Griddle, which I know you don't like, but can you just eat something and pretend to like it for me? I mean, she is going to be your mother-in-law in a few months. It would be nice if you could just pretend that you can eat breakfast with her at her favorite place in L.A. and not make a big deal about it."

I want her to shut up. I say, "Okay." It doesn't work.

"And don't be rude and order something that's not on the menu. The last time we went there, you asked the guy if they could make you a plate of scrambled eggs with nothing else in it. How embarrassing. If you want scrambled eggs, just get an omelet or something and cut it up."

When we get in the terminal we find out her mom's flight is fifteen minutes late, which Casey insists is a perfect amount of time to go look in the gift shop. I flip through an issue of *Hustler* that someone has already taken out of the plastic and left on the rack. Casey flips through Oprah's latest issue until she sees me staring at a pair of huge tits and a shaved pussy.

In a forced whisper she says, "Put that down."

I pretend not to hear her and flip the page to see another bitch spreading her friend's cunt open in preparation to lick it.

Casey walks over to me and closes the magazine while I'm still holding it. A naked bitch on the cover grabbing her own tits is still plainly visible to anyone walking by. Casey says, "How could you be looking at that right now?"

"It was the most interesting thing on the stand."

"My mother's going to be here in"—she checks her watch—"ten minutes. You can't be looking at that."

"You were the one who wanted to come look in the gift shop."

"Just put it back."

Even though I decide it's not worth getting into a fight over and put the *Hustler* back, the angry dissatisfaction I felt last night hits me tenfold and the thought of spending another second with Casey without fucking her makes me want to kill somebody.

She puts her magazine back and I walk with her to the baggage claim area, where we're supposed to meet her mom. I see at least a dozen other guys standing with girls. I wonder how many of them fucked their girlfriends last night.

Ten more minutes or so pass and Casey tries to explain to me how important it is to choose just the right kind of wedding invitation. She says that even though I won't be involved in the process of choosing the invitations, it's important for me to understand why she and her mother end up choosing whichever invitations they choose. She further explains that she wants something new and hip, but still traditional enough that her grandparents won't think she's moved to Hollywood and gone crazy. Then she laughs.

I try to imagine what she'd look like thirty pounds lighter. I can't. Her mom finally comes down an escalator and out to meet us.

She says, "Give me a hug, Casey. Long time no see." Then she laughs.

Casey says, "So did you get a hotel or did you decide to stay at my place?"

"I thought I'd stay at your apartment tonight so we can talk about a game plan."

"That's a great idea."

"So are you guys ready to go get some breakfast?"

We wait for her bags and drive to the Griddle, one of my least favorite places to eat.

chapter twenty-three

The Griddle

I figure Casey won't be fucking me for at least a few days anyway, so I order the plate of scrambled eggs with nothing else in it that Casey has forbidden me to get. Casey and her mom both pretend not to hear me when I ask the guy if they can make it for me. Even though I've already ordered it, before the guy leaves our table I throw in the following knife twist for good measure, "Now you're sure there'll be nothing else in the eggs?"

He says, "No. It'll just be eggs. I mean, it's not on the menu, but we can make it for you."

"Thanks."

Then he leaves. Casey's mom can't stand that I ordered a plate of scrambled eggs with nothing else in it. She doesn't even look at me as she says, "Do you always order things that aren't on the menu?"

I say, "Sometimes. Not always."

She still can't deal with it. She says, "It's just kind of strange. They have a whole variety of items that contain scrambled eggs. I just don't know why any one of those dishes isn't good enough."

And it's right then that I know I never want to see this woman again. I never want to hear her voice and I never want to placate her just to make Casey happy and I never want to deal with her in any way.

The waiter comes back with our drinks just as Casey's mom is getting fired up about my eggs. She calms down. As he leaves, she changes the topic of conversation entirely with, "Casey, your father wanted me to tell you that he's really sorry he couldn't come out and he wishes he was here, but he has to work."

Casey says, "Yeah, I know. He already told me."

Their voices trail off into nothing as I stare at this guy and girl sitting a few tables away from us. The girl isn't amazingly hot, but she's pretty good-looking and has what looks to be a nice set of tits. They're all over each other. The guy is rubbing her stomach and she's running her hands through his hair. Every now and then they kiss like they're going to fuck each other right there at the table.

I guess I watch them for a while because I'm still watching them when our food comes to the table probably ten minutes later.

As he gives me my eggs, the waiter says, "Here's your special plate of scrambled eggs with nothing else in them."

I say, "Thanks."

Casey and her mom both cringe again.

He leaves after asking if we need anything else and the following conversation begins:

Casey's mom takes a bite of her blueberry pancakes and says, "So after we eat I thought just you and I could go back to your place, Casey, so we can get started on everything."

Casey says, "Yeah, that sounds good. You won't mind just dropping us off, right?"

I say, "No."

Casey's mom says, "You wouldn't want to be involved in this anyway. It's really very boring . . . unless you're a woman." Then she laughs. So does Casey.

It's right then that I realize I never want to be Casey's chauffeur again.

I chew my eggs while I stare at the guy and girl who are definitely about to go somewhere and fuck after they finish their waffles. I try to remember a time when Casey was like that, and even though the memory doesn't come easily, there definitely was a time. I decide that all bitches eventually cool down and lose interest.

Then Casey says, "I'll just give you a call tomorrow morning and maybe we can all go out and eat breakfast again or something."

Her mom says, "Well, maybe we should just play it by ear."

Casey says, "Yeah, I guess you're right."

It's right at that moment that I realize I never want to be dismissed or taken for granted by Casey or her mother again. I never want to play the role they expect of me. For a split second I feel bad for the guy who I'm sure is going to be in this situation a few years from now, but at that moment it becomes crystal clear to me that when I walk out of the Griddle, I will not be engaged to this woman's daughter.

In the following minute that passes, nobody says anything, but the blood pounding in my head and my teeth grinding down on pieces of scrambled eggs and Casey licking the jelly off her lips and the fake smile that's been on her mom's face since we walked in and the general rage that's built up in me over the course of our relationship all boils down to the following seven words:

I say, "I don't think we should get married." As the words come, I feel no immediate liberation. I feel no significant change. But something, some dark, twisted knot in the pit of my stomach that I never really even knew existed, seems to loosen up a bit—just a little bit.

Her mom says, "Excuse me?"

Casey's mouth is just hanging open, half full of chewed toast. I don't really want to say anything else so I wait for her mom to say, "Did you just say you don't want to get married?"

I say, "Yeah."

Casey's mom drops her fork on her plate, wipes the corners of her mouth with the napkin that's been in her lap since she sat down, and says, "I have never been so insulted in all of my life."

Casey still hasn't said anything.

Her mom says, "You let Casey's father and me come all the way out here, find an apartment for you to live in . . . I just . . . I can't believe it. Do you realize you've wasted over a year of Casey's life? That's a year and a half that she could have been looking for someone who actually wanted to marry her."

I try to imagine who that poor guy would have been. I picture a fatter version of myself with glasses.

Casey's on the verge of tears. She finally says, "Do you still want to be boyfriend and girlfriend?"

I feel like I'm in the seventh grade telling Amber Pearson that if she won't let me touch her pussy then I don't think we should "go" together anymore because Amanda Long said she'd let me touch hers.

I say, "No, I don't think so."

"So you want to break up?"

"Yeah, I think so."

"And not see each other anymore . . . ever?"

"Yeah."

And Casey's out of commission. She just breaks down sobbing and choking and saying, "Why?"

Casey's mom moves her chair around the table and puts an arm around her daughter. She looks at me and says, "Look what you've done." Then to Casey she says, "Everything's going to be fine, honey. You'll find a husband. This doesn't mean anything."

Casey just keeps saying, "Why?"

Casey's mom stands up, forcing Casey to stand up with her, and says, "We'll be out by the car," and walks out, leaving me with the tab. As I pay it I realize a couple of things:

1. I do actually feel kind of bad about the whole thing but I am glad that I ruined Casey's mom's favorite breakfast place in L.A. by dumping her daughter in it.

And

2. I still have to give Casey and her mom a ride back to Casey's place.

chapter twenty-four

The Drive to Casey's House

Casey's house is probably about forty-five minutes from the Griddle, thirty with no traffic. There's traffic.

Casey and her mom sit in the backseat while I drive. Casey rocks back and forth sobbing and saying, "Why?" as her mom hugs her and keeps repeating, "It's going to be fine. We'll just get to your apartment and forget all about him."

As we come to a dead stop on the 405 in minute four of our drive, I wonder why her mom didn't just tell me to go fuck myself and get a cab for her and Casey to take back to Casey's apartment. As we lurch forward again I ask her.

"Are you sure you guys don't just want to get a cab? I can drop you off at a hotel or something."

Casey's mom says, "You just broke my little girl's heart and probably ruined any chance she has at getting married for at least the next year. The least you can do is drive us back to her apartment."

I say, "Okay."

Surprisingly, the drive back to Casey's apartment isn't that uncomfortable for me. Having cut Casey loose gives me a feeling of detachment from anything she must be going through and that's comforting.

Every now and then Casey says something like, "Isn't there any way we can like just talk this through?" or "I just don't understand. Can't you give me some chance to like change?" to which I say, "No, I don't think so." Then she goes back to crying so much she can't talk or properly breathe.

Her mom throws out things like, "I can understand realizing that you don't want to be with somebody after a few months, but waiting a year and a half to end something—after you've proposed, no less . . . that's just plain rude. And after all her father and I have done for you. Well, I can tell you this much, you won't be missed at any of the Childress family functions," and, "Do you honestly think you're going to find another family as giving as ours? Because you're not. The Childresses were the best thing that ever happened to you and you're going to realize it one day, but it'll be too late because Casey will be gone. She'll be married to someone else who deserves to be part of our family."

For a second I imagine Casey fucking some other guy. It doesn't bother me at all. I imagine her sucking some other guy's cock, which gets the same reaction. The thought of her getting gangbanged by the Lakers doesn't make me mad or queasy or sad or anything at all. I go back to just imagining one guy fucking her. I start to feel sorry for the guy.

Casey snaps me out of the image by saying something new: "Is there someone else?"

And even though technically there isn't, the question makes me think immediately of Alyna and what she's doing and if the fact that I'm single would change how she felt about me at all. I say, "No."

"Then why do you want to do this? I just don't understand."

I kind of feel like I do owe her an explanation, but I know telling her the truth—that I can't stand to be around her and I hate her mother and I wish she would fuck me more—will ultimately end up with her promising to change and forcing me to give her a chance to work out our problems. I also think about explaining that I never really wanted to get engaged. Maybe telling Casey's mom that the night we got "engaged" was actually a misunderstanding, that I never actually proposed. I think about seeing the look on her face when I tell her that I just went to Casey's apartment that night because she promised to fuck me, but then never did—kind of like how I supposedly agreed to marry Casey and never will. But I decide it's not worth the effort of a conversation, so instead I just say, "I just need to be by myself."

"Then we don't have to get married. We can just date and I'll give you your space."

Her mom says, "Don't cater to him. If he doesn't want you for who you are, then you don't want him." I want to smash my car into a pole just to see Casey's mom fly through the windshield.

Casey says, "Yes, I do, Mom. I love him."

I say, "I don't want to date."

Casey says, "Then we can just be friends and like start dating when you feel comfortable with the idea of it again."

Her mom says, "You're giving him too much. If you want him back, you make him come back on your terms."

I change my mind about smashing my car into a pole. Instead, I realize I'd rather get into some kind of accident that would result in Casey's mom being trapped and me having to save her, so for the rest of her life she'd know the man who ruined her daughter's life also saved hers.

I say, "Terms? I don't want that either."

Casey says, "Then whatever you want, just like let me have a chance to give it to you."

Casey's mom says, "He doesn't deserve you, Casey. Just let it go. He's not worth it."

And I'm so sick of Casey begging, and her mom being a cunt, and my imaginary car crash scenarios that I decide to just come out and say it. "Okay, you want to know what I want?"

She says, "Yes," truly believing that whatever it is I'm about to say is going to show her the way to keep me forever.

I say, "Okay, I want to fuck twice a day minimum or at least have my dick sucked. I want you to swallow. I want to butt-fuck you every once in a while and I want you to like it. . . ."

By this point I'm sure her mom is having an aneurysm, but I can't stop. I feel like every word I say should have been said a million times before over the course of our relationship. I feel like every word I say should come as no shock to Casey, but I know they do. I feel like every word I say makes up for every load I should have shot in our relationship.

For those reasons I keep saying, ". . . I never want you to tell me a stupid fucking story about shit I couldn't care less about again. I want you to get rid of your cats. I want you to lose about fifteen pounds off your ass. I want you to never want to get married or have kids. I want you to like video games. I want you to think retards are funny. I want you to not care if I say 'fuck' in front of your mom. I want you to wish Marie Osmond was dead."

The Marie Osmond line is too much for Casey's mom. She says, "Why would you ever want Marie Osmond dead? She's one of the most courageous women of our time."

I remember a line from some shitty movie Casey made me watch a month or two ago because it was one of her favorites. I decide to use the line on her. "I guess I just want you to be something you're not."

I don't know if she remembers that the line is from the movie or not, but she goes back to crying. Her mom goes back to hugging her and telling her that everything's going to be okay, and I turn up the volume on my stereo and listen to Dr. Dre's "Can't Make a Ho a Housewife," which I'm pretty sure makes me smile.

Veggie Love

I start my hunt for Internet pornography by going to Pengus-Picks. Pengus-Picks always has at least a few clips that interest me on the site itself as well as several links to other portals. After downloading a few clips from the main site, I click a link to one of the portals. Then I click on a link that reads "U GOTTA C THIS."

I'm taken to a page that has three free movie clips: cucunt.mpg, squashfuck.avi, and cantaloupe.mpg. The idea of bitches ramming vegetables in their cunts doesn't necessarily turn me on, but the novelty of it is interesting enough for me to download all three clips.

Cucunt.mpg is forty seconds long and depicts a woman sliding a sizable cucumber in and out of her cunt three times before inserting it in her anus and then licking it.

Squashfuck.avi is fourteen seconds long and depicts a man inserting a small squash into the cunt of the same woman from cucunt.mpg.

Cantaloupe.mpg is thirty-two seconds long and depicts a different woman forcing a small but entire cantaloupe into her cunt and wincing in pain.

Despite the fact that I don't actually find the idea of women using vegetables as dildos arousing, there is something about the looks on their faces as they're doing it and the idea of using something that you normally eat as a misshapen dildo that gives me a hard-on.

I loop the clips in my Windows Media Player and jerk off. I get through the second playing of the third clip, cantaloupe.mpg, before I shoot a load that goes all over my hand.

As I get up to get some toilet paper from the bathroom, the phone rings. I answer it with my clean hand. It's my mom. She wants to know if I got the sweater she mailed to me and she wants to know if it fits.

The sweater is sitting next to my dresser in the box it was mailed in, still unopened. I say, "Yeah, I got it. It fits fine."

My mom says, "You'll wear it then?"

"Yeah."

"Good, because sometimes I buy you things even though I know you probably won't wear them." The semen is dripping down my hand.

"Mom, I need to go."

"Why? What're you doing?"

"Nothing, I just need to get going."

"All right. Well, I just wanted to make sure that sweater will work and I miss you and I love you."

"You, too."

"I also wanted to see when you were thinking about coming to visit next."

"I don't know. I'd have to check my work schedule." The semen is about to drip off my hand onto the floor.

"Well, check it when you can and let us know."

"Okay."

"Well . . . I guess good-bye then. I love you."

"I love you, too."

"Bye."

"Bye."

The semen drips off my hand onto the floor. I hang up the phone, wipe my hand with some toilet paper, and get the spot that dripped on the carpet. Then I try on the sweater. It fits.

chapter twenty-five

The Day After

I wake up, turn on the TV, and jerk off to an episode of *Real World vs. Road Rules* in which the contestants are involved in a challenge that requires the girls to wear bikinis. I get dressed and go to the gym. On my way there, I imagine fucking every girl I pass. I imagine some of them sucking my cock before I fuck them. When I finish working out there are twenty-six messages on my cell phone. I dial my voice mail and listen to the following:

"Just give me a chance. We don't have to like get married if you don't want to, not right now at least." End of message. "Call me when you get this, I have to talk to you. I just like don't understand why you're doing this." End of message. "Don't ignore me. I know you're there and I have to talk to you. Call me as soon as you get this." End of message. "My mother and I are going to get something to eat, so if you call in the next thirty minutes and we're not here, call back." End of message. "I just wanted to say that I can change. If there's something you think I'm not giving you, I can give it to you. If you still care about me at all, just call me back." End of message.

And it continues for the next ten minutes. I listen to every message, waiting to hear something that will trigger any feeling in me at all. She's crying on some of the messages, mean on others, pleading on others, but in none of them does she say anything that elicits any emotional response from me.

I delete the messages and play World of Warcraft for the next four hours. My phone rings every ten minutes for the duration of my game and each time I let it go to voice mail.

I take a ten-minute shit during which my phone rings three more times and then I listen to the new messages. Two are from Casey. The other one is from my mom. She says she forgot to ask me when Casey and I are coming to visit them again. She also wants to know if it's okay to sell all of my old He-Man toys at her next garage sale. She asks me this question once a year and my answer is always no. I delete the messages and put on a DVD called *Cum Drenched Butt Sluts*. I select scene number eight, an anal fucking and blow job scene that's been my favorite for some time.

Despite the number of times I've seen this exact scene, the look on the woman's face when the guy takes his cock out of her ass and puts it in her mouth still entertains me. She clearly doesn't like the way it tastes and she clearly doesn't like the way he rams it into the back of her throat, nor does she like the way he shoots a load of semen in her eyes and hair. I find this scene entertaining in a way that has never aroused me or made me want to jerk off. The scene that follows features two women fucking one guy. This scene does make me want to jerk off. As I start to, the phone rings again. I turn up the volume on my TV and decide to finally talk to Casey as I jerk off to this scene, hoping she'll hear the fucking in the background and wondering if I'll be able to maintain any kind of coherent conversation as I cum.

I answer the phone. It's not Casey. It's Alyna. I stop jerking off and turn down the volume as fast as I can, but I'm pretty sure she heard the guy say, "I'm gonna wreck that hole."

She makes no mention of it as she says, "Hi."

"Hi."

"Listen, I know this is probably really weird to you, but would you want to go get something to eat sometime?"

It is weird to me, she's right. But it's not weird enough to make me forget about how much I want to fuck her. "Yeah, but what about your boyfriend?"

"He's not my boyfriend anymore. What about your fiancée?"

"She's not my fiancée anymore. She never really was."

"I just, I don't know, I thought there was something between us that night, you know?"

"Yeah."

"I mean, I didn't dump my boyfriend over it or anything. We were headed in that direction anyway, but I just—I kind of felt something that night and I thought I'd give it another.try, a real try, if you wanted to. And now you're single, too?"

"Yeah."

"Well, then it just kind of seems like we should at least give it a real try, right?"

"Yeah."

My call waiting goes off as Alyna and I make plans for our second date. I ignore it. After the plans have been made I turn my phone off, restart the scene on the *Cum Drenched Butt Sluts* DVD after the butt-fucking and throat fuck, restart jerking off and finish to a part that features the two bitches in the scene doing the sixty-nine while the guy fucks the top bitch doggie style and occasionally gets his balls licked by the bitch on the bottom.

I wonder if I could get Casey to do the sixty-nine with another bitch while I fucked them by telling her it's the only way I'd take her back. I wonder if she knows any girls who would do the sixty-nine with her. I somehow think Alyna might be more likely to.

Rubbernecking

I'm driving through Westwood looking for parking when I see a bitch walking down the street. I can't tell if she's hot or not. I have to know if she's got decent tits or a redeemable ass. I have to know. So I take a good three-second stare at her. She's probably about forty-five, droopy tits, flabby ass, and haggish in the face.

I look back to the road just in time to see my front bumper make contact with the back bumper of the car in front of me that's sitting at a red light. We both pull over next to the Fatburger and get out to check the damage to our cars and exchange information.

The guy who was driving the other car says, "I was stopped at a red light. What the hell were you doing?"

"I was looking at a woman walking down the street."

"What?"

"Sorry."

"Sorry? You had your head so far up some woman's ass you didn't see my car stopped right in front of you, and all you can say is sorry?"

"Your car looks okay."

He looks it over, sees I'm right, and says, "It might look like super-ficial scratches, but who knows what damage we can't see."

As the guy keeps talking about the cost of what possible damages I might have done to his car, I see the woman who caused this whole thing waiting for her crosswalk sign to turn green. She's worse than I originally thought. She is hideously ugly and her body is absolutely repulsive. I smashed into a car for her.

The guy's still talking about something as I try to think about all the times I've been in near wrecks because I was trying to see if some bitch walking down the street was hot. There are a lot, and in most instances the bitch is not worth the possibility of a wreck.

The guy says, "Here." He's waving something in my face. It's his insurance information. I take his, give him mine, and wish that old hag would have at least been a hot college bitch wearing tight pants.

chapter twenty-six

Letter from Casey's Mom

It's been a few days since I dumped Casey and she's finally stopped calling. When I come home from the gym, there's an envelope with my name on it taped to the front door of my apartment. I try to remember what Casey's handwriting looks like but can't.

When I open the envelope I find out that it's not from Casey, it's from her mom, and this is what it says:

Dear Breaker of My Daughter's Heart,

I know you might find it strange that I'm writing you a letter instead of Casey, but you should know she's finally come to her senses and decided to never speak to you again after what you did. I told her she should write you a letter just so she could get out everything she needs to get out, but she refused. Well, I don't quite have the same restraint.

I can't believe you dated my daughter for so long and even went so far as to propose to her only to end things the way you

did. *You are the most miserable and ungrateful person I think
I may have ever had the displeasure of meeting and I for one
have absolutely no regrets that my daughter didn't wind up
marrying the likes of you. My only regret is that she wasted so
much of her own time and so much of her family's time on you.*

*I consider myself lucky because Casey's sister has found a
man who loves her for who she is and has been able to give me
a grandchild. But I also consider myself very unlucky in that
I'm not positive Casey will ever be able to give me the joy of a
grandchild because I'm sure it will be a long time before she's
ready to try men again and you're to blame. I hope that stays
with you.*

*Just for the record, when Casey told us she was engaged to
you, I was not immediately happy, and even after trying to convince myself that it was a good thing, I was never fully satisfied
with my daughter bringing someone like you into our family
and neither was Casey's father.*

*I wish that I could somehow warn every woman on the
planet what a cruel and unfeeling person you are so in the
future other girls won't suffer the same misery my daughter has,
but after witnessing your behavior this weekend in the Griddle
I have no doubt that you will remain alone for the rest of your
life, and that thought comforts me a great deal.*

*In closing I'd just like to let you know that when you come
to your senses in a month or so and realize that you threw
away the best thing that ever happened to you by ending your
relationship with my daughter and with the Childress family,
it will be too late. Casey will never accept your apology and
neither will I. You have made the biggest mistake of your life.*

*Sincerely,
Anne Childress*

I fold the letter back up and put it back in its envelope. I know I will probably never read the letter again, but something makes me want to keep it, so I put it in the latest issue of Playboy, which is sitting on my coffee table.

As I take a shower I wonder if I should write Casey's mom a response letter. I decide against it based on the lack of interest I have in ever communicating with her again. I wonder if I should write a letter to Casey. I decide against this based on the possibility that Casey might misinterpret something I write as a chance to get back together and start calling me every five minutes again.

In the shower I reach for the soap and notice Casey's sponge thing. I remember a specific time we fucked in my shower and she washed my cock with that sponge thing after we finished. I wash my cock with her sponge thing and get an immediate hard-on, but refuse to jerk off on principle.

chapter twenty-seven

Psychosis

It's 2:32 A.M. and I'm walking toward the front door of my apartment building after a long and unsuccessful night of playing wingman for Todd while he tried to pick up bitches at the Westwood Brewing Company. I see something that almost makes me fake an aneurysm so I don't have to deal with it. Casey's sitting outside the front doors by the call box. She's already seen me and there's nothing I can do. Even though I know the following conversation is unavoidable, I try to pretend I don't see her sitting in front of the door I have to walk through as I reach for my keys in preparation to enter.

She says, "I've been sitting out here like all night. Even though my mom told me not to, I had to come over here. Where have you been?"

"Out with Todd."

"I can't do this. I don't know how to do this."

"Do what?"

"Not be us."

She starts crying like a little kid. I don't say anything. I just stand there watching her sob and wondering how I'm ever going to get her off my porch without actually calling the police and having her forcibly removed.

She says, "Why? Why do you want to do this to me?"

I still don't say anything. It's becoming even more apparent to me that this situation could very quickly unfold into the worst moment of my life.

"I just don't understand it."

I still don't say anything.

"Say something."

I say, "Uh, it's pretty late and I'm tired. Maybe we could talk about this later."

"I came all the way over here and sat on your porch for five hours. I'm not leaving until you talk to me."

I don't say anything. I put my key in the door, open it, and walk in. Casey just sits there. I go to my apartment and look out the window at Casey, still sitting there. I watch her for five minutes. She doesn't move except to cry every now and then. Then she stands up and starts screaming.

She says, "You fucking bastard! I hate you and I'm not leaving here until you talk to me! Just come out and talk to me!"

I go into my bathroom and take a long-overdue shit as Casey keeps screaming on the front porch. I'm sure some of my neighbors can hear her screaming but she never uses my name, so I don't care. She just keeps screaming things like, "You're a fucking son of a bitch," and "I'm sorry I ever let you have sex with me," followed by, "I just want to talk," and "Please give me a chance to work it out."

As I wipe my ass she's still screaming. When I get out of the shower she's still screaming. When I get in bed, she's still screaming. When I jerk off thinking about the possibilities of fucking Alyna on our next date, she's still screaming.

I wonder if she'll be asleep on my front porch when I leave for work tomorrow morning or if someone will call the cops before then or if she'll just get tired and go home.

UCLA Party

Todd and another friend of mine whose last name is Marquis are over at my house. We've been drinking beer for the last three hours and playing Madden when Marquis makes the following suggestion: "Dude, we should go to a fucking college party around here."

Todd says, "Do you think we can even pass as college-age anymore?"

Marquis says, "Fuck it. Who gives a shit if we can? What're they gonna do, fucking kick us out?"

I say, "They might."

Marquis says, "So we fuckin' leave then. But if they don't kick us out—free fuckin' booze and free fuckin' eighteen-year-old pussy."

Todd says, "Fuck it, I'm in, dude."

I agree. We all knock back one for the road and walk out the door in search of a party in the area. As we walk Todd says, "So once we get to a party, what's our story?"

Marquis says, "We're fuckin' baseball players from USC. One of our friends who transferred to UCLA last semester invited us over here."

I say, "What do we tell 'em when they ask who the friend is?"

Marquis says, "Fuckin' Jim."

Todd says, "Jim?"

Marquis says, "Fuckin' Jim. There's always a fuckin' Jim at a party, dude."

Marquis' logic is apparently sound enough for Todd and me because we don't ask any more questions before we find ourselves walking up the steps to an apartment from which loud music and drunk college bitches pour out onto the balcony.

We walk in seemingly undetected and make our way to the kitchen where a keg is being pumped by a gigantic thick-necked guy who is either fat or muscular—I'm not sure which. Thick-neck says, "Where's your cup, bra?"

Marquis says, "Some bitch knocked it outta my hand on the fuckin' balcony."

Thick-neck gives him a new cup. "Bros before hos. Here you go, bro." Marquis gets a cup full of beer from Thick-neck, then says, "My buddies here lost their shit, too." Thick-neck supplies us with beer and continues to pump the keg as we walk off into the pitch-black living room.

I sit down on a couch next to a hot bitch and start to notice that Todd, Marquis, and myself are the shortest guys at the party by at least a foot and underweigh all the guys at the party by at least a hundred pounds. The hot bitch says, "Hey, who are you?"

I say, "A friend of Jimmy's."

"Oh."

I can't believe it fucking worked.

The hot bitch says, "Are you on the football team?"

"No, I play baseball for USC."

"Oh, cool. Freshman?"

"Sophomore, you?"

"I'm a sophomore too—on the soccer team. It's kind of noisy in here, do you want to go out on the balcony?"

"Sure."

She takes my hand and we go out on the balcony, where there are three other guys and three other girls. The guys all seem to be bigger than the ones inside. They shoot me a look when they see me. The hot bitch notices and says, "He plays baseball for USC." The guys' scowls turn to head nods and a few guys say things like, "Cool," and "Baseball, a'ight," before turning back to their respective college sluts and getting back to trying to fuck them.

The hot bitch says, "So how do you like L.A.?"

"Okay, you?"

"I'm originally from Phoenix, but I like it here okay. Do you have a girlfriend at USC?"

"No. You have a boyfriend?"

"No. I did, but now I don't."

"Oh."

"Yeah, it's cool now though. He was a complete asshole. You probably saw him in there pumping the keg."

I immediately picture Thick-neck tossing me off the balcony or caving in my fucking skull with the keg.

"Yeah, I think I saw him."

"Well, we're through, even if he doesn't think so."

I look back inside and see that Marquis and Todd are talking to a few hot bitches of their own and know there's no way they'll leave this party. I'm fucked. I say, "I feel kind of sick, I think I should go to the bathroom."

She takes my hand and says, "The line's probably horrible. You can use the one in my bedroom."

She leads me through the living room crowd, thankfully out of Thick-neck's line of sight, and into her bedroom, closing and locking the door behind her. She lies down on her bed and points to the adjoining bathroom. She says, "Bathroom's in there."

I go in, look in the mirror, can't draw a bead on my face—still too drunk. Fuck it. I walk back into her bedroom and say, "I really think I should go."

She shakes her head and pats the bed beside her. "No, stay here for a few more minutes. You'll feel better. I promise."

Two things fight for dominance in my head: this hot bitch's tight eighteen-year-old ass and Thick-neck's fists. The ass wins by a landslide. I sit down. She starts kissing me and shoots a hand down my pants. Forty-five seconds later, she's sucking my cock. I wonder if she wants to fuck and I wonder if she has any rubbers. I'm about to ask her when somebody knocks at the door. "Cammie, come dance with me." It's fucking Thick-neck.

She rolls her eyes, takes my cock out of her mouth, and says, "Richard, I don't want to dance with you."

"Come on, babe. It's your favorite song." I try to listen to the song through the door to gain some insight into what kind of an eighteen-year-old college slut Cammie might be, but it's too garbled.

I look around for a window, but strangely Cammie doesn't have one. I am positive I'm going to die at the hands of Richard the thick-necked keg pumper.

He says, "Cammie, come on, just one dance."

Cammie does a few more head bobs on my cock, then says, "Okay, I'm feeling kind of sick, just give me fifteen minutes, then I'll give you one dance."

He says, "All right, babe. I'll be at the keg if you feel better sooner."

She says, "I fucking hate that asshole," then gets right back to work on my cock. It's a fairly well-executed blow job. I've had better, but not many. As Cammie starts to play with my balls I kind of wish I was getting a blow job from the twenty-four-year-old version of Cammie so she'd have a little more experience, but then my thoughts come back to the fact that I'm getting my dick sucked by an eighteen-year-old hot college bitch and I'm about to blow my load.

I say, "Do you have any condoms?"

She stops sucking my cock and says, "I want you to finish in my mouth."

I have no problem with this. I say, "Okay."

As she sucks my cock, I assume that she's just into swallowing. But after I shoot my load in her mouth and then sneak back out into the party and watch her give Richard his promised dance as well as a minute-long tongue-kiss, I realize she was just using me.

chapter twenty-eight

Second Date

I ring Alyna's doorbell for a second time, meet her hippie roommate for a second time, make small talk for a second time, and wait for Alyna to come out of what I assume is her bedroom for a second time.

She walks in front of me out of her apartment complex and I see that her ass is as good as I remember. I decide that if tonight leads to any point at which there might be even a remote possibility I can fuck her or get her to suck my cock, I'll try my best to make sure it happens.

We get in my car and I reach to put the keys in the ignition. She grabs my hand, stops me, and says, "Does this feel kind of weird to you?"

"No."

"Really?"

"I don't know, maybe a little."

"It feels really weird to me."

Fuck. It's over before it even started.

I say, "You want to call it off?"

"No. No. It's not necessarily weird in a bad way."

She squeezes my hand and I feel her fingers, kind of hard and wiry. I wish those fingers were squeezing my dick.

She says, "Let's go."

I start up the car and we head off. The ride is pretty uneventful. We never really address either of our breakups or how we felt about our first date. She tells me about last night's episode of Conan O'Brien, which I missed, and I tell her about the new 50 Cent video. At one point she laughs at something I say and puts her hand on my shoulder as she's laughing, which forces her to turn her tits at me. That's when I notice the button-up shirt she's wearing gives me a slight glimpse of one of her tits. I take it in. It's nice. I want to be sucking it.

We get to the Smoke House in Burbank, which I remember Casey taking me to a few times. It's an interesting place if nothing else and if the date itself goes sour, the senior citizen lounge act will be entertaining.

We get a table kind of by the stage and order a few drinks to start the following conversation:

She says, "So why'd you and your girlfriend break up?"

"She thought we were getting married and I didn't."

"I guess that's a pretty big thing to disagree about."

"Yeah, I guess so. Why'd you and your boyfriend break up?"

"He was a complete dick and I was tired of dating a complete dick."

I wonder what it was about him that made him a complete dick. I don't ask her. I'm sure I'm fully capable of duplicating whatever it was. I just say, "Fair enough."

She says, "Do you think it's too soon to be dating other people?"

"No."

"My boyfriend and I were dating for almost a year and a half, and I know you're supposed to have some time by yourself before you jump back into dating and all that, but I don't really feel like I need any time. I'm over him. I was over him while we were dating. What do you think?"

"I'm pretty much the same way."

We get our drinks. She raises her glass and says, "Let's do a toast."

"To what?"

"To . . ." She thinks. ". . . seeing what happens."

"Sounds good."

We clink glasses and drink.

We talk about a lot of things through the course of our dinner and have at least three more drinks each. I find out she's a senior at UCLA. She has two brothers—one is older and lives in New York and does something on Wall Street and the other is one year younger and plays baseball at Arizona State. Her mom and dad were high school sweethearts who still live in the town they were born in. She's twenty-one but has never gotten a driver's license. She's only been in two serious relationships. She won't give the exact number of people she's slept with, but it's under ten. She has freckles on her shoulders. When she was seven years old she found nine hundred dollars in a garbage bag behind the dumpster in her alley. When she was ten her brother threw the metal lid of a coffee can at her like a Frisbee and it cut the two middle fingers on her left hand to the bone. As a result she has no feeling in the tips of those fingers.

I tell her similar information about myself and the date seems to be going well. When she gets up to go to the bathroom, I watch her ass and think about it naked spread over my face as we do the sixty-nine.

When she comes back, she puts a hand on my shoulder as she walks around the table, which I take as a good sign.

She says, "So you ready to hit the road?"

"Sure." I pay the bill and we leave.

In the car she says, "So do you want to check out my apartment? My roommate's supposed to be spending the night at some camp-out thing."

"Yeah."

Although this kind of offer would normally mean a girl is ready to be fucked, I can't be sure because of the strange circumstances surrounding the date and her behavior on our first date. Nonetheless, it's well worth my time to see what happens.

Once we get inside her apartment she gives me the grand tour, ending at her bedroom, which is decorated in a pretty normal college girl kind of way. There are more pillows than necessary on her bed, a poster of Einstein on her wall, and a little bookshelf with college philosophy books and classic literature on it. In the corner she has a thirteen-inch TV.

She sits on her bed and slips her shoes off. I notice a picture stuck in her mirror of her and her ex-boyfriend. I wonder if she forgot to take it down or if she left it up on purpose. I don't ask.

She says, "Do you want to watch some TV?"

"Okay."

She turns on her TV and I sit down next to her on her bed, closer than I need to. She doesn't move away. She says, "You know, I'm sorry about our first date."

I don't know why I say it, but it seems right to say, "Me too."

She leans in and kisses me. It's a good kiss, one that makes me ready to fuck her immediately. I reach up and put my hand behind her head, and she does the same to me. We kiss for a few seconds before she lies down, taking me with her.

Then she stops and says, "Wait."

Fuck.

Then she sits up, unbuttons her shirt, and takes off her bra.

Fuck yes.

Her tits are un-fucking-believable, rock hard, perfectly round B cups. She takes my hands and puts them on her tits, then kind of moans. She drops back down on top of me and we start going at it. She half rips my shirt off and unzips my pants before I know what the fuck is going on. She shoves her hand down my pants and starts jerking me off. It's been a long time since I've been with a girl who's this enthusiastic about dick. For a split second I'm sure I'm going to blow a load in my pants, but I hold it back.

As she's tugging at my cock, I reach down and unzip her pants, which she helps me take off. She lets go of my dick for a second and pulls off her underwear before yanking off my pants and boxers so we're both completely naked in her bed. Despite the number of times I've jerked off to this exact fantasy, I never imagined it could be this good.

My cock is harder than I can remember it being in a long time when she starts jerking at it again.

She says, "This is what I wanted to do the first time we went out."

"Me too."

"I'm glad we didn't, though."

"Me too." I say it without really knowing what the fuck I'm saying or what that could even mean. All I can focus on is her hand on my cock.

She says, "Do you like it soft," and she kind of teases my dick with her fingers, "or hard," then she squeezes my cock and yanks on it kind of hard.

The fact that she's so aggressive and vocal about this entire event is again about to make me blow my load, so I take the opportunity to shift my focus to her.

I slide a few fingers into her pussy, which is already pretty wet, and say, "How do you like it?"

She kind of grinds on my hand at her own pace and I give as much resistance as I think she might like.

She says, "Just like that," with her hand still on my cock, but not as intent on jerking me off.

I finger her for a while listening to her moan and feeling her hand on my cock until I feel her pull away. I've gotten enough head to know that as she starts kissing me on the neck and then on the chest that her mouth's headed for my dick.

A few seconds later I'm not disappointed as she has one hand on my balls and her mouth on my cock. It's a pretty good blow job. Not quite the best I've ever had, but definitely good. I stop wondering if this is going to be a precursor to fucking when I realize I'm about to cum. I reach down and squeeze her shoulder to give her fair warning, but she keeps sucking and right as I cum she squeezes my nuts a little, which is a new experience for me and not unenjoyable, then swallows the entire load I shoot in her mouth with a little giggle. This is more than pleasantly surprising. It confirms my hopes that Alyna is a girl who not only genuinely enjoys sucking cock, but also fully enjoys all aspects of the act. She keeps sucking my cock for a minute or so after I've shot my load, which is also a new experience for me that I find much more enjoyable than the nut squeeze.

When she finishes she crawls back up and lies next to me on her back, rubbing my chest and kissing me on the neck in a way that lets me know she's ready for her turn.

I spread her legs and bury my face in her cunt, which is easily the best-looking pussy I've ever seen. It's well trimmed and neat with smallish lips and a decent taste. I flick my tongue at her clit for a few seconds before really going to work and putting a few fingers in her as I eat her out. After twenty or thirty seconds of this, she's kind of writhing around and moaning with her hands on my head pulling my face deeper into her pussy. She accidentally pulls a little too hard once and hits my nose against her pubic bone, which hurts a little, but not enough to stop me from doing my work.

Once she gets completely worked up and she's about to cum, she pushes me away, rolls over on her stomach, gets up on all fours with her ass in the air and her legs spread so her pussy's kind of open and sticking out.

She says, "I want to cum like this."

I've only ever seen a guy eat a girl out from behind in a porno movie, but I have nothing against it as I spread Alyna's ass from behind, which I'm dumbfounded by when I look at how perfect it is again. I get off the bed slightly so my face is at her ass level and pull her back so she's still on all fours at the edge of the bed as I lick her cunt from the back.

She keeps backing into my face as I'm eating her out, which causes my nose to actually touch her asshole. I'm surprised to find that it smells good, kind of like pears or some kind of berry. I wonder if she uses scented toilet paper or actually sprays some kind of body spray in her asshole on a regular basis, or maybe she just thought that at some point tonight she'd wind up with my nose in her ass so she used the spray, based on an educated guess.

Her nice-smelling asshole makes me less apprehensive about really cutting loose, and a few times I notice my tongue getting a stray lick in on the asshole itself, which she seems to genuinely enjoy. This makes me think that at some point I could possibly fuck her in the ass.

My neck starts to hurt from the weird angle my head's suspended at but her perfect ass in my face and her escalating moaning makes me want to finish her off like this. So I continue for a few more minutes, ignoring the burning pain.

Right after one of her loudest moans she says, "Spank me."

Holy shit. I have spanked girls I've fucked in the past and some have even liked it. But none have demanded it of me. I hit one of her ass cheeks.

She says, "Harder."

I hit her harder.

She says, "Again."

I get in about seven or eight solid slaps before she cums like a ton of bricks, shudders a little, and then collapses in a heap on her bed. She rolls over on her back and I lie down next to her.

She says, "That was great."

"Yeah, it was."

I'm kind of curious as to why we didn't fuck, but more than curious I'm refreshed by the immensely satisfying and enthusiastic blow job she delivered and her clearly expressed and unique preference for being eaten out.

Just before we both fall asleep I wonder if Alyna will fall in love with me.

chapter twenty-nine

Post-Lunch with Carlos

After eating the same lunch we eat every Saturday at the CPK in the Beverly Center, Carlos and I are across the street at the music store in the Beverly Connection in the DVD section shopping for his mom's birthday present.

Carlos holds up the Vin Diesel *Pacifier* DVD and says, "You think my mom would like this? I would love to suck his cock."

"I'm sure he'd love that."

"You never know. Anyway that's neither here nor there. I still can't believe you and Casey are kaput. I mean, despite all the shit you always complained about, I thought you guys would wind up married—maybe divorced down the line, but married at some point. That is funny though about her mom writing you that letter. Do you still have it?"

"Yeah."

"I want to read it. I love shit like that." He picks up a *Spider-Man* DVD and says, "I think I remember my mom telling me that she and my dad saw this movie like three or four times." He flips the DVD over and reads the back as he says, "Tobey Maguire . . . I'd suck his dick so fucking good."

"Is he gay?"

"You don't have to be gay to have your dick sucked." He looks through some more DVDs and then says, "And you still haven't talked to her since she showed up at your house stalker-style?"

"No."

"Jesus fucking Christ, that's pretty cold. But maybe it's for the best. You don't want her getting the idea that you want her back in your life if you don't. I fucked this one little Chinese hardbody for about a week and a half before I got sick and tired of getting poked by his two-inch pushpin and dumped him on Valentine's Day. But I kept talking to him, you know, just to be nice, and he somehow thought that meant he could drop by anytime and try to make me cum with his little nub. Jesus, that was a long two weeks. Anyway, like I was saying, it's probably better you don't talk to her."

"I agree."

He holds up an *Assassins* DVD and says, "My mom likes Stallone. Do you think either one of these guys would let me suck their cock?"

"I don't know."

"And now what's the deal with this new girl? She sucked your dick and you ate her out, and she's the same one you went on that other date with?"

"Right."

"Do you think it's a little quick to be jumping right back into another cunt?"

"I'm not jumping into anything. It was just a date."

"For me, wrapping my lips around a cock is just a date. For any girl, though, sucking some guy's dick is not just a date. Didn't you say she just got out of some long-term relationship, too?"

"Yeah."

"I don't know. I mean, don't get me wrong, I'm all for getting off as much as you possibly can in this life, but this looks like trouble to me."

"Trouble was being engaged to Casey. If Alyna's trouble, at least she's trouble with a perfect fucking ass."

He holds up *Ace Ventura* and says, "She hates Jim Carrey. Maybe I should get her this. I don't know why, but I've always had a crush on him. I think it has something to do with that scene in the second one when he crawls out of that rhino's ass naked." He puts the DVD back on the shelf and says, "I mean, did she snuggle up to you after you guys finished or did you guys fall asleep together or anything?"

"We fell asleep in her bed, but we weren't snuggled up or anything."

"Did she touch you at all?"

"Yeah. She has a small bed. It couldn't be helped."

"Then in the morning what happened?"

"I got up and left."

"Jesus, did you even say, 'Thanks for the blow job?'"

"I kissed her and we both said we had a good time and all that, then I left."

"Well, just be careful. After getting out of something like you had with Casey, I think it's very easy to fall right back into the same trap if you don't watch out. And you didn't even give me any time to convince you that women are all evil bitches and you should give guys a try."

He laughs at his joke, then picks up a *Wizard of Oz* DVD and says, "This is it. She fucking loves this stupid movie. So many fags love it, too, but I fucking hate it. All those little midgets and that fucking song that every guy I've ever fucked knows by heart and actually starts fucking singing when we're watching it. I don't know how many times I've had to sit through this piece of shit just so I could get some cock up my ass. I almost don't want to buy it on principle alone, but . . I'm getting it. My mom will like it. You getting anything?"

"No."

At the register, the girl ringing us up is hot as fuck in that indie-rock-slightly-Emo just-out-of-high-school kind of way. Nice little tits, dyed black hair, nose ring, tattoo peeking out of her shirt and probably weighs a hundred pounds. I immediately imagine myself fucking her doggie style in some back room of the record store. A few seconds in, I start thinking about Alyna in the back room of the record store and end up continuing to think about her all the way back to my house, where I jerk off to the memory of her sucking my cock.

chapter thirty

Casey's Shit

Casey hasn't tried to call me for almost a week, which is why it kind of surprises me when I pick up the phone and hear her say with forced confidence, "When's a good time for me to come get the things I have at your apartment?"

"Uh, I don't know."

"Well, I have some stuff that I need to get back. You can't keep it."

I don't think she does have anything at my apartment, but after a year and a half of dating it makes sense that she would, so I don't argue.

"When do you want to come get it?"

"Today if I can."

"Okay. I'll be here."

"I'll be over in an hour."

She hangs up. I think about finding whatever shit she's talking about and putting it all in a box on the curb so she can just take it and go instead of hanging around my apartment longer than necessary, but I don't really know which shit is hers and I'd probably end up giving her something of mine by mistake, which she'd take to mean something it didn't. I'm also fully aware that this is, more than likely, just a ploy for her to see me again, maybe in hopes of luring me back to her fat ass. I hope that playing along will give her some sort of closure so I never have to see her again. I decide I should play an old Xbox game. I decide to play Mech Assault 2 until she shows up, which turns out to be an hour later.

When she comes in she says, "I'm sorry about that night I showed up here. How have you been?"

"Okay."

"So have I. I started my next Groundlings class."

"Great. I didn't know which stuff you were talking about."

"I didn't think you would."

She rummages through a pile of papers and *Playboys* on my coffee table. Her mom's letter falls out onto the ground and she picks it up.

"Is this from my mom?"

"Yeah."

"What is it?"

"A letter."

"Obviously it's a letter, but like why would she write you a letter?"

I shrug my shoulders, knowing she wants to read it more than anything. She puts it back in the *Playboy*, closes the magazine, and tosses it down on the coffee table a little too nonchalantly.

"My Groundlings teacher said I have the most potential of anyone in the class."

"Great. Do you know exactly what you have over here?"

"Just some things."

She goes in the closet and pulls out an umbrella that I think my mom gave me when I moved to L.A.

She says, "Like my umbrella."

She opens a cupboard in the kitchen area, pulls out a box of tea, and says, "And my tea."

She walks back into the bedroom and comes out still holding just the tea and the umbrella. She says, "Are you doing anything right now?"

Fuck. I should have just thrown some of my shit in a box and left it on the curb.

"No."

"Do you want to go get a cup of coffee with me?"

"I don't think so."

"Just like to talk."

"I don't think so."

"Why?"

"I just don't want to."

"It's because I came over to your house and yelled at you and now you think I'm a psycho."

"No, I just don't want to."

"Well, then, let's have dinner this week."

"I don't think I can."

"Why can't you just have dinner with me and talk to me about this whole thing?"

"It's better like this."

"Like what?"

"Just over."

"No, it's not."

"Sorry."

She starts to tear up. She starts crying. She says through sobs, "Aren't you even going to hug me?"

I wish I was anywhere else. I think about Alyna. I think about telling Casey that I ate Alyna's pussy and she sucked my cock.

"I don't think so."

Her sobs become convulsive. She sits down on my couch and cries into her hands.

"Why? I just like don't understand why."

I don't say anything.

"Can you just tell me why you're doing this?"

"I already did."

"Because you want something I'm not?"

"Yeah."

"That doesn't even like make sense. I was something you wanted for a year and a half and now I'm just not? What happened?"

"I don't know."

"You have to know. If you broke up with me you have to know."

I don't say anything again. I know that anything I say will only prolong this already annoying situation.

"I mean there has to be something that changed."

I stand as still as I can and try not to breathe. For a split second I think I might be able to coax her into sucking my cock or fucking me, but it's probably not worth the effort.

She says, "It was the engagement, wasn't it?"

Please something happen. A car wreck right outside my door. A gunshot through my window. A fucking phone call for fuck's sake. As I think this my cell phone actually rings. Casey sits on the couch, still crying as I answer it. It's Alyna, who I've only talked to once in the two days since she sucked my cock.

She says, "What're you doing?"

"Nothing."

"I'm done with work. Can I come over?"

"When?"

"Now."

"I haven't taken a shower or anything."

"That's fine. Neither have I. We can take one together. I'll be over in ten minutes."

She hangs up. The slightly less than comfortable familiarity she's approaching in whatever kind of relationship we might be on the verge of having makes me a little uneasy, but the thought of soaping up her ass and tits in my shower generates a spark of excitement that alleviates it; and the crying-ex-girlfriend-sitting-on-my-couch situation seems slightly more pressing.

I say, "Okay, you have to go."

"Why?"

"Because I'm tired of arguing about this." Even as I say the words it hits me that I owe Casey nothing, but something makes me think telling her about Alyna would make the entire situation worse. I wonder if Alyna has any interaction with her ex-boyfriend and if it's similar to mine with Casey.

She says, "Well, I'm not leaving until I get an answer or until you at least promise to get coffee with me."

"Fine."

"Fine what? The answer or the coffee?"

"Coffee."

"When?"

"I'll call you."

"No, you won't."

"Yes, I will."

"You promise?"

"Yes."

"Okay, but I'm holding you to it."

She gets off my couch, wipes the tears off her face, and leaves.

I sit on the couch where she was sitting for about two or three minutes thinking about the last time Casey and I fucked. I wish I had blown a load on her stomach or put my dick in her ass or done something to signify it as the final time I would put my cock in her. Alyna rings my doorbell, shifting my thoughts back to her soapy cunt in my shower.

She walks in and says, "Hi," then kisses me, sees the tea that I now realize Casey left sitting on the coffee table along with what I am now sure is my umbrella, and says, "I would have never guessed you for a tea drinker."

The shower we take five minutes later yields a pretty good and immediate soapy hand job that leaves me no opportunity to even attempt fucking her. Instead I repay the favor by making her cum as I finger-fuck her up against my shower door. The dinner we eat afterward at Jerry's Famous Deli is filled with conversation about trivial things that ignore the nature of what seems to be a burgeoning relationship, but nonetheless is the only conversation either of us wants to have.

The 98 Percent Rule

Todd and I are eating lunch at a Quiznos in North Hollywood. Sitting across from us at two different tables are an unrealistically hot bitch who we decide must be a porno actress and an old lady who looks like she died two weeks ago.

Todd says, "If you had to fuck the old ugly one, but then you get to fuck the hot one, would you do it?"

"What's the rest of the scenario?"

"There is no rest. That's it."

"What about disease, and pregnancy, and subsequent chances to fuck the hot bitch?"

"No. You don't get any of that."

"See? So there's more to the situation here. You have to lay it out completely."

"Okay, here's your scenario. You're lying in bed at one A.M. and the old bitch materializes in your bed completely naked and starts sucking your cock."

"Okay."

"Now, while she sucks, she says, 'If you fuck me, not just let me suck your cock, but actually stick your dick in me, then right after you blow your load, the hot porno bitch will show up and fuck you, too.' And you get no diseases, there're no pregnancies, no one knows about it, and both bitches vaporize as soon as you blow your load."

"And I'll be magically ready to fuck immediately after I've just fucked the old bitch?"

"Yeah."

I think it over. I look at the old bitch, at her gunt, at her wrinkly, jerky lips as she eats a cup of Quiznos clam chowder. I realize that given Todd's theoretical situation I think I would fuck her even if the hot bitch wasn't a follow-up.

I say, "In your theoretical situation I'd fuck the old bitch even if there was no hot bitch."

"Dude, that is fucking vile."

"You would, too."

"What? No fucking way."

"Yeah, you would. If no one will know and there's no risk involved, what do you care if she's old. She's still got a pussy, right?"

He realizes I'm right. "Yeah, I guess I would fuck her. Would you fuck any bitch on this planet given that same situation?"

My gut reaction is to say yes, but logically that can't be true. I hedge my bet.

I say, "Maybe not all of them. In the age range of seventeen or so to dead, I'd probably fuck like ninety-eight percent."

A decent-looking mom walks in with two little kids. She's kind of fat.

Todd indicates her with a head nod and says, "Is she ninety-eight percent?"

"Yeah."

There's an old, insane-looking homeless bitch on the street corner.

Todd points to her and says, "Dude, is she ninety-eight percent?"

"Uhhh . . . yeah, sure."

"Holy shit. You'd fuck her?"

"Yeah, if she vaporizes right after I do it, what do I care?"

"If she's ninety-eight percent, then what's a two-percenter look like?"

"I don't know. I'll let you know when I see one."

We finish our sandwiches and on the entire ride back to work we don't pass a single two-percenter. I wonder if the fact that I live in Los Angeles has anything to do with it or if I should just change my range to ninety-nine percent. It's probably L.A. I decide to leave it at ninety-eight percent.

chapter thirty-one

Introducing Alyna

Over the course of the last week Alyna's sucked my cock once and given me one hand job in the shower. I've eaten her out once and fingered her once, also in my shower. These statistics are enough to make Todd want to meet her.

I pick Alyna up at nine and we go to a bar called Daddy's, where we meet Todd and two girls sitting in a booth with him who I assume did not come with him. One of the girls is short and fat with a pretty cute face and small sloppy tits that are poorly concealed in a shirt that no girl that chubby should be wearing. The other girl is surprisingly attractive for having such a fat pig as a friend. As we sit down Todd says, "What's up guys, this is Sandra and Debra."

Debra, the short fat one, says, "It's Devra, with a *v*, like vagina."

In addition to being short and fat, Devra is drunk.

I introduce Alyna to everyone around the table.

Todd says, "So, Alyna, what do you do?"

She says, "I'm a student. This is my last year, though."

Todd says, "Cool."

Sandra, the hot girl, says, "Where do you go?"

Alyna says, "UCLA."

Devra the fat pig says to me, "And are you guys like boyfriend and girlfriend or are you fair game?" Then she laughs a weird laugh that almost sounds like an eight-year-old kid and I imagine the cellulite that must be on her ass and thighs rippling as I fuck her.

Alyna looks at me. I refuse to say anything.

She says, "No, we actually both got out of relationships not too long ago and I've sucked his dick once and he's eaten me out . . . oh, and we've given each other hand jobs in his shower, but it's not that whole boyfriend-girlfriend thing yet, so I guess he's fair game."

I want to fuck Alyna right there.

Devra the fat pig looks at me with an open mouth. Judging by their similar slack-jawed expressions, Sandra and Todd also seem to be a little surprised by the bluntness of what Alyna just said. I smile and kiss Alyna on the cheek. She smiles back.

Todd says, "Uh . . . I'm going up to the bar to get some drinks. You guys want anything?"

We put in our order with Todd and he leaves us with Sandra and Devra, whose mouth is still hanging open, making her look even more like an actual pig to me.

Alyna says, "So what do you guys do?"

Devra the fat pig says, "I work at an ad agency as a project coordinator."

Sandra the hot one says, "I'm a graphic designer at the same place."

Devra says to me, "And what do you do?"

I say, "Nothing important."

That ends whatever conversation might have been about to happen. We sit in silence for another minute until Todd comes back with drinks for the whole table, which seems to erase the uneasiness everyone was feeling after Alyna told them she sucked my cock.

As we all drink and talk about nothing important, Sandra the hot girl explains that since moving to Los Angeles she's only dated jerks and can't seem to find a guy that takes her seriously. Devra the fat pig explains that all the guys she goes out with just want to have sex and then never call her again. Sandra further explains that her problem isn't in the guys calling her back. They call her all the time, it's just that they only call her to have sex. I can see Todd mentally constructing the best possible strategy to result in fucking at least one of them tonight, preferably the hot one.

He says, "I hate the dating scene. I've had my heart broken enough to know that it's rough out there, especially for a guy who just wants to meet a nice girl and doesn't want the whole fast-paced L.A. thing."

It's a strong strategy.

Alyna leans over and whispers in my ear, "Does your friend really think that's going to work?"

Sandra the hot one and Devra the fat pig say almost in unison, "I know what you mean."

I lean over and whisper in Alyna's ear, "Yes."

Alyna drinks the last of her cosmopolitan and says, "I'm getting another drink, anybody want anything?" I ask her to get me another Dewar's and then watch her perfect ass leave the table in a tight black skirt. When I turn my head back to the conversation at hand, I notice Todd was also watching Alyna's ass. He notices me noticing him and then gives me the thumbs-up. The two girls he's trying to fuck tonight are oblivious as they talk about a new lip gloss that Sandra bought at the Grove.

I look at the bar to see if Alyna's close to getting our drinks and see that some guy is talking to her. He's sloppily holding a drink and standing as close as he possibly can to her. I wonder if he's thinking about fucking her or getting his dick sucked as he tries to pick her up. My gut reaction is to go to the bar under the guise of seeing if Alyna needs help so I can tell this asshole to go fuck himself, but I don't know if that's something I have the clearance to do at this point in whatever relationship it is that we have. So I watch the following:

The guy says something to her.

She gives no reaction.

The guy says something to her again and motions his drink toward her, possibly asking if he can buy her one.

She shakes her head.

The guy says something else and Alyna looks over at me, rolls her eyes, and mouths, "I fucking hate this," as she indicates the guy with a thumb point.

It's in that one second that I have an overwhelming urge to hug her, to fall asleep with her, to wake up with her, to smell her hair, to do everything with her except fuck. Then she turns around to pick up our drinks from the bar and I get a perfect shot of her ass again, which replaces my previous impulses with the more familiar set of urges to fuck her in every way imaginable.

She comes back to the table with a fresh round of drinks. We all talk about movies, TV shows, and records we think are good and bad and other completely boring bullshit. Todd and the hot girl seem to be doing most of the talking as the fat pig tries to interject here and there but must know she has no chance of scoring any guy once her hot friend shows even the most remote amount of interest.

Neither Alyna nor I contribute much to the conversation. Instead we drink our drinks and she puts her hand in my lap. Over the course of the next thirty minutes, her hand moves from gently resting on my leg to semi–jerking me off through my pants. Todd and his two bitches are oblivious to what's going on under the table, which at one point is me fingering Alyna under her skirt and her about to make me blow a load in my pants by rubbing my cock through them.

As the table conversation dives into further boredom with a change in topic to the sensibility of leasing cars versus buying them and how the reverse is true in the real estate world, a slightly drunk Alyna leans over with her hand still on my cock and whispers the following line in my ear: "I want to go back to your place and fuck your brains out right now."

I say, "Well, ladies, it was nice to meet you. Todd, I think we should be going. We're getting kind of tired and I've got to be up early in the morning for some things."

He says, "What? What things do you have to be up early for?"

"Just some things."

"Like what? You don't have to be up early for shit."

I'm kind of buzzed and far too ready to fuck to think straight. I say, "I have to make a phone call."

This seems to confuse everyone at the table enough to allow our dismissal.

Todd says, "Oh. Well, Alyna, it was nice meeting you. I'm sure we'll be seeing more of each other around." I can't tell whether he's trying to hit on her or he's giving our burgeoning relationship a drunken vote of confidence.

She says, "Nice meeting you, too."

The fat pig and the hot bitch both say something like, "Good night, nice meeting you," but I don't care enough to actually decipher it.

As we leave I shift my hard-on to make walking more comfortable. When we get in the car Alyna says, "Jesus Christ, I thought we'd never get out of there," and she kisses me hard with a wet mouth.

When we get back to my place, she kind of pushes me down on my bed, takes my pants off, and starts sucking my cock. Without taking her mouth off my dick she somehow takes her own clothes off and maneuvers herself around into the sixty-nine position. Once again I notice her asshole smells like some kind of berry or melon and once again I enjoy it.

She sucks my dick as I eat her out, then just as I'm wondering if she's going to make good on the offer to fuck my brains out, she climbs off my face and sits on my dick. I don't really do much except lie there while she grinds on my cock.

I don't know if she can somehow sense it or if it's just lucky timing, but every time I'm about to blow a load she gets off my cock and says something like, "Fuck me doggie style," or "I want you on top."

It seems like we've been fucking for a while, but as she cums and the sound of her cumming makes me blow a gigantic load in her pussy, I look at the clock and notice that we've only been going at it for ten minutes. I wonder if she's in any way disappointed. I'm far from it. Even in the few seconds after I've expelled what must be one of the biggest loads of my life, I am fully aware that this is quite possibly the best single sexual experience I've ever had, barring maybe the first time I had my dick sucked by Jennifer Gladson my sophomore year in high school.

She lies down next to me, panting. She says, "That was amazing."

I say, "Yeah."

She doesn't really snuggle up to me, but just kind of lays a hand on my stomach and we both just look at my ceiling, breathing. The berry or melon smell from her asshole is still in my nose, which I find pleasant. I think momentarily about a conversation we had last week in which she explained that she's been on the pill since she was seventeen and it's the only form of birth control she'll use because she hates rubbers. I wonder if she was lying, or if maybe she's forgotten to take it recently and my giant load is impregnating her. Despite my overwhelming urge to ask her these questions, I remain quiet and just stare at my ceiling.

After ten or fifteen minutes pass and I'm almost asleep, I feel her hand on my dick and her lips on one of my nipples. She says, "You got another round in ya?" Judging by the speed with which my dick becomes hard, I guess I do.

chapter thirty-two

Halo 2

The next morning I wake up and Alyna's in my bed next to me, staring at me. She says, "Morning."

I say, "Good morning."

"Last night was pretty incredible."

"Yeah."

"I think we should see if we can relive a little of it this morning."

I don't know why Alyna would only suck my dick and jerk me off until last night, but apparently whatever kind of seal she had on sex has been broken. We fuck each other in a slow, controlled rhythm that makes us both cum about thirty minutes later. Then we get up, take a shower, and go into my kitchen area to look for breakfast. As we pass through the living room she notices my array of video game systems and says, "You have an Xbox 360?"

"Yeah."

"Do you have Halo 2?"

"Yeah."

"Are you any good?"

It's a strange challenge that excites me almost as much as the thought of her ass grinding against my crotch as I fuck her. We hurriedly eat two bowls of Fruity Pebbles and sit down to play Halo for the next few hours. Alyna's not the best Halo player I've ever seen and is less than a challenge for me, but I'm legitimately impressed at the level of skill she does have, and her genuine enthusiasm for the game is beyond rare for a girl.

As we play she admits to being a minor video game junkie and attributes her interest and skill to having two brothers who constantly played video games and refused to let her play shitty girl games like Tetris or Bubble Trouble when they were growing up. I want to meet her brothers.

After we play against each other on several maps and she vows that one day she'll beat me, we go online and get into a few team games. In each of them she hops in the driver's seat of the warthog and I get on the turret. She's a good driver and we do well. She says, "I love this game. I can't wait until the next one comes out."

I instantly remember a day that Casey agreed to play Halo with me. She played for a grand total of three minutes and complained that she didn't understand the controls before asking me if we could play Tetris or Dance Dance Revolution, which she later forced me to buy. When I told her that I didn't have Tetris and I didn't want to play Dance Dance Revolution because it's a shitty game, we ended up going to the Beverly Center and looking at couches in Crate and Barrel for three hours.

As the next game queues up and we can already hear the voices of some of the players who have entered the queue with us, I wonder if Alyna could ever spend three hours looking at couches.

I say, "What are your plans for the rest of the day?"

"Nothing."

The game starts and she hops in a warthog on the beach. I get on the turret.

She says, "Why?"

"I don't know, I was just wondering."

I take out a few players with a round of machine-gun fire.

She says, "Do you want to do something with me today?"

"If you want to . . . I mean, I don't want to . . ."

"Rush things?"

"Yeah."

She drives up a ramp and deposits us on the opposite side of a wall, where there are three enemy players waiting, one with a power sword. She runs him over and I take out the other two with the machine gun.

She says, "I don't want to rush things either, but if we both want to hang out with each other, then nobody's rushing anything, right?"

She spins the warthog around and we're staring down the sights of a guy with a rocket launcher.

I say, "I guess not."

We both jump off the warthog just in time to see a rocket blow it apart and both of our shields go down to half. We both whip out battle rifles and deliver a few short bursts to the rocket launcher guy's head. He goes down.

She says, "I think we should just do what feels right."

"Me too."

"Besides, I'm going to be out of town this weekend so we'll have plenty of time to not see each other."

"Where you going?"

She picks up the guy's rocket launcher and blows up an enemy player who's at a turret in the main base, then says, "I'm going back home. I haven't seen my parents at all this semester and they said they'd fly me back for a weekend because they miss me so much."

"You need a ride to the airport or anything?"

She runs out of rockets and trades her rocket launcher for a sniper rifle she finds on the ground. I slightly regret the airport offer. I don't want her to think it means more than it does.

Alyna says, "You don't have to do that."

"Don't worry about it. I'd like to do it." I have to back up my original offer.

"Okay, then yeah, I guess I need a ride."

She crouches behind a rock and waits for her shield to get back to full. I run over beside her and my cell phone starts ringing.

I say, "Dammit. Why do people always call right in the middle of a good game?"

She says, "Get it. I'll protect you." Alyna keeps playing while I answer it in the bedroom.

It's Casey. She demands that I have coffee with her as I promised and wants to know if I was ever going to call her to set it up. I explain that I've been busy and ultimately schedule our coffee date for the upcoming weekend before hanging up.

When I get back I see that Alyna's been trying to fend off enemy players from our position and my controller's vibration is evidence of this task's difficulty.

She says, "Who was it?"

"*L.A. Times* trying to sell me a newspaper subscription."

As soon as I pick my controller back up, the vibrations are replaced with stillness and my character's accompanying death grunt.

Jenna's Picture

I'm looking through some old boxes for the Nintendo Power Glove that I got for my seventh birthday. As I take some old books from college out of a box, a picture of my old girlfriend Jenna falls out of one. It's a picture that I took of her on the beach when we went to Martha's Vineyard one summer.

I am surprised that seeing this picture makes me stop looking for the Power Glove and sit down to think about that summer and about Jenna, who I realize is now married to the shark-toothed manager of NASCAR Superstore and possibly has given birth to his shark-toothed child.

I remember that she liked to fuck outside and we fucked that summer on the beach, not far from the exact location she's standing on in the picture. I wonder if her shark-toothed husband fucks her outside. I wonder if she likes it when he jerks off in front of her. I wonder what my life would be like if she had stuck to her plan of moving to Los Angeles when she graduated. I wonder if she's fat.

In the picture she's far from it. She's wearing a bikini that accentuates her already ample C-cup tits. She's standing at an angle so her ass, which was always a little too flat for my taste, but still a great ass, looks better than I remember it. Her stomach is defined but not overly muscular.

I try to remember our first few dates and can't. For some reason I remember a specific date we had sometime in the middle of our relationship when she dragged me to a Renaissance fair and paid a fat ugly high school girl in a wench costume two dollars to kiss me. I remember her rubbing my back once when I was sick. I remember renting *The Natural* with her because she had never seen it. I remember her telling me that when she was a little kid she thought Frisbees were gas-powered.

I put the picture back in the book and put the book back in the box.

When I try to jerk off to memories of fucking Jenna I can't cum, so I spend ten minutes downloading some Internet porn and end up blowing my load to the image of a skinny, pale girl with smaller than average tits and a mole right above her pussy taking it up the ass and saying, "That's it—clean it out, clean it out."

chapter thirty-three

Coffee with Casey

I've spent almost every night with Alyna for the past week, but it surprises me that I feel something close to real sadness as I get her bag out of the back of my car and hand it to her outside the American Airlines terminal at LAX.

She kisses me. Then she hugs me and says, "Thanks for the ride, mister."

"No problem."

"I'm gonna miss you."

"I'll miss you, too."

She hugs me again, tighter this time. I feel her rock-hard tits press against me.

She says, "This is stupid. I'm only leaving for the weekend. I'll see you in a few days."

"Okay."

She gives me one more tight hug and then squeezes my ass before she says, "I'll call you from my parents' house."

"Okay."

As she walks into the terminal she blows me a kiss. I genuinely wish she was staying. I watch her ass as she walks through the sliding doors into the check-in area, then I get back in my car and leave.

I meet Casey about forty-five minutes later at the coffee shop she demanded I go to in order to prevent her from showing up at my place every night at two A.M. I'm fully prepared for a psychotic outburst.

When I walk in, she's already sitting down trying not to look too eager. She's wearing a tight shirt that shows off how decent her tits are, and since she's already sitting down, I don't get a glance at her big ass, which makes me wonder if she's somehow miraculously slimmed her ass to a normal size since we broke up. I decide to go with the odds and believe that her ass is the same size if not bigger due to dealing with the emotional stress I must have caused her.

I sit down at the table with her.

She says, "I wasn't sure you were going to come."

"I said I would."

"I know."

She takes a drink of her coffee. A group of ten or so college-age girls all wearing UCLA women's soccer sweat suits walk in. Casey notices me checking them out. I don't care.

She says, "So like let's talk."

"Okay."

"Okay."

She takes another drink of coffee, wanting me to say something. I don't want to say anything. I don't want to be sitting here. I want to be back at my apartment fucking Alyna up against my bedroom wall.

Casey says, "So . . . do you miss me at all?"

"No, I don't think so."

"What do you mean you don't think so?"

"I mean no."

"You don't miss me at all?"

"No."

She starts to tear up and I want her to cry in this coffee shop. I want to be the guy sitting across from her as she's sobbing like a stupid fucking kid right in front of the UCLA women's soccer team.

Casey says, "We were together for a year and a half and you don't miss me even a little?"

I give a little pause for impact. "Not at all."

"Are you happy?"

Even when I was with Casey, I never considered myself unhappy, but the marked difference in the amount of enjoyment that I get from my life without her in it is undeniable.

I say, "Yeah."

She says, "Happier than when you were with me?"

"Yeah."

"Why?"

The answer is clear and simple: Alyna. Alyna fucks better and more, she has an amazing ass, and she genuinely seems to like me more than the idea of being married by twenty-eight no matter what. Even though I want Casey to self-destruct right in front of me and I know telling her about Alyna will snap her like a twig, I don't.

Instead I say, "I don't know. I just am."

"Well, I don't like understand that."

"Neither do I."

"Well, if you don't understand it, then why did you break up with me?"

Casey's voice has risen loudly enough by this point in the conversation to get the attention of the soccer team, who are now poorly disguising the fact that they're listening to every word we say.

"I just had to."

"You had to?"

"Yeah."

"Why?"

"I told you I don't know."

"Can't you give us another chance?"

"No."

"I think I deserve another chance."

"I can't do that."

"Why can't you? Like what's so bad about seeing if we can work through this?"

"There's nothing so bad about it. It's just not going to happen."

"You wouldn't go out on a date with me?"

The thought of going on a date with Casey and trying to see how many holes I could put my cock in before the night ended does pique my interest, but my unyielding urge to run out the front doors of the coffee shop and never see Casey again for the rest of my life holds more weight.

I say, "No."

Casey's close to losing it. She slows down and takes a long swig of her coffee. I look at the UCLA women's soccer team and they all quickly try to look at something else. Casey also notices that they've been watching us.

She says, "Can we go back to your apartment and talk about this?"

"Why?"

"Because this is like a private conversation and I don't really want to be having it in public."

"I think we should stay here."

"Why?"

"It's better that way."

She drinks more coffee.

She says, "You know, my mom always told me she never liked you."

"You should have listened to her."

"I just can't believe you're doing this."

"It's already done."

"How can you just stop loving me?"

In possibly one of the most honest moments of my life I say, "I don't think I ever really did."

And that's the end of Casey's emotional fortitude. She starts bawling like a baby. The UCLA women's soccer team doesn't even try to conceal their voyeuristic interest in what's going on or their apparent contempt for me, judging by the scowls on their faces.

I offer nothing to Casey, no words, no hug, nothing. Instead I get up out of my chair and turn to leave. As I take my first step away from the table I decide to get in my car, which is parked across the street, and sit for the next ten minutes to watch Casey cry. But I don't get to my car. I don't even take another step before Casey pukes out the following sledgehammer to my nuts:

"I'm pregnant."

My asshole clenches so tight that I'm pretty sure I tear my sphincter.

Milla Jovovich

She's standing right in front of me in the bread aisle at Ralph's on Sunset holding a basket half full of fingernail polish, and I watch her fill up the other side with five bags of powdered donuts. I wonder if I knocked up Milla Jovovich if she would have an abortion, but I would probably be okay with whatever Milla decided to do.

I lose any memory of the purpose of my visit to the grocery store. I'm holding a packet of superglue and a can of beef stew, both of which I reason I must have had some need for or I wouldn't have been holding them. All I can think about is jerking off to Milla Jovovich's nude scenes in *Return to the Blue Lagoon* as a teenager. I can also think about seeing her tits and cunt in *The Fifth Element* and *Resident Evil*, which I promptly do when she squats down to get another bag of powdered donuts off the bottom shelf.

I specifically key in on the scene in *Resident Evil* when she wakes up strapped to a medical examination table wearing only a piece of paper and her pussy is clearly visible. I follow her into a checkout line.

As she checks out, she uses a Ralph's card, which the computer says yields her no savings on the brands of fingernail polish and powdered donuts she chose to purchase. She pays with a credit card and asks to have her items put in a plastic bag.

I watch her ass as she walks away from the checkout counter. It's fucking perfect beyond belief.

I rush the cashier through my checkout procedure and pay in cash, carrying my beef stew and superglue out of the store without a bag to expedite my departure. I'm not sure exactly why I'm in such a hurry to watch Milla Jovovich walk to her car but I am.

I see her get into a black Escalade. I get in my own car and fail to resist the urge to follow her, which I do until I see her pull into a driveway at a house in the Hollywood Hills that looks like it must cost more than it's worth.

That night at home, I eat the beef stew and imagine what it would be like to fuck Milla Jovovich. I wonder what my unfounded odds of ever fucking her are. I give myself a 1.33 percent chance based on the following criteria: (1) I live in Los Angeles, where she must spend a significant amount of time, increasing my chance of running into her randomly; (2) she married the guy who directed *The Fifth Element*, who is a fucking toad; and (3) she is a supermodel/actress, and all of those types love to party and love to fuck.

Satisfied with my odds, I put on my *Resident Evil* DVD and jerk off to any scene that features her in little or no clothing. I blow a load but still can't remember what I bought the superglue for.

chapter thirty-four

It's Official

Over the course of about a month and a half Alyna and I have fucked enough for me to know the following things: She likes it when I spread her ass cheeks apart in doggie style and press my thumb on her asshole; she can't cum unless I talk dirty or spank her; and she loves to have me stick my cock halfway in, then jerk me off so I shoot a load in her pussy.

But as we eat Combo Burritos at the Taco Bell by the Beverly Center, I'm not thinking about any of these things. I'm thinking about the fact that Casey is fucking pregnant. I only vaguely remember the last few times we fucked, and even though I know a large percentage of those times ended with me blowing my load all over her face/ass/stomach, I do remember at least a few times that I shot my load in her cunt because she said she didn't like it when I came on her face. I shouldn't have let her manipulate me. This entire thing could have been avoided. I wonder if Alyna would care if I had a kid.

I'm chewing on a piece of Combo Burrito and thinking of ways to have Casey accidentally die when Alyna says, "If we were out somewhere and ran into some friend of yours that I haven't met, how would you introduce me?"

"I'd say . . . this is Alyna. How would you introduce me?"

"I don't know, I might say something like . . . this is my boyfriend. What do you think of that?"

I chew a piece of my burrito as I give it some thought. I say, "I wouldn't mind." Strangely, I really wouldn't.

"And you wouldn't mind if I was your girlfriend?" I wouldn't mind this, either.

I say, "No. Would you?"

"Obviously not, or I wouldn't be asking. I just felt like we see each other so much and I like you a lot and it seems like you like me just as much. . . . We might as well be official."

I search for the uneasy paranoia this conversation should be building in me, but it's not there. What is there is a strange sense of relief, which doesn't bother me as much as it should. I'm actually happy to have another girlfriend, and not because a girlfriend means free and easy fucking, but because my new girlfriend is Alyna. I almost feel like telling her about the impending life-ruining child I'm about to have with my ex-girlfriend but decide that until the kid exists it's not worth bringing up.

She says, "You don't feel weird about it being so soon after both of us just getting out of relationships?"

"No."

"Me either. Does it make you feel weird that you don't feel weird?"

"No."

"Me either."

"Does it make you feel weird that I don't feel weird?"

"No."

"I'm driving you crazy with this, right?"

"No."

"So then it's official. You're my boyfriend and I'm your girlfriend?"

"Yeah."

"Does that kind of excite you?"

As we talked I hadn't thought about it, but now that she brings it up it does kind of excite me. I've never had a girlfriend that I've found as attractive as Alyna, nor have I had one that I've wanted to spend as much time with.

She says, "You know what we should do to celebrate?"

"What?"

She says loud enough for the lady hobo sitting in the corner to hear, "We should go back to your apartment and fuck."

I've also never had a girlfriend who's wanted to have sex enough to propose it in a Taco Bell in front of a hobo.

We finish our Combo Burritos as Creed's "(Can You Take Me) Higher" starts to play on the Taco Bell radio system and the lady hobo stands up, raises her arms to the heavens, and sings along with Scott Stapp.

Back at my apartment I've been fucking Alyna up against my bedroom wall for a few minutes and I'm about to blow my load. The thought of fathering two children with different women drives me to pull out and shoot semen all over her ass and legs. As I fall back onto my bed and Alyna goes to the bathroom to clean herself up, I wonder what my kid is going to look like and wish I was dead.

chapter thirty-five

Alyna Finds My Stash

I'm sitting on the couch half watching the World Series of Poker on ESPN2. Alyna is kneeling between my legs with one hand on my balls and the other jerking me off while she sucks the head of my cock. I blow a load down her throat just as a pro poker player goes all in on a pair of aces and loses to an amateur who draws two queens on the flop to match the queen he has in the queen/ten hand he chose to stay with.

Alyna sucks my cock for a few more seconds, then says, smiling from my crotch, "Did you like that?"

"Yeah."

"I hate yeast infections because we can't have sex, but I kind of like them because I get to give you blow jobs all the time."

I wish I had never met Casey. I wish I had never fucked Casey. I wish she wasn't pregnant with the ruination of my life. Alyna says, "I'm getting a drink. You want something?"

"No. I'm good, thanks."

She walks into my kitchen area, leaving my cock hanging out of my pants. I move to start buttoning them back up and she says, "Just leave it. I want to see if I can make you cum again after I get a drink."

I wonder how difficult it would be to have Casey killed.

I watch a few more hands of the World Series of Poker. The amateur guy gets dealt the same hand—queen/ten—and goes all in again and wins again, knocking another player out of the final five. Despite having just shot a load down Alyna's throat, the thought of her wanting to suck my cock again starts to give me another hard-on.

As the next hand is being dealt, Alyna says from the kitchen, "Hey, what's this Bloussant stuff?" and I quickly realize that in the cupboard above my drinking glasses I still have half a case of unused breast-enhancing drug that I never slipped into Casey's food. I don't know what my explanation will be. The truth is probably not the best choice. As I think for a few seconds, Alyna reads one of the bottles and says, "Why do you have a breast-enhancing drug?"

I don't leave the couch. With my dick losing its semi-hard-on but still hanging out of my pants, I say, "My old girlfriend kept it over here."

"Why?"

"She didn't like to keep it at her house."

"Why not?"

"I don't know, I think she didn't want her cats to get into it." This immediately conjures images of Casey's cats walking around with gigantic tits.

Alyna comes out of the kitchen with a bottle of Bloussant in her hand and a glass of Dr Pepper in the other. She says, "Did this stuff work?"

"I don't really know."

"Do you think she'll want it back?"

"Probably not."

"Do you care if I try it?"

I wonder if there's any way on the planet that Alyna wouldn't mind the fact that I'm going to have a kid with my ex-girlfriend.

"No, go ahead."

"It can't really work, right?"

"It's supposed to."

"I have to try it."

She puts the bottle of Bloussant down on the coffee table next to her glass of Dr Pepper, then takes my cock in her hand and says, "You think you can handle another one?"

She already has her mouth on my dick when I say, "I don't know, I guess we'll have to see."

As she sucks my dick for the second time in fifteen minutes I try to picture her B-cup tits getting bigger. I put my hand down her shirt as she sucks my dick and squeeze her tits, trying to imagine them a full cup size bigger. I like her tits as they are and I'm not completely sure increasing their size would improve their overall quality, but her enthusiasm to willingly use an unproven breast enhancer is an attractive enough personality trait to make her tits somehow feel better in my hand.

The second load I blow proves to be a little too much for her mouth to handle. She swallows some of it, but some of it drips out of her mouth onto her cheek and chin and onto my dick.

She comes up from sucking my dick, laughs, and says, "Do I have anything on my face?"

As she smiles at me with my cum dripping off her chin, I can't help laughing too, partly because of the humor of the situation, but mostly to mask the utter despair I feel closing in around me when I think about the fact that the best thing I've possibly ever had is going to be destroyed by a fucking mistake that's growing in the womb of a girl I hate.

Subway Whore

After thirty minutes of a drunken argument about the necessity and quality of the Los Angeles subway system, Todd and I find ourselves waiting at the Hollywood terminal to test it out at one A.M. Next to us a family with a retarded kid and what I assume to be some kind of junkie also wait for the next train. Todd elbows me and points in the general direction of a hobo, crouching by what I make out to be a log of human shit near the stairwell and says, "Dude, check out that guy with his deuce."

The retarded kid sees the feces at the same time Todd does and starts screaming, "Mommy, he poodied! Mommy, that man poodied on the ground!" which gets no reaction from the hobo, who remains crouched by his work. This goes on for a while.

When the subway train finally pulls up, I convince Todd to get on a car that does not contain the retarded kid, which turns out to be a mistake because the car we do get on contains a weatherworn woman who can't be any younger than fifty-five with eyes that don't really focus on anything holding a brown-stained teddy bear that at one time was pink, and a black guy in an Adidas sweat suit who I'm pretty sure is carrying at least a knife, but more likely a gun.

The train pulls away from the terminal and our fate is sealed.

Todd says, "So what do you think now?" and I'm reminded that there was an original reason for us to be on the subway.

I say, "Uh, I still think L.A. can do without it."

"Whatever, dude. This is the fucking shit."

Todd and I don't say anything for the next few minutes. Then the old lady with the bear says what I think is the following: "Kiss my bear and I'll suck your cock."

I'm positive she didn't actually say this and I'm drunk enough to say, "Excuse me?"

And she says again, "Kiss my bear and I'll suck your cock."

Todd says, "Did she just say kiss my bear and I'll suck your cock?"

The old lady says, "You bet your ass I'll suck those cocks."

Todd and I are both stunned into silence. She says again, "Kiss my bear and I'll suck your cock."

I shoot a quick glance at the black guy in the Adidas sweat suit just to see if he's getting any of this. He seems to be unfazed by what's going on and I don't know if any of this means anything to him until he says, "Well, you gonna kiss her fuckin' bear or what?" And it becomes suddenly clear to me that this man is the bear-wielding old lady's pimp. I immediately wonder if I'm going to be forced to accept a blow job from this aged and most likely disease-ridden whore at gunpoint, and worse, made to kiss her bear in order to receive the blow job.

I look at Todd, who's dazed.

I say, "Uh, no, thanks."

The pimp says, "You two faggots or somethin'?"

The old whore scratches out a laugh and then says, "Hey, faggots, you kiss my bear and I'll suck your faggot cocks."

For some reason my immediate reaction is to defend my sexuality to the pimp and his whore, so I say, "No, we're straight."

The pimp says, "Then kiss her fuckin' bear."

Todd finally chimes in, "I don't think so, man."

The whore says again, "You kiss my bear and I'll suck your cock."

The pimp says, "If you ain't gonna kiss her bear then you gotta get off this train."

I wonder how close the next stop is and hope we get to it before we're killed.

For the next five minutes the whore insists that we kiss her bear so she can suck our cocks, and the pimp keeps asking us if we're sure we're not faggots. When we get to the next stop, across the street from Universal Studios, Todd and I get off the train and make our way aboveground, where we take a cab back to the bar we originally came from in Hollywood.

As we sit back down at the bar and order two beers, Todd says, "Hey, dude, was that bitch on the subway ninety-eight percent?"

Despite the possibly life-threatening situation we managed to narrowly escape, I force myself to imagine getting head from the repulsive whore and then fucking her so I can accurately answer Todd's question.

I say, "She's about as close to a two-percenter as you can get, but if it's disease-free and she disappears right after I fuck her and her pimp's not around . . . I'd fuck her."

Todd says, "Me, too."

chapter thirty-six

Dinner with the Mother of My Child

I'm waiting outside Casey's apartment for her to come out so I can take her to a dinner she forced me to agree to, where she wants us to talk about the baby and how we're going to raise it.

When she comes out to the car she catches me a little off guard by saying, "Hey, why don't we skip the dinner, go back into my apartment, and have crazy sex?"

I'm pretty shocked by this, but even more shocked by my reaction as I say, "I think we should go eat dinner." It doesn't take me long to search for an answer as to why I passed up free grudge-fucking with my ex-girlfriend—Alyna. I don't want to cheat on Alyna. At face value, not wanting to cheat on Alyna should bother me, but as I stare at Casey I'm almost calmed by the fact that at the moment I really only want to fuck Alyna and no one else.

Casey gets in the car, puts her hand right on my dick, and says, "Then after dinner, I want you to come back here and fuck me silly." Despite the fact that Casey is carrying the doomseed of my life in her gut, this gets me pretty horny, but as soon as I get a hard-on I start

thinking about Alyna and I know I don't want to fuck Casey. I'm genuinely surprised by this seemingly impregnable psychological defense I
seem to have developed.

As we drive, I make sure to hit the brakes a little harder than I need
to at each stop in the hopes of jarring the fetus loose and causing an instant miscarriage. As I come to the fourth or fifth abrupt stop, it doesn't
seem to be working. Nonetheless, I stomp the brakes whenever traffic
allows, reasoning that it only takes one good one to bust the fetus loose.

We pull into the valet at Lawry's and it doesn't seem like the fetus
is detached. I walk into the place behind Casey and kick her back foot
so she trips on herself going up the stairs, still hoping to jar the fetus
loose. She shoots me a pissed-off look that I explain away by saying,
"Sorry, it was an accident," but the unborn life-ender in her gut seems
to be doing fine.

We sit down, get our water and bread, and then it starts.

She says, "So what do you think we should name it?"

I am a statue.

She says, "I was thinking Willamena for a girl and Kerry for a boy.
What do you think?"

I hate both of these names. I say, "Casey, do you really think we
should have this baby?"

"Uh . . . yeah. What else would we do? Give it up for adoption?"

"You could have an abortion."

"An *abortion?!?* Why would I abort a child that was conceived
through love?"

"Do you remember the conversation we had in the coffee shop a
few days ago?"

"Yeah, but you were just confused. You didn't know what you were
saying. This baby, our baby, is going to bring us back together and
make you see that you still love me, that you never stopped loving
me."

I want to open the salt shaker and dump it in my eyes.

The waiter comes over and takes our orders, giving me a quick breather from the worst conversation I've ever had in my life. Then he leaves and it's back on.

She says, "Don't you want to see what a baby that's half me and half you would grow up to be like?"

I think about this for less than a second and say, "No," with more certainty than I've ever had about anything in my life.

"But that will change once you actually see the baby. They say no man can stop himself from crying when he first sees his little baby."

"I don't want a baby. Have an abortion."

"No. I'm not having an abortion. We're having this baby and starting a family."

"What?"

"I'm sure if you just apologize to my parents and tell them you were like confused when you blew up on my mom and everything, they'll forgive you and we can still get married."

"I don't want to get married."

"Well, I'm not having a child without being married to the father."

"Then get an abortion."

"I can't believe you're being such an asshole about this."

She wants me to say something. I don't.

She says, "It was meant to be. I mean, if I was on the pill and still got pregnant, then this baby is meant to come into this world and we're meant to be its mother and father."

Now she really wants me to say something. I don't.

She says, "Well, aren't you going to say something?"

"Get an abortion."

She says, "I am not getting a fucking abortion," right as the waiter brings our drink orders to the table. He pretends he didn't hear it, but he must have. I wonder briefly if he's ever been privy to any identical dinner conversations.

She says, "We're going to get married. We're going to have this baby and we're going to start a family."

"I'm not."

"What do you mean, you're not?"

"I'm not starting a family."

"You don't have a choice. I'm going to have your baby. You're going to be a father."

"But I don't have to be around for it. All I'm required to do is pay you, which I'll do as the law dictates." I'm hoping this line of reasoning will make her realize she doesn't want to have a baby if the father won't be around.

She says, "You wouldn't want to see your child grow up?"

"No."

"Why?"

"I just don't want to."

"You wouldn't want to help me raise *our* child?"

"No."

"Why?"

"Same reason."

Our food comes. Over the course of the meal, Casey continues to try to convince me that the best thing to do is to get married, have the child, and start a family. I stand firm in my disinterest in her plans.

On the drive home I continue to try to jar the fetus loose with more abrupt driving maneuvers.

At the end of the night, she once again invites me in to have "crazy sex." Upon my refusal she reaches for my pants and says she won't take no for an answer. She explains that she's missed me and "my penis." Although I'm very tempted to fuck her just to see if a few deep thrusts might knock the fetus out of her uterus, my genuine affection and respect for what Alyna and I have keep me from leaving my car.

Once I finally get Casey to go back inside her apartment by promising to at least think about getting married, I drive to a party where I'm supposed to meet Alyna. As I drive I wonder if Alyna ever had an abortion or ever would. I assume she would but is careful enough to not get pregnant in the first place.

chapter thirty-seven

Ex-Boyfriend Duane

Other than Alyna's hippie roommate Simone, I haven't met any of her friends. Despite her telling me that she really doesn't have many friends and the party I'm at is being thrown by more of an acquaintance, I feel uneasy about the fact that I want to make a good impression, which I find even more unsettling than the party itself. I can't remember the last time I was conscious of trying to make someone happy or giving a shit about something I normally wouldn't.

As soon as I walk in Alyna takes my hand and guides me through the packed apartment. My dick brushes a couple of hard college asses as we make our way to the kitchen and a counter full of Ralph's brand hard liquor and various bottles of juice. Alyna makes herself a screwdriver and I pour myself a blue plastic cup full of scotch from a jug with a Distiller's Preference label on it and a price tag that indicates the entire gallon was a price-conscious $6.34. Even though I immensely enjoy getting drunk with Alyna, I drain the scotch in one swallow in an effort to numb the memories of my dinner with Casey and the thoughts of my bleak future.

Alyna leads me around to two girls standing by an open window. Alyna says, "Okay, I'll introduce you to these two girls. They're both complete bitches and one of them supposedly got crabs last semester from the other one when they were drunk and got dared to rub their pussies together."

Alyna introduces me.

One bitch says, "Hi. I'm Carolyn."

The other one says, "I'm Mandy."

I say, "Nice to meet you," as I'm imagining them both naked rubbing their cunts together in a drunken frenzy, which isn't bad considering they've both got late-teen bodies that haven't yet started to show the signs of wear associated with too much drinking and little to no exercise on a steady diet of eating anything they want.

The conversation I wade through yields nothing interesting aside from Alyna starting to get semi-drunk and moving her hand from the middle of my back down into my pants and pinching my ass from time to time.

As I move my hand down her pants to reciprocate, I notice she's wearing a thong. My hard-on is almost instantaneous. As I squeeze her rock-hard ass, I wonder how long it will be before she loses it, before she gets cellulite, before she becomes an old woman eating a cup of yogurt in the airport. Somewhere in the pit of my stomach the unrealistic but not entirely impossible scenario of her ass never losing its firmness and fuckability gives rise to a giddy excitement that combines with the first sip of a new plastic cup of scotch to make me feel better than I've felt in a while about anything.

The two bitches use a momentary lull in the boring conversation to announce that their drinks are empty and they have to get refills. As they leave I wonder why I was so worked up about making a good impression. A completely hot bitch who's a little taller than Alyna with slightly bigger tits comes over to talk to us, and the hope that somehow Alyna and this girl would have no problem double-teaming me is accompanied by the urge to make the best impression of my life.

The hot bitch says, "Hey, Alyna. Who's this?" in a way I interpret as indicative of her entertaining the idea of fucking me.

Alyna introduces me as her boyfriend and the hot bitch's formerly flirtatious tone changes to something closer to repulsion as she says, "I'm Brooke." I've always wanted to fuck someone named Brooke.

Brooke says, "Is he the reason you haven't been hanging out as much?"

Alyna says, "No. I mean, we've been spending a lot of time together, but I don't know. . . ."

Brooke says, "Does Duane know you have a new boyfriend?"

Who the fuck is Duane? I think he's Alyna's ex-boyfriend but I'm not sure. I am sure that I'm slowly starting to hate Brooke. As she continues to talk to Alyna like I'm not in the room, I imagine myself fucking her doggie style, pulling her head back by her hair. I imagine her crying somewhere alone. I imagine her pregnant and fat—like Casey.

Alyna says, "I don't care if Duane knows."

Brooke says, "Well, he'll find out soon enough."

And fucking Duane walks up, puts his arm around Brooke, and says, "Hey, Alyna, how's it going?" with a forced confidence and nonchalance that make him seem more drunk than he probably is.

Alyna introduces me to her ex-boyfriend.

Duane says, "Yeah, I think we met once before, but that was when I was still fucking Alyna."

Brooke laughs.

Alyna says, "Jesus Christ, this is why I fucking dumped you. You're a complete dick."

Duane misuses the phrase "That's what *she* said." Then he says to me, "So aren't you like thirty years old or something?"

Alyna answers before I can. "You know what, Duane, he's not thirty, but even if he was, it doesn't matter because I sucked his cock three times today and it stayed hard every time. So no matter how old he is, he can make me happier than you."

The fact that Alyna and I are both well on our way to being completely shit-faced helps me explain away the slight insult I feel at her reduction of our relationship to its sexual components.

At this point I've noticed that a small group of people who have obviously followed the mini-drama of Duane and Alyna in their circle of friends have gathered around us, unfortunately for him.

They watch, waiting for the rebuttal from Duane that never comes. He takes a drink from his cup and opens his mouth to say something, but instead puke comes out. His puke lands mainly on the floor and his shoes, but some of it gets on Brooke. The small crowd that's gathered around the scene disperses with the spread of Duane's cloud of vomit stink.

Alyna says, "Let's get out of here."

We leave and walk down the street to IN-N-OUT, where I buy Alyna a number one plain. We get our food and sit down.

She says, "I'm sorry about that. I didn't know he was going to be there."

"It's okay."

"I know the last thing you want to see is my asshole ex-boyfriend who's still not over it."

"Is that true about him not being able to get hard-ons?"

She kind of laughs and says, "Yeah, it is, actually."

"Why'd you stay with him so long?"

She laughs again and says, "There's more to a relationship than sex."

Hearing those words come out of her mouth scares the shit out of me for two specific and conflicting reasons. Reason 1: My earlier disappointment at Alyna's trivialization of our relationship dissolves, meaning that I actually want her to think there's something more between us than just sex. Reason 2: Casey used that exact phrase more times than I can count as an excuse to not have sex.

At the moment reason number two seems more pressing, so I say, "But that's one of the most important parts, right?"

"Oh yeah. Don't get me wrong. If I don't get sex once a day I go crazy."

"So didn't he drive you crazy?"

"Yeah. I guess it just took me a while to realize it. Why'd you stay with your girlfriend for so long?"

It's the first time anyone's asked me this and the first time I've even thought about it. It wasn't the convenience, it wasn't the boring sex, it wasn't the unemotional response I had to everything she did, it wasn't the disinterest with which I approached everything about her. As I chew my plain number one sitting across from Alyna, I pinpoint the single exact reason I stayed with Casey for a year and a half.

I say, "I guess I just didn't think there was anything better."

Alyna smiles, thinking I'm talking about her specifically as the "anything better." I don't ruin it. I smile back knowing to a large degree her smile is justified.

She says, "Do you still talk to her?"

I'm pretty sure Alyna wouldn't care if I did still talk to Casey, but fear of any conversation that could lead to my accidentally divulging the existence of my unborn child causes me to say, "No."

"When was the last time you did?"

I don't count the time she showed up on my doorstep or the time I had coffee with her and she told me she was pregnant or the time we ate dinner and I tried to convince her to have an abortion thirty minutes before I showed up to the party we just left when I say, "I don't know. Months ago."

"Do you think she's okay with everything?"

I say, "Probably."

We finish eating our number ones and then go back to my apartment, where Alyna insists on fucking in front of an open window. As we do, some people walk by on the street outside, but I don't think they notice because the lights are off.

We rest for a while and then have sex again. This time it's less aggressive, slower, with us lying side by side, and it ends with her falling asleep a few seconds after we both cum. I stay awake for a few minutes trying to imagine how pissed off Duane must have been when Alyna explained to him that she sucked my cock three times today.

I try to imagine Casey sucking some guy's cock just to see if it elicits any reaction. It doesn't. I throw in another guy fucking her doggie style while she's sucking another guy's cock. Still nothing. I think about her getting fucked in the ass and the cunt while she's sucking some other guy's dick who I imagine to be Persian. Still nothing. I end up falling asleep imagining Casey sitting in the middle of a basketball court as the entire Lakers roster surrounds her, coating her in a six-inch-thick layer of semen, and I still feel nothing except the growing paranoia created by the rising probability that the cum-drenched girl sitting center court will soon be the mother of my child.

Gwen Stefani

No Doubt's first CD plays in Alyna's car and I still don't understand why anyone has ever bought any of their records or why Alyna and almost any girl I've ever known loves their shitty music.

This mystery remains unsolved as Alyna and I pull into the underground parking garage at the Virgin Megastore on Sunset with the intent of buying Jefferson Airplane's *Crown of Creation* because mine has been lost. As we come up the elevator and the doors open, we see a giant mob of teenage girls standing in a line that snakes around the side of the building out onto the street.

We walk into the main courtyard area of the shopping center and the crowd's source is revealed to be Gwen Stefani. She's inside the store signing copies of her various CDs, posters, and other crap.

Alyna looks at me and says, "Holy shit. I didn't know she was gonna be here. Do you mind if I go get something autographed?"

I tell her I will meet her back here and go and buy my CD, which takes me all of five minutes. I head back to meet Alyna in the mob. The line hasn't moved, and I find Alyna near the end.

The line we wait in isn't entirely unpleasant. I'm surrounded by teenage girls dressed in self-empowering belly shirts and thongs that rise up out of their pants. I wonder if the doomseed growing in Casey's gut will turn into one of these mini-bitches in fourteen years. There are a few other guys in the crowd, but I think they're fags. Alyna keeps telling me how sorry she is and how much she thinks this sucks, but I know she's enjoying it just as much as the teenage girls are. This should bother me more than it does.

The two girls directly behind us in the generally disorganized crowd that's supposed to be a line we're standing in have the following conversation:

One girl says, "I can't believe we're going to meet her."

The other one says, "I know. It's so awesome."

The other one says, "Seriously, she's like the raddest girl ever."

The other one says, "I know. I have like two posters of her."

The other one says, "Which ones?"

The other one says, "The one where she's punching all tough like and the one where she's dressed up in a pretty dress all girly."

The other one says, "I have the one where she's punching hanging over my bed."

The other one says, "Me, too."

I grab Alyna's tit over her shirt and squeeze it, which is a behavior I've gotten her used to. She turns into the squeeze, hiding it between our bodies, but not discontinuing it. But then she grabs my wrist and lowers my hand and says, "There are little kids here. Wait till we get back to your place." It's the first rejection of this type she's ever given me. I dismiss it based on the legitimacy of her argument.

I end up being forced to listen to another conversation, this one slightly more interesting than the first, between two girls who I roughly estimate to be about fifteen.

One bitch says, "Paul wants me to suck his you-know-what. Have you sucked Kenny's?"

The other bitch says, "I did it once."

The other bitch says, "What was it like?"

The other bitch says, "Kind of weird. It was totally like shoving a Blow Pop down your throat."

The other bitch says, "Did he, you know . . . finish?"

The other bitch says, "No. I had to do it with my hand."

The other bitch says, "Why didn't he?"

The other bitch says, "He said I was doing it wrong. But he hasn't even tried to go down on me, so I couldn't care less."

The other bitch says, "I don't know if I want Paul to be down in that area."

The other bitch says, "Does he ever use his hand on you?"

The other bitch says, "Yeah, sometimes."

The other bitch says, "And do you like it?"

The other bitch says, "Yeah."

The other bitch says, "Then think of how good a tongue would feel."

The other bitch says, "Yeah, I guess you're right. Maybe I should make some kind of deal with him. I'll do him if he does me."

The other bitch says, "You totally should. I think I'm going to do that to Kenny next time he wants me to suck his thing."

The other bitch says, "I can't believe we're about to see Gwen."

The other bitch says, "I know, it's so cool."

The other bitch says, "Do you think Gwen sucks Gavin's you-know-what?"

The other bitch says, "I bet she doesn't have to."

The other bitch says, "She's so awesome."

That's when I tune out and notice that even though we're still far from being next in line, Gwen Stefani is in my line of sight. She is hot as fuck. Her hard little tits are pushing out against a wife beater that has the word ROCKSTAR printed on it in rhinestones.

I imagine what she's like in the sack. My gut tells me that away from her public image, in the confines of whatever room she's being fucked in, she's completely submissive. No matter how much girl power she has, I imagine Gavin Rossdale's dick has more power. I wonder what the two girls behind us in line would think of her if they could see her with a load of Rossdale's cum sprayed all over her face.

Over the course of the next twenty minutes we make our way to the head of the line. Once there, Alyna hands her a poster she bought inside and we have the following conversation with Gwen Stefani:

Gwen Stefani says, "Hi there, who should I make this out to?"

Alyna says, "Alyna."

Gwen Stefani says, "How do you spell that?"

Alyna says, "A-L-Y-N-A."

Gwen Stefani says, "Cool name."

Alyna says, "Thanks."

Gwen Stefani signs the poster and hands it back to Alyna, then says, "There you go. Rock on."

For some reason I say, "Thanks," and we head back out into the mob.

When we get back to Alyna's apartment, she puts the poster up on her bedroom wall and fucks me like a crazed animal. I don't know if it was getting Gwen Stefani's autograph or the fact that I offered no concrete objection to waiting around to get it that got Alyna so amped up, but I don't question it.

As I look over at Gwen Stefani kicking at nothing in particular to display her unique style and empowerment, I pull out and blow a load all over Alyna's tits.

chapter thirty-eight

Two-Month Anniversary

It's been exactly two months since Alyna and I have officially referred to ourselves as boyfriend and girlfriend and in celebration we're eating at a Tex-Mex place on the coast called Marix that Alyna said was one of her favorites. I'm eating a burrito, trying not to think about my baby in Casey's stomach that Alyna still doesn't know about.

She says, "Does it seem like we've been dating for two months?"

I don't know what a good answer to this question is. I say, "No."

"I know."

I guess that was what she wanted to hear.

"So what do you think of the food here?"

"It's good."

"I'm glad you like it. I love this place."

She picks up her margarita, extends it out toward me, looks in my eyes, and says, "Let's do a toast."

I pick up my beer and clink her glass as she says, "Happy two-month anniversary."

"Happy two-month anniversary."

As what is potentially the culmination of importance in our two-month relationship is happening, Cameron Diaz walks right past our table, luring my gaze away from Alyna's eyes and making it refocus on her own unimaginably perfect body.

I stare at her for at least five or ten seconds, remembering every time I've seen her in a bikini or her underwear in a movie before realizing that I'm in the middle of my own anniversary toast. I try to turn back to Alyna as nonchalantly as I possibly can in case there is some chance to explain away my lightning-quick loss of interest in our special moment and I see that Alyna herself is staring at Cameron Diaz.

Alyna says, "God, she is so fucking hot."

Casey would have been in tears by now, questioning me about what our relationship means to me, etc.

Alyna says, "I think if I ever had sex with a woman it might be Cameron Diaz."

It takes every ounce of self-control I have not to go over to Diaz's table and ask her if she wants to have a threesome with Alyna and me. The odds obviously aren't good that she'd say yes, but lightning has to strike somewhere. I remain seated, reasoning that although I might be able to gawk at Cameron Diaz's ass on my two-month anniversary without incurring any ill feelings, I probably wouldn't be able to solicit a two-girl orgy with my girlfriend and myself.

As we finish our dinner, we both can't help taking a few more glances at Diaz, who's here with a group of friends, some of whom are guys. I try to imagine being in Cameron Diaz's circle of friends but can't because I can't get past the thought of her licking my balls while Alyna eats her out as I fuck Alyna doggie style.

About halfway through our dinner, I get up to take a piss and purposely walk too close to Diaz. She smells good.

Outside the pisser there's a guy selling flowers. I'm not worried about the possibility of not getting fucked tonight, but I decide to buy Alyna some flowers anyway, knowing it will make her happy. When I get back to the table and give them to her, I say, "Happy Anniversary."

Alyna smiles a big smile and says, "Look at you. You're the perfect little boyfriend." Then she leans across the table and gives me a kiss. As she kisses me I'm looking with one eye semi-open at Diaz, who I'm surprised to see is looking right back at our table, smiling a kind of "oh-isn't-that-cute" kind of smile. Again, I have to swallow down the impulse to invite her into a threesome.

We finish eating and I take one last look at Cameron Diaz, trying to imagine what her pussy looks like before paying the bill and going back to my apartment.

When we get inside, Alyna thanks me for the flowers and hugs me. She says, "Happy anniversary," and then kisses me and says, "Take me to the bedroom so we can have two-month-anniversary sex." I comply.

Once in the bedroom she sucks my cock a little and I eat her out some. We fuck for a few minutes and then she says, "Wait." I'm kind of scared to hear what's coming next, but when she says, "Let's do something different for our anniversary, something neither of us have ever done with anyone else," I'm interested.

She rolls over onto all fours and says, "Have you ever fucked one of your other girlfriends in the ass before?"

Of course I have, but none of them ever had an ass as rock hard and perfect as Alyna's.

I say, "No."

She says, "Neither have I, let's do it."

I can't believe I say, "You sure?"

But she erases my mistake with, "Yeah, I want to see what it's like. Do you think we need to lube up first?"

"Maybe."

We do the sixty-nine for a few minutes with me licking her asshole, which has the melon smell that I've now become familiar with. She seems to be genuinely getting off on it. This leads me to believe she may actually enjoy getting fucked in the ass, which would be something I've never experienced with another girlfriend.

After her asshole and my cock are sufficiently dripping with each other's saliva, she rolls back over onto all fours and says, "Okay, go slow at first."

As I put my cock in her asshole, she pushes her ass back toward me, forcing my dick in a few inches. The little moan she lets out isn't specific enough to let me know if she likes my dick in her ass or if it's hurting her. She pushes back again until I'm almost balls-deep in her asshole. This time the moan is accompanied by her saying, "Oh my god. That feels so good," letting me know she likes it.

I fuck her in the ass and reach around underneath her to play with her clit. Her ass is so tight I can barely move without cumming. Despite my efforts to remain totally still so as not to make myself blow an early load, Alyna keeps moving her ass back and forth, forcing my cock in and out of her.

I think about dogs getting hit by cars, my grandma, and the time I cut my knee open with the tin lid of a can of corn so deep I could see the bone. This helps me last until Alyna cums, the sound of which overcomes any repulsive or familial imagery I might be able to conjure, and I blow a massive load in her ass. As I pull out I can feel her asshole contracting around my cock. I wonder if I can get another instantaneous hard-on and start ass-fucking her again immediately. On second thought, the soreness that might result from a double inaugural ass-fucking might discourage her from ever doing it again. I pull out humbly.

As we lie in my bed she says, "Wow. That was really, really good."

"So you liked it."

"Yeah. I always thought I might, but Jesus Christ, that was almost better than normal sex. Do you like it?"

"Yeah."

"So you wouldn't care if we did that from time to time."

"Nope."

We lie there for a few minutes and then she says, "Hey, I want to tell you something and I don't want it to freak you out."

She's pregnant too, she has AIDS, she used to be a man, I have no idea what's coming as I say, "Okay . . ."

"I don't know if there's an easy way to say this so I guess I'll just say it. . . .

She's been fucking someone else. She's still fucking Duane. She's getting back together with Duane and they're getting married. Duane's in the closet with a video camera and a gun.

She says, "I'm in love with you . . . I love you."

I give in to my trained reaction and hug her, then say, "I love you, too," and I think I actually might.

"You don't have to say it back just because I did."

"I'm not just saying it back."

"You really love me?"

"Yeah," and I think I really do.

She kisses me all over the face and rolls on top of me. I wonder if my semen is going to drip out of her ass and onto me as she says, "I know this is going to sound stupid, and I don't really believe in fate or destiny or any of that stupid shit, but I kind of feel like we're meant to be together."

I don't believe in any of that shit either. Casey did. This is the first moment in our relationship that I feel slightly uneasy about how good she makes me feel. I just smile back. She hugs and kisses me again, then says, "So we're in love. Does being in love make you horny?"

She kind of grinds her cunt on my dick and it starts hardening up.

"Do you want to fuck me in the ass again?"

"If you want to."

She sits up a little and reaches back to grab my dick. Just before she inserts my cock into her ass for the second time in twenty minutes, she says, "Happy anniversary, I love you," and I wish Casey would have been into ass fucking on the night I impregnated her.

chapter thirty-nine

Another Chance Encounter

Alyna and I are in the Beverly Center because she thinks the Bloussant is working and wants to see if a C-cup swimsuit will fit her. We're holding hands as we walk into a store called Everything But Water and I'm ready to spend up to thirty minutes staring at Alyna's tits as she tries on different bathing suits, but instead I get one mind-shattering second of staring Casey right in the eye as she looks up from a swimsuit rack to see Alyna and me walking toward her.

Casey doesn't waste any time with pleasantries. She says, "Who's this?"

I'm too stunned to speak. I wonder what the odds are of a terrorist attack on the Beverly Center occurring right now.

Alyna takes over. She says, "I'm Alyna, his girlfriend. I think we met once before. I think it was actually in the Beverly Center, too."

Casey says, "His girlfriend, huh?" She shoots me a look. "Yeah, I remember that. That was like back when we were engaged. So what are you up to?"

I think she's talking to me so I respond, "Nothing."

Casey looks at Alyna and says, "So what do you do, Alyna the girl-friend?"

Alyna says, "Oh, I'm a senior at UCLA."

Casey says, "Wow, you must be all of eighteen years old."

I say, "She's twenty-one."

Casey says, "That's just great. So what are you going to do when you graduate?"

Alyna says, "I don't know yet. I haven't really given it much thought."

Casey says, "Well, good luck with that."

We all stare at one another for a few awkward seconds, then Al-yna says, "Look, I'm going to go try on a few suits. You guys should catch up."

Casey says, "Yeah, we should catch up . . . because we haven't talked to each other in such a long, long time."

Alyna says, "Nice meeting you again," then heads off to the back of the store, out of earshot.

Casey looks like she wants to kill me. She says, "A *girlfriend?* I'm guessing she doesn't know that you're going to be a dad, right?"

I shake my head.

Casey says, "A fucking girlfriend?!? And she's twenty-one. We're going to have a baby. How could you get a twenty-one-year-old girl-friend?"

"I like her."

"Do you love her?"

The only thing I want to do less than have Alyna find out about my unborn child is have a conversation about my feelings for Alyna with Casey. I shrug my shoulders.

Casey says, "That means you don't. Look, I don't want to make like a big scene, so here's what you're going to do. You're going to break up with that little slut. Then next Sunday, my mom's going to be in town. You're going to go out to dinner with us and apologize to her for the last time she was out here and you're going to tell her that everything is fine between us and that we're going to get married just like we planned."

"No, I'm not."

"Then your new little girlfriend is going to find out that you're about to be a daddy."

I'm too scared to think it through rationally. I'm too horrified by the entire situation to realize that I could lie to Casey now, not break up with Alyna, and figure out something else later. I'm too terrified of letting Casey get her way and too filled with rage to think straight.

I say, "Fuck you."

Casey says, "Have it your way."

As if on cue, Alyna walks up from the back of the store with a bathing suit in her hand. Casey looks at me and musters up all of her Groundlings training as she says, "You bastard. I can't believe you didn't tell her that I'm pregnant with your child." Then she slaps me and walks off into the mall, leaving me to stare into Alyna's eyes, which tell me she's already questioning every minute of our relationship.

Alyna says, "Is that true? Did you knock her up?"

I want to lie, but not to Alyna. I say, "Yeah."

Alyna says, "That fucking sucks."

"I know."

"Will she get an abortion?"

"I don't think so."

"Fuck. That really fucking sucks."

She stands there and repeats, "That fucking sucks," a few more times, not in reaction to my life being ruined but in reaction to a relationship that could have been something really amazing getting flushed down the shitter right in front of her.

In the car on the way back to her apartment, she says that she really has fallen in love with me, but she can't deal with a kid being thrown into the picture. She breaks up with me. Luckily she's too distraught at the thought of our relationship ending to realize the logistics of

Casey's pregnancy and my knowledge of it mean that I have been in contact with her beyond anything I've ever admitted.

When we get to her apartment, she hugs me and kisses me and says good-bye. I think about telling Alyna that I don't love Casey and I don't want anything to do with the baby in her gut. But the entire situation seems too far beyond repair. There's no point.

As she gets out of the car, she cries a few tears and says, "This really fucking sucks," one more time.

As I watch her go up the stairs to her building, my sadness at the loss of Alyna turns quickly to unbridled rage for the cunt who took her away from me.

chapter forty

Carlos's Gay Party

I walk into a party with Carlos that he invited me to when I told him that Alyna broke up with me because I got Casey pregnant. The first thing I notice is that there are no women at this party.

I say, "Is this a gay thing?"

Carlos says, "Of course. What kind of parties do you think I go to?"

"Why'd you invite me to a gay party?"

"It's better than staying home by yourself."

"No, it's not."

"Well, maybe you'll meet a cute boy who'll give you a blow job and make you realize how stupid you were to ever stick your dick in a pair of meat curtains in the first place."

Then Carlos says, "I'm going to go mingle," and abandons me in the middle of an apartment full of fags.

As I go to the fridge to get a drink I run into a guy who says, "So you're here with Carlos, huh? I didn't think he had it in him."

"Excuse me?"

"To get somebody as hot as you."

"We're just friends."

"Oh, I know. I'm just friends with every guy I've ever let fuck me in the ass, too."

"I'm straight."

"What?"

"I'm straight."

The gay guy says, "Then why'd you come to this party?"

"Carlos invited me."

"Yeah, but he told you we all suck each other off at the end of the night, right?"

I'm thrown into a catatonic state by the impact of the guy's statement. Then he squeezes my arm and says, "Just kidding," followed by a gay laugh.

He says, "We fuck each other in the ass . . . just kidding again. But he did tell you this was like an all-gay party, right?"

"No."

"That little shit."

Carlos comes back from wherever he was. He says, "Tedward, you better not be trying to suck my friend's dick. He's straight."

Tedward says, "I know, that's what he said. Why'd you bring him here?"

Carlos says, "He told me he didn't have anything to do tonight. His girlfriend dumped him because he got his ex-girlfriend pregnant."

Tedward says, "I'm so glad I'm a fag. I couldn't handle some whore telling me she was pregnant and not really knowing the truth."

It has never really occurred to me that Casey could be lying. I say, "What do you mean not knowing the truth?"

Tedward says, "Women lie constantly to get their way. They can be seriously bitter cunts. At least with a guy you always know they want to fuck and you always know they're not pregnant."

Carlos says, "He's right. I fucking hate deceitful bitches. You know you should find out if Casey really is pregnant before you go throwing your life away and marry her or some stupid shit."

I say, "How do I do that?"

Carlos says, "Get one of those home pregnancy kits and make her pee in it."

I say, "She's not going to agree to take a home pregnancy test."

Carlos says, "You'll figure out some way to do it if you really think she might be lying."

Tedward says, "As enthralling as this conversation about cunts is, I must conclude my participation in it. It was nice to meet you"—he shakes my hand—"but I'm off to find a cock to suck." Then he moves off into the crowd.

Carlos says, "He's an even bigger slut than I am, and that's saying something."

I say, "Do you really think she could be lying?"

Carlos says, "Does a cunt smell like rotten fish?"

There is something comforting about the possible hope this suspicion has created in me. I don't want to talk about it anymore for fear I might change my mind and accept her declaration of pregnancy as fact when I now know some doubt exists. I want the doubt.

I say, "So why didn't you tell me this was an all-gay party?"

"If I did, would you have come?"

"No."

"Exactly. But now that you are here, drink your drink and be my wingman."

"You want me to help you pick up gay guys?"

"Of course. Why do you think I invited you? Fags are attracted to straight guys like moths to flame. All you have to do is just stand here and get hit on, then when you tell them you're straight they'll have to talk to me."

"Jesus Christ." I'm gay bait.

"Just shut up and do it, here comes our first victim."

A gay guy comes up to me and says, "I'm Jim. You've got a great ass."

I can't even begin small talk. I just say, "I'm straight."

Jim says, "Hey, man, I wasn't hitting on you, I was just saying you've got a great ass."

Carlos jumps in, "How is that not hitting on somebody? And what about my ass?"

Jim says, "Are you straight, too?"

Carlos says, "Nope."

Jim looks at Carlos's ass and says, "Eh, your straight friend's ass is better."

Carlos says, "Fuck you. How dare you."

Jim ignores Carlos and says to me, "So you're straight, huh?"

I say, "Yeah."

Jim says, "You ever wonder what it'd be like to have your cock sucked by a guy?"

I say, "Nope, sorry."

Carlos jumps back in, "Oh, and you're a fucking bottom?"

Jim says, "Yeah, so?"

Carlos says, "So get the fuck out of here."

Jim says, "Fine," and walks off back into the party.

The same scenario plays itself out at least a dozen times, with Carlos getting a couple of phone numbers and ultimately blowing some guy in a back bedroom while I deflect gay advances for twenty minutes. When he comes out of the bedroom with the guy he just blew, he says, "I told you it would work."

After the party I go back to my apartment with a new sense of the possible future—one in which Casey does not have my seed growing in her womb, one in which Alyna and I are together, one in which I still have no idea how to secretly administer a home pregnancy test to Casey.

As I close my eyes and reflexively start going through a mental list of things that I hate about Casey, I stop on one item—she never flushes the toilet after she takes a piss.

Finger in the Two-Hole

Todd and I are at Barney's Beanery after work. He's been staring at the same bitch for the past thirty minutes, assuring me that as soon as she notices him looking at her, she'll come over and talk to him. She's looked directly at him multiple times and has made no movement in this direction.

I say, "It might help if you weren't leering at her."

He says, "Dude, you gotta let 'em know what you want. I don't want her coming over here asking me for my phone number. I want her coming over here asking me to suck my dick. And P.S., dude, I don't really need advice on picking up women from the guy who fucking locked himself into eighteen years of prison with a bitch he doesn't even like."

"It's not my choice at this point."

He says, "Whatever, dude. Okay, fuck this shit."

He walks over to the girl and her two friends and somehow gets them to come over and sit at our table.

I don't remember any of their names even as they say them, and

nothing any of them says holds even the most remote amount of interest for me, until one of the girls who is moderately attractive and not
too fat launches into the following story:

"I work for this catering company that does big events for famous
people and movie openings and things like that. And this one time
we were doing a private party at Joel Silver's house. And I was walking around serving drinks and everything. And Bruce Willis and Mel
Gibson and all of these crazy famous people were there. And it was
completely surreal. And so I'm handing a drink to Keanu when I hear
this weird voice behind me go, 'Come here, I want to show you something.' And I turn around and it's this huge '80s movie star. And he's
going, 'Come back here, I want to show you something amazing.' And
he takes me by the arm and kind of starts pulling me back toward the
pool house. And so I go, 'I have to work. I can't really leave.' And he
goes, 'It's okay, you're with me.' And his wife is completely watching
the whole thing go down, but he's still pulling on my arm, going, 'Just
come with me for a few seconds.' And so I finally just go, 'I really can't,
I'll lose my job.' And he goes, 'Okay, then just go into the bathroom,
stick your finger up your asshole, and then come out here and let me
smell it.' And I couldn't believe it."

She keeps talking, but I think I got the only important information
in what turns out to be a story that lasts for ten more minutes about
how many crab cakes Chris Rock ate. I wonder if her story is true.

I wonder what the storyteller's asshole smells like. I wonder if it
smells as good as Alyna's.

chapter forty-one

The Test

I have done more preparation for this night than possibly any other in my life. I have purchased a home pregnancy kit. I have agreed to meet Casey and her mother for dinner but insisted on picking them up at her apartment before we leave, knowing that I'll be invited in for a few minutes and Casey will piss before we leave, as is her habit, and that she will not flush the toilet, as is also her habit. I have invited Alyna to meet me at the bar of the restaurant in which I will be dining with Casey and her mother. She doesn't know that Casey and her mother will be there and assumes that I just wanted to have dinner with her to talk about how things ended. I am hoping to surprise her by publicly unveiling the possible truth about my pending fatherhood. I have rehearsed the "I know you're not pregnant and here's the proof" speech, making slight dramatic alterations to increase the amount of emotional duress I can cause both Casey and her mother without making Alyna think I'm a psychotic monster. I have done all of this as I pull up to Casey's apartment with the home pregnancy kit tucked away inside my jacket.

I knock on her door, which is opened by her mother, who offers me a hug unprompted. I do not hug her back. As she presses her small and shriveled tits against me, she says, "Casey explained everything. You were just confused. I understand this is a big decision and it's better that you came back to it after having doubts. It only makes your bond that much stronger. Luckily we can salvage some of the initial wedding planning we did."

I offer nothing in response. As she lets go of me I hope more than I've ever hoped for anything that in a few hours I'll be able to crush her soul one more time.

Casey comes out of her bedroom with a giant smile on her face, oblivious to the sledgehammer I hope to deliver to her psyche tonight.

She says, "Well, are we ready to get going?" and it seems completely possible that she's going to walk out the door without peeing.

I'm about to ask her if she needs to pee when she says, "Just let me use the ladies' room and then I'll be ready."

As Casey pisses, I can almost feel the home pregnancy kit getting warmer in my jacket pocket. Her mom says, "You should probably wait to apologize to me until we're at dinner, you know, so it can be just right and so Casey can hear it, too. I think she'd like that."

I say, "Okay." I can hear Casey washing her hands in the bathroom as I stare at her mom, imagining myself waving the negative pregnancy test result in her face, telling her to fuck off and walking out with Alyna.

When she comes out I say, "I think I need to use the restroom, too. I'll be right back."

Casey says, "Hurry, the reservations are in twenty minutes," as I shut the bathroom door behind me.

I walk to the toilet bowl and lift the lid. There below me in all its golden glory is a bowl full of Casey's just-squirted piss. I pull out the home pregnancy kit. The directions require the possibly pregnant woman to hold the end of the strip in her urine stream for three to five seconds.

I dip the strip in the toilet for three to five seconds. The directions further require you to wait for seven minutes while the chemical effect takes place, producing either a blue or a pink result. Over the course of the next seven minutes, I'm sure Casey will knock on the bathroom door to ask me what's taking so long. Instead I hear her ask her mom the same question and her mom actually cuts me some slack by saying, "Leave him alone. He's probably nervous about this whole thing and he's having some bowel trouble."

At the end of seven minutes, the strip is neither pink nor blue, but instead the same tan color it was when I pulled it out of the box. Further examination of the directions reveals the following line:

Grip the strip firmly while urinating. If the strip is accidentally dropped into the toilet bowl, the test's results should be considered invalid as water will dilute the necessary chemical reaction.

Fuck.

Realizing there's no place I can safely dispose of the strip or the box in Casey's bathroom without leaving a clue to my clandestine pregnancy test, I wash the strip off, put it back in the box, and put the box back in my jacket pocket, hoping that I don't smell like piss. Then again, if I do smell like piss, maybe it will make the night even worse for Casey and her mom.

I leave the bathroom and we all get in my car to drive to the restaurant, where Alyna is going to meet me at the bar and my plan is going to fall apart miserably.

We walk into the restaurant, Lala's, one of Casey's favorites, and I don't see Alyna at the bar, which is small enough for me to conclude that she is not here yet. We take our seats at a table near the bar. We get bread and water, and Casey's mom starts in immediately.

She says, "So, now that we're all here and sitting down to a nice dinner and everything is happening like it was supposed to . . . do you have something to say?"

I'm on the verge of sweating visibly as I think about how Alyna is going to react to this whole thing and about whether Casey is actually pregnant. I don't say anything. Casey nudges me.

I say, "Uh, yeah. I, uh, I'm sorry for everything that happened last time you were out here."

Her mom says, "Well, that wasn't very heartfelt."

My heart is about to jump out my fucking throat. All I can picture is Alyna crying when she sees me with Casey and her mom and I can offer no explanation for inviting her here to meet me.

I apologize for the apology. "Sorry."

Her mom says, "Listen, it took a lot for me to accept the idea that you were getting back together. I mean, don't get me wrong, I like the idea of Casey getting married a lot more than I like the idea of her having to spend another year looking for another husband, but you seem a little ungrateful for my forgiveness."

I'm momentarily jarred out of my paranoia by a quick shot of hate. I want to tell her mom to fuck off, but it's not part of the plan, even though the plan doesn't exist anymore. Every time someone walks through the front door, I know it's one person closer to being Alyna and one second closer to being the last time I ever see her again.

I apologize again. "I'm sorry." It's all I can say.

Her mom says, "That's fine, I guess."

Casey says, "Good. Now that that's out of the way, let's talk about the wedding. We should have it in a few months, I think—just like we had planned."

Her mom says, "I agree. No sense in letting the planning we've already done go to waste."

I can't sit at the table anymore. I have to leave. I have to think, somehow salvage my plan.

I say, "'Scuse me. I have to go to the bathroom," then leave the table without bothering to look at their reaction.

In the bathroom I pull out the pregnancy test, hoping against all hope that it has changed to some discernible color. No luck, still fucking tan. A guy is taking a massive shit in one of the stalls. Still, the smell of his deuce is preferable to the company of Casey and her mom.

I wash my hands and think about a few ways out of this:

1. Climb out the window.
2. Fake a stroke.
3. Force myself to shit my pants so we all have to leave before Alyna gets here, which should be any second.
4. Throw myself in front of a bus.

And then it hits me—I can just go on with my plan. I may not have the concrete evidence to back up a nonpregnancy accusation, but I might not need it. The accusation alone might be enough to bring out the truth. I'll have to sell it, and once I go down that road I won't be able to turn back. But I really have no other choice. Worst-case scenario—I'm still the father of Casey's unborn child and her mom still hates me. Nothing lost, really.

I rinse my hands off, splash a little water on my face, and prepare to initiate a public scene.

As I walk out of the bathroom, I see Alyna sitting at the bar. She says, "Hi," with sadness.

I say, "Hi. Watch this and no matter what happens, don't leave."

I don't give her a chance to respond before I walk up to Casey and her mom, pull out the pregnancy test, and say loudly enough for most of the tables in the place to hear, "Casey, I know you're not pregnant."

I've never seen someone's face when their heart explodes, but I'm pretty sure that's what I'm looking at as Casey's mom falls out of her chair and her mouth and eyes get big enough to make her look like a cartoon.

I keep going, "When you pissed at your house, I did a little test and it came back negative."

Casey's mom looks at Casey and says, "Pregnant?" in a way that makes me realize Casey never told her, which gives more weight to my current paper-thin argument.

The whole place is stunned into silence. No waiters or managers are telling us to shut up. No one is saying shit. They're all just watching us.

Casey says, "Mom, I was going to tell you after we were married," which takes my argument back down a notch.

Nonetheless, my course of action is set. I continue on with, "Casey, you're not pregnant, I have the results right here."

Casey looks at her mom lying on the ground, panting and heaving like someone shot her, then she looks back at me, like she's deciding something. Then she says, "I am pregnant. Your test must be wrong."

There's no turning back. I say, "These things are ninety-nine-point-nine percent accurate," having no real idea how accurate they are. "Do you think you're the point-one percent that the test failed on? Not likely."

From the ground her mom says, "I can't believe you had premarital sex. Oh my god. Your father is going to be so disappointed in you."

The line about her dad does something visible to Casey, who starts to cry. It physically hits her, changing the look on her face from wrongly accused innocent pregnant girl to Daddy's biggest disappointment.

Casey says, "Fine. I'm not pregnant."

Holy motherfucking shit. With those three words, Casey releases me from a prison that never existed in the first place. I'm washed over with an immediate and palpable sense of euphoria, like I just woke up with a hard-on after having a nightmare that my dick got cut off.

As Casey admits her lie, I look across the room at Alyna for the first time. She has a weird look on her face. I can't tell if she's happy or horrified. I turn back to Casey, who is now helping her mom back up to her feet, and toss the pregnancy test at her. I want to say something really cool or really mean to drive a nail into her coffin, but instead I say, "Here," and walk over to the bar where Alyna's sitting, grab her hand, and walk out the door.

On the street Alyna says, "So I guess you didn't really just invite me out for drinks."

"No."

"That was fucking insane, by the way."

"Are you mad at me?"

"Mad? No. I'm happy. For the past week I haven't been able to eat. I haven't been able to sleep. I haven't been able to do anything except think about the possibility that I might never see you again and you'd be stuck in some shitty life raising a kid you don't want with a girl you don't love."

What I feel for Alyna as I hear her say this is more than affection, more than respect. It's unquestionably love.

She puts her arms around me, kisses me, and says, "Why did you invite me here to see all this, though? You could have just told me you found out she wasn't pregnant."

"I didn't want you to question it, I guess."

"Well, you accomplished that goal."

"So what do we do now?"

"Pick up where we left off. But what about your ex-girlfriend and her mom?"

"Fuck 'em."

As Alyna and I walk to my car, I don't think about what's happening inside the restaurant. I don't think about Casey's world being shattered. I don't think about how she and her mom are going to get home. I think about Alyna, her perfect ass, her lips around my cock and fucking her doggie style as I press on her asshole with my thumb. And more than that, I think about waking up with her tomorrow morning.

Hot Girls Give Gay Guys Partial Handjobs

I'm at a bar with Todd. He's drunk and reacting to the story about Casey being forced to admit that she wasn't pregnant.

He says, "Holy shit, dude, that is some good-ass shit. It makes sense, too, that one night she was all over you, trying to suck your cock and shit in the car. She wanted you to fucking drop some seed in her hole so she could get pregnant and make her lie true. Dude, you're fucking lucky to be done with that crazy bitch. Here's to being done with crazy bitches."

He raises the pitcher of beer he's drinking from and we toast to being done with crazy bitches.

He nods in the direction of a girl and her less attractive friend in our vicinity and says, "See that hot bitch over there?"

I say, "Yeah."

Todd says, "I wanna try out a new technique I read about on the Internet. But I need your help."

I say, "What do I have to do?"

Todd says, "Pretend I'm gay."

I say, "What?"

Todd says, "Dude, just do it," and then walks over to the girls, points at me, and says with an overly affected gay lisp, "See my friend over there? We have a bet and I was wondering if you guys would come over and help us settle it."

Hot girl says, "Sure."

Less attractive girl says, "Okay," and they both come over.

Todd says, "So here's the deal. I'm gay."

Hot girl says, "Okay," just as confused as I am by this point.

Todd says, "My friend here seems to think that no man is 'too gay' to be aroused by a hot woman, which we have a ten-dollar wager on. Now I know this is a weird request, but to help us settle the bet, I was wondering if you'd be interested in trying to, you know, arouse me."

Even as I hear the words come out of his mouth, I can't believe he's saying them. I've known Todd to use some extreme measures in the past, but this is by far the most insane I've ever seen him. I'm ready to witness a drink getting thrown in his face, a slap, a bouncer tossing him out when she starts screaming rape, but instead she smiles and says, "And you're gay, right?"

Todd says, "Queer as a three-dollar bill, honey," with his thickest gay lisp yet.

She says, "All I have to do is get you hard?"

Less attractive girl says, "This is nuts," but in an encouraging way.

Todd says, "You won't be able to, but yeah, that's the bet."

She says, "And I can do anything I want to you?"

Todd says, "Well, within reason. I mean, we are in a bar here."

She gives her drink to her friend and says, "Okay."

What I witness in the minutes that follow makes me want to cry.

She puts her hand under Todd's shirt and bites his ear, then takes a step back and looks at him.

Todd says, "Nothing."

She gives him a fourteen-second tongue kiss while pressing her B cups against him, then steps back and looks at his crotch, which gives no conclusive proof one way or the other.

Todd says, "Still nothing."

She says, "Are you sure? Not even a little bit?"

Todd says, "Limp as a noodle."

She musters up her strength for one more attack. She leans in close to Todd's ear, whispers something, and then puts her hand down the front of his pants and starts jerking him off right in front of me and her less attractive friend, who seems to be more entertained by the show than even Todd is as she says, "Yeah, get that thing," and takes another drink of her Long Island iced tea.

After what I estimate to be a minute and a half of solid tugging at Todd's cock with the hot girl saying, "It feels hard, is that it?" and Todd saying things like, "It's not totally hard. That doesn't really count," she finally says, "That's a hard-on," and pulls her hand out of Todd's pants.

The hot girl then puts her hands in the air in victory and says something like, "Whoo-hooo! I gave a fag a boner," then to me, "Looks like you win ten bucks."

Later that night at Alyna's apartment, she refuses to believe me as I recount the night's events to her, which sound too fantastical to be real even to me as I say them. Her main problem with the story's plausibility is Todd's ability to suppress an erection when a hot girl is kissing him and rubbing his chest and eventually jerking him off for well over a minute.

I offer that the girl might have been drunk enough to take Todd's word that he didn't have a full erection or Todd might actually have some kind of superhuman erection-suppressing ability.

Alyna asks me how long I think I could suppress a hard-on if a hot girl was tugging at my cock. She then gives me a hand job and I suppress my erection for twelve seconds.

chapter forty-two

Casey's Underwear

I keep most of my pornographic videocassettes and DVDs in the living room with the rest of my home video collection. But there are a few choice DVDs that I keep in my bedroom closet for quick viewing on the DVD player in my bedroom. This is what I tell Alyna after she asks me if I have any porn because she wants to watch one with me and do everything they do in the movie.

As she goes into my closet, I hope she picks out *Cream Queens 3* so we can reenact the scene in which a bitch puts a popsicle in her cunt and then eats it. Then I realize that I don't have any popsicles and decide to hope for her to choose *Tit Bangers* because I've only titty-fucked her a few times and I wouldn't mind doing it again.

As she says, "Hey, what's this?" I'm already forming my explanation for the *Teeny Weenies* DVD given to me as a gag gift, which I left in the closet along with the box of lube Todd packed with it for my twenty-fifth birthday. But to my surprise she's holding up a pair of Casey's old underwear.

I say, "I think those are a pair of my ex-girlfriend's underwear."

"Why do you still have them?"

"I don't know. They must've gotten thrown in there at some point and she never got them back."

Despite the fact that this explanation is probably exactly true, I don't think Alyna buys it.

She says with a malicious smile on her face, "You don't take them out from time to time and sniff them?"

"No."

The sight of Alyna standing at the foot of my bed completely naked holding Casey's underwear is strange, but even stranger is the sight of Alyna putting on Casey's underwear, which she does.

"These are kind of big."

"She had a big ass."

"Do you like big asses?"

"I like your ass."

"Do I have a big ass?"

"You have a perfect ass."

She walks around my bedroom in Casey's underwear.

She says, "I want you to show me how you fucked her."

"I don't really want to do that."

"Why not? Did you guys do some seriously weird shit?"

"Not as weird as this."

She gets on top of me with her back to me and grinds her ass on my cock.

She says, "Did you like it when she'd do this? Did you like her big ass on your dick?"

I actually kind of did like her ass on my dick, but it was rare that she'd put it to use in our sexual encounters. As I look at Alyna's ass in Casey's underwear I start to become painfully aware of the fact that the underwear fits Alyna a little too well. By no means does she fill them out like Casey did, but neither are they grossly oversized on her.

This semi-alarms me, but I convince myself that it's some trick of my mind brought on by the mental overload created by seeing my current girlfriend in my old girlfriend's underwear.

Feeling that my dick has become hard enough for insertion, Alyna reaches down, moves the part of Casey's underwear covering her pussy to the side, and guides my cock into her. As she rides me, she looks back occasionally and smiles a weird kind of smile that I don't know quite how to take. But when her head is turned away from me and all I see is her ass in Casey's underwear bobbing up and down on my cock, I try as hard as I can to imagine that I'm really fucking Casey.

When I reach out and actually touch Alyna's hard little ass as she rides my dick, the illusion is broken, but for the most part I do a good enough job that I might as well be fucking Casey.

I blow my load to the memory of fucking Casey doggie style on a hot summer afternoon when she was drenched in sweat from jogging.

chapter forty-three

Cap and Gown

In two weeks Alyna will graduate with a bachelor's degree in film studies from UCLA. This never crosses my mind as she's sucking my cock an hour before we're supposed to go pick up her cap and gown at the UCLA bookstore.

The blow job started with me asking her to suck my cock, which doesn't strike me as out of the ordinary until I realize I've never had to ask before. This realization would bother me significantly if it wasn't immediately overshadowed by something I find vastly more important and disturbing as I blow my load—she does not swallow. Not only does she not swallow, but she doesn't even let me finish in her mouth. Instead, as I'm about to cum, she takes my dick out of her mouth and jerks me off in a dozen or so quick strokes that send streams of my semen all over her hands and my dick and balls.

Although she's never done this before and I much prefer her normal technique of swallowing my cum and then sucking my cock for roughly thirty postejaculatory seconds in order to rid my dick of any semen that might not have gone down her throat initially, I have no intention of bringing it up with her until she says, "Oooh, you made a mess."

I have to say, "No, you made a mess."

"Hey, I got you off, didn't I?"

"Yeah, but you usually swallow."

"I know."

In the least accusatory tone I can muster, I say, "So why didn't you?"

She says, "I don't know. I just didn't feel like it."

There are four explanations I can conjure for what she just said: (1) She's fucking somebody else whose semen she's more interested in swallowing than my own; (2) she's lost her taste for semen altogether, which seems unlikely based on several months of evidence to the contrary; (3) she just didn't want to do it before she gets her cap and gown, which makes no sense but seems plausible for a girl; or (4) she's lost her will to suck dick, which is a more serious issue and one I'm not willing to entertain.

I accept her answer at face value and walk to my bathroom to mop up my seed with toilet paper, which takes me longer to get out of my pubic hair than I would have imagined.

When we get to the bookstore, there are roughly seventy-five to a hundred other students also there to get their caps and gowns. I overhear some of the following dialogue:

"I have a few interviews lined up, but nothing that I'm really excited about." . . . "Yeah, we'll probably get engaged over the summer and then start looking for a house next year after we've saved up some money." . . . "Dude, I don't give a fuck. Tell him I'll pay for two kegs and he can pick up the other two. . . . "I don't know, I've been thinking about going to grad school." . . . "Moving in with my parents." . . . "My uncle has a houseboat he said I could live on for a while."

As Alyna and I approach the table where a fat bitch wearing glasses sits sorting through cap and gown orders, a semi-hot bitch wearing gym attire stops us with, "Hey, Alyna."

Alyna says, "Hey, Jenny," then introduces us and explains that Jenny was her freshman year roommate. Judging from Alyna's response to her greeting I don't think they've talked much since freshman year.

Jenny says, "So can you believe we're graduating?"

Alyna says only semi-patronizingly, "It's pretty crazy."

Jenny doesn't catch it. She says, "I know. I thought I was gonna be here for freaking ever." Then she asks me, "Are you graduating this year, too?"

I say, "No," and wonder if I really look enough like a college student to warrant that question from her.

Jenny says, "So what're your plans after the big day?"

Alyna says, "I don't know. My parents are coming out here . . . ," which is something I remember she told me about a few days ago but I had forgotten until now. She continues, ". . . We'll probably go out and eat or something."

Jenny laughs. "No, silly, I mean what are you going to do with your life? Do you have a job lined up or anything?"

Alyna says, "No, we haven't really figured out what we're going to do yet," and they keep talking but the word "we" is ringing so loud in my ears that I can't hear what else they say.

It's true "we've" never talked about what "we're" going to do after graduation, but "I'm" not going to do anything significantly different from what "I'm" currently doing, which is wish I was fucking Alyna instead of listening to her talk to this bitch who has somehow posed a question that elicited the "we" response from her.

I don't particularly dislike the fact that she used the term "we" when talking about the possible direction of her future, but I'm far from being comfortable with it. I wonder how much further down the road she has thought about our relationship beyond the next time we're going to fuck.

The ringing dies down in time for me to hear Jenny say, "Well, good luck," and although this wish of good fortune most likely has nothing to do with me, I wonder if the part of the conversation I missed included Alyna detailing her plan to somehow force me into marriage.

Jenny leaves, we pick up Alyna's cap and gown, and just as we're leaving the bookstore she says, "What do you think we should do?"

I say, "I think we should go back to my apartment and fuck."

She says, "I mean when I graduate."

I say, "I think you should do whatever you want to."

We don't talk any more about it as we walk back to my apartment, where I steer our foreplay in the direction of a blow job and contemplate attempting to see if Alyna will refuse to swallow my load again, but my urge to fuck her in the ass wins out and she cums bent over a chair as I hold one of her legs up in the air and ram my cock into her ass a little harder than I think I ever have before.

Scarface Part 3

I'm in the Beverly Center looking for something to wear to Alyna's graduation. I go into Banana Republic and find a decent pair of pants and a shirt.

I walk up to the counter to pay, but nobody's there to complete the transaction. A gay guy walks by and says, "Is someone helping you?"

I say, "No."

He gets on a telephone and makes the following storewide page: "Amy to the front register, Amy to the front register." Then he says, "Someone will be right with you," and disappears somewhere in the back instead of selling me the clothes himself.

When Amy comes to the register I almost shit my pants. Amy is Scarface, who I haven't dealt with since she last called me and I rejected her offer to take me on a date. In the light of day I notice that Scarface has a hot little body, but her hairlip is more repulsive than I remember.

I'm not positive she remembers me as I toss my shit down on the counter in front of her, but when she says, "So how've you been?" I'm pretty sure she knows exactly who I am.

I have to say, "Fine. You?"

"Oh, pretty good. You know, just working."

I wonder what Scarface is like in the sack as she slides my credit card through the machine. I imagine she would let me do anything I wanted to her, even if it caused her physical discomfort or even pain. That is slightly interesting to me. I decide that anything Scarface would let me do to her if I tried to fuck her Alyna would more than likely do with me willingly. As a result I make no small talk with Scarface as she wraps up my clothes.

As I sign the receipt and she gives me my card back along with my bag of clothes, she says, "Hey, I've got a break coming in like five minutes. Do you wanna go get some Starbucks?"

I look at my watch and say, "You know what, I'd actually really like to, but I have to be at my friend's house in fifteen minutes."

She says, "Oh, yeah, that's cool. I just thought maybe, you know. It's cool."

I don't say anything as I exit Banana Republic with my graduation outfit. I get into my car in the parking structure and realize the possibility of this interaction causing Scarface to call me again is not entirely implausible. I hope that she's lost my number as I pull onto Beverly and head back to my apartment, where I jerk off thinking about Scarface eating Alyna out while I fuck her.

chapter forty-four

The Final Final

Alyna hasn't fucked me for the past week, citing the importance of spending every free moment she has studying for her final exams. I accept this excuse only because I have no choice. I do find it strange, though, that she is able to go a week without fucking for finals, or any reason for that matter, based on our previous once-a-day minimum, which has held fast since the third or fourth time we fucked. Despite the fact that she seems to genuinely miss having sex with me, I'm still more alarmed at her ability to omit it from our relationship entirely and feel no significant regret at her decision.

Alyna's last final is at 11:00 A.M. and she's promised to meet me for lunch at my apartment so we can break the dry spell. I've already resigned myself to taking a long lunch despite the consequences at work, which will likely be none. She gets to my apartment at around 1:10 and proceeds to tie me to my bed and fuck me. She alternates between riding my cock, sucking my dick, and jerking me off while she licks my balls, switching her method each time I'm about to cum.

She sits on my dick and plays with her clit as she rocks back and forth. Seeing this makes me blow my load, which she in turn says makes her cum because she can feel my dick throbbing in her cunt.

She gets off my cock and lies down next to me, leaving me tied down. She seems to have genuinely missed fucking me, and based on her performance, most of my concerns about her ability to go without sex are alleviated.

I say, "Untie me."

She says, "Nope."

"What? Untie me."

"Nope. I just took the last test I'll ever take in my life and now I want to spend the rest of your lunch hour doing whatever I want to you. So you're just going to have to lie there and let me do it."

I think back to the first time I saw Alyna on the plane and wondered what she was like in bed. My memory of the event is cut short by Alyna's hand on my cock. She massages it kind of slowly, never letting it get fully hard.

I say, "What're you doing?"

She says, "Whatever I want."

She takes the hand that's not on my dick and starts playing with her clit, then says, "I want to see who I can make cum first."

It's me. I shoot a load all over her hand and all over myself about two minutes after she really gets into giving me a bona fide hand job.

She cums roughly a minute later and then says, "That was pretty fun. I want you to do that to me sometime."

I say, "How about right now?"

She says, "Nope. You don't get to do anything but cum for the next"—she looks at the clock—"thirty minutes."

I say, "I'm taking a long lunch."

"What does that mean?"

"It means I probably have more like an hour."

"Oooh. Then you're definitely not getting untied."

She gets up to get a towel, then comes back and cleans all of the cum off my dick and out of my pubic hair. Then we lie there together for a while.

I say, "What if you fall asleep?"

She says, "Then you're fucked."

She rolls on top of me and looks me in the eyes, then says, "I wouldn't do that to you."

I say, "Thanks."

She takes a second and then says something that makes what was shaping up to quite possibly be the best lunch hour of my life take a nasty turn. She says, "I want to talk to you about something."

She's sitting on top of me and I'm tied down.

She says, "I already know this is going to completely freak you out, but I don't care. . . ."

Not only am I completely freaking out, I'm already trying to rationalize one of three things: (1) how I could have missed the fact that Alyna somehow used to have a dick; (2) how I'm going to cure the herpes that she gave me; or (3) what name would best suit a child I don't want to have.

She says, "What do you think about marriage?"

"What?"

"I know on our first date we both said we thought it was stupid and all of that, and I'm not saying right now. I'm not even saying in the next five years, but what do you think about it in the far, far future?"

I can't believe this is happening to me. I keep waiting for her to tell me that she's just kidding, but it never comes. I'm almost hoping she'll tell me she once had a dick, but she just keeps saying, "Come on, what do you think?"

And as I force myself to actually think about it, I'm surprised to find that the idea of marrying Alyna—as she said, in the far, far future—does not make me want to smash myself in the nuts with a sledgehammer.

I say, "I don't know, why are you asking me this?"

She says, "I don't know. I'm sure it's just because I'm graduating and I don't really know what I want to do with my life and I've just been thinking about a lot of things lately, mainly things that have to do with where my life goes next."

I try to get out of my bonds, but I get nowhere.

I say, "I thought you said in the far future."

"Yeah, I did. I mean, I'm just thinking about what kind of life I could have five or ten years down the road, and I'm not saying this is definitely something I want, but thinking about a life with you doesn't scare me."

I try to imagine being married to Alyna and it doesn't scare me either. It doesn't excite me, but it gives rise to no ill feelings, which is far more than I could have said for a life of being married to Casey. I also realize that this is in no way an admission to myself that I want to marry Alyna.

She says, "I don't want this to turn into some big thing. It's just something I've been thinking about lately and I wanted you to know. I don't want to get married right now, and I don't even really know if I ever do. But the idea of it doesn't sound as bad as it used to. That's all."

I say, "Okay."

She says, "Okay? Are you really okay with this?"

"Yeah." Her terms were vague enough to make me think this might actually be true.

"It doesn't make you want to break up with me?"

She shifts her weight on me and I can feel her wet pussy brush my cock.

"No." This is without a doubt true. Despite her recent slip into a territory I had hoped never to visit again with a girl, she's still hands down the best girlfriend I've ever had.

"Do you still love me?"

Her wet pussy kind of settles right on my cock.

"Yeah."

"Good. I'm glad we talked about this."

She sits back a little and slides her pussy lips along my cock, which is now hard again.

"Me too."

She kisses me and reaches back behind her ass to line my dick up with her cunt. She says, "My mom might bring this up when you meet her," then sits back, and my dick slides into her as she fucks me for the next forty-five minutes.

chapter forty-five

Graduation Day

Alyna stayed at her apartment last night with the excuse that she didn't want to be worn out for her big day. So I jerked off twice before falling asleep and realized that since Alyna and I started dating, the number of times I jerk off in any given week has dropped significantly. Barring the week of her final exams, I estimate my rate of jerking off while dating her to be once or twice a week, usually only to get to sleep if Alyna and I aren't together on a given night. I realize I have never snuck away as Alyna slept to jerk off. The feeling of accomplishment and forward progress I get from this realization makes me eager to see her.

I take a shower and put on the clothes I bought at Banana Republic. Alyna's graduation is in three hours, but I'm supposed to meet up with her so we can go to breakfast and she can introduce me to her family, who she is picking up at the airport.

When I walk into the diner where I'm supposed to meet them, I see Alyna, her dad, who reminds me in no specific way of Casey's dad; her mom, who is a shorter, fatter, uglier version of Alyna; and her two brothers, neither of whom has a wife or children in tow. They all seem nice enough. And it begins.

The brothers give me a few words of caution about dating their sister and let me know not to treat her badly. The mom tells the brothers to back off and the dad keeps asking me what it is I do, even though I've told him multiple times that I don't really do anything important or interesting.

All in all it seems to be going fine and I'm feeling very close to dodging the bullet of a conversation I don't want to have with my girlfriend's parents until Alyna's mom says, "So you guys have been dating for a pretty long time."

And the bullet hits me right between the fucking eyes

Nobody says anything. Nobody wants her mom to say anything else.

She says, "Now that Alyna's graduating, what do you guys think you'll do?"

I don't know exactly who this question is directed to, but I don't answer. I just take a bite of toast and hope that Alyna will field the question, which she does.

She says, "Mom, I don't know."

Her mom says, "I mean, your father and I got married the week after we graduated from high school, and look at us now."

I can tell Alyna's dad wants to make some kind of joke but he holds it in. I wonder how many weeks after they were married he learned to do that.

Her mom keeps going. "Alyna, you're going to stay out here, right?"

She says, "Yes, Mom. We've already had this conversation."

Her mom says, "Well, if you two love each other, you should at least be living together just to test it out if you don't want to get married right away."

I think about faking a stroke or a seizure so I don't have to listen to her mom anymore, but I don't. Instead I just sit there and let her mom go on and on about how good marriage is. I wonder what her mom would think if she knew I've had my dick in her daughter's ass. I wonder if she's ever taken it up the ass from Alyna's dad.

As she continues to extol the virtues of marriage, an uneasy suspicion works its way through me. It seems more than likely to me that the conversation Alyna had with me about marriage when she had me tied up naked to my bed with my dick in her hand was the direct result of some previous conversation she had with her mother.

I take a sip of my water, which by this point is just ice cubes, to quell the boiling heat in my intestines. I honestly don't know what her mom says for the next ten minutes. All I can think about is that if Alyna and I were to have a daughter, someday Alyna would be telling all the same shit to some poor son of a bitch who just wants to fuck our daughter.

Alyna's parents pay for breakfast and the last thing I remember her mom saying is, "You guys seem like you're practically married now," before we all get in our cars and drive to Alyna's graduation.

I have the amazing privilege of sitting next to her mom during the ceremony.

Laura Ziskin gives the commencement address. I wonder how many cocks she's sucked. I try to remember who spoke at my own graduation but can't. Then the dean comes out and starts handing out diplomas.

As the students start to walk across the stage, Alyna's mom says, "Oh my gosh, doesn't she just look so good in her little cap and gown?"

I look at the stage, where her mom indicates Alyna's sitting, but I can't make her out. She looks the same as all the other twenty-one-year-old girls sitting in their bookstore-rented caps and gowns graduating with degrees in film studies so they can say they went to college before they locked some poor asshole into marriage and kids.

I look out in the crowd of family members and see if I can tell which of the guys are watching their girlfriends graduate knowing their lives will be over as soon as she crosses that stage.

They call her name, "Alyna Janson." She stands up, walks over to the dean, looks out in the crowd, gives her mom a big smile and wave that's caught on at least a dozen pictures snapped by every member of her family, shakes the dean's hand, takes her diploma, and walks back to her seat, where she's once again indistinguishable from everyone else.

The next student does the same thing. And the student after that does the same thing, too.

I hear Alyna's mom whisper to her dad, "Do you remember when we graduated college?"

Then her dad whispers back, "We'd already been married four years and David was a month old."

Her mom whispers back, "I just can't believe our baby is done. She's an adult now."

Her dad whispers back, "We raised her good and she'll do the same for her kids. We did good, Mom. We did good."

I am repulsed by Alyna's dad calling his wife "Mom," and wonder if I had children with Alyna if she'd call me "Dad" or "Father."

That night after I fuck her and pull out to blow my load all over her stomach and tits, I ask her that specific question. Instead of answering it she says, "Have you been thinking about having kids?" with too much enthusiasm to allow me to fall asleep for the rest of the night, despite sneaking into the bathroom twice to jerk off.

Diamonds in the Rough

Over the course of my computer-literate life, I've downloaded countless hours of free Internet pornography. On those very rare occasions when I find a clip that is worth repeated viewing, I put it in a folder on my desktop called "Diamonds in the Rough."

As I'm jerking off and downloading movie clips, I find one such clip called cumsisteranna.wmv, in which one girl rides a guy's cock while another licks at his balls, stopping every now and then to take the guy's cock out of the first girl's cunt and suck it before putting it back in and stroking the guy's balls while the first girl keeps fucking him.

I've seen clips like this before and none have seemed as remarkable. I can't quite tell what makes cumsisteranna.wmv stand out. I decide it must have something to do with a subconscious reaction to camera placement or lighting that my untrained eye can't decipher.

I stop jerking off, and as I drag the file into the Diamonds in the Rough folder, I notice that the folder has reached 698MB. The frequency with which I find a clip worthy of being added to the folder is so minuscule that I never would have imagined having enough material to burn an entire disc of porn. I'm almost amazed as I clear my Windows Media Player library and drag all of the files from Diamonds in the Rough into the new library for review.

The first clip that plays is called xxx040.mpg. It features two slightly skinny girls using a double-headed dildo to fuck each other doggie style. The clips that follow are of varied style and subject matter, but for the next forty-five minutes. I watch the porn without jerking off. Instead of the urge to blow a load, the clips strangely conjure nostalgic memories of the girls I was dating when I downloaded them and the computers I downloaded them on.

One specific clip, cumslutsav2.mpg, a fourteen-second clip in which a girl gives a slow, lubricated hand job to a guy whose face you never see, I remember setting to download before I went to fuck my high school girlfriend Katy at one A.M. and coming back two hours later to find it only 76 percent complete on the first Internet-ready computer I ever had.

Another clip, t246.avi, in which a girl deep-throats a dick for thirty seconds without coming up for air, takes me back to Jenna and the time I fucked her in her parents' laundry room while they were in the next room watching *The Omega Code* on the Trinity Broadcasting Network, which in turn reminds me that she is now married to a guy with fucked-up teeth and probably has a kid.

There's a clip of a girl fucking a mechanical dildo doggie style called sybian43.mpg that I jerked off to once while Casey was taking a shower. I blew a load all over myself and had to go into the bathroom she was showering in and pretend to be pissing so I could clean myself off.

I realize the last clip, cumsisteranna.wmv, which I just put in the folder, is the first Diamond in the Rough I've come across since dating Alyna.

As I drag the contents of the entire folder into my Roxio CD burner window and hit the burn button, I wonder how many more Diamonds in the Rough I'll find over the course of our relationship.

As the disk burns I jerk off to an elaborate fantasy involving all the girlfriends I've ever had fucking each other in Jenna's parents' bedroom.

chapter forty-six

Long Story Short

In the week after Alyna's graduation we fucked twice. She gave me one blow job, but finished it by jerking me off. She cited anxiety about her future as the reason for her decreased sex drive.

In the month after Alyna graduated we fucked four times, each time in the missionary position, except once with her on top. She sucked my dick twice, but only after I asked.

In the sixth-month period after her graduation we celebrated our one-year anniversary and fucked forty-seven times, thirty-three of which were initiated by me. I came on her tits six times, each time believing that shooting some of my load "accidentally" on her face might jar her from her increasingly problematic lack of interest in sex.

In the year after Alyna graduated we fucked seventy-four times, the last twelve to fourteen of which were almost like fucking a corpse. During this time, Alyna held various part-time jobs at flower shops and coffeehouses and began taking acting classes at various acting studios. I fucked her in the ass seven times. I jerked off three hundred and thirty-four times, only fantasizing about Alyna twelve times when I actually blew my load.

The relationship has very clearly run its course and this is its final state. I'm surprised this doesn't enrage me more. Instead, Alyna's lack of desire to fuck has given birth to a rapidly growing disinterest in her that strangely hasn't been replaced by interest in anyone or anything else.

It will never be like it was. It will never be better than this.

chapter forty-seven

The End

After an entire morning of lying in my bed watching TV and not fucking, we're sitting outside eating lunch at Swingers in Santa Monica.

She says, "So I think I've figured out what I want to do with this whole acting thing."

I take a bite of scrambled eggs.

"I mean, I like taking acting classes and everything, but I don't think I'm getting anywhere with it. I need to change it up a little."

I take another bite.

"I'm not sure straight acting is what I really want to do anymore. I think I want to try to be like a funny actress, you know, on a sitcom or something. Some of my friends from school are going to take some comedy classes at Improv Olympic and I think I'm going to do it with them, then try to go on some auditions or something. I mean, I live in L.A., right? I might as well give it a shot."

I look over through the big glass wall at a guy sitting across from his girlfriend inside Swingers. She's talking about something as he eats his scrambled eggs and stares into space. I'm pretty sure she's telling him that she wants to be a comedic actress and I'm also pretty sure that they lay in his bed for the entire morning before coming here and I'm also pretty sure she didn't fuck him either.

As Alyna keeps telling me how much fun she thinks comedic acting class will be, I come to a sudden realization that is as horrifying as it is liberating. The uneasy feeling in the pit of my stomach for the past five or six months isn't due to the fact that Alyna seems to have lost her desire to fuck me. It's caused by something else entirely and knowing its source alleviates it completely.

Alyna has slowly become Casey. Aside from her ass, which I'm sure will eventually match Casey's, Alyna has become everything in Casey that made me not want to marry her. Or maybe she was like Casey from the very start but she fucked me so much in the beginning I couldn't see it. Either way, this realization changes something in me.

I look at all the other bitches in Swingers and they all might as well be Casey, or Alyna, or whoever they are.

I take another bite of scrambled eggs knowing that any bitch I ever fuck will ultimately become any other bitch I've ever fucked and they'll all become the fat old bitch eating yogurt in the airport. I look at Alyna and see Casey, Jenna, Katy, and every bitch I've ever fucked or gotten head from or a hand job or even thought about while I jerked off. There is nothing better. There is no fucking escape.

That night we're lying in my bed, both completely naked, watching Conan O'Brien. As Conan interviews Molly Shannon I try to think of all the possible excuses Alyna might use to avoid fucking me tonight. She uses one I did not think of, which is that she's too excited about going to sign up for Improv Olympic classes, and unwittingly sets the following inevitable conversation in motion:

"Alyna?"

She rolls over and says, "Yeah?"

"I was thinking about some things today."

"What things?"

"Just about us and about you."

"What about us and me?"

"Alyna . . ."

"What?"

"Will you marry me?"

Her lack of hesitation as she accepts disgusts me. I wade through an hour of faked joy and hugs and kisses and assurances that we are going to be happy forever. After Alyna calms down, I wait for her to fall asleep without touching my dick and then go to the bathroom and jerk off.

acknowledgments

Mom, thanks for always encouraging me to write and be creative. I'm sorry the end result of that encouragement is something you will not want to read.

Dad, thanks for teaching me self-discipline and thanks for giving me a good education. I know this isn't the same as playing pro-baseball, but it's still pretty cool.

I love you guys and I hope this book doesn't lose you any friends or anything.

YASMINE

GALENORN

MAUDLIN'S MAYHEM

A BEWITCHING BEDLAM NOVEL

BOOK 2

A Nightqueen Enterprises LLC Publication

Published by Yasmine Galenorn
PO Box 2037, Kirkland WA 98083-2037
MAUDLIN'S MAYHEM
A Bewitching Bedlam Novel
Copyright © 2017 by Yasmine Galenorn
First Electronic Printing: 2017 Nightqueen Enterprises LLC
First Print Edition: 2017 Nightqueen Enterprises, LLC
Cover Art & Design: Earthly Charms
Editor: Elizabeth Flynn

A Nightqueen Enterprises LLC Publication
Published in the United States of America

Acknowledgments

Thanks to my beloved husband, Samwise, who is more supportive than any husband out there. (Hey, I'm biased!). He believes in me, even at times when I'm having trouble believing in myself. Thank you to my wonderful assistants—Andria Holley and Jennifer Arnold. And to my friends—namely Carol, Jo, Vicki, Shawntelle, and Mandy. Also, to the whole UF Group gang I'm in. They've held my hand more than once this past year as I've made the jump from traditional to indie publishing. It's been a scary, exciting, fast-track ride and I'm loving it.

Love and scritches to my four furbles—Caly, Brighid (the cat, not the goddess), Morgana, and li'l boy Apple, who make every day a delight. And reverence, honor, and love to my spiritual guardians—Mielikki, Tapio, Ukko, Rauni, and Brighid (the goddess, not the cat).

And to you, readers, for taking Maddy and Aegis and Bubba into your heart. Be cautious when you rub a kitty's belly—you never know when you're petting a cjinn! I hope you enjoy this book. If you want to know more about me and my work, check out my bibliography in the back of the book, be sure to sign up for my newsletter, and you can find me on the web at Galenorn.com.

Brightest Blessings,
~The Painted Panther~
~Yasmine Galenorn~

Welcome to Maudlin's Mayhem

As the van eased out of the parking spot, the side door opened and I was stumbling toward it, pushed along by whoever had hold of me. I tried to resist, my legs noodling under me. I started to sink toward the ground when another pair of arms swept me up. I found myself staring at a broad chest, clad in a dark shirt and denim jacket. I tried to look up, to see the face of whoever was holding me, but he was wearing sunglasses and some sort of a hat. Hazily, I wanted to tell him that it was nighttime, he didn't need the glasses, but that seemed like it wasn't the right thing to say.

Confused, I rested my head against his chest. He smelled like cigarettes and brandy, and I winced, the stench of smoke making me gag. As he lifted me into the van, I saw three others there, though I couldn't make out any of their features. And then, I was resting on a blanket on the floor, and as I drifted off, I felt someone tying my hands and feet. The last thing I remembered thinking was who was going to tell Aegis where I went, and that it was a damned good thing Bubba was staying the night with Mr. Peabody.

Chapter 1

"I CAN'T BELIEVE I have to interview for a new housekeeper. Trina didn't even work here for two months before she up and ran off." I slapped the table with the latest copy of the *Bedlam Crier*, which contained the classified ad I'd submitted the day before. Hopefully, someone would answer it before the end of the day, because I was getting tired of wasting my spells on creating holeos to clean the B&B. I might be a powerful witch, but I didn't have unlimited energy, and at some point, I wanted to do something besides create automatons to scrub the toilets.

"What happened to her? She get pregnant?" Sandy took another sip of her drink.

We had decided to celebrate the upcoming holiday by getting a jump start on spring. Since we were nearing Ostara—the spring equinox—we decided on a tart, bright flavor to fit the bill. The blender was full of a mixture of lemon sorbet, spiced rum, limeade, and a little grenadine. The drink was surprisingly nifty, especially after the third round.

"Trina and her boyfriend are selkies, you know. He got a job out on the peninsula near Port Townsend, so he was moving to a new pod. If Trina continued to work here, that would put a damper on their relationship. I get it, but *damn it*. She was a pretty spiffy worker." I tossed back the last of my drink and held my glass out for a fourth round.

Sandy poured out the last of the drinks and held up the empty blender. "Another batch?"

I shrugged. "You know, we really should have something to eat. I forgot lunch and I doubt if I'm going to be in any shape to make dinner."

"When are you *ever* in shape to make dinner? You're lucky Aegis is a good cook." She snorted, peeling herself out of her chair. "Do you have any potato chips? With all the lime in these drinks, it feels like we should have some salt to go with it."

"You're thinking of margaritas. Yeah, in the cupboard." I started to hum the "Coconut" song as she foraged for goodies. Sandy and I had a high tolerance for mind-altering substances. After all, we had three hundred years of practice at being party girls. But I knew I wasn't going to find my answer to the cleaning problem at the bottom of a blender.

I let out a sigh. "Well, the ad just came out today so hopefully, I'll get some sort of response." I paused. "Now, if I could just take care of that damned Ralph Greyhoof. You know, he actually egged my front door the other morning when he was drunk off his ass? Took my holeos an hour to wash it off."

"He's an idiot. He won't let go of the feud, will he?"

"No, and I was willing to let the past go." Ralph Greyhoof and I had come to a temporary truce for a while but that was shot to hell. One of the Grey-hoof boys—they were a band of satyrs—he owned the Heart's Desire Inn, or should I say *brothel*. And he was always accusing me of trying to steal his business.

"No," I said, giving her an evil grin. "But this morning I left him a little surprise. I found a glo-wing and thought maybe Ralph needed a pet, so I left it just inside his door."

Glo-wings were gorgeous little caterpillars that happened to multiply like crazy. As their name suggested, they glowed non-stop. They didn't destroy anything except plants, but they spread like crazy, and required a massive amount of elbow grease to remove. You had to remove them all, because just one could repopulate the entire species. Later in the year, they went into stasis, then burst forth as beautiful autumn moths, but when they were in their caterpillar stage, they were nothing but nuisances.

"Oh man, you're just escalating matters."

"Too bad. He started it and I'm tired of his horny face." I raised my glass. "Here's to payback."

"I'd be cautious if I were you," Sandy said, sipping her drink.

"*M'rrow.*" Bubba wandered in, swishing his tail.

He had a feisty look in his eye, one that only led to trouble. As the gorgeous, massive orange tabby leaped up on the table to stare me in the face, I reached out, singing as I gave him an ear rub. He began to purr and I swept him into my arms, dancing with him.

"You want some catnip, Bub?"

Bubba liked to party as much as we did. I found his stash and sprinkled some on the cat bed sitting near the kitchen door that led to the backyard. He bounced down and began to purr, rolling on the green fleece.

Sandy gave him a long look. "He's been awfully good lately. You think he's up to something?"

"I never know what's going on in that furry brain of his," I said. "Cjinns are always cunning. They pride themselves on it. But he's saved my ass more than once, so if he acts out now and then or wants to get stoned, I say go for it." I tossed him a squeaky mouse and he rolled over, raking it with his back claws in a nip-induced frenzy.

"All the same, I wouldn't touch his belly if I were you. Not with as much as we've been drinking. You'd end up with Alice from *The Brady Bunch* working for you." Sandy handed me a bowl that she'd filled with potato chips, along with a tray of lemon bars. "A little sugar wouldn't hurt us either."

"Aegis made those for our guests. But what the hell, they'll never miss them." I glanced at the clock. Five P.M. "I never thought I'd wish away time, but with the waxing year, he has to sleep later and later. *That*, I don't like."

"How long till sunset?" Sandy peeked out the

sliding-glass door.

"About seventy minutes, give or take a few."

Vampires were bound to sleep during the day. At least *most* of them. I'd recently had an eye-opening experience that almost landed me dead, but had also netted us some pretty powerful information about a secret society of Aegis's kind. Even *he* hadn't been fully aware of it, but we were keeping our mouths shut because the ramifications were huge and we really didn't want to set ourselves up as targets.

I was about to dive into the lemon bars when my cell phone rang. Or rather trumpeted. I grimaced. I had recently bought a new phone and hadn't bothered to set new ring tones yet.

"I don't recognize the number."

"Maybe it's somebody answering your ad."

"That would be wonderful. Hold on while I take this."

Sandy nodded, pulling out her own phone to check her texts while I took the call.

"Maudlin Gallowglass here."

"Ms. Gallowglass? I'm Thornton Weston, calling about your ad in the *Bedlam Crier*. I'd like to apply, if the position's still open."

I blinked. I had no problem with a man applying, but apparently, my subconscious had been expecting a woman because his voice threw me off guard. It was deep and rich, and made me think of smooth, black coffee with just a hint of sugar.

"Why...well, *of course* you can. The job's still open. Can you come by for an interview at ten tomorrow morning?" I thought about setting up the interview for evening, when Aegis was awake, but the last thing I needed was him chasing off a potential employee just because he was male. While Aegis was all kittens and cupcakes when he was in his domestic mood, my vampire boyfriend had a protective streak a mile wide, and it reared its green-eyed head at the most inopportune times. I needed a housekeeper now, not in two weeks after we had worked through his *"But it's a man, will you be safe"* rhetoric.

"I'll be there at ten, resume in hand."

"Good. See you tomorrow." With that, I hung up and Sandy and I went back to our impromptu pre-spring party.

"I DON'T CARE what you say, you're not going to hire him until *I* get to meet him. You just call him back and change the appointment for when I'm awake." Aegis tried to stare me down, but I was having none of it. Besides, he might have been imposing, except for the fact that he was wearing my kittens-and-bows apron over his black leather pants and holding a copper mixing bowl in one hand, and a wire whisk in the other.

"If I think he can do a good job, you damned well bet your pearly fangs I'm going to hire him. Why don't you just use the mixer for that?" All of the yummy afterglow of the booze had fled my system. I was perched on the counter near Aegis, and I reached out with one foot to lightly tap his ass.

He gave me one of his "Are you kidding?" looks.

"You really know nothing about cooking, do you?" He quirked his lips into a slightly snarky grin.

I stuck out my tongue at him. "I know how to fry an egg. Beyond that, I know the names of my best friends—Chef Pizza-Joint, Chef Chicken-Chicken, and Chef-in-a-Can. Now tell me why you're using a whisk for those egg whites."

He shook his head, still whisking away. The egg whites were whipping up into a nice foam. "You're incorrigible. It just so happens that egg whites are best whipped by hand in a copper bowl. It's faster than using a mixer and you get better results. So if you really want lemon meringue pie for the guests tomorrow, you'll quit back-seat baking and let me do my job."

"Yes, sir," I said meekly.

"And don't you and Sandy go eating it all before we have a chance to offer it to the paying customers. I can't just whip another one up in the middle of the day, you know." He paused, leaning against the counter next to me. "Did the two of you *really* eat the entire pan of lemon bars I made? I'm glad you liked them, but it's a wonder you both aren't puking your guts out."

"We have a high tolerance for booze and sugar, built up through centuries of practice." I wrinkled my nose. "Don't guilt trip me about my love for food and drink."

"I won't, if you quit complaining about the fact that I want to make sure you're safe," he shot back.

I rolled my eyes. "We have strange men in the

house anyway. That's what it means to own a bed-and-breakfast. Don't forget, we take in strangers and give them a place to sleep. Maybe kindly old Mr. Mosswood is a serial killer."

Aegis laughed, setting the bowl down. "Oh, Maddy, I love you. You crack me up. If Mr. Mosswood is a serial killer, then I can walk out into the sun and just get a nice tan."

Mr. Mosswood was rapidly becoming a long-term guest. He had checked in three weeks ago, and kept extending his stay. He was slight, about five-seven and thin as a reed, and he was quiet and polite to the point of annoying. He wore a suit and hat that reminded me of something out of the 1950s—and I had lived through the fifties, so I knew they were genuine vintage.

Mr. Mosswood had thinning hair and wore round glasses. I thought of them as spectacles, because he seemed to be stuck in a time period long past. He was human, and he said he was gathering information for a book he wanted to write about the history of Bedlam. He paid on time, tipped well, and was a tidy man, so I welcomed him as long as he wanted to stay.

"Don't you dare. Seriously, though, you never really know. Some of the worst killers have been the quietest. I'm sure Mr. Mosswood is thoroughly benign, but we know nothing of his background." I leaned forward. "But he proves my point. He's staying here, and he's up and around while you're sleeping. If he *were* a murderer, you wouldn't be able to save me during the day. So why worry when I interview someone for a housecleaning job?"

Aegis pressed his lips together, regarding me as though I was an annoying gnat, and I knew I had won the argument. Finally, he plastered a kiss on my forehead, then bopped my nose with his finger. He smelled like musk and cinnamon, like dark knights on an autumn evening. My knees quivered as I stroked a long strand of his wavy jet black hair back from his face. His eyes were pools of coffee, tinged with crimson around the edges, and he was strong and fit, with a voice that made me melt.

"You know, you should finish making that pie, before the egg whites go flat," I murmured.

"I don't care about the egg whites," he whispered, gathering me into his arms.

I squirmed, feeling him press hard against me. The egg whites might be going flat but something else wasn't. But I didn't complain as he carried me up the stairs, ending the conversation with a long, sweaty session in bed.

THE NEXT MORNING, I slid into my new jeans—black stretch denim with a lot of give to accommodate the padding of my butt, which was, as I liked to call it, *curvalicious*. I pulled on a short-sleeved V-neck silk shirt with cap sleeves. The deep green set off the teal of my eyes, and the rich brunette of my hair. I also had big boobs, which was fine with me. In fact, I was about as hourglass as they came, in terms of my figure.

I scooched my feet into a pair of black leather

ballerina flats—I was about five-eight so I could do flats without feeling short—and fastened my pentacle around my neck, along with a rope of moonstone beads. The pentacle was about two inches in diameter and stood out against my shirt. I fastened on freshwater pearl chandelier earrings, then took a few minutes to slap on a quick ten-minute face at my vanity.

Bubba was next to my makeup mirror, watching. He cocked his head as I pursed my lips to apply my lipstick—a bright fuchsia. I hated any pinks that weren't magenta or fuchsia, but neon colors and jewel tones rocked my world.

"Mrow." Bubba reached out one paw to tap my arm.

I paused, trying not to jog the lipstick onto my face. "Bubs, hold on. I'll feed you in a minute. I'm almost done."

Bubba waited a beat until I raised the lipstick to my lips again, then—more firmly—smacked me on the hand with his paw.

"Bubba! Look at what you did!" I frowned at my reflection. A bright pink line of lipstick ran jaggedly down my chin. "Gee thanks, Bub."

As I reached for the makeup remover, I swear, Bubba snickered at me. He pulled his paw back, then began to groom it as though he had no clue what I was talking about.

"That cat is a menace." Franny rose up beside me. As in, through the floor, to hover a foot above it.

I jumped. "I told you to stop doing that! And Bubba's not just a cat. He's a cjinn."

Franny was the house ghost—or B&B ghost, now that I'd converted the place. And she was moody as all get out, always finding something to bellyache about. But over the past six months, I had actually gotten used to the depressed spirit and she had lightened up a little.

I poured a little makeup remover on a cotton ball and wiped the lipstick off my face. "I haven't seen you for a couple of days. Where have you been keeping yourself? You can't leave the house, so I know you weren't on vacation."

She shrugged. She was dressed in the dress she had died in—a sky blue muslin gown à la Jane Austen, over which she wore an ivory corset and a matching lace shawl. She was pretty in a serious sort of way, with blue eyes and blond hair spilling out of a messy bun.

"Oh, this and that. I watched the gardeners plant the new roses from out of the library window. Thank you, by the way, for setting up the computer e-reader for me." Franny flashed me a rare smile. "I just read a marvelous book by a Mr. Mark Twain. It's called *Tom Sawyer*."

I grinned. I had been around during Twain's time, and figured she would like some of his work. "Glad you liked it."

Franny loved to read. In fact, that was how she died. On a warm August day in 1791, Franny had been walking along the second-floor hallway, reading, and she missed the first step as she turned to go downstairs. She broke her neck in the fall and had been trapped here ever since. Franny had spent a long time alone until I had bought the old mansion. Those who could see her had run in fear until Aegis moved in. And he had pretty much ignored her. When I bought the house, I gave him hell for treating her like she didn't exist.

Franny loved to read, and she missed it most of all. So I had set up a spare computer in the library. I kept the computer on constantly, and the e-reader program was always open. I had programmed it to voice control and since Franny could speak as clearly as I could, she could command it. I programmed in some basic commands—*Turn Page, Go to Page, Open New Book, Close Book.* Now she could read to her heart's content. Every few weeks, we'd go through the online bookstore and add a few new books for her.

I finished with my lipstick and sat back. I was about as presentable as I was going to get for the morning. Bubba let out another squeak.

"Yeah, yeah, Bub. I'll feed you. Franny, come on down to the kitchen if you like. I have someone coming at ten, but if you want to talk..." I left it open ended. Franny resented any trace of pity, for which I didn't blame her, but she also liked to chat. Granted, she was angsty as hell, but I couldn't help but feel that I should treat her as one of my permanent houseguests. You didn't just ignore someone because she had a chip on her shoulder about being dead and stuck in a house.

She brightened. "All right. I can tell you what I found out about your guests—"

I stopped in the doorway, glancing at her. "What did I tell you about spying?"

She rolled her eyes. "I know, but can I help it if

I happen to be around when they don't know I'm watching?"

Shaking my head, I headed down the stairs, listening to her ramble on about Mr. Mosswood's habit of rubbing his scalp with rose-scented lotion, and how Mrs. Periwinkle, a very old witch who seemed to have misplaced her marbles along with her late husband, had been trying to convince the grandfather clock to tell her where we kept the hidden treasure. What treasure she was talking about, I had no idea.

AT TEN O'CLOCK, prompt to the second, Thornton Weston was sitting in my parlor. He was human and in his early thirties. He was also a fine-looking piece of man flesh. Five-ten, pale blond hair in a Euro shag, trim but not overly thin, with a wisp of a beard and deep blue eyes that sparkled when he said hello. He was dressed in jeans and a polo shirt, but it was obvious he belonged in a leather blazer. I could easily see him driving some classy little number like a Jaguar or a Lotus. In fact, everything about him smelled like old money, so why was he applying for a housekeeping job?

"Are you sure you're interested in this job? It's not very glamorous. You'd be cleaning the mansion every day. You won't be responsible for laundry, except for the sheets and blankets in the guest rooms. We have three rooms for paying customers, a personal guest room, and my bedroom. You'd be cleaning the guests' rooms every day, the other two bedrooms once a week. We have six baths—they need to be cleaned daily. The kitchen gets cleaned every day, and it *must* be spotless due to health code regulations. You won't need to cook, but you may be called upon to wait tables occasion-ally. There's the daily dusting and tidying things up in the living room, library, parlor, and grand ballroom. I have someone to wash the floors once a week and windows once a month, so you don't have to worry about those."

As I paused, he shrugged. "I've had worse jobs. I'm not afraid of a little work."

"We have a maid's room on the main floor, which would be your living quarters, and a butler's pantry. You'll eat in there. Room and board are included in your salary. I take care of Bubba's litter box. Oh, and whatever you do, please *don't* pet his belly." I didn't want to tell him that Bubba was a cjinn until I knew him better. There were people who weren't above trying to steal the creatures for their own use.

Pausing, I let the information settle. "So, are you interested?"

"Definitely. What are the official hours?"

Surprised, I said, "The job is full time, but since I won't ask you to be on call 24/7 unless there's an emergency, you'll have Tuesdays and Wednesdays free. They're our least busy days. We ask longer-term guests to waive daily cleaning for a reduced rate, so you only have to clean their rooms twice a week. Right now, we have two of them, actually."

"The job sounds good to me, especially the live-

in part. I'm between apartments right now." He
flashed me an easy grin.

I glanced down at the resume again. He had
worked in a number of hotels in housekeeping, as
a bellhop, and desk clerk, but his employment history was sketchy, especially for the past five years.

"Why the gap in work the past few years?"

He shrugged. "Let's just say I've been in an
abusive relationship and I finally got out after a
bad breakup. I had to leave quickly. All I own are
in a couple of suitcases, and I have nowhere to go.
I happened to see your ad in the *Crier* yesterday
and thought this would be perfect with my background."

As someone who had spent too many years in a
bad marriage, I knew how easy it was to get suck-
ered into a relationship that tangled you in knots.

"Well, I have your number. Let me run your
references and see what they have to say. I'll call
you by tomorrow." I shook his hand and walked
him to the door. As we passed through the living
room, Franny popped out, took one look at him,
and vanished.

He paused, letting out a short laugh. "Let me
guess. House ghost?"

"Right. She's disruptive at times, but overall
she's a good egg. We've adopted her." I shook my
head. "Sometimes it's just easier to play the hand
you've been dealt. She came with the property and
so she's part of the B&B."

"The 'we' you refer to... You and... Are you married?" He glanced around as though he expected to
see someone else magically pop into view.

It was my turn to laugh. "Not anymore, but my new boyfriend helps me run the place. I should tell you, just in case you have issues with the idea. I'm involved with a vampire. His name is Aegis and he's the lead singer of the Boys of Bedlam, an up-and-coming band. You might have heard them down at the Utopia nightclub."

Thornton stiffened. "Aegis? The rock star vampire?"

"That would be him. But he has a heart of gold. Loves kittens and cupcakes. He bakes most of the goodies for our guests." When I had first encountered Aegis, in addition to his gorgeous bad-boy self, I had come face to face with his private passions—kittens, jigsaw puzzles, baking, and reading mysteries. He loved *Murder She Wrote*. We watched a lot of re-runs.

Thornton thought for a moment. "I guess it could be worse," he said, reaching for the door. "I'll wait for your call."

As I walked him down the porch steps, I found myself hoping his references would check out. Not only did he have experience, but he seemed personable and he could probably charm the pants off my guests. But then, as I turned to go inside, a large crow appeared on the porch railing and began to caw.

I started to ask it what it wanted, but a shiver raced up my spine as clouds began to sock in, covering the pale blue sky. Within less than sixty seconds, lightning flashed, thunder roared, and I was soaked to the skin as the storm opened up. The crow let out a single echoing caw and flew away. Chilled to the bone, I turned and ran inside, wondering why I was suddenly frightened.

Chapter 2

SO, IT'S TIME for introductions. My name is Maudlin Gallowglass. My nicknames range from *Maddy*—which most people know me by these days—to *Mad Maudlin*, and *the Mad Wonder*. Remember that old folksong "Boys of Bedlam"? Also known as "Mad Tom of Bedlam"? Well, I'm the "Mad Maudlin" they sang about. And Tom was my boyfriend. It's a long, colorful history that I'll go into later, but let's just say that I was known as one of the more powerful witches to come out of the UK during the 1700s, and I also happen to be one of the most famous vampire hunters in history.

Yes, yes, I know the irony, I was a vampire hunter and now I'm bedding one. Well, actually in love with one, if I'm honest. It doesn't make sense, but when you really look at life, not a whole lot does.

Anyway, I'm Maddy, and I'm now the owner of the Bewitching Bedlam B&B. I live in the town of

Bedlam, on the island of Bedlam, which is part of the San Juan Islands in Washington state, near Lopez and Orcas in the Haro Strait. My Bedlam is nothing like the Bedlam of the songs—that was a mental institution back in jolly old England, and if you were committed there, it was pretty much a death sentence.

My Bedlam is a magical island filled with magical people. The PretCom community is strong here. While the city was founded by a group of witches a long time ago, plenty of Otherkin live here besides those of us with magical blood. Shifters and Weres are common, along with Summer, Winter, and Woodland Fae.

We even have a nest of vampires, run by Essie Vanderbilt, the Queen of the Pacific Northwest Vampire Nation. Having a vampire queen on the island isn't all that pleasant, especially since she tried to set me up to be killed. But there's no way to prove it was her. Since Rachel, one of her lackeys and Aegis's ex-girlfriend, took the fall for it, all I can do is keep an eye out. Luckily, all that's left of Rachel is a pile of dust.

Bedlam has a population of about six thousand people, and we also boast one of the greatest magical schools for witches—Neverfall Academy. If I was born during the current day, I'd give just about anything to attend there.

Life's a lot different for young witches today.

When I was born, the witch hunters were rampant, searching for my kind to burn us at the stake, string us up, drown us. Torture was par for the course and we did our best to hide.

Of course, most of those killed by the Inquisition weren't really witches, but innocents who were disliked by their neighbors, or who had enough money to matter. Once branded a heretic, the accused land owner lost their land, their money, and most important—their lives. And the Church grew rich. Tom and I ran from them, always keeping a hop and a skip ahead. But the fires and the witch hunters followed us, raging across the continent and into England.

Anyway, those are dark thoughts for dark days. I met my best friends back then—Sandy, who went by Cassandra, and Fata Morgana, who was even more wild than I was.

After my Tom vanished, Sandy and Fata helped me hunt down and destroy the vampires who were feeding across the countryside. Then, finally, the fires I drove them out with ended up scorching my soul. After that, the three of us ran wild, partying, hanging with the satyrs and the nymphs. Finally, the madness dissipated and we moved on to new things and new lives. Fata disappeared into the mists, but Sandy and me? We stuck together, best friends forever.

Eventually, as the decades rolled by, Sandy moved to Bedlam and I moved to Seattle. Then, a few months ago, she persuaded me to move to the island. I'm now High Priestess of the Moonrise Coven, a duty I consider sacred.

So yeah, that's my life. That and the Bewitching Bedlam. I bought the old mansion to rile my ex, but unexpectedly, I fell in love with it. And with its squatter—Aegis.

Now, Maddy the vampire hunter is in love with a vampire, and the proprietress of a fancy-schmancy bed-and-breakfast. And you know what? I'm happier than I've ever been.

"MADDY? MADDY!" SANDY bellowed out my name from the kitchen. I had invited her and Max—her new squeeze, a weretiger and the owner of a chain of clothing shops—over for dinner. Of course, that meant that I had placed a call to the best pizza joint in town and ordered four pizzas. I'd asked Sandy to pick up dessert on the way over. She carried in two cheesecakes—one New York–style cheesecake with raspberry topping, and one chocolate cheesecake.

"What?" I glanced up at the clock. It was almost six-ten. Aegis would be getting up soon.

"I can't find the pizza cutter!"

"Be right there!" I glanced over the shopping list one more time. Thornton was going shopping the next day and I wanted to make sure that everything Aegis had asked for was on there.

Thornton had checked out. Even with the gap in his employment history, I had taken a chance and hired him the day after the interview. Now, I couldn't imagine what I'd do without him. He was one hell of a housecleaner, and he had taken the inn in hand and not only was he keeping it in tiptop shape, but he had compiled a list of necessary repairs. He had been working for us for about a week, and already, Aegis and I had come to rely on him more than we wanted to admit.

I put down my pen and hustled out of my office to join Sandy and Max. As I entered the kitchen, I caught them kissing.

"Max and Sandy, sitting in a tree, K-I-S-S-I-N-G!" I laughed as they broke apart.

Sandy had met Max during the week after New Year's. They had had a rather harrowing experience together, even as I had been trapped by an avalanche. But our misguided vacations hadn't been in vain. The time had brought Aegis and me closer together, and Max and Sandy had found one another. They fit together in a way that I had never seen Sandy fit with anybody else.

Max winked at me. He was a little shorter than Aegis, but he had wavy hair the color of wheat and his eyes were the color of dark soil. A scar ran down the side of Max's face. I hadn't asked him where he got it, and so far, he hadn't volunteered the information. He routinely dressed in designer wear. Sandy, on the other hand, was wearing her usual yoga pants and crop top—she was lean and toned, as blond as the morning sun, and as rich as Max appeared to be.

"Don't bother us, woman, we're busy."

"Yeah, well, get busy in a room, you two. No fornicating on my kitchen floor." I winked at them. I motioned for Sandy to move aside. She was searching in the baking drawer for the pizza cutter. "That's the wrong drawer. That's the baking drawer. The pizza cutter is with serving pieces."

"You have a baking drawer?" Sandy stared at me

like I was out of my mind. "Since when?"

"Since Aegis. You know how much he likes to bake. I finally caved and let him arrange the kitchen the way he likes, since he does most of the actual cooking. We have a baking drawer, and a serving drawer, and a stirring drawer, and a cupboard for bake ware, and a cupboard for stemware—not the good crystal, which I keep in the china hutch. I told him he had free rein as long as I get to arrange the bar."

Sandy laughed. "That makes sense. You lucked out, you know. Since you refuse to hire a cook, landing Aegis is the next best thing. The man makes a mean brownie."

"As long as his red velvet cakes don't have blood in them, I'm good." I opened a bottle of merlot and poured out four glasses.

"I still can't get over the fact that vampires can eat and drink. I never knew that before." Max was slowly getting used to hanging around Aegis. They didn't have a lot in common, but they were polite and kept searching for something to share.

"Yes, but they never gain weight, and the food and booze don't give them any energy. They need blood to actually recharge. Without enough blood, they'll go into their predatory phase, and if they're starved long enough, they'll slip into a form of hibernation."

Max paused, then softly said, "Sandy's told me a little about your background. If I'm not being presumptuous, how does it feel to go from vampire hunter to..."

"To being the lover of a vampire?" The question

was highly personal, but by now I was used to Max and he didn't offend me. While it wasn't something most strangers would be comfortable asking, I understood the curiosity, and I didn't mind talking about it to the weretiger.

"How much of my background did Sandy tell you about?"

"Just that you're the original Mad Maudlin and that you hunted vampires together with another friend." Max frowned. "If I've overstepped, please—you don't owe me any explanation. I wasn't sure if the question was too personal."

"It is...very personal, but I like you, and Sandy obviously likes you. So..." I handed them their wine and slid onto one of the counter bar stools, crossing my legs as I cupped the goblet in my hand, swirling the wine gently in the glass.

"I was once in love with a witch, a man named Tom. He was incredible, and oddly enough, he was a musician, too. Back in 1659, I met Fata Morgana. She's actually the one who introduced me to Tom. He was a distant cousin of hers. We fell in love. The three of us traveled together all over what's now the UK, and through Europe. We were chased by witch hunters a lot. We were good at what we did, and we developed a certain notoriety. On a trip to London in 1699, we met Sandy. We all hit it off really well, and she joined us on the road."

"You met Fata on the shore, didn't you?" Sandy carried the pizzas over to the table. Max followed her with plates and forks.

"That's right. I was standing on the edge of the ocean, in the area now known as Seahouses. I was out on the sand, watching the waves, when I saw a big swell headed for shore. As it drew near, I realized that a woman was riding the wave in. She was actually emerging out of it, arms spread wide, head back, as she stood atop the crest of the highest wave. As the water crashed along the beach, she leaped off and ran over to me, laughing. Her hair was flame red, and she was wearing a long black dress that looked like it was made of seaweed at first. She danced around me, then took my hands and said, 'Have you ever ridden the wild ocean?' And that…was my first meeting with Fata Morgana."

"When did you meet Bubba?" Max asked.

"Oh, in 1687, and he's been with me ever since. I rescued him from a burning barn. I had stopped near a Faerie barrow to see one of the Aunties when I smelled smoke. A farmer's barn was on fire—it had a thatched roof and you know how dangerous those are. One stray spark, it's *boom, crash,* and you can kiss your livestock and livelihood good-bye."

I whistled to Bubba, who was sitting by his food dish, watching us. "Isn't that right? You were just a baby when I found you, weren't you, Bub?" He padded over and leapt onto the stool next to me, letting out a loud *purp.* I ruffled his fur. "I have no idea what happened to his mother or the rest of the litter. Anyway, so Bubba and I have been together a long, long time."

"When did you begin to hunt vampires?" Max looked intrigued.

"A while later. You see, a group of them caught

Tom. He sacrificed his life to save mine. They turned him. I wanted revenge. With Sandy and Fata at my side, I became the scourge of the vampire nation until my fires burned brighter than those of the witch hunters. But fire can scorch the soul, so after a while, I retired. To answer your question, it's been a process of adapting. Of accepting that not all vampires are evil—that like us, they have a choice."

I carried my wine over to join them at the table, glancing at the clock again. "Aegis should be getting up—"

"Right about now." Aegis popped his head around the kitchen door and joined us. "Sorry I'm late. I needed a shower." He kissed me and waved at Sandy and Max. "Pizza?"

"Yes, love. Sit down and join us." I patted the chair next to me. Aegis sat down, accepting the glass of wine I offered him. "I was just telling Max about how I met Sandy, Fata, and Bubba."

Aegis nodded. "A lot of water under the bridge there."

"You're not kidding about that." I paused as the doorbell rang.

"I'll get it." He excused himself and headed for the living room.

I glanced back at Max. "I lost Tom in 1720. We were out in the woods, working on a spell for a girl from some village. She had broken her leg in several places. Nobody asked us to help, but we knew that without our magic, the break wouldn't heal right and she'd be lame. We didn't realize that a group of vampires had followed us. They apparently had caught our scent—witches' blood is an aphrodisiac for vamps."

"I didn't know that, either," Max said. "I would think that witches don't have a great love for vampires, then?"

"Mostly, no. Anyway, long story short, the vampires cornered us. Tom pushed me behind him and told me to run. I didn't want to, but the next thing I knew, a unicorn appeared, with a Fae warrior riding his back. I snatched up Bubba, the warrior grabbed hold of me and pulled us onto the unicorn with her, and we raced away. We were so fast the vampires couldn't even see us. We vanished into a swirl of mist and fog, and before I knew what had happened, Bubba and I were in a Barrow Mound."

Aegis returned, carrying a package. He glanced at me, a questioning look on his face. "You're telling Max about Tom?"

"He was curious how I went from vampire hunter to being a vampire's mistress." I smiled at him. "What's that?"

"I don't know. It's addressed to you." He handed me the box. "You order anything recently?"

"I'm the queen of online ordering." I took the box. "Anyway, as I said, I ended up in a Barrow Mound. I was there for twenty years. When Bubba and I found our way out, Tom was long lost to the vampires. I reconnected with Sandy and Fata, and together we combed the country and part of the continent for those vamps. We killed...so many. There were weeks when all I could smell was the stench of blood. About ten years after that we took down an entire village of them and I lost my fire.

Figuratively, not literally. I just couldn't go on."

"That's when we ran wild, in our party-hearty stage," Sandy said. "Finally, the scene grew old. Satyrs and nymphs are a lot of fun, but you can only drink so much wine, fuck so many cocks, eat so much pussy, before you want something else in life."

Aegis arched his eyebrows. "Sex, drugs, and rock 'n roll, huh?"

I laughed. "Well, I had the sex and drugs all right. Now I've got the sex, rock 'n roll, and the occasional bender. But I've also got the Bewitching Bedlam, and that makes all the difference." Turning back to Max, I reached for the pizza wheel. "And that is how I went from vampire hunter to vampire lover, in a long nutshell."

As we dove into our meal, I realized just how grateful I was that my life had turned out like this. I would always mourn Tom, but I was happy now, and that's what mattered.

WE WERE SITTING in the living room, watching an old movie—*Night of the Living Dead*—when I remembered the package. I hopped up, grabbing the empty potato chip bowl, and dashed into the kitchen.

After refilling the bowl, I picked up the box. It was small, about the size of a brownie. Maybe it *was* a brownie, I thought. I carefully unwrapped the paper. Inside sat a red velvet box that remind-

ed me of a jewelry box. Aegis must have been trying to surprise me. He often slipped trinkets onto
my nightstand while I slept, and I'd find them the
next morning. He also loved sending me flowers.

I flipped open the lid on the box. In the center sat a brooch. The rose gold heart had a ruby
centered under the point, and was both delicate
and elegant at the same time. It wasn't my usual
style, but as I lifted it off the cushion, I found
myself mesmerized by the piece. It was lovely, and
looked vintage. Smiling—it had to be from Aegis—
I pinned it to my shirt. Then, refilling the bowl of
chips, I returned to the living room.

"Thank you, I love it!" I handed Sandy the bowl,
then leaned over Aegis's shoulder, wrapping my
arms around his neck. "It's so pretty, and you're so
thoughtful." Kissing him on the forehead, I nuz-
zled his hair with my nose.

He laughed. "Well, I'm glad you think so, but
what are you thanking me for? I haven't made that
pan of Turkish delight that I promised—not yet, at
least."

I snickered and slid onto his lap. "Maybe not,
but still...I love you to pieces."

"Whatever you did, you did it right." Max
reached for a handful of chips.

"It must be my natural charm," Aegis said, winking at him.

"No, seriously, thank you." I was starting to get
annoyed. I liked to joke around as much as the
next person—probably more—but I wanted him
to realize just how much I appreciated the brooch.
"The pin. This one." I pointed above my left boob.

"The box that came to the door? Thank you, I love it."

Aegis stared at the heart, a furrow forming on his brow. "Love, I didn't buy that."

"What do you mean? If you didn't, who did?" It was my turn to frown. If not Aegis, who on earth would send me expensive jewelry? Even though the piece was simple, I could tell it hadn't come cheap. Rose gold and a ruby that size weren't exactly the stuff of petty cash.

"Was there a note?" Aegis asked.

Sandy muted the television as she leaned over to check out the heart. "That's gorgeous. And I can tell you right now, that's real. I have a thing for gems and metal—I can tune into them." Sandy actually had a thing for *money* in general. She could sense fake designer wear, costume jewelry, and counterfeit bills a mile off. If she said the brooch was real gold and ruby, I believed her.

Confused, I slid off of Aegis's lap. "I don't think so. Let me go look."

As I headed into the kitchen, my head started to pound. I winced as I picked up the box. Nothing. I flattened out the paper it had been wrapped in, thinking that somebody might have written a note on the inside, but nothing. I peered at the address label. The handwriting wasn't familiar, and now that I looked at it, I realized there was no return address. The velvet box revealed nothing out of the ordinary—just the puffy little cushion the brooch had rested on. I even slit the material and peeked inside, but there was only cotton.

Leaning against the counter, I realized that I was

more than annoyed—I was now anxious, as well as on the verge of a headache.

"Are you okay?" Sandy asked as she peeked into the kitchen. She glanced around. "So, no clue yet?"

I shook my head. "No note. No return address. I wish I could be sure Aegis isn't messing with me—you know, playing a joke."

"He isn't. He's out there complaining to Max about men who send jewelry to other men's girlfriends. A little jelly, isn't he?"

I laughed through the growing ache in my temples. "Oh, he's got a jealous streak, all right. I don't know if it's just him, or if it's his vampire nature. But he's not a brute and he's not stupid about it, so I can deal." I tossed the box back on the counter. "I just want to know who sent this. It's like when you can't remember the name of a song. The more you try to figure it out, the more frustrated you get."

"Why don't you come back and finish watching the movie? Chances are, a friend sent it and just forgot to enclose the note. I've done that any number of times." She wrapped her arm around me. "Would you like me to get some Throb-Be-Gone tablets for you?"

I winced, my head aching more by the second. "Yeah, they're in the medicine cabinet. Andy made up a fresh batch the other day just before I dropped in there, and I'm glad that I thought to pick up some."

Andy McGee owned McGee's Apothecary. He was the local pharmacist and he made the best tonic in the world. Come to think of it, I hadn't been taking it regularly. I usually took one tablespoon a day and it kept me fit as a fiddle, but the past few weeks I'd been so busy with the B&B that I had all but forgotten about it. That must be what was happening. I'd let myself get rundown and it all hit at once.

Sandy headed off to the bathroom and I poured myself a glass of water, sipping it slowly. I'd had a lot of caffeine and booze over the past couple of weeks, and was probably dehydrated.

Aegis entered the kitchen. "Are you all right, love?"

I shrugged. "Headache threatening to turn into a migraine. Sandy's grabbing me some Throb-Be-Gone from the bathroom. I'm just a little rundown and overtired. If you don't mind, I think I'll call it an early night and go to bed."

He wrapped his arms around me, pulling me close. "I don't mind," he said, burying his face in my hair. "I've got a lot of cooking to do for tomorrow, so I'll take care of that and make sure the bookings are all organized. I have rehearsal tomorrow night. We're writing a couple new songs so next week's going to be pretty booked up. But let's make sure to get some time together," he added, kissing my neck.

"It's a date." I gave him a quick kiss.

Sandy returned, and Aegis moved aside so I could take the medicine. As I swallowed the capsules and went to bed, I realized that I still didn't have a clue as to who sent me the heart. As I stripped out of my clothes and slipped under the covers, I decided that it didn't matter for now. I placed the heart in its box on my nightstand, and—

as Bubba jumped on the bed and curled by my feet—I closed my eyes and drifted off to a dreamless sleep.

Chapter 3

I WOKE UP, feeling one hundred percent better. As I sat up, pushing the covers back, the sun burst through my window and I realized that I had slept in. I glanced over at my phone, and there was a note beside it.

Love, I turned off your alarm. You needed the sleep and I've asked Thornton to serve the guests their breakfast. You were right—he's a gem. Can we keep him? XXOO ~A.

There was a single red rose in a bud vase next to the phone, along with a tea dish holding a blueberry muffin. I smiled as I picked up the rose and smelled it. The fragrance was as deep and rich as the color was, and as I replaced it in the vase, I thanked my lucky stars again that Aegis was part of my life.

As I slipped out of bed, I looked around for Bub-ba. He was almost always there to greet me in the morning, but today, there was no sign of him. He was probably cadging breakfast off of Thornton. Bubba was fickle when it came to food—feed him and he was your pal for life. Rub his belly, and you were in his merciless grasp. Laughing, I headed for the shower.

After a quick rinse off, I braided my hair back, put on my makeup, then slid into a black A-line skirt and slipped on a green tank top. I was wear-ing my prettiest purple bra and, as I adjusted the girls beneath the shirt, I brushed my fingers over my nipples, thinking about Aegis and how much I wished it were his fingers instead of mine. Shiver-ing, I thought about pausing for a quiet moment with Bob—my neon green vibrator. But a glance at the clock told me there wasn't time for any hanky-panky this morning, even if it was a solo affair.

As I pinned on the brooch, I again felt another shiver run up my spine, but this time, the shiver was less *horny* and more *startled*. It wasn't a bad feeling, more like somebody had brushed against me with an ice cube.

Shaking my head, I resolutely picked up my muffin, grabbed my purse, and headed for the door. After a quick check-in with Thornton, who was already hard at work scrubbing the downstairs bath, I headed for my CR-V, keys in hand, ready to start the day.

FIRST STOP WAS mandatory: Bouncing Goats Espresso Shack. I couldn't function without my caffeine and BG was *the* place to get a good latte.

I pulled up to the microphone and was startled to see Gillymack's face staring at me from the camera. Gillymack was a local celebrity of sorts—infamous rather than famous. He was notorious for raising hell with the Greyhoof boys. Except Gillymack was a Meré who had been cast out from his home after accidentally setting off a hand grenade. He ended up blowing up the underwater lair of his people and the olders didn't take kindly to that.

The Meré were the merfolk. When not found in lakes, they mostly stayed in the waters around Bedlam Island, though a few dared the coastal waters over by Ocean Shores. Most of the merfolk on this side of the continent sought out lakes and rivers because the Pacific Ocean could be so wild and dangerous.

They could stay out of water for up to eighteen hours at a time, but then they would rapidly lose their stamina after that, until they went swimming under the water again. It was a lot like our need for sleep. Don't get enough sleep and it wears on you. Except for the Meré, staying out of water too long would kill them. One day, they could handle. Two days were iffy. Three, and they could easily die. When they came ashore, they lost their tails and fins, much like the selkies when they transformed into human shape. But the merfolk needed the water even more than the Sealkin.

"Gillymack, what the hell are you doing here?"

Everybody knew that he had an allergy to work and basically lived off the begrudging charity of others.

He rolled his eyes. The Meré were tasty to look at, at least in their human forms, but I knew better than ever tangle with one on a romantic level. They were selfish lovers and they also had a nasty tendency to pass along STDs—not the usual kind, either. Fishrot and brine-itch were two of the most common, and both required hefty doses of antibiotics to clear up.

"Sheriff ordered me to pay restitution for a little accident that I had last week. She also made it a condition of my release that I earn the money myself. So I'm stuck with the day-drag for a few weeks until I can make seven hundred dollars to pay off the Hoffmans."

I tried to suppress a laugh. The Hoffmans owned a beach house down by the shore of Bedlam City Park, a dawn-till-dusk beach park. "What did you do?"

"I might have gotten pie-eyed and crashed, uninvited, at their place for a few hours." He grinned at me, and his lifeguard good looks gave him a roguish, please-trust-me vibe. "Say, Maddy—you wouldn't by chance have some work I can do to pay off my fine in a less...banal way, would you?"

That *did* make me snort. "The fact that you know the word 'banal' is good for a tip, but no, Gillymack, I am not fronting you the money, and I am not hiring you. I bet you did more than break in to their house. What did you steal? And I'll have a triple-shot chocolate thunder mocha."

He put in the order. "Please pull through to the window ahead."

As I eased forward—there was a line forming behind me—I quickly searched my purse for a stray ten-dollar bill. I wasn't about to hand him my credit card. I didn't trust him, even if he handled it in plain sight the entire time.

When I got to the window, he handed me the drink and I gave him the tenspot. "Keep the change. So, tell me, what on earth did you do to warrant a seven-hundred-dollar fine?"

He shrugged, winking. "I might have taken a pisser on their designer sofa. But hey, I was asleep. I didn't know what I was doing."

And *that* was classic Gillymack. As I choked down a cough and drove off, I thought once again how much more entertaining it was to live in Bedlam than back in Seattle.

AFTER A STOP at Freddie's—a chain department store—I eased into a spot by the dry cleaner's. Aegis had asked me to pick up his leather pants. He owned more than one pair, but as he said, you just can't wear leather pants more than a few days in a row without them becoming ripe. Even though he didn't sweat, they picked up his scent and trust me, vampire balls and dick? Give off a heady lusty scent, indeed.

The Boys of Bedlam had a gig coming up in a week at the Rainbow Dance Machine—a new club.

They usually played at the Utopia, but Jack-Az, the owner, was on his annual pilgrimage to his home in the Black Forest. Black Forest as in *Germany*. The crusty old bear shifter didn't trust anybody else to run the joint while he was going, so the Utopia was closed for the month of March.

I picked up the pants, dropped off my ritual gown, and chatted for a few minutes with the owner. As I came out of the shop, I was so engrossed in my thoughts that I ran right into a woman who was passing by, tripping her up.

"Pardon me, I'm sorry!" I knelt by the prone woman. She was pale as cream, with jet black hair and ruby lips, and as she pushed herself up, I couldn't help but stare. She had the biggest boobs I'd ever seen. I was big, but she had to be a J-cup at least.

She cleared her throat. "Eyes up here, girlie."

I shook my head, blushing. "I'm sorry. I didn't mean..." Pausing, I finally found my words. "I didn't mean to trip you up. Here, can I help you?"

I held out my hand and she took it, leveraging herself to her feet. She was too thin for those breasts, I thought. Either they were silicone or she wasn't human. She was also wearing the weirdest outfit I had seen in a long time, and I had seen just about everything.

She had on a mid-calf poufy skirt. The skirt was red, and over it, she was wearing a black dirndl apron, and a white shirt. A big blue bow was affixed to the top of her hair, looking way too goofy to even try to pass for the Lolita look. White knee socks and black patent Mary Janes completed the slightly deranged, cartoonish look. As she brushed herself off, I tried not to stare.

"Are you hurt? I hope I didn't—"

"No, I'm not hurt. I've got so much material in this skirt I'd be well padded if I fell off a cliff." She paused, frowning. "You have a cigarette?"

Maybe it was time to back away slowly. "Um, no, I don't smoke. If you're all right—"

"Then maybe you can point me to the nearest hotel. My friends and I need a place to stay for a few days while we're here on...a job. Our host told us to find a hotel because his is fully booked." She let out a sigh as if the weight of the world had just landed on her shoulders.

I tried to keep my mouth shut. I knew I'd regret it if I didn't, but somehow I found myself opening my lips and the words just tumbled out. "I own a bed-and-breakfast. The Bewitching Bedlam. I have two open rooms. Possibly three."

While Mr. Mosswood was still at the B&B, two days back, old Mrs. Periwinkle had suddenly sprung the news that she had bought a house and was leaving for home to complete arrangements before moving to Bedlam. The house happened to be next door to me, so she was going to be my neighbor. The news both delighted me and made me worry. The slightly addled Mrs. Periwinkle was going to have a working kitchen, including a gas range.

The long shot was, as a result we had two guest rooms available, plus my private guest room that I could rent out if I wanted.

The woman stared at me for a second, then

nodded. "If you don't mind if we double up in the rooms, that would be great. Or triple up. We can make do with sleeping bags if necessary."

Triple up? I instantly regretted making the offer. "I'm really not sure—"

"Gimme your address, doll, and we'll be over in an hour, after we finish for the day."

Blankly, because I couldn't seem to find the words to tell her no—after all, I had knocked her down pretty hard—I handed her my card. She took it, nodded and started down the street.

"Wait a minute," I called, turning around. "I'm Maddy. What's your name?"

She glanced over her shoulder. "Just call me Snow, babe. Just call me Snow."

I SAT IN my CR-V, hands on the steering wheel, practicing my speech. "I'm sorry, but it looks like we don't have the room after all. Here's a brochure that lists several other hotels in the area. I suggest you try the Viola Hotel. They're sure to have the room." I said it over and over until it rolled off my tongue. Then I called Sandy.

"What up?" She was panting, so I knew she was on her treadmill.

"*What up* is that I think I just invited Snow White to stay at the Bewitching Bedlam."

The panting stopped. "Come again?"

"I just knocked Snow White down in front of the dry cleaner's, and ended up inviting her to stay at the Bewitching Bedlam."

Sandy spoke very slowly. "Honey, does your head still hurt? I thought I just heard you say you knocked down Snow White—"

"Oh, stop it. I'm perfectly fine, except that I seem to have stepped into the world of the Grimm Brothers. Snow White doesn't really exist, does she? I mean, this has to be cosplay, right?"

Most faerie tales were based on true stories, but somehow the thought of Snow White being a thirty-something, cigarette-smoking, dirndl-wearing goth girl who was about to descend on my house with her dwarves had thrown me for a loop.

Sandy was laughing so hard she was gasping for air.

"Excuse me, but this is a *real* problem."

"Right," she gasped out. Then, after a moment, she sobered enough to talk. "Maddy, love. Whether or not she actually exists doesn't matter. What does matter is you have someone who either *thinks* she's Snow White, *is* Snow White, or is *playing* the role of Snow White on the way to your house. If she makes you uncomfortable, tell her to find another place to stay."

"I hit her hard enough to knock her on her ass. By accident, of course, but I kind of feel like I owe her something."

"Did you break any bones?"

"Well, no."

"Did you draw blood?"

I let out a sigh. "No."

"Then you owe her nothing. Seriously, though, I am coming over to your place. I need to see what the cat dragged in." She snickered. "Speaking of cats, you didn't make any stray wishes on Bubba's belly, did you?"

I glared at the phone. "You're just being contrary now. Shuddup. I have to go buy something to eat. Aegis forgot to make me anything for lunch, and he warned me that if I ate the snacks for the guests' tea again, he would let them go hungry."

Sandy let out another laugh, this one from the gut. "Oh, Maddy. I'll see you in an hour." And with that, she hung up.

I FINISHED MY errands—stopping at the post office to pick up my forwarded mail, then at Geek Parade to pick up my new laptop. My old one still worked but it had been making some odd noises lately, and I didn't want to wait until it bluescreened me or refused to boot up. Last stop was at the Chicken-Chicken Shack for a bucket of chicken, coleslaw, and mac 'n cheese. I arrived home ten minutes before Snow was supposed to come over. Sandy was waiting for me in the kitchen. Thornton had let her in.

"He's handy, I'll tell you that," she said. "And delicious to look at."

I stared at her. "Oh, Sandy, you *didn't*. What about Max?"

"For fuck's sake, just because I say a man's handy doesn't mean—" Sandy stopped, then raised her mocha at me. "You have me there, but no, I *didn't.* Nor am I planning to. I just meant that not only is the place whistle-clean, but he makes a mean mocha."

Relaxing, I slid into a chair at the table, setting my bags on the floor. "Thank gods, because I really don't want to find a new housekeeper *again.*" I glanced around. "Say, have you seen Bubba?"

She shook her head. "He's probably in some snit over something. Is that chicken I smell?"

I nodded. "Yeah, for us. Not for Snow White, or whoever the hell she is. I swear, this town attracts all types, doesn't it?" I set the chicken and sides on the table as Sandy grabbed plates and silverware and set them out for us.

"Well, look at the name. You name a town after an asylum, what do you expect?" She helped herself, piling her plate high. The woman ate and ate and never gained an ounce. I ate and ate, and ended up with a nice layer of padding.

Thornton peeked in the kitchen. "A Miss White to see you...with her...friends." The look on his face was a mix of bewildered and amused.

"Oh, man. Show them into the living room. I'll be right there." I wiped my hands on a napkin and smoothed my skirt. I glanced at Sandy. "Come with me for reinforcement?"

She snickered. "I wouldn't miss this on a bet."

As we entered the living room, I found myself staring at Snow, who was now wearing a skin-tight red dress that barely covered the down-under region of her world. Standing behind her were seven dwarves. Real dwarves. As in *hi-ho, hi-ho*, Tolkienish grumpy men, short in stature but bulky in muscle. They were all bearded and wearing man-buns. The fact that they were clad in jeans along with muscle-tops did nothing to comfort me, nor did the fact that the room was now full of musky man-scent.

"Hey," one of them said. He had bright red hair and a well-trimmed beard. "We appreciate the lodgings. Every place in town seems booked up and we thought we were staying at our host's inn, but apparently not. Mercury retrograde, you know—miscommunications are flying."

Behind me, Sandy choked back a snicker. I tried to elbow her but she dodged just in time. She sat down, watching with what I could only peg as a snarky glee.

"So, who's your host?" I figured it best to find out who had invited this group to town. I found myself wondering just what they did. Entertainers, perhaps? Musical group? Maybe they entertained at kids' parties?

"You might know him. Ralph Greyhoof. He runs the Heart's Desire Inn."

I closed my eyes and counted to ten.

Of course it was Ralph. It was always Ralph. I really didn't want to know what kind of gig Snow was playing at Ralph's, or why. I was about to tell them *No dice, find another place* when Thornton appeared at the doorway.

"Maddy? There's a phone call you might want to take. In your office." He looked so serious that I let out a sigh and nodded.

"I'll be back in a moment. Sandy, keep our guests...entertained."

As I slipped out of the room, I ran over all the excuses I could think of as to why I couldn't let them have the rooms. Maybe I'd get lucky and they couldn't pay, so I could say *No money, no room.*

"What's up?" I frowned as Thornton handed me the phone.

"It's the bank. The lady said there's an emergency with your account."

"All right." I brought the receiver to my ear. "Maudlin Gallowglass here. How may I help you?"

"Ms. Gallowglass, this is Amanda, down at Bedlam Star Credit Union. I'm afraid that Mrs. Periwinkle's check has bounced. I thought I'd call you because once I process the NSF fee, it will leave your business account overdrawn."

Overdrawn? *How the hell.* I stared at the phone. "But I have fifty-five thousand dollars in that account. How could it be overdrawn?"

Amanda let out a *tsk*ing sound. "This morning you moved fifty-four thousand dollars to your account in Dubai. The transaction was processed online. That means when we deduct the $1,420 for Mrs. Periwinkle's check and the NFS fee, it will leave you overdrawn by almost five hundred dollars."

My stomach lurched. "I don't *have* an account in Dubai. I'll be right down. Don't go anywhere and don't process that check yet, please."

I slammed the phone down, sweating. I had bought the mansion outright, and paid in cash for all the renovations. That fifty-five thousand dollars was the rest of my savings. How could they have transferred all my money to a foreign account without my permission? While I was pissed at Mrs. Periwinkle for bouncing a check on me, I realized that if she hadn't, I wouldn't have known about this for a while. I raced back out to the living room.

"I'm sorry, I *have* to go downtown to talk to the bank about something." I stared at Snow and her retinue. As much as I didn't want them in the Be-witching Bedlam, if my savings was gone for good, then I needed cash. "Three rooms. Sandy and Thornton will settle you in. One hundred bucks a night per room, with twenty-five dollars per extra guest. Cash in advance."

And with everybody staring, I raced out of the house and jumped in my car. Whoever the scam-mer in Dubai was, he had better pray I didn't find out his name. Because once I found him, he'd be staked out on top of an anthill, covered in honey. Red ants. Under the blazing sun.

Chapter 4

"LET'S GO OVER this once again." I was ready to smack the nice credit union representative over the head with a sock full of pennies. "I didn't go online this morning and I didn't transfer money to a stranger's account in Dubai. I don't live in Dubai. I've never even been to Dubai. I don't own a bed-and-breakfast in Dubai. Why the *hell* would I transfer money to Dubai?" My voice rose perilously close to a screech.

Amanda finally called the manager.

"It's about time. I've only been asking to talk to your manager for the past twenty minutes." I was grumpy and not inclined to be particularly diplomatic.

While Amanda ran over what had happened with the tall, professional-looking woman wearing a blue pantsuit, a tidy blond chignon, and heels that jacked her up to at least six-three, I tried to control my anger.

The manager—whose nametag read "Emily Chambers"—sat down at the desk, motioning for Amanda to back away. Her hands flew over the keys as she examined my account. I tried to practice my deep breathing. The meditation always worked in magic, but I kept coming back to the image of a generically squirrelly scam artist, grinning as he rolled around on my money.

"Here we go. Yes, this morning at three A.M. we logged a transaction to transfer fifty-four thousand dollars. It was automatically logged as suspicious. Normally, someone should have contacted you, but...oh dear. Oh dear."

That didn't sound good. "Oh dear *what*?"

The bridge of Emily's nose suddenly furrowed as she ran her fingers along a line on the screen. "Well, for heaven's sake, it looks like the alert was canceled by—some program that I don't recognize. The transaction was approved and put through."

I rubbed my forehead. "You can transfer it back, right? No problems?" I knew I was being wildly optimistic, but sometimes grasping at straws seemed the thing to do.

"I'm sorry." Emily flashed me a patient smile. "We'll return the money to your account, of course, but this is going to involve alerting the police and the FBI. This appears to be an international incident. I have to talk to my supervisor in the main branch of the credit union about how we're going to go about this. I estimate a ten-day lag before we'll be able to take the hold off your account. In the meantime, we'll waive any NSF fees that come in because of this." She beamed, as if the problem were solved.

"You have to be joking. Ten days? I had fifty-five thousand dollars in there—" I jumped up, leaning on the desk. "I want access to my money. This is the credit union's fault—"

"Yes, I know, and I'm so sorry about this. But there's nothing I can do to rush this through. But we *will* fix the matter, I guarantee you that. Meanwhile, I'll raise the limit on your credit card for the next month, to give you leeway."

Emily Chambers quickly grabbed my hand, shook it, and took off.

BY THE TIME I left the bank, I wanted to punch somebody hard. Or kick something. Or throw a few bottles. Or slam a fireball into the side of some building. Preferably my ex's house. Not that he had anything to do with this, but the way the credit union had jacked me around felt exactly like all the ways he had tried to deal with me.

I contemplated going somewhere out in the woods and blowing off some steam, but somehow I doubted that the wood nymphs—who were legion in our area—would appreciate my version of target shooting. Neither would the dryads, come to think of it.

So I once again found myself pulling into the drive-thru at Bouncing Goats Espresso Shack. Gillymack was nowhere in sight, for which I was relieved. I was too pissed to laugh at his jokes or humor him. I ordered a quad-shot white chocolate cherry mocha.

On the way home, I called the sheriff. My cell was plugged into the VOXware unit I had bought for my CR-V and I was wearing my headset. The phone rang twice and then a calm, level-headed voice answered.

"Delia Walters here. What's going on, Maddy?"

"You have caller ID, I see."

"Yeah, I do." Delia sounded busy, but friendly. We knew and liked each other. "So what's up?"

"I have a problem. My credit union should be contacting you today at some point, but I'm lighting a fire now. Somebody in Dubai hijacked my checking account and stole fifty-four thousand dollars from me. The credit union okayed the transaction rather than contacting me."

"Holy fuck. I'll be over later. I'm the only one manning the fort right now, but I can come over at five, when the night shift comes on watch."

"Thanks. I want to find these scum suckers and smash them flat."

"I don't blame you."

As the call disconnected, it occurred to me that I'd better run a virus check on the computer. Maybe a trojan had gotten through, or something equally as dangerous. Whatever the case, I was out a buttload of money and even though the bank promised to reimburse me, it sounded suspiciously like I wouldn't be seeing a penny for some time.

I pulled into my driveway and slammed out of my car, taking care not to spill my mocha. My mood had gone south about as far as it could go. As I headed into the house, through the kitchen, I found Sandy sitting there, a traumatized look on her face. Snow White and her retinue of burly men were nowhere to be seen.

Sandy glanced at me as I slumped into a chair. "Do you know what your newest guests do for a living?"

I rolled my eyes. "I have a pretty good guess. I really don't want to know, do I?"

She let out a strangled laugh. "It seems that Ralph Greyhoof and his brothers are running a sideline. They make bargain-basement porn flicks and sell them on the net."

The thought of the Greyhoof boys at the helm of a seedy porn industry didn't faze me at all. It seemed all too fitting. "Lovely. Which means that Snow and her boys..."

"Are porn stars in his latest flick, *Snow White and the Seven Whorves*."

I blinked. "That's a horrible name. It doesn't even...oh, never mind. So, did you find out who Snow really is? I don't think she's human."

Sandy rubbed her forehead. "I really wish I had some brain bleach. There are things that—once you know about them, cannot be unknown."

"That bad?"

She nodded. "I have no idea how he did it, but it seems that Ralph decided having the real thing would be better than hiring actors. Snow says he considers himself to be the next Alfred Hitchcock, only of the porn brigade. Anyway, he did some-thing that brought Snow White and the dwarves out of the book. Before he'll let them return, he's making them act in his movie."

"You have to be kidding. That's sex slavery." I pulled out my phone. "I'm calling Delia. He has to be breaking some law—"

"Nope. Because when you think about it, technically Snow White doesn't exist, not in this form. The only reason she's here is that he's created an automaton, like our holeos. Only she's a lot more substantial. If the spell's broken, she'll vanish back into the book. So no, he's skirting the law in a most unsavory way."

Sandy crossed to the fridge, where she brought out a plate filled with chicken and macaroni and cheese. "I made sure to save your favorite pieces," she said, sliding it into the microwave. "So, tell me what happened at the bank? Who do I need to kill?"

That's one thing about best friends. They always knew how to make you feel better.

"Thanks—I'm starved. And as to our target, well, somebody in Dubai is living it up on my money." I told her everything that had happened. "I need access to my money. I mean, it's not like I'm going to lose the house or starve, but that's *my money*. I need reserves while we continue to keep the business running. Aegis has offered to help before, but I'm pretty sure he doesn't have as much as most vampires accumulate. Rachel cleaned him out, for the most part. Or at least, I think she did. And while it's a lot easier for him to make money than me, I have no desire to be a burden on him. Especially financially."

I finally ran out of steam and sat there in silence, drinking my mocha while Sandy brought me the plate of food. "Where's Bubba? Did you see him? I could use a good dose of that fuzzy love right now."

"I haven't seen him." Sandy glanced around. "Maybe we should go look for him? By the way, I set up Snow and the boys in their rooms and got the cash from them. You're going to have a word with Ralph about setting his creations free on the community, aren't you?"

"You know me all too well. I'm looking for a punching bag right now."

I began to call for Bubba. Sandy and I searched through the main floor, then ran up to the second floor. Bubba wasn't anywhere to be found, and he wasn't in Mr. Mosswood's room, either. Then I dashed downstairs to see if he had somehow gotten himself locked in the basement. Sandy followed, slowly. She was leery of my basement—it still had a creepy feel to it.

There were any number of cubbyholes where he could be hiding, but I motioned for Sandy to wait while I slipped into Aegis's lair. There, sitting in the rocking chair, was Franny, staring at his coffin. And curled on top of the coffin was Bubba. He lifted his head as I slipped in the room.

"Bubs...where have you been? How did you get locked in here? Are you okay?" I lifted him into my arms and he curled up against my shoulder. "Do you feel okay? I've been looking all over for you."

Franny cleared her throat. "He was here when I got here a few minutes ago."

I stared at her. "Do you sit and watch my boyfriend's coffin very often?"

She shrugged. "Only when I need to think. I always leave before he wakes up because he says it freaks him out to have me watching him."

"Then maybe you could respect his wishes and not do it." I carried Bubba upstairs and over to the table, where I lay him down and examined him. That he was letting me turn him this way and that and prod him wasn't a good sign.

"Is he okay?" Sandy had followed me.

"I don't know. He's awfully quiet. Cjinns don't get sick very often, so I'm not entirely sure what the problem is. I need to visit the doctor." There were several specialists in the PretCom community who took care of all variety of Supes. "Who do you take Mr. Peabody to?"

Sandy looked at me. "*Really?* Mr. Peabody is all skunk. I take him to a vet."

"Okay. Then I guess..." I frowned. I hadn't needed a doctor in years, except when Aegis's ex-girlfriend Rachel had messed me up a few months back. "I suppose I can just call the clinic and ask."

"Here, let me call them for you. I have them on speed dial."

At my look, she gave me a quick shrug. "Remember, I'm taking care of Derry's daughter, Jenna." Derry, Sandy's friend, was on an extended world tour. "She's thirteen and kids are at the doctors on a perpetual basis, it seems. Two weeks ago, she fell while she was doing some wildcrafting. I got a call from a nurse at Neverfall that my ward had broken two fingers, cut her lip on her tooth, and had a badly bruised knee. It was two in the morning. I gather they were learning to harvest mandrake."

"Oh, yeah. And mandrake always has to be harvested under the cover of night."

She paused, then said into her phone, "My friend needs to bring her cjinn in for a checkup.... We're not sure, but he's lethargic and hasn't eaten today." She waited for a moment, then pulled a notebook out of her purse and scribbled something down. "Farrows? Dr. Jordan Farrows, at three P.M. tomorrow? All right. The name? Maudlin Gallowglass... Oh, of the cjinn? Bubba. Yes, I said Bubba. All right. Thank you."

She dropped her phone back into her purse. "The nurse said that if he gets worse, go to Urgent Care, but if he stays like this, you have an appointment tomorrow with—"

"Let me guess. Jordan Farrows? Thanks. Where's the place located?"

"The Bedlam Medical Center, third floor, room 311. That's where Farrows's office is. Be there at three. I'll text the info to you to make sure you have it." She reached out and ruffled Bubba's head. "Hey, little dude. You want me to rub your belly?"

But Bubba merely looked at her, then quietly got up and gingerly jumped to the floor. As he headed over to his bed by the rocking chair, I found myself really beginning to worry. Bubba and I might argue, but he was my heart and soul, and I couldn't imagine life without the little guy.

DELIA ARRIVED SHORTLY after five. Aegis was still asleep and would be till after seven, thanks to the damned daylight saving time that we'd just switched over to. Sandy had gone home, and I was trying to figure out how to deal with my overly full B&B and my empty bank balance. But mostly, I was just concerned about Bubba, who had eaten a little, then gone back to sleep.

Delia Walters wasn't just the sheriff of Bedlam, but she was a werewolf as well. She wasn't a great beauty, but she was smart as a whip and as tough as one, too. Her hair was strawberry blond, and until recently she had worn it in a long braid. But today, she was sporting a new 'do—a short shag that skimmed her collar. The new cut brought her into the twenty-first century. Short, sturdy, and entirely focused on business, Delia was a whirlwind. Nothing got past her observant eye, although her logic sometimes interfered with her intuition. She had a tendency to go by the book, even if it didn't fully jibe with the facts. But she was good at her job, and I liked her.

She took copious notes as I told her what had transpired at the credit union. After I finished, she tucked her pad and pen back in her pocket.

"They haven't called the station yet. I'll bet they're trying to lawyer up before you sue them. I'll drop by tomorrow morning and light a fire under Ms. Emily Chambers." She paused, then asked, "Have you lost your credit cards recently? Checkbook come up missing? Do you use their online banking system?"

"No, no, and yes. I suppose someone could have

gotten my information some other way. I do a lot of online shopping and have my Spell-Bay account hooked up to my bank account."

"Not the best idea. Change your passwords immediately and have someone check out your computer. The hackers are so good now that it's almost impossible for most AV software to catch all the .exe programs. All it takes is one click of the mouse on a suspicious email and boom, you've opened yourself up to strangers the world 'round. I hear there's a new wave of scammers and hackers focusing on PretCom instead of humans."

"Why?" That didn't make sense to me. We were fewer in number than humans and usually more dangerous.

"Think about it. We live a lot longer and generally accumulate a lot more wealth. How many humans do you know with over fifty thousand dollars in their bank account?"

"But I got that money from selling my condo. That's all I came away from the divorce with. Craig saw to that." I wanted to protest, but then stopped. "Though when you think about it, I guess you're right. Not all PretCom are rich, not by a long shot. But a number of us have a tidy amount in savings, especially vampires and witches. The Weres and Shifters don't seem to accumulate as much."

"That's because we don't use magic very much. It's easier to make money when you have glamour at your disposal, or magic to invoke abundance." She laughed. "I'm not picking on you or Aegis. Frankly, like all werewolves, I'm scared of magic, but because I'm the sheriff, I need to keep my fear under control. So I do. But if I wasn't? Don't get me wrong—I like you, Maddy, but I wouldn't want to be your neighbor."

I nodded. Werewolves, especially, had an anathema to magic. And to vampires. And to humans. And to modernization. Delia wasn't a typical member of the pack, that was for sure. Most of the werewolves I knew worked in physically demanding jobs—construction, shipping, park rangers, and forest service personnel, that sort of thing. Their innate fear of fire kept most of them from becoming firefighters, but they made excellent soldiers, lifeguards, and personal trainers.

"So how are things otherwise?" Delia gave me a long look. "I heard a rumor you have a bunch of guests."

I blushed. "Yeah. I have...some very unusual guests. Apparently, Ralph Greyhoof is trying to become a linchpin in the low-budget porn industry." I told her about Snow. "Apparently, I'm now housing porn stars. Porn stars who aren't even real people—who are fresh out of the pages of a fairytale. Honestly, if this happened to anybody else, I'd laugh my head off."

"Be careful. Greyhoof's been on a tear lately and he's not happy at you. I'd love to bust him for illicit activity. Unfortunately, filming a porn flick isn't against the law. Neither is using automatons or holeos in the production of it. But I'll figure out some way to shut him down."

"I wish you would. I wish they'd just move."

"Those brothers are going to be the death of me, I swear. I've got files so thick on all of them that I had to commandeer an entire drawer in the cabinet for them." She laughed and stood up. "Okay, Maddy. I'll call you after I have my chat with Emily tomorrow. Hopefully, we can get them to fast track your case. I'm also calling the FBI."

And with that, she put her hat back on, and headed out.

I glanced at the clock. Still another hour before Aegis woke up. I knelt beside Bubba again. He glanced up at me, looking bereft. But his nose felt cool, and he lazily licked my fingers when I tickled him under the chin.

"Just make sure you stay well, Bub," I said softly. "I really can't deal with you being sick right now. Or ever. You're my special guy, you know?"

Bubba touched my hand with his paw and let out a soft *"Purp."*

As I carried the dishes and cups to the sink, Thornton entered the kitchen. He glanced at Bubba, then at my face.

"Let me take care of those." He took the tray from me. "Why don't you and Bubba go rest?"

Grateful, I accepted. At this moment, that was all I could think of doing.

Chapter 5

BY THE TIME Aegis joined me, I had fallen asleep next to Bubba. I woke as he lightly cupped my shoulders and placed a kiss on my neck.

"Maddy? Maddy, are you okay?" He sounded worried.

I shifted and rubbed my eyes. I had fallen asleep in my clothes and now they were tangled. Aegis sat back, giving me room to sit up and shake them out. I glanced over at Bubba, who was still sleeping quietly. Without a word, I burst into tears.

"Hey, what's wrong? Thornton said you weren't feeling well? Are you sick, love?" Aegis wrapped me in his arms, pulling me close as the sobs came thick and furious.

"Noooo. *I'm* not sick," I said, hiccupping on the phlegm. I cleared my throat. "I think Bubba is. We have an appointment tomorrow to see the doctor. I'm worried about him." I pressed my lips together, trying not to break out in a fresh round of tears. But my heart ached. I loved Bubba, and the thought that something might be wrong with him tore me apart.

"What's wrong with him? Hey, little dude, can you tell us what's wrong?" He reached for Bubba but I stopped him.

"Let him sleep. If he's sick that's the best thing he can do until we get him into the doctor. Today's been a total mess. Dubai ate all my money and we have porn stars staying in the guest rooms." The words tumbled out in a rush. I rubbed my head. Even though I didn't feel sick, I was a little woozy and I felt flushed.

Aegis kissed my forehead again. "What do you mean? Dubai? Porn stars? How can so much have happened since I went to sleep last night?" He handed me a tissue.

I wiped my eyes and blew my nose as I checked on Bubba. He was breathing softly and evenly, and didn't show any signs of distress. "I guess we can leave him here, but I want to make certain he doesn't go hide under anything in a different room, so I'm going to close him in here. He has a litter box in the bathroom here, too."

"Good idea. Go wash your face and then you can tell me about everything while I fix you some dinner." He patted me on the ass as I headed toward the bathroom. I washed my face, thinking I did look a little flushed. But then again, I was stressed, and I'd been sleeping on my stomach, which I seldom did, and my face had been pressed against the pillow. I went to the bathroom and washed my hands, and finally, straightening my skirt and top, returned to the bedroom. Aegis and I headed downstairs after gently closing the door to keep Bubba in my room.

Thornton was bustling through the kitchen, carrying a stack of dishes.

I glanced at the clock. "What's going on? We don't serve dinner—"

"Snow and her gang ordered pizza and asked for dishes to eat it on. I figured you wouldn't mind since they paid cash. The delivery driver said they tipped him a hundred bucks, by the way. You might want to rethink your room charges if they stay a second night." He grinned. "Franny was with them, asking them about what it's like to live in a book. I don't think they quite knew what to say. And don't worry, they're all dressed."

I shuddered at the image that conjured up. I really didn't want to think about a gang-bang scene starring Snow and her entourage. "Fine."

Aegis headed to the fridge. "What do you want for dinner? It's already eight."

I sat down on one of the stools at the counter, leaning my elbows on the granite. "Soup would be good, and biscuits?"

"Chicken soup?"

I nodded. One of my go-to comfort foods was always chicken noodle soup and those biscuits in a can that were all fluff and no substance. Aegis shook his head, but he was smiling as he opened the cupboard to pull out a can of soup and preheated the oven.

"So tell me what happened today. What's going

on with Dubai? And why do we have a bevy of porn stars upstairs? Thornton told me we were hosting a kinky fairytale revue." He plunked a bottle of water down in front of me. "Drink."

I pulled a long sip of the sparkling mineral water, then wiped my mouth and launched into the gritty details. "So Delia's going to try to hustle the credit union into gear and I'm going over to see Ralph Greyhoof and read him the riot act."

"You don't *need* to tangle with Ralph. You already escalated this little feud of yours when you turned him in for illegal fireworks last month. And the month before that, when you cast a spell on the snow in his yard so that it all melted and flooded his basement."

"He deserved everything I've done. He wouldn't stop whining about the weather and I got tired of listening to him. I was just helping out." I tried to play innocent, but Aegis may have had a point. The illegal fireworks? Yeah, my complaint was justified. But the flooded basement—that might have been going a tad too far.

"Well, I may not need to, but I'm feeling bitchy as hell and ready to rumble." I upended the bottle and finished the water, burping as I finished. "Excuse me."

"Um hm. Leave the satyrs alone. You don't need them pissed at you again."

"Pissed at me? It's not my fault they're running a brothel masquerading as an inn. It's not my problem that he decided to bring Snow White out of a storybook and force her to act in a porn movie for him—"

Aegis laughed as he stirred water into my soup—half a can. I liked it strong. "She and the dwarves could have refused."

I blinked. "Ralph won't let them return to the pages until they finish the movie."

Aegis stopped in mid-stir. "You have to be kidding me."

"Nope, but since technically Snow White doesn't exist, there's no way Delia can stop him. Snow and the boys are pretty much constructs, like my holeos, only they're more substantial and they have more autonomy. He yanked them off the pages and now he won't put them back until they finish working for him." I poked at the water bottle, feeling all grumpy again. "I *really* want to go over and yell at him."

Aegis snarled. "I want to go over and beat the crap out of him. Constructs or not, that's a fucking horrible thing to do to somebody." He set the pan on the stove, but didn't turn on the burner. After he popped open the biscuits and lined the baking sheet with them, he slid them into the oven. "Dinner in twelve minutes."

"*You* go over and it makes matters a little dicey. I go over and all he can do is badmouth the business. I promise I won't try to turn him into a frog." I fluttered my eyelashes, smiling at him. "Please don't try to stop me."

Aegis let out a gruff snort. "After what you just told me, I don't think I'd have the heart to stop you. All right. At least let me put an infusion of cash into your anemic bank account. I told you I do have a stash."

"You might need that someday, and it can't be that much, right? You were squatting in the house when I bought it."

"I was squatting in the house because I didn't think I'd want to stay here, doofus. And I have more tucked away than you think I do." He arched his eyebrows. "I can front you what you need. Hell, I'll give it to you, if you like."

I stared at him. "I thought you weren't that well off. I always assumed—"

"That because I'm a vampire, I'd own a big mansion if I had money? I was always too much of a nomad. That changed when I met you, Maddy." He turned on the soup, glancing at me, a serious look on his face. "I feel at home here. At home, with you."

Once again, the sense that we belonged together, that somewhere, deep inside, we had known each other over the centuries, hit home. He leaned across the counter to stroke my face. "I love you. I *know* you."

Catching his fingers in mine, I brought them to my lips and kissed them slowly, my heart beating so loud I knew he could hear it. I pressed my lips to his palm. "I *know* you. I don't know how we were brought together, but it feels as though it had to happen."

We stood there for a moment, just basking in the sensation of touching one another. Then, he slowly withdrew his hand and pulled the biscuits out of the oven, ladled up my soup, and pushed the bowl over to me. A plate of the biscuits followed, along with butter and honey, and for the first time all day, I felt calm.

As I buttered one of the biscuits and spooned up the soup, he began rinsing off the dishes and stacking them in the dishwasher.

"So," he said, wiping his hands on a dish towel, "will you let me help you out? After all, the Bewitching Bedlam is important to me, too."

Heaving a long sigh, I finally nodded. "All right. When you put it like that, okay. But we're going to the credit union and make a new account that we both can access."

"Sounds good to me," he said, brushing a strand of his hair back. "I have rehearsal tonight. You don't mind if I go, do you? If you want me to stay home because of Bubba, I will."

I shook my head. "No, but before you go, would you be interested in a little dessert?" I was tired, the day had seemed interminably long, and the food hit me like a sledgehammer. I probably would have fallen asleep if I hadn't already had a long nap. "I don't want to wake up Bubba, though."

Aegis laughed. "Let's go in the parlor. We can lock the door and nobody will disturb us."

Finishing up the last biscuit—I could easily eat the whole can of ten, and usually did—I wiped my hands, popped a mint, and followed him into the parlor.

AEGIS LOCKED THE door and leaned against it, eyeing me with those silken eyes of his. I caught my breath, holding it as I shivered. My hand fluttered to my throat as he slowly began to walk toward me, his hands on his belt buckle.

"Undress for me, Maddy. Let me see your beautiful naked body." He liked to watch me, liked to see me take off every speck of clothing.

I slid the tank over my head, dropping it on the back of the sofa, and then reached around to unhook my bra. As my breasts bounced free, he let out a low laugh—one that whispered *I'm hungry and I'm going to eat you up.* I stroked my breasts, lingering over my nipples, and Aegis's eyes grew bright, his lips curving into a cunning smile.

"Now, the skirt."

Reaching for the side zipper, I slowly lowered it, taking my time. Aegis grunted as I began to shimmy it down over my hips until my panties were showing. They were purple hip huggers, with a gold design embroidered on them. As the skirt dropped to the floor and I stepped out of it, I hooked my thumbs on both sides and began to lower them, as well.

"You're so fucking gorgeous." Aegis paused, slaking me with his gaze.

Feeling more naked than nude, I slid my hands down my hips, tilting my head to give him a coquettish look. "Like what you see?"

"Yes." His voice was throaty.

"Want what you see?"

In answer, he slid his jeans down, and his cock popped up, erect and strong and hard. "Hard as a rock, and ready." As he undressed, I debated on whether to play the come-and-catch-me game we played, but then decided I just wanted him. Now. Here. Without any subterfuge.

I crossed to the rug in front of the fireplace and knelt, sitting back on my knees. Aegis blurred for a second, and then, faster than I could see, he was behind me, holding me against his chest, his arms curling around me. I leaned back into his embrace, tilting my head to the side as he pressed his lips to my neck.

"You drank recently, right?" I didn't want to break the mood, but the scent of my blood—and he could smell it right through my pores—was like ambrosia.

"Yes, when I woke. I had two bottles of blood. So, love, no worry. As much as I want to taste you, I can control myself," he murmured into my ear. "Let me love you."

As he cupped my breasts, I relaxed into his embrace, closing my eyes as he fingered my nipples, squeezing gently, twirling them with two fingers. His cock was hard, pressed against my back, and my own desire heightened, my sex throbbing for his touch.

"Lean forward on your hands and knees," he whispered.

I obeyed, leaning forward. He let go of me and turned, lying on his back as he slid between my legs. He reached up, took hold of my hips with both hands, and brought me down onto his face, slowly positioning me until his tongue massaged my clit. As he began to suck, I let out a soft moan, undulating against the feel of his tongue against me, of his hands on my skin. The tension built quickly, making me dizzy. I tried to catch my breath and couldn't, and then—abruptly and without warning—a ripple began to swallow me up. Startled, I yelled out his name as I came, hard.

"Already? You really were hungry, weren't you?" He laughed, pulling me down to lie on top of him. His cock pressed hard against my belly and I ached, wanting him inside me. Oh, great mother of all that was sexy, I wanted him deep inside.

"I want you. All of you," I said with a ragged pant. "Come inside?"

Aegis lifted my hips. "Climb aboard, babe."

I slid down his cock, enfolding him with my pussy. I was wet—so wet that I felt like I was dripping, and his girth slid neatly inside, widening me, stretching me with one good hard thrust that pierced my core, forcing my lower lips apart.

"Ride me, babe. Ride me hard," he said, his eyes flashing with crimson rings around their deep brown.

I began to rock, then leaned forward so that I could balance my hands against the floor to either side of his chest. I swiveled, every nuance of his shaft exploring my inner core. He began to thrust, holding my waist tight as he pumped deeper into me. After a moment, the room was silent, heavy with only the sound of our breathing. Aegis flipped me over, driving himself between my legs, thrusting so hard that it felt like he was penetrating every fiber of my body. He bent down, catching one nipple between his teeth, and sucked hard. The sensation rippled through me from my breast down to my cunt, exploding as he lowered one hand between my legs, and tweaked my clit again.

"You like this? You like me in you?" His voice hung heavy with lust, like grapes on a vine that were almost ready to burst.

I nodded, my teeth chattering. I couldn't speak, I was so caught in the web of passion we were building between us. All I could do was wrap my arms around him, moaning his name in little sighs, each one a little higher than before. In turn, he drove himself faster, letting out a series of grunts, whispering my name as I spiraled, caught by the vortex of hunger that was building around me. And then—I could stand it no longer. I quit resisting and let out a stifled scream as I tumbled into the orgasm again, coming so hard my lips tingled.

Aegis stiffened between my legs, holding me taut, a guttural cry lodged in his throat. A moment, and he thrust a few more times and then, he relaxed in my arms and draped forward against me.

I slid my arms around him as the sex haze tumbled around us, pulling us into a whirl of love and satiation and the rain of rose petals that fell gently around us, thanks to my magic.

WE SHOWERED TOGETHER and dressed, and Aegis left for rehearsal shortly after. I petted Bubba, who was awake but still lying on the bed. "Dude, you need to get better. I love you, you crusty old cjinn. Quit scaring me."

A knock sounded at my bedroom door and I

answered. It was Thornton.

"I'm sorry to bother you, Maddy, but Snow wants to know if you have any booze in the house." He gave me one of those "I can't believe I have to ask this" looks.

I frowned. Snow might be paying well, but she wasn't getting my stash. "Tell her no. If she wants liquor she can go to a nightclub or bar or the store." I opened the door a little wider. "If you want, I'll go tell her. In fact, it's only nine-thirty. I think I'm going to go give Ralph a talking-to."

I had put on jeans and a light knit tank top, and I slid my phone in my pocket, shut my bedroom door behind me, and before Thornton could say a word, headed out the door.

It wasn't far to Ralph's place. The Heart's Desire Inn was only a mile or so away, which was part of the problem. At least for Ralph. He really didn't like the fact that I had opened a bed-and-breakfast so close to his place. But truth was, we had entirely different clientele, even though he didn't want to admit it.

The driveway in front of the inn was pretty packed. It looked like they had a full house, which was good in one way. It would keep Ralph and his brothers from spouting off about how I was stealing their business. I slammed out of my car, tossed my purse over my shoulder, and headed inside. As I entered the lobby, sure enough, Ralph was there, behind the counter. Which meant his brothers were probably off on a bender. They took turns roughhousing with their friends.

"Yo, Ralph." Nobody else was in the lobby as I

crossed to the desk. The inn was about one and a half times the size of my B&B.

He frowned as I came into view. "What do *you* want?"

"I'm here because your skanky actors showed up, asking for a place to stay and I really wish you'd make certain you have room for a bunch of horny dwarves and their queen bee before telling them to go forth and find accommodations. What you're doing is bad enough without sticking me with the porn star brigade. At least they can pay their bill but damn it, what the *hell* are you thinking?" I was getting louder as I went. Sex had relaxed me, but all my irritation of the day came sweeping back.

He gave me a side-eye look. "Maddy, you're pushing it."

"No, *I'm* not the one pushing it this time. You are. You were last time. You're always falling into some screwball thing. It's bad enough you helped a vampire set me up to be killed—"

"You just can't let it alone, can you? That's the trouble with witches. You have long memories and you nurse grudges like a baby on a tit." He slammed his hands on the counter, leaning across to glare at me.

Ralph was six-three, muscled up the wazoo, and wore shorts revealing his silky brown goat legs. The hair on them shimmered—at least he kept himself clean. His eyes were wide and slightly slanted, the color of rich topaz, and his hair hung to his butt. Usually he kept it braided, but today it was hanging loose. I also knew he had a huge cock.

Not from experience—at least not with him, but from my past exploits I knew full well that satyrs were always over-endowed. They were horny as hell, usually fun, but self-serving in far too many ways. And, unfortunately, for me *and* the rest of Bedlam, Ralph and his brothers weren't exactly the brightest bulbs in the socket.

"I'm not the *only* one who nurses a grudge. Not three weeks ago I found out you hired away my gardener. I booked him in advance and all of a sudden, he couldn't take on my landscaping be-cause he 'forgot' about a project he was doing for you."

Ralph snickered. "It's not my fault you don't know how to keep help. You think I don't know it was you that sicced the glo-worm on me?"

"Ralph? I wanted to ask you—" A woman's voice echoed from around the corner. A second later, she appeared. She was gorgeous, with big boobs and a tiny waist and big, curvy hips, and she was wear-ing a pair of short shorts and a crop top that barely covered her nipples. Her hair, long and red, was caught back in a ponytail, and she was carrying a plant and a trowel. "Oh, I didn't know you had company." She gave me a long look, cocking her head to the side.

"I'm not company, exactly," I started to say.

"This is *Maudlin Gallowglass*," Ralph said. I wasn't sure why he exaggerated my name, but then figured he must have told her about the murder and everything that had come out of it. "Maddy, this is Honey. She's...a distant cousin."

All satyrs were male, and their mothers were

usually nymphs. If a human woman and satyr mated, the result would be half-satyr and male, or human and female. If the mother was a wood nymph, then the child would either be nymph—female, or satyr—male. Occasionally, a nymph would have fraternal twins, which made for an interesting family portrait. Honey appeared to be human. I quit trying to calculate the dynamics there.

"I'll be with you in a minute, cuz," Ralph said.

Honey gave me a long look, a cunning smile curving on her lips. A shiver raced up my spine, but I couldn't figure out why. She nodded to Ralph, then darted back around the corner.

Ralph turned back to me. "Listen to me. I'm not doing anything illegal. You know the sheriff can't ding me on using constructs in my productions—"

"*Productions?*" I snorted. "More like, cheap bargain-basement knockoffs. This seems crass even for you, Ralph. When the fuck did you decide that you could become the next Hugh Hefner?" I followed his suit, slamming my hands on the counter next to his, and staring right back at him.

Ralph's nostrils flared and I swear I saw steam rising from them. After another moment, he slowly pulled away from me, crossing his arms. "Go home, Maddy. Keep your nose out of my business. Nobody held a gun to your head to force you to give Snow and her boys a room. Right?"

I clenched my teeth. I hated it when I lost an argument to somebody I didn't respect. Ralph and I used to be buddies, but once he had decided I was trying to put him out of business, his friendliness had turned to watchful sarcasm.

I straightened up, staring at him. "You're right on that. I admit it. But damn it, Ralph, I wish you'd think about what you're doing. Even if she's a construct, that doesn't mean what you're doing is right. You're acting like a sleaze, and you know it. You just don't give a fuck anymore, do you? All you see are dollar signs. That's all that matters."

And with that, I turned and left a lot more quietly than I had come.

As I arrived home, Thornton was standing at the kitchen door. He frantically waved for me to hurry in. Crap. What was wrong now? I raced across the lawn, hurrying inside.

"What's going on? What happened? Is Aegis okay? Is Bubba okay?"

"I don't know," he said, his eyes wide. He nodded toward the stairs. "You'd better go check. I went to look in on Bubba a few minutes ago and... well—"

Fucking hell. I took the stairs two at a time, hurrying up to my room as my heart sank. As I reached my door, I slammed it open, not giving a fuck if I disturbed Mr. Mosswood or the dwarves.

I glanced around the room, scanning for Bubba. And then, I saw what Thornton was talking about. Bubba was nowhere in sight, but a man with long red hair was sprawled across my bed. He was buck nekkid, deeply tanned, tall, and muscled. He gave me a hesitant smile as I froze.

"Rub mah belleh?"

And that's when I really lost it.

Chapter 6

I GLANCED INTO the man's eyes. No. It couldn't be. *Nope, no, no, no, no.* Nopedy-nope, even.

"Want to rub my belly, Maddy?" His voice was deep, but trembling, and he stroked his stomach with long, strong fingers. He wasn't hard, thank gods, but even so, he was mighty impressive. I prayed he'd keep his hands on his abs. *Please don't reach any lower.*

Then, realizing that I really was seeing what I was seeing, I let out a strangled squeak. "Bubba...is that you, Bubba?"

He blinked, slow, just like a cat. "What happened to me?"

Thornton, who was standing beside me, had turned red as a beet. He was looking every which way but directly at Bubba. "Want me to call Aegis?"

"Please. Please do. Call him *now*. And Sandy. I need them both."

As he slipped out of the room, I cautiously approached the bed. Maybe somebody was playing a joke on me. Maybe this was really just Sandy's way of trying to get a laugh out of me. Maybe I had slipped into an alternative universe and the gods were fucking with me.

"Sit by me?" The man who might be Bubba patted the bed. "I'm lonely."

I licked my lips, trying to figure out what to say. As far as I knew, cjinns couldn't turn into human form, so what the hell had happened? Had he made a wish and rubbed his own belly?

No, a voice inside whispered. *That's ridiculous. He's been with you for over three hundred years. If he had wanted to be human all that time, he would have become human sooner. Bubba gets what Bubba wants, usually.*

I gingerly sat on the edge of the bed. "Are you really Bubba?"

He wrinkled his nose, frowning. "Bubba. Who else would I be?" And then he held out his hand, examining his fingernails. As he brought his fingers to his mouth and started licking them, I could only stare, trying to figure out just what the fuck to do.

He rolled to a sitting position, turning his head to the side. His tongue darted in and out a few times. Finally, with a frustrated look, he turned to me. "I can't reach my shoulder. How do you ever stay clean? You smell so good, I know you've figured out a way. Though I never see you grooming." He leaned forward, and I knew where he was aiming.

"Stop that!"

He blinked, straightening up. "Why?"

"You can't reach your balls, thank gods." The thought of him "grooming" himself the way he knew how sent a freak flush through me and I stumbled to my feet. "Bubba—if you are indeed *my* Bubba—you can't groom yourself with your tongue right now. Do you understand what's happened?"

"No, only that you seem to understand me better than usual." He gave me a squirrelly look. "What do you mean, 'what's happened'?"

"Don't you see the difference?"

"What difference?" Again, the confused, suspicious stare.

I reached for his hand. "Here, give me your... paw. Please?"

He cautiously reached out and took my hand. "What's going on? I feel strange." He was starting to sound a little freaked out.

"I know you do, Bub. Come on." I pulled him off the bed. He stumbled a little like a toddler trying to take steps as I led him over to my vanity. I took him by the shoulders, moving him so that he was facing the mirror. "Do you know what a mirror is?"

"The see-yourself glass? Yeah."

"Look at yourself, Bubba. What do you see?" I stepped away in case he freaked out.

Bubba raised his eyes, staring at his reflection in the mirror. One blink. Two blinks. On the third, he let out a shriek. "Oh hell, oh hell, what the hell? What the hell happened to me? I'm so butt ugly.

I'm one of *you!*" He whirled around, pointing at me, and promptly unbalanced himself so that he went tumbling forward, faceplanting on the floor.

"Ow! I meant to do that!" he mumbled.

I knelt as he turned over, groaning and reaching for his groin. "That hurt, Maddy. I hurt myself."

"I know, Bub. And yeah, somehow you've been turned into human form. I'm sorry. I don't know what's going on, but I'll find out. Meanwhile, let's get you up and get some pants on you—don't protest. You can't walk around with your dick hanging out for everybody to see."

Bubba sat up, looking terribly forlorn. He glanced up over at me, then rubbed his head against my arm. "I'm scared. I've never changed shapes before. I don't like it."

I held his head, comforting him. "I know, Bub. I know."

THORNTON RETURNED, BRINGING with him a robe and some underpants. They had to be his, because Aegis usually went commando. "Here, I brought a couple things for him to wear. Both Aegis and Sandy are on the way."

"Pet me?" Bubba's head butted my leg. He was lying down, and he reached out to grab hold of my ankle.

"Bubba, you need to let go. Come on, stand up. Pretty please?" I cajoled him to his feet and, with Thornton's help, got him into the underwear and the robe, neither of which he liked.

"This binds. This is stupid. Why do you wear this? I want pets. I want my belly rubbed." He continued to grumble, tugging at the legs of the briefs, until we got him back to the bed.

I motioned for him to sit down. "Just rest for a moment, Bub. I need to think."

What could cause a cjinn to turn into a human? And how was I going to return him to his regular form? This was going to take some doing. I ran through any number of spells that could turn an animal into a human, but they didn't quite fit. For one thing, Bubba was a cjinn. Any typical spell that worked on animals wouldn't be able to affect a magical creature. For another, even if it was a spell, who the hell had cast it—and how?

"Snow."

"What?" Thornton asked.

"The only stranger I've had in this house in the past twenty-four hours has been Snow and her dwarves. Damn it, I knew better than let them stay here. You watch Bubba. Don't let him leave this room—and no matter how much he begs, do not rub his stomach!" I headed for the door, slamming it behind me. As I rounded the corner of the second-story hall, I was ready to wipe my feet on the first person to cross me.

I came to Snow's door. There was a lot of whispered giggling inside and the sudden belief that they were rehearsing a scene under my roof filled me with rage. I slammed open the door, ready to order the entire lot outside. But instead of an orgy, the eight of them were sitting around on the bed and chairs, eating pizza and playing poker. A pile of pennies and nickels sat between them, and they all looked startled when I came barging into the room.

"Maudlin? Is everything all right?" Snow frowned, standing.

"You're all clothed."

"We tend to wear clothes when we play poker. Why, what's going on? Do you want us to get naked for you?"

One of the dwarves—I had no clue which one, except he was the most gorgeous of the group—winked at me.

"No! I don't want you naked! And I don't want my cjinn naked either, especially in human form. Who's the wiseass who turned him into a human? I want you to reverse the spell immediately." I ran out of breath at the same time I ran out of steam.

Snow shook her head. "What are you talking about? None of us work magic. I'm a princess. These guys are dwarves and you know very well just how well dwarves and magic get along. As in, not so much."

I held her gaze. Her eyes were clear and she was telling the truth.

"You really didn't do it," I said.

"I don't even know what you're talking about, but no. I didn't do anything to you or whoever it is you're worried about." She gave me a cool stare. "The only one I'd like to do something to is Ralph. And it's not what he's been begging for."

I paused, thinking. "I might be able to help you on that, but first I have to take care of a problem."

"Listen, hon," Snow said in a waitress-friendly voice, "if you can help me exact some revenge on him, then I'm forever in your debt."

"Right. I'll think about what we can do. Meanwhile, sorry for barging in on you." I hurried out the door, closing it softly behind me. As I headed downstairs, I stopped at my room and motioned to Bubba. "Come on, Bubba. We're going to the kitchen."

"Food? Time to eat?" He jumped up, his eyes bright, and shot past me, out of the room, thundering down the stairs.

I facepalmed, shaking my head. "What am I going to do, Thornton?"

"Feed him?" Thornton gave me a blank look.

"Wiseass. Come on, help me corral him before he damages anything." I froze. "What do I do if he still has his powers?"

"Might I suggest Valium?" And with that, Thornton motioned to the door. "Go."

By the time we got to the kitchen, Bubba was sitting on the counter, opening his third can of cat food. "I've got thumbs!" He hadn't eaten any of them, yet, but seemed entranced with the idea of being able to open his own breakfast.

I quickly took the cans away. "Hold on now, Bubs. You're in human form now. We don't eat cat food."

"Why?"

"Because it's not formulated for human bodies." It seemed the easiest explanation all the way around. I swept the cans off the counter, handing them to Thornton. "I'll make you something to eat." At Thornton's laugh, I turned around. "I can cook eggs. I can make a sandwich."

"Why don't you and Bubba sit down at the table and I'll make him a sandwich." Thornton shooed us out of the kitchen proper.

I led Bubba over to the kitchen table and motioned for him to sit down. "So. Bubba, can you tell me anything about what happened? Did someone come in the room? Do you know if they cast a spell on you? Earlier today you didn't seem to be feeling well. What was wrong?"

Bubba tilted his head, staring at me sideways. "You look different now. Smaller." He paused, then said, "I remember feeling tired and I just wanted to sleep. When I woke up, everything looked different." He wrinkled his nose. "My nose—something's wrong. I can't smell nearly as much as usual."

"That's because humans don't have the ability to smell as much as a cat does, Bub. And even though you're a cjinn, your body's used to doing cat-stuff."

Thornton brought over the sandwich and set it down in front of Bubba just as Aegis came in the backdoor. He took one look at Bubba, who was still wearing the robe and boxers, and his jaw dropped.

Bubba poked at the sandwich. "How do I eat that?"

"Pick it up in your paws...your hands. Hold it, and bite into it," Thornton said, showing him how to hold the sandwich.

I motioned for Aegis to follow me into the dining room. "We have a problem."

"What happened?" Aegis peeked around me, staring back into the kitchen. "Are you sure that's him? Bubba is a California boy?"

"Apparently so. And yeah, trust me. Bubba tried to groom himself and it was obvious he hadn't realized that he wasn't as bendy as he usually is. He's scared and he's grumpy." My smile faded. "I have to find out what's going on. The only person I can think of who might try to do this to him is Snow—and I confronted her. I'm convinced it wasn't her. Or maybe Ralph."

"Why would Ralph turn Bubba into a human?" Aegis paused. "Don't tell me you went over there? Maddy, I thought we talked about this—"

"No, *you* talked about it. And for what it's worth, Snow wants a little bit of payback on Ralph as well. I don't think she appreciates her starring role in *Snow White and the Seven Whorves*." I shook my head. "But Ralph couldn't have done this either, because I came home from his place to find Bubba transformed. I'm worried about him. What if this is permanent? What if he's really sick?"

"Call the doctor and ask if he can see you for an emergency visit. I'll pay for it." Aegis motioned to my phone. "Go on, call."

The front door opened and Sandy came in. I motioned for her to talk to Aegis as I put in a call to Dr. Farrows and begged him to come over.

"He'll be here in twenty minutes," I said as I hung up.

Aegis had filled Sandy in while I was on the phone and now, she was staring into the kitchen. "I can't believe that's Bubba," she whispered.

"*Believe it.* And I want to know how and why. Let's go in. I warn you, he's still very much Bubba

87

the cat." I glanced at Aegis, who smiled.

Thornton was back at the counter with Bubba's sandwich. "Apparently, Bubba does not like pickles. Or tomatoes."

"More meat. And whatever that white goop is, I don't like it." Bubba was examining his nails. "Why are these so short?"

"Because—white goop?"

"Mayo," Thornton said. "Noted: Bubba doesn't like pickles, tomatoes, or mayo."

Aegis pulled me aside. "Before I forget, here— put this in your purse."

I glanced at the piece of paper. It was a check for twenty-five thousand dollars. "You have to be joking."

"Nope. That should tide you over till they get your money back, and if it doesn't, there's more where that came from. Put it in your purse and don't leave it lying around." He sat down next to Bubba. "Hey, Bubba. You know who I am?"

"Vampire. Aegis. You do things to Maddy." His eyes flashed.

"Enough about that!" I dove into the conversation. "We really don't need to rehash what you're used to watching." I decided right then and there, once we had Bubba back into his usual form, he wasn't going to hang out in the bedroom with us when we were having sex. Nope.

Sandy stifled a laugh. "Bubba, did Maddy ask you if any strangers came near you today? Or even last night? Or, did anybody rub your belly and make a wish?"

Bubba pulled open his robe to flash his six-pack

abs. "You want to rub mah belleh?" His eyes were wide as he patted his stomach.

"I swear, it's like breathing, isn't it?" Sandy glanced over at me.

I nodded. "I think getting people to rub his belly is an innate part of his nature." To Bubba, I said, "Close the robe, Bubs. We're not rubbing your belly. Why do you even want your belly rubbed?"

Bubba smiled at me. "Because, you rub my belly, I make your wishes happen. It's what I do. Maddy, I don't like being human." He rubbed his belly, but nothing happened and his smile slid away and he started fidgeting, looking anxious. Before I could answer, he had slid under the table with his new, meat-heavy sandwich.

"Where is that doctor?" I motioned for Sandy and Aegis to back away. Bubba was nervous, I could tell that much. It had to be scary, and I was beginning to realize just how much the cjinn relied on the feline part of himself. Bubba could never manage as a human because he wasn't human by nature. He needed his cat form to feel secure.

"Watch for the doctor, would you?" I nodded to Sandy and she headed to the front door. I turned back to the table and slowly got down on my hands and knees, crawling under the table with Bubba. He had finished his sandwich and now he gave me a wide-eyed look and curled up on the floor, his head on my lap. I stroked his hair, feeling sorry for him. He really didn't understand what was happening and while we could talk to him now, he seemed more confused than when he was in his cat form.

"It's okay, Bubs. We'll find out what's going on. I'll figure out how to make it right." I hated promising something I wasn't sure I could deliver, but he seemed so forlorn.

"I'm scared, Maddy." He sniffled and I realized he was crying. I rubbed his ears, hoping that the familiar sensation would calm him down.

Aegis peeked under the table. "I'm going to look around the house and see if I can find anything that might suggest why this happened."

"Thanks. Something had to trigger this." I paused as the doorbell rang. "Hold on, that might be the doctor."

Sure enough, it was Farrows. Short, with black wavy hair and a ruddy face, he was a youngish doctor, or looked youngish, but I knew that he was a powerful witch—a healer by specialty—and he was probably older than I was. He entered the kitchen.

"So, you said you have a sick cjinn? Where is the little guy?" He was talking to Aegis, who pointed under the table at us.

"He's right here, Dr. Farrows. Bubba wasn't feeling good, and then, tonight, we're not sure what happened but he ended up in human form. Come on, Bubs, let the doctor look at you." I tapped on Bubba's shoulder.

He shook his head. "No. Don't know him."

"Bubba, you need to let the doctor examine you. He might be able to tell what's going on." I used my *I mean business* voice. Bubba glanced up at me and I gave him a stern look.

"Don't want to," he grumbled, but crawled out from under the table.

The doctor stared at him for a moment. Then, without a word, he set his bag on the table and opened it. He draped a stethoscope around his neck, and then took out several interesting-looking instruments. I wasn't sure what they were, but he laid them out on a cloth on the table.

"Come on, Bubba. Let me take a look at you." Dr. Farrows had a soothing voice, and Bubba slowly responded, allowing the doctor to steer him to a chair.

Bubba sat very still, staring straight ahead as the doctor checked his heart, ears, eyes, and then held a square electronic gadget against Bubba's chest, looking at the screen on the front of it as it registered a number of waves that looked like sine curves. After making a few notes, he took out a circlet made out of some sort of metal and fitted it around Bubba's head. He pressed a button on the side of it and stared at his tablet. I peeked over his shoulder and saw a number of undulating curves rolling by on a graph. Finally, the doctor cajoled Bubba into letting him take a quick blood sample, to which he added a pale blue powder. The blood foamed up and turned bright magenta.

"I think we've found the problem with this...little...guy. He's under a curse." Dr. Farrows turned to me. "He's the victim of a hex, though I'm not sure what kind yet."

I stared at Bubba. "He's been *hexed*? Who on earth would have want to hex my cjinn? Can you do anything? Is this hurting him?"

"First, yes, it can harm him if he stays too long away from his natural form. His magic stems from his very nature. He can't use his magic now, and the longer he stays in human form, the more chance there is he'll lose it altogether, even if he does transform back. Also, his mindset isn't geared toward being human. This is causing him great distress." He paused, looking at Bubba, who was staring at him, eyes wide with fear.

"Bubba, you stay here, all right?" The doctor motioned to me. "Let's talk in the other room."

I followed him into the living room. "What can you do for him? Can you break the hex?"

"Not at this point, but what I can do is to place him in stasis. That will keep him from panicking and it will prevent the hex from draining his magic. But I can only keep him that way a couple weeks. If Bubba were human to begin with and changed into a cat—or a cjinn—it would be different. He would still have the mental and emotional facilities to cope with this. Humans and other bipeds are much more open to change. But cats... and cjinns...they're creatures of habit and routine. Stress that routine to any significant degree and it can send them into shock."

My heart began to race. "Stasis? What about the curse?"

"I'll start researching to figure out just what kind of hex he's under. Until I know more, I don't want to try random curse-breakers. It could make things worse." Dr. Farrows glanced over his shoulder at the kitchen. "Ms. Gallowglass, do you know anybody who could want to cause him harm? Or you?"

I froze. "Me? You think somebody hurt Bubba because they're mad at me?"

He shrugged. "It's a distinct possibility. But if I'm going to put him in stasis, I need to do so now. The sooner we get him into a calm state, the better. And I don't want to leave him here. If I keep him at my clinic, he'll be safer."

"Safer than here at home?" I was starting to feel frantic. A sick feeling raced through my stomach. Had I inadvertently caused this? Who could be mean enough to target Bubba if they were mad at me? "Wouldn't it be better to keep him in familiar surroundings?"

"He won't know the difference, and if somebody is mad at you, then they won't be able to hurt him any more than they have. Have you noticed anything else going on that's odd? Anything that might lead you to believe that somebody has a gripe against you?"

I pressed my hand against my lips. "Oh great gods, the money."

"Money?"

"Somebody stole fifty-four thousand dollars from me. They skimmed my account. But they're in Dubai."

"A person doesn't have to live overseas to send money to an account there." He patted my arm. "Ms. Gallowglass—"

"Maddy, please."

"Maddy, I think you might want to talk to the police. It seems somebody is intent on making your life miserable. Meanwhile, let's get Bubba squared away. I can keep him in stasis for two weeks without it affecting him in any negative way. I can give him a sedative until we get him to the office, where I can put him in stasis. I want you to convince him that it's just a shot to help him relax, because I don't want to scare him any further."

We returned to the kitchen. I sat by Bubba and began to stroke his hair back from his face. "Listen, Bubs, the doctor is going to give you a shot to help you relax. I promise, it will help you feel better. Please let him?"

Bubba looked up at me, and his gaze was so trusting that it just about broke my heart. "Okay, Maddy. If you say so."

"I do, Bubs. Remember, we love you, little guy. No matter what form you're in."

The doctor prepared the shot. "Bubba, this may sting a little but it won't for long, and you'll feel just fine after a few minutes. It will help you sleep for a little bit, all right?"

Bubba nodded. "Sleep's good. I like to sleep."

As Dr. Farrows injected him with the medication, I held his hand. I swore to all the gods that once I figured out who the hell had messed with Bubba, I was going to have a field day on their ass.

Chapter 7

BUBBA SLUMPED IN the chair within seconds after the shot.

"I'll call my assistant to bring the ambulance around. He'll help me take Bubba back to the clinic and get him situated. He'll be in a magic-proof chamber, which is also sealed against vampires." Dr. Farrows stopped, glancing at Aegis. "No offense meant."

"None taken. Just take care of him." Aegis looked as worried as I felt.

"I'll start tomorrow morning trying to figure out just how he was hexed. Meanwhile, as I told Maddy here, she'd better start looking around for somebody who means her harm. They could be targeting her friends and loved ones, so I suggest you take care and be alert. All of you." With that, Farrows took out his phone and put in a call to his assistant.

I explained to Sandy and Aegis what the doctor was going to do. "He thinks I'm being targeted." I turned to Aegis, who had rearranged the sleeping Bubba so that he wasn't sliding off the chair. "I have a thought, but I want to wait until he's gone to talk about it. Meanwhile, I also want to get Snow and her dwarves out of here. I don't for a minute think she did anything, but if I'm a target, it could put my guests in danger too. And Mr. Mosswood, for that matter."

Aegis nodded. "Better safe than sorry. I'll make arrangements at another hotel for them. If I have to, I'll bunk them with friends. Sandy, can you stay awhile?"

She sat down next to Bubba. "Of course. Jenna's staying at the school this weekend. Neverfall is having its spring fling and she's actually taking part in it."

We waited another fifteen minutes before Farrows's assistant arrived, and I watched morosely as they strapped Bubba in a stretcher and carted him out to the ambulance.

"Should I go with you?" I asked, anxiously patting Bubba's forehead. He was asleep—actually far deeper than sleep—but I still wanted to feel like I was doing something.

"Really, there's not much you can do. I suggest you get some rest. Come see me tomorrow and I'll show you where we're keeping him so you can reassure yourself that he'll be all right. Around ten A.M.?"

I stood back, letting the doctor and his assistant do their jobs. "All right. Tomorrow."

As they drove off, all I could think about was how Bubba, regardless of his shape and the fact that he was a powerful spellcrafter, was just a scared little tabby inside.

SANDY STAYED WITH me as Aegis ferried Snow, the dwarves, and Mr. Mosswood to a hotel, and she agreed to stay the night. When he returned, we gathered around the fireplace in the parlor, drinking wine and eating cheese and crackers. I let out a long breath, and then asked Aegis the question that had been haunting me since Dr. Farrows first suggested that someone might be targeting me.

"Do you think the Arcānus Nocturni are after me? We took out Luke, but that doesn't mean the rest of them don't know who I am. He certainly had a grudge against me."

Sandy straightened up. "What are you talking about?"

I swallowed. Hard. I hadn't told her much about the vacation Aegis and I had taken shortly after the New Year, and I didn't want to reveal too much even now, but she had to know at some point. "Sandy, during the trip to the chateau? I discovered that there's a secret society of vampires called the Arcānus Nocturni. I didn't tell you because the less you know about them, the better. But now..."

"Who are they and what should I know?" Sandy understood the concept of a need-to-know basis.

Aegis spoke up. "The Arcānus Nocturni is an organization of ancient vampires. They're all old—usually far older than me. They can walk abroad in the sunlight. Vampirism is a disease that was originally brought to Earth by those who walk among the stars."

Sandy let out a soft breath. "Vampires who can walk under the sun?" She pressed her hand to her chest. "I just felt my heart stop. Do you know what this could mean for vampire–human relations?"

"It would bring the fang-haters out in full force. As long as humans feel they have an upper hand, and the only one they have over vamps is the ability to go out in the sun, then there's a chance a treaty can be reached. But the moment that they feel like they have no safe harbor, then all peaceful talks will go out the door." I licked my lips. "The vampire I fought during our trip was after me because of my past. It was a personal vendetta. But given the worry we have over Essie, and then what I found out about the Arcānus Nocturni, I'm not sure what to think."

Sandy turned to Aegis. "What's your opinion on this? Do you think that some vampire from this society hexed Maddy?"

"I don't know." He darkened. "I did some more research into them, but they're hard to pinpoint. I can barely find a mention of them in the library—and I'm talking the private section of the library, where you can look at books but not check them out. All I found out is that some of the members walk about in the highest business circles today, but as to who they are? There's no telling. There are no member rosters listed. The few mentions of them on the internet are brief and listed as rumors. I found one reference to a writer who was writing a book on obscure societies but he vanished and they never found his body."

"What do you know about them personally?" Sandy asked.

"Just what I've told Maddy. I've heard of them. Most old vampires have. But they've never approached me and I've never attempted to approach them. I'm not old enough to belong to their cult." He shrugged. "They're dangerous, though."

"It sounds like it. So let's stretch this a bit. It might not be them. Who else would want revenge on you?" Sandy asked. "Rachel is dead."

"Rachel's dead. Who else have I pissed off in the recent past, besides Ralph? I don't think even he would hurt Bubba." Then I paused. "Craig. My ex. He was pissed out of his mind when I bought the mansion and sold his condo. Doesn't matter that I was the legal owner, he loved that beige cubicle, precisely because I was awarded it during the divorce settlement. Could he have hired somebody to throw a hex on Bubba? He never liked him, even though he thought Bubba was just a cat."

Aegis let out a little growl. "Want me to pay a visit to him?"

Quickly, I shook my head. If Aegis paid a visit to Craig, chances were, Craig would turn up in a cemetery. "No, let's think about this for a while. Meanwhile, the doctor is right. We should get some sleep."

"I'll keep watch till sunrise. No sense taking any

chances." Aegis motioned toward the stairs. "Go to bed, and rest easy."

But even though I tried to sleep, I couldn't help but think about Bubba. Finally, around two A.M., I fell asleep from exhaustion.

MORNING ARRIVED TOO soon. I managed about five hours of sleep, but at seven, I was awake. I automatically looked for Bubba, but then remembered what had gone down. My heart sinking, I dragged myself over to the closet and dressed in jeans and a V-neck T-shirt. As I zipped up my ankle boots and applied my makeup, once again, a flare of anger ran through me. I wanted to find whoever it was that had been messing with me. I wanted to hurt them bad.

I headed downstairs to find Thornton making breakfast. Sandy was sitting at the kitchen table, blurry-eyed. I glanced up at the clock. Seven-twelve.

"Aegis must have just gone to bed. Sunrise in three minutes," I said.

"He actually went downstairs at six. Left me here. Said he had some things he wanted to do." Thornton set a plate of pancakes in front of us, along with bacon and orange juice. "Given what went down last night, I figured you'd be up early and would need a good start."

I yawned, stretching. "I'm still exhausted, but I want to get a start on today. I need to talk to Delia.

See if any odd vamps have been spotted around Bedlam." I paused. We were expecting a guest tomorrow. "I also need to cancel tomorrow's guest. I don't want anybody staying here until we figure out what the hell's going on."

"That blows." Sandy speared a pancake with her fork, spreading butter and syrup on it like they were going out of style. "Thanks, Thornton. You really can handle a spatula."

"I learned at...yeah, I can." He smiled, then headed out of the room. "I'm going to clean all the rooms and get them done, just in case you're able to take in guests again before the end of the day. Think positive, and all that."

"So how do I go about this? I'm sick over Bubba." I followed Sandy's suit, even though I wasn't that hungry. As I bit into a piece of bacon, I felt just how tired I was. "I'm so exhausted. I need more sleep."

"Take care of business and then take a nap this afternoon." She pursed her lips. "Since *you're* the coven's High Priestess, we can't very well go consult her about the issue. What about talking to Auntie Tautau? She might be able to give you some advice."

Auntie Tautau...that made sense. If anybody would be able to help, it would be her.

The Aunties were a group of incredibly powerful witches. They were aligned to no coven, no circle or group. They were, in fact, often regarded as harbingers of fate. Nobody quite knew what made a witch an Auntie, or how they came to be, but Auntie Tautau knew how to *arrange* things. The question was, would she agree to help? If she didn't, no force on Earth could push her into offering a hand.

"I'll go see her after I talk to Delia. You want to come with me?"

Sandy frowned. "I wish I could, but I have a board meeting this morning that I can't miss. My ex will be there, and you know Bart. He's a by-the-book type of guy. At least when it comes to business. And I need to check on Mr. Peabody. But I think you should go talk to her, at least. The worst she can do is say no."

"True that." I stabbed half-heartedly at my pancake. "All right, I'll go talk to Delia, then stop off at Dr. Farrows, and then go see Auntie Tautau. I also need to put Aegis's check in the bank. As much as I hate borrowing money, I want a cushion in there."

We finished breakfast, and then, leaving the Bewitching Bedlam in Thornton's capable hands, were off for the day.

MY MEETING WITH Delia went all right—she was even more concerned after hearing about Bubba, and she promised to check around to see if any strange vamps had been spotted in the area. I didn't tell her why. I didn't want to tell anybody about the Arcānus Nocturni yet. But I warned her to be cautious if she did find any new vampire activity around town. In turn, she cautioned me to leave Essie alone and let her check in with the vampire queen.

Essie Vanderbilt was the Queen of the Pacific Northwest Vampires. She had started out as a Voudou priestess, born in 1844, and when she was turned, she retained some of her powers.

The vampire nation was divided into regions, and each region was ruled autonomously. We weren't sure if there were any shadow puppets governing the vamps, other than the distant influence of the Arcānus Nocturni. But Essie didn't like anybody dipping their fingers in her pie, so I rather doubted she'd be willing to allow any outside elements into her rule.

What we knew about Essie wasn't a lot, but we did suspect her of attempting to gain traction in Bedlam, outside of the Moonrise Coven's influence. The coven dictated how vampires could interact on the island, but Essie was always seeking ways around our rules. Any new vamps in the area were supposed to check in with her, and she was supposed to cooperate with us, but we had learned the hard way that was only for show.

After leaving the sheriff's office, I headed over to see Dr. Farrows and Bubba. All the way, I fretted about what to do if something had gone wrong, but as his receptionist guided me back to his office and he came out, smiling, I tried to relax.

"Bubba. Is he okay?"

"Yes, Bubba is fine. I'm doing my best to figure out what kind of hex he's under. Here, let me take you to see him. He won't know you're here, but it will put your mind at ease."

He led me to a back room that could only be entered via a code-lock. He punched in the code and, as we entered the room, I felt the hush descend over my magic. The doctor was right—there would be no magical use here.

"Why doesn't the cloaking shield negate the curse?"

"Oh, it does, but only in here. Look." He led me over to a bed where a big orange tabby was curled up asleep.

"Bubba! He's back to his normal form."

"Only in here. Unless I can figure out what hexed him and how to break it, in two weeks we'll have to bring him out of stasis and the moment he walks out of this room, he'll be back in human form." Dr. Farrows frowned, leaning against the bed. "I've been testing his blood and so far I've ruled out standard transmogrification spells. So we know that over-the-counter hex-breakers won't take care of this. I'll have another go this afternoon after I see patients."

I stroked Bubba's fur, burying my nose in his side. He was breathing rhythmically, and I wished for all the world that I could just scoop him up and take him home. After one last kiss on his tummy, I turned to the doctor.

"Find out what's wrong with him, please? He's been with me over three hundred years. I can't..." As tears filled my throat, I stopped talking.

"I know, Maddy. I know. Come on, let's leave him be." He escorted me out of the room. "I've only had the pleasure of treating one other cjinn, but they are lovely beings. And they're loyal, you know. You win the trust of a cjinn and they'll stick by you forever."

That didn't help any, and the waterworks really did start to flow. I hung my head. As he handed me a tissue, I blew my nose and dried my tears. Thank gods for waterproof eye makeup.

"Thank you, Doctor."

"Jordan, please." He paused, then said, "I don't mean to be forward and this isn't the right place or time, but...the vampire who was in your kitchen. Are you and he..."

"Dating? Yes, we are." I smiled at him.

He flashed me a rueful smile. "I thought as much, but it never hurts to ask. All right, Maddy, I have patients to see. But I'll take care of Bubba and do my best to figure out what's wrong."

"Thank you. He's my sweetie and I can't bear to think of what might..." I stopped as the tears threatened again. "Thank you. I'll call you later today."

As I headed out the door, I thought that Jordan Farrows was one heck of a nice guy.

I STOPPED BY Auntie Tautau's but she wasn't at home. Or she wasn't answering her door. Either way, I left a note for her and then sat in my car, trying to figure out what I wanted to do next. Finally, I headed to the credit union.

"Have you figured out who stole my money and when you're going to replace it?" I asked Emily Chambers as soon as I walked through the door. She happened to be standing by a teller's station.

She jumped—apparently she hadn't seen me enter—and turned around. Her face fell as soon as she saw who was talking. "Ms. Gallowglass, I'm sorry. I didn't see you enter. Please, follow me." With a swish of her pencil skirt, she led me back to her office.

I slumped in the chair across from hers and rested my hands on the arms, crossing my legs. I wasn't in any mood to be brushed off. "Did the sheriff visit you this morning?"

Her eyes narrowed, but she pasted a smile on her lips. "Why, yes, thank you for contacting her. I was going to talk to her after I talked to the FBI, but that saved me the call."

"You do know that I'm the High Priestess of the Moonrise Coven, right? So I need access to my funds." The two really had nothing to do with one another but it didn't hurt to let her know that I really didn't appreciate being shunted around and that I had more pull than she wanted to know about.

She cleared her throat. "The sheriff made that clear, yes. And I'm happy to tell you that we've made your funds available again. Because your account was compromised, however, we created a new account for you. I hope that's acceptable. We called Mrs. Periwinkle about the check and she apologized. She wired the money." She sorted through her desk and handed me a packet of information. "You'll have new debit cards within five days."

"Good." I took the sheaf of papers. "And you might add this check to the account, please?" I scribbled my signature on the back of Aegis's check and handed it to her.

She glanced at the amount, then stared at me for a moment. "Aegis is one of our biggest account holders." It was a question without being poised as a question.

"Yes, and he's also my boyfriend."

That put things into motion. She swung out from behind her desk. "I'll be right back with your receipt."

Well, one problem solved, thanks to Delia. I contemplated cashing out my account and going to another bank, but truth was, they were all about the same. Sticklers for rules and regulations, and the customer always seemed to be the last in line for services. By the time she came back and handed me the receipt, I was ready to go.

"I want to be informed if you figure out just who wormed their way into my account. Thank you, Ms. Chambers. You know where to reach me." I didn't wait for her reply but strode out of her office and out of the bank.

I WAS AT loose ends as I returned to my car. Sandy was busy. Aegis was asleep. We didn't have any guests to attend to. Bubba was in stasis. As I reached for the door handle, I glanced up at the sky. No rain today, but it was overcast and cool—forty-five degrees. I thought about taking a walk, or going out to the beach, and finally decided on the latter. I could use a dose of water energy. I ran fire, and occasionally when the blaze grew too bright, there was nothing like a trip to the beach to calm me down. Now, feeling as melancholy as I was, it seemed like the perfect place to sit and think and try to figure out what the hell was happening.

I drove across the island to the Enchanted Sands park—a county park that was open dawn till dusk with a few camping spaces for those who reserved them in advance, and once again found my thoughts returning to Bubba. As I had told the doctor, he had been with me since 1687. I had saved him from a fire, and it was because of my own fire that I had been able to carry him to safety. He had been so young, and so frightened.

As I pulled into the parking lot and turned off the ignition, I closed my eyes, returning to that time when Bubba and I had first found one another, and saved each other's lives.

I HAD BEEN on my way to visit one of the Aunties. There was one living in a small village near our home, and while my mother hated her and warned me never to go near her, I had secretly formed a friendship with the crone, sneaking over to visit as often as I could.

The week had been rough. I was staying at home again for a while, in between runs with Tom, Sandy, and Fata, and it wore on my nerves. My mother was berating my father, *again*, and I had lost my temper with her, *again*. It was after he had been attacked by wild dogs, before he had managed to get a job with the Society Magicka.

Zara, my mother, had been particularly cruel, calling him a loser and telling him she wished he had died during the attack so she could at least remarry. I couldn't take it any longer.

"You *bitch*. Leave him alone. He was out hunting to fill your belly, and you gave no thought to the fact that he almost lost his life for you and for us. So help me, I hope to hell you hurt yourself so bad that one day you're the one who's disabled and can't take care of yourself. Then see just how welcome you'll be." I smacked her across the face, hard, and ran out as she began screaming at me.

I decided to go see old Auntie Berma, who lived deep in the woodland, to ask if she could help us. Auntie Berma had a reputation for loving children and hating adults, and all the kids in the area knew they could go to her when things were bad at home and she'd be there to listen and—If she could—help out. I was now an adult, but she had watched me grow up and we had a gentle friendship that transcended age.

I ran barefoot through the tall grass, moist with dew, darting between the raindrops that threatened to come. We were in a glen protected by magic so the witch hunters couldn't find us, though now I was pretty good at sensing them. As I took a shortcut through the Singing Grove, a Faerie Barrow in a tall circle of stones that continually hummed with a resonating pulse, I paused.

The smell of smoke filled the air. Curious, I began to follow the scent, traipsing through the woods till I came to a clearing.

I was on the outskirts of Joseph Stanton's farm. He was a mandrake farmer, and all the witches came from far and wide to buy their roots from him. He also sold eggs and pork, bacon and milk. Joseph's wife was the local herb woman, and taught wortcunning to all the young witches, and her laugh made everybody around laugh with her.

But something was wrong. The smell of wood smoke was too strong for the early evening, and I could hear the crackle of flames. I darted along the side of the house—it looked empty, and I remembered they had decided to take a caravan around the countryside selling herbs and eggs and vegetables. As I passed the house, I saw the barn was blazing. The thatched roof had caught fire and it was raging out of control.

I started to run back to the village, so that I could find someone skilled in water witchery to put out the blaze, when I heard it. A faint cry, almost like that of a cat. I paused, listening, and then heard it again. But in that mew, I heard fear and a cry for help.

I raced over to the barn and tugged open the door. The flames were licking at the walls, and the roof had already fallen in several places. The cries were coming from the nearest corner to the door, but a wall of flames stood between me and them. I caught my breath, wondering if I could do it. My element was fire, and I was considered quite powerful for my age. I had never been able to fully merge with the flames, even though I could summon them.

As I squinted through the smoke, I saw a sparkle from the corner—it was a kitten, small and ginger, with long hair, and he was crying frantically. The flames were making their way toward him. With a deep breath, I closed my eyes and reached into the fire, whispering to it, feeling its vibrant hunger against my heart. The flames were eager, gobbling the wood, burning brighter as they went. I focused on their need, and then whispered the spell I had seen my mentor practicing.

Flames burn brightly, flame and spark,
But your wall must break and part.
Move aside, form a door,
Flame and fire, I implore.

As I opened my eyes, I was startled to see them obey. The flames parted, forming a door. I knew I had to move fast, so I dashed through the break in the wall and grabbed the kitten. Then, before the flames could cascade back together, I raced back through and out of the barn. The next moment, the entire ceiling collapsed and the barn was engulfed in the frenzy of the fire.

I held up the kitten. He looked at me, and with a gentle tap, touched my face. I knew that I had found a dear friend. In my heart, I knew we were meant to be together. Carrying him close to me, I headed toward Auntie Berma's, knowing she would be able to help me with him.

SHAKING OUT OF my memories, I slid out of the car and walked across the beach to a log by the shore. As I settled down, I thought about how long ago it had been that I first found Bubba. I wasn't ready to let go of him. Not at all.

Chapter 8

AS THE WAVES crashed in, I stared at the water, resting my arms on my knees. I thought back to the discussion of the night before. Now that we knew Bubba was under a hex, I needed to find out who did it and why.

There were any number of ways to curse somebody. Most witches were cautious about dabbling with darker magic because it could backfire so easily. I had never really feared putting whammies on people because I reserved them for when the situation was dire and the person in question really deserved it. But then, again, I was strong with my magic, and I had learned long ago that sometimes, you had to stand up for yourself.

The scent of seaweed and brine swept over me. To the east, I could see the coast of upper Western Washington. To the west, I could see a faint glimpse of Saturna Island. Bedlam was north of

Orcas Island, exposed to the winds that swept down from the north, out of the Strait of Georgia and the Salish Sea. The Pacific Ocean fueled this area, sweeping in from the Strait of Juan de Fuca. The waters were cold, even in summer, and deep and dark.

When I had moved away from Seattle, I had left the city behind and with it, my ex. But now, I wondered—had he finally figured out how to have his revenge on me? Was Craig behind the hexes?

He was human, and he was one of the bad ones. Our relationship had started out great, but then again, sociopaths are often charming. By the time I left, I felt like a shadow of myself, and I was embarrassed by how I had let him beat me down. But it happened. It happened to a lot of women, even strong ones, when they let down their guard. I knew one thing for sure: I'd never let it happen again.

I stared at my phone, debating. If I called him and asked him point-blank, of course he'd deny it. I needed to see him face to face to know if he was lying. And that was a trip I wasn't sure I was prepared to make, yet.

I ran through my list of everybody who could want to hurt me, and it was a long one. From my vampire hunting days to now, I had acquired a number of enemies—on all sides of the fence. Finally, I decided there was nothing else to do but carry on with business as usual, as much as I could, while I tried to figure out who was out to get me.

As I stood and stretched, a wave came crashing in near my feet. I stared at the sea foam for a moment, then turned and crossed the beach back to my car. Even if I did have to cancel guests this week, there were still a gazillion chores on my list. I might as well get busy.

I WAS HALFWAY through grocery shopping when I came to a stack of canned diced tomatoes. Aegis had asked for three cans so he could make a spaghetti sauce. As I reached for the top can, someone pushing their cart down the aisle bumped into me and, instinctively, I jerked to get out of their way, stumbling into the stack of cans. Like a teetering pile of dominos, they came down, scattering across the aisle in a thunderous clatter of metal on linoleum. I groaned, trying to back away, when I accidentally slipped on one and ended up on my butt, in the middle of the floor.

"Fucking hell!" I didn't swear all that much, but when I did, I went for it. "What the hell?" As I struggled to sit up, cans rolled every which way. The other shopper—I recognized her as belonging to one of the local weretiger packs—let out a snarl of surprise, but then instantly was on her knees beside me.

"Are you okay? Do you need help?" She helped me sit up, a look of concern on her face. "I'm so sorry—that was my fault! I didn't think I was that close to you. I knew I should have worn my glasses. Stupid me."

She sounded so concerned that I felt bad for my outburst.

"I'm... It's all right. Accidents happen." I tried to stand up, but as I put pressure on my wrists to brace myself, my right thumb sent a jolt of pain through my hand and I let out a cry.

"My thumb!" I held up my hand, staring at it. My thumb looked bent in a way it shouldn't bend, and it was rapidly swelling and turning color. "I think..." I tried to move it. As I shifted it backward, the pain flared, throbbing, but it didn't hurt the same way that it had when I tried to put weight on it. "I think it's sprained."

The Muzak playing in the background was annoyingly cheerful. Right about then, one of the stockers came running over, skidding to a halt when he saw the cans filling the aisle.

The moment he saw me, I saw the glassy hint of terror in his face. Lawsuit city, he was probably thinking. He quickly knelt beside me. "Are you all right? Hold on, please. Let me get the manager." Before I could answer, he was gone.

"Afraid of a lawsuit," my weretiger companion guessed. She winked at me. "You could make out like a bandit, you know."

"I've had enough of bandits," I said, feeling grumpy. "Can you help me stand up?"

She was athletic, and had no trouble bracing herself as she leveraged me to my feet. As I cautiously checked myself out, holding my thumb as still as I could, one knee began to twinge, and I tasted blood.

"You cut your lip," she said. "I'm Rhonda, by the

way. Rhonda Castille."

"Hi. I'm Maddy Gallowglass." I licked my lip and sure enough, that's where the blood was coming from. At least I hadn't broken a tooth.

Right about then, the manager came barreling around the corner. "Ms. Gallowglass, are you all right?" He kicked his way through the cans, barking an order for the stocker to clean them up. "Do you need me to call an ambulance? The medics?"

I stared at my thumb. Driving with that was going to be a bitch, at least until I got it splinted. "If someone could just drive me to my doctor, I'll be all right, I think."

"It was my fault—" Rhonda started to say, but I cut her off.

"It was nobody's fault. An accident." I stared at my cart ruefully. "I really needed to shop, too."

"I'll take you to the doctor," Rhonda said. "It's the least I can do."

I let out a sigh, then nodded. "Thanks, then if you can drop me back here, I can finish getting my groceries and go home." I turned to the manager. "Can you please put three cans of tomatoes in that cart, and keep it for me? I don't think there's anything frozen in it."

"Will do. Here, Ted." He turned to the stocker. "When you finish picking up those cans, put three of them in this cart and then tag it with Ms. Gallowglass's name and put it in the back till she returns for it. And for the sake of the gods, clean this mess up pronto."

Rhonda asked them to keep her cart as well and led me out to the parking lot. The back window of her Toyota Highlander had those stick figure decals—a mom, four kids, and two dogs. Which meant she was either a single mother, a widow, or she was pissed at her husband and had pulled his decal off.

She bundled me into the front passenger seat, then plugged her phone into the GPS. "Where do you need to go?"

I went to the same doctor as Sandy—it had been easier than finding someone new when I moved to Bedlam. "Dr. Karen Osgood. She's on Rushwood Drive."

Rhonda plugged in the instructions and the GPS navigator began guiding her. As we eased out of the parking lot, I leaned against the headrest and tried not to move my thumb.

"I own the Bewitching Bedlam B&B. What do you do?" I really didn't relish the silence of a ride with a stranger.

She flashed me a smile. "I heard about your inn—and you—when the woman from your coven was murdered. Bad business, that."

"Rose. She was a friend," I murmured.

"I'm an accountant. I run my own business, Castille's Accounting. My husband started it, and after we got married, I became a partner in the firm. He was killed two years ago when he drove into Seattle. There was a lot of ice that year on the West Seattle Bridge, ending up in a five-car pileup. He was unlucky enough to be wedged between a big van and a semi-truck."

I blinked. That was a lot of information to take in. "I'm sorry."

She gave a little shrug, and a flash of pain crossed her face, but all she said was, "Life sucks, sometimes. But we had four kids and I had to pick up the pieces."

I steered the conversation away from painful memories. "Thanks so much for giving me a ride. I don't think my thumb is broken, but I'm not going to be able to do much until it's set. They really shouldn't block the aisles with stacks like that. It's much safer to put the cans on the shelves."

She let out a laugh. "You know how businesses are—make use of every inch of space. I don't like going into some antique or china boutiques because I'm afraid of breaking things. I may be a weretiger, but you'd think I was a proverbial bull in the china shop."

It was my turn to laugh. "I'm not graceless, but honestly, I sometimes think that Murphy's Law follows me around just waiting for an opportunity to prove itself."

We continued the banter until she eased the SUV into the doctor's parking lot. She turned off the ignition and jumped out, coming around to open the door for me. "Here, this will be easier than you trying to use that hand."

Holding my right hand in the air, I headed into the doctor's office with Rhonda following me. Thirty minutes later, I walked out again, sporting a wrist guard and a brace on my thumb. The pad below my thumb was also inflamed, so the doctor wanted me to wear the brace for three weeks.

"Thank gods I'm left handed," I said as we drove back to the market. At that moment, my phone rang. I managed to get it out of my purse and answered. It was Sandy.

"Can you meet me at the Blue Jinn for lunch? I need to talk to you about something. It's important."

That Sandy dove right in told me something had happened. "I'll meet you there at twelve-thirty. If I'm a little late, don't panic."

Back at the supermarket, I thanked Rhonda for her help and paid for my groceries. I'd have to pick up the rest of what I had come for later. As the bagboy carried them to my car, I glanced at the time. Twelve-ten. If I went home first, I'd be late. There was nothing that could spoil in the bags, so I decided to drive straight to the Blue Jinn.

Navigating wasn't nearly as difficult as I had thought. I just kept my thumb straight and used one hand to grasp the steering wheel. I passed the central park in the town square, where it was all decked out for Ostara. Bedlam celebrated all the holidays with gusto, and every six weeks like clockwork, the park would spring to life in a flurry of decorations marking the season. A group of schoolchildren were there, testing out their magic as they enchanted the bird baths and other statues to glimmer and glow.

The Blue Jinn was along Exxo Street, and I managed to find a parking space in the crowded lot. As I entered the diner, the noise and aromas from the lounge hit full force and I realized I was starving. The Blue Jinn had a stage for live music and dinner theater, and the lounge for drinks and finger food. I motioned to the hostess.

"I'm joining Sandy Clauson."

She consulted her table chart and then nodded, motioning to one of the nearby waitresses. "Please escort Ms. Gallowglass to table 14B."

I followed the waitress, who led me to a small booth near the windows overlooking the outdoor seating area. It was still too cool and rainy to sit outside, but the center fountain in the courtyard was flowing. It was a statue in the shape of a dolphin leaping out of the water, and water burbled out of its blowhole, and also from its mouth.

Sandy was already in the booth, poring over a menu, a tequila sunrise in hand. She was still wearing her sunglasses, and that meant something was up. She glanced up when I arrived.

"I'm glad you made it." She pointed to her drink. "Want one?"

I shook my head. "Water, please, and raspberry herb tea. I took a pain pill and the doctor suggested not mixing them with alcohol. While they won't make me drowsy on their own, he said that the combination would put me out like a light."

"Pain pill?" Sandy lowered her glasses and, judging by the red swollen eyes, I knew she had been crying.

"Um hmm." I held up my thumb. "Sprained it a good one at the grocery store." I waited until the waitress left to get my drinks and then leaned forward. "What's going on? You look like you've had one hell of a cry-fest."

She pressed her lips together, then nodded. "Yeah. I have."

A sudden fear ran through me. "Not Max...or

Jenna or Mr. Peabody? Are they all right?"

Again, Sandy nodded. "Yeah, they are. But you know I was supposed to go to a board meeting today?"

"Right, for your restaurants."

"Well, while I was changing for it, I got a call. My ex died. He had a heart attack at five-thirty this morning. They couldn't get hold of me till about an hour ago. I can't believe he's gone." She paused, then added, "And I can't believe that I still care this much," as a sob escaped her throat.

I pressed my lips together. Finally, I reached my good hand across the table and took her hand in mine. "I'm not surprised. You two were friends. He couldn't help it that he didn't realize he was gay until later on in life. Or at least, wasn't ready to admit it to himself. And you guys...you still love each other. How many times have you had dinner together in the past few years?"

She pulled out a tissue and blew her nose. "Once a month, on the clock. Every month. Yeah, we are...*were*...still friends. I wanted the best for him and he wanted me to be happy. After I got over the initial shock, I knew that I didn't want to carry a grudge."

I leaned across the table and took her hands in mine, squeezing her fingers gently. "Sandy, if you didn't care about him, then you wouldn't be hurting. Face it, you guys were meant to be in each other's lives. Just not the way you originally thought."

She worried her lip, holding tight to my hands. "You know he broke up with his boyfriend recently? His mother and father weren't happy at all when they found out he had left me and that there weren't going to be any grandbabies. I'm going to have to take care of the arrangements for the general service." She paused. "He focused more on his business than his magic, but would you preside over the Cord Cutting when it's time?"

I patted her hand as I let go. "Of course. I'd be happy to help. I liked Bart."

That much was true. Though I had never quite forgiven him for hurting Sandy the way he had, I also liked the guy. We had had many a late-night movie binge together, the three of us, until I had married Craig and Bart came out.

"Thanks. So tell me, what happened to your thumb? And how's Bubba doing? Did you get to see him?"

"Are you sure you want to know? You must be swimming in thoughts—"

"No, take my mind off Bart, please." She sounded so forlorn that I mustered up a gusto I didn't feel and, as we segued onto other subjects, I found myself thinking about how it never failed to shock when a friend died. No matter how many people had left your life, you never got used to it.

I WAS WALKING back to my CR-V when the sound of skidding tires filled my ears and I whirled to see an out-of-control pickup truck come sailing my way. Terror fueling my reflexes, I leaped out of the way just in time to avoid being creamed by the massive vehicle. The truck spun out, slamming into the side of the parking lot, which was basically a concrete retaining wall separating the restaurant from a small park. The driver was trapped, unable to get his door open. I raced toward the truck, Sandy hot on my heels, as a trail of gasoline trickled down from the gas tank.

"Crap—gas! Nobody light up!" I screamed at a couple of guys headed toward the truck. One of them was dangling a cigarette from his lips.

He must have heard me, because he came to a halt, falling forward as he lost his balance. The sudden jolt dislodged the cigarette and it flew out of his mouth, landing in the pooling gas. Sandy and I froze as it blazed to life, the flame traveling up the trickle of gas into the gas tank. An explosion reverberated through the air as the truck caught fire.

Frantic—the driver was still trapped—I raised my arms and focused on the fire. Fire was my element. Fire was my strength.

Flames eat flames, please depart.
Veil of flames, I bid thee part.
Open the way, bridge a path,
Hold back the fire's wrath.

As I chanted the spell, a break in the crackling flames opened up right in front of the passenger-side door. I focused on keeping the flames apart as Sandy ran forward. She grabbed the door handle and screamed—the metal was hot—but she didn't let go till she had wrested it open. By then the other man—the one without the cigarette—was by her side. He motioned for her to move. He crawled in the cab of the truck and a moment later, as I struggled to keep the hungry flames from gobbling up the truck, he emerged, dragging the unconscious driver. Sandy was calling 9-1-1 and we could hear sirens in the near distance.

"Clear—he was the only one in the truck!" the man called to me.

But the man who had been smoking was unconscious, as well. The force had knocked him silly, and a few wisps of the flame were heading directly for him across the pavement. Another bystander darted in to drag him out of the way. As everybody cleared from the path of the flames, I released them and they roared together, a ravenous monster of flame and fire, as thick black smoke rose from the truck.

The fire department and ambulance rolled into the parking lot and I hurried over to Sandy. Her right hand was burned, blistered across the pad directly below her fingers where she had grabbed hold of the handle. As the medics began to assess the condition of the two men, I made her join them to be treated.

"I'm all right—"

"You are not. Those are at least second-degree burns. Now hush up and let them treat you."

She nodded, tears in her eyes. "They hurt."

I gathered her in my arms and kissed her forehead. "I know they do. We'll do some healing work on them later, after the process has started."

She sat down on the tailgate of the medic unit. I wandered over to watch the burning truck. Why had the driver lost control? Was it just coincidence? But I really didn't believe in coincidence, and I had the sneaking suspicion that whatever force had hexed Bubba, had also caused my bank account to be pirated, and my thumb to be sprained. And now, I had almost been hit by a truck. When that hadn't happened, two men I didn't even know and Sandy had ended up taking the brunt of the attack. Whatever was going on, it was clear that I was being targeted and anybody around me was in danger because of it.

Chapter 9

DELIA SHOWED UP, recording what information she could find. Then, after the men were taken to the hospital and Sandy's hand was tended to, and the fire department managed to put out the fire, Sandy and I sat in my car, staring at the restaurant.

"Well, this proves it, Sandy. Somebody cast a hex on me and if anybody gets in the way, it puts them in danger. I *have* to find out who's responsible." I leaned forward, resting my head on the steering wheel. "I'd cast a Divining spell but I'm not sure it would work in this case. If I'm being cursed, then my magic is probably a little wonky. I'm almost afraid to find out."

"At least you were able to hold back the flames." Sandy regarded her hand. "It's been a shitty day all the way around, hasn't it?"

I nodded. "Last night wasn't much better. Come

back to my house?"

"Sure. Better to hang together when the shit hits the fan than try to dodge it alone."

"I feel like a magical Typhoid Mary."

"Well, you don't look it, if that's any comfort." And with that, she returned to her own car and followed me back to my place.

IT WAS THREE P.M. by the time we got back to the house, and Thornton took one look at our bandaged hands and began mixing a pitcher of margaritas. The pain pill had worn off with my adrenaline, so I decided against a second one. Self-medicating sounded better. I broke out the chocolate sandwich cookies and cheese tortilla chips. Lunch seemed a million miles away and holding back those flames had been difficult, at best.

As we retreated to the parlor, I glanced around.

"Bubba?" But the moment the name was out of my mouth, I stopped. Bubba wasn't here, I reminded myself. Bursting into tears, I tossed the food on the coffee table and slouched down on the sofa, crossing my arms across my stomach as I leaned forward, unable to do anything but cry.

"I'm sorry," I blubbered. "I can't stop thinking about Bubba."

Sandy sat next to me, reaching out to brush my hair back from my face. "Maddy, it's okay to cry. You love him. He's part of your life. He's been part of your life for hundreds of years, and you guys have a special bond."

"I want that bond to be with a fluffy orange cjinn, not some confused ab-happy human," I stuttered through the tears.

"I know. We'll figure this out. I promise you, we will." She frowned, looking around. "Dry your eyes. I'm going to ask some questions that you might not have been able to think of given the state you're in. First: when did weird crap start happening? I don't mean run-of-the-mill weird crap, but really oddball stuff?"

I hiccupped, trying to think. She handed me a tissue and I wiped my eyes, then blew my nose. I had lost my housekeeper, but that was less hex and more hormones.

"I guess...with the money in my bank account disappearing. Then Bubba. I had an accident in the store today and hurt my thumb. Then the truck." I paused, then raised my eyes to meet her gaze. "You don't think Bart..."

Sandy slowly shook her head. "No, love. Bart wasn't good at keeping his health up, and he had a history of heart disease in his family. The signs were all there, he just didn't read them until too late."

"I wonder what's going to happen next?" I felt queasy as a future of one disaster after another opened up before me.

"Stop right there. We don't know what's going to happen and there's no use borrowing trouble. Hold off on speculation until we figure out what the hex is. Now, did—" she paused as my cell phone rang.

I glanced at the Caller ID. Dr. Farrows. Feeling a

lump of panic rise in my throat, I answered. "Hello? Is Bubba okay?" The words poured out and I gulped a sob at the end.

"Bubba's fine, he's still in stasis," he said. "I just thought you might like to know that I've managed to dig up some information on the type of hex that hit Bubba."

Breathing deeply, I put him on speakerphone. "Anything you can tell me would help. I've had another not-so-fun-filled day."

"Well, the hex is pretty specific. It seems to be a form of Dirt Magic."

I stared at the phone. "Dirt Magic? Isn't that a little like Voudou?"

"Yes, though Dirt Magic is more street-magic, not formalized ritual. The only people I know who use Dirt Magic have origins either in the South, or they came over from the Old Country."

"Right. That I knew."

Dirt Magic was a slapdash form of Old World hexing—real Baba Yaga–level curses that could easily travel down through families. Though it was often seen as a poor man's magical system, the realities were that Dirt Magic was complex and utilized a wide variety of roots. It required precision in weaving the roots to produce the required effect. Dirt Magic had a lot in common with Voudou, and sometimes, the practice of one led right into the practice of the other.

"You have to find the object that brought it into the house. Dirt Magic always requires an anchor. I think you'll find the hex came in attached to something, and that something most likely has a glamour over it so that you can't spot it. That's all I can tell you for now, but I'll try to find out more."

As he hung up, I turned to Sandy. "Crap. Somebody's using Dirt Magic on me."

Sandy stared at me. "Dirt Magic? That can be nasty juju. The practitioners usually don't worry about backlash because by the time they cast spells like that, they're powerful enough to deflect most retaliation from their enemies." She nodded at the fire in the fireplace. "You should put that out. You know how much Dirt Magic likes fire. And you run fire, love."

I ran fire, Sandy ran air magic, and Fata had run water magic. Together, we had mustered up enough earth magic to form a balanced arena. But fire fueled a lot of hexes, and my own fire was probably stoking the flames.

"Crap. That means I should restrain my magic as much as I can until I find what's anchoring the spell, because any spark of fire could trigger something else to happen."

"Were you using flame before the accident in the parking lot?"

I thought back. "No, but I've been thinking about the night I found Bubba, and I was running flame strong that night. And I've been ticked off right and left, which strengthens the fire. In fact, I recently came to the conclusion that I need to start chilling out more because the flames seem to be building and I don't want them to get out of hand."

Sandy snapped her fingers. "Dirt Magic often goes hand in hand with Voudou. And who do we know who used Voudou?"

I frowned, trying to go through the miles-long mental checklist of magical friends in my circle. "I don't think I know anybody."

"Oh, yes, you do. But she's not part of the magical society here on Bedlam. Maddy, we do know someone who was a Voudou priestess. *Essie Vanderbilt*. Remember, she's the granddaughter of Marie Laveau."

Crap. I had totally spaced that fact. "You don't think Essie's after me again?"

"You're now the High Priestess of the coven, and she no longer has her fingers in the pie because Linda is in the Witches' Protection Program." Sandy suddenly stopped talking, her fingers on her lips.

Linda had been the High Priestess until recently. She and her daughter—whom Essie had essentially held hostage—were now in the Witches' Protection Program. Even though we understood why Linda had done what she had, the fact was she compromised both the Moonrise Coven and the entire community of Bedlam by allowing Essie to influence her. Essie didn't appreciate our interference, nor did she appreciate my refusal to play ball with her.

Sandy looked around till she found a notepad and scribbled out a note.

You think maybe the house is bugged?

I frowned. I hadn't even thought of that possibility. *I don't know*, I wrote.

Just then, Thornton came in. He stared at us, a

puzzled look on his face. "Is something wrong?"

I flashed Sandy a warning look. "Not really, Thornton. We just... Would you bring us a couple bottles of water, please?"

He excused himself and, a moment later, returned with our water. I glanced at them, making sure the seals hadn't been broken, and then handed them to him.

"If you could open these, please? With Sandy's burn and my sprained thumb, we have a bit of an issue with lids right now."

"Sure thing, Maddy." He twisted open the caps, then excused himself again and shut the door behind him.

I felt a bout of paranoia growing. The thought that Essie might have cast a hex on me was scary enough, but what if she *had* somehow bugged my house? I held out my notepad, scribbling another sentence.

Do you know if Essie can work Dirt Magic as well as Voudou? I need to talk to Auntie Tautau. She could tell what's wrong, I'm certain of it. But she was gone when I stopped there this morning.

Sandy took a long pull on the bottle, then motioned for me to follow her. We traipsed into the backyard, shutting the kitchen door behind us. I had bought a picnic table and benches once the snow had melted, and now we wandered over to sit under one of the apple trees, ignoring the chill.

"All right," Sandy said. "I wouldn't put it past Essie to learn all she could about that. Most vampires don't bother with magic, but the fact is, Essie will do whatever it takes to protect her seat on the throne, and she knows better than to trust you. She knows she can't manipulate you. And we know she wants to establish more than just her penny ante kingdom here."

"But why now? What set it off? I feel like there's more to this issue than just Essie suddenly deciding to make a move. Something isn't clicking for me. I feel like I don't have all the pieces to the puzzle." I sorted through everything I could think of that had happened since my account got hacked.

"Did anybody new come into your life recently? Beside Snow and the dwarves, I mean."

"I can't think of...wait." I glanced back at the house. "Well, there's Mr. Mosswood, but I really can't see him as the problem and he's been here several weeks. A few other guests came and went without anything seeming askew."

"Anybody besides guests?"

"No. *Wait*. Trina left and...*Thornton*. He's new. I hired him about a week before the shit hit the fan. Sandy, you don't suppose he's working for Essie? He's not a vampire."

"Maybe not, but that doesn't mean much. Essie has a lot of human groupies. You know how some of them get crazed about the vampire thing. They geek out over the blood-and-goth set and line up for a chance to get fanged. You have to admit, the proximity between when he showed up and when all this freakshow stuff started happening—it's way too convenient." Sandy winced and stared at her hand. "Damn, this hurts."

"It will, for a while."

"Sucks. Anyway, did you check out Thornton's references?"

"Yes, and they all checked out. Except..." I paused, thinking for a moment. "He has a gap of about five years between his last job and now. He said he was in a relationship that didn't work out and that he had been out of the workforce during that time. I know that happens, so I just let it be—especially when everything else checked out all right."

"You need to find out where he was during those five years." Sandy paused as a butterfly circled around the table. She held out her hand and the gorgeous swallowtail landed on her finger. A few moments later, the butterfly took wing again and flew off.

"I think you're right, but how do I go about it without sounding like I'm prying? And if he *is* in cahoots with Essie, won't I alert them by asking? I suppose I can start with Delia. If he has any sort of record, she can tell me."

I glanced at the sky. The clouds were building again, but we wouldn't see rain before nightfall, by the smell of the air. The storm was out over the water and was moving slowly onshore. The birds, though, were picking up on the incoming moisture, and singing loud and clear about it.

"Sometimes, I think about the way the world was when we were young. No technology, really, beyond primitive basics. Cities were few and far between, and the world seemed so incredibly large. Now, everything seems so immediate and close together. I sometimes miss those days." I shrugged. "But I don't miss the backward attitudes. The witch hunters and the slavers and the bigots—"

"Oh, we still have those," Sandy said. "Unfortunately, there will always be people who hate what they don't understand. Or hate who might threaten to tip the status quo that might be in force. I'd like to say I think we'll see a day when peace governs the land, but honestly? Right now, I'd like to just see peace govern one city."

I leaned my elbows on the table. "So how's it going with Max?"

A smile crept across her face. "Good. It's so good that it's scary. You know me—I shy away from any real relationships because, hey, I'm over three hundred and I've never found one that has lasted."

"Honey, you find a relationship that outlasts sixty or seventy years, let me know."

"Right. Let me just put it this way. It's too soon to tell, but I'm having fun and he hasn't pissed me off yet. And that's a miracle."

"I guess we give thanks for whatever sort of miracles come our way." I let out a long sigh. "I guess I should call Delia while we're out here, huh?"

Sandy leaned her elbows on the picnic table. "Yeah. I think you should."

I pulled out my phone and, once again, put in a call to the sheriff.

DELIA HAD PROMISED to find out everything

she could. She *wasn't* pleased to hear that Essie might be up to her old tricks again. And she was none too happy to hear that someone was practicing Dirt Magic in Bedlam.

"Dirt Magic isn't forbidden, but we discourage it, you know. Linda wrote that into the charter." Delia paused, and I could hear the tap of her pencil on the desk. "Maddy, given you're the High Priestess of the Moonrise Coven, I think you need to understand that you *will* attract enemies. I don't think that fact has set in yet. Essie wasn't the only one who was out to snare Linda into her own agenda. There are other groups on the island who would love to have you in their back pocket."

I sobered at her tone. "I am starting to get the picture."

"We haven't gotten around to discussing this yet, but you need to be aware that Bedlam isn't as rosy on the underside as it seems on the surface. There are dark secrets in this town. My father was sheriff before me, and I remember the days when he would come home, unable to talk about the problems on the job, but he would pace the floor half the night."

"I thought you took over from your grandfather?"

"I did. He retired when I was old enough for the job. But my father was sheriff for a while before that. Ma begged him to quit. She wanted him to buy a little farm where we could just sit back and raise chickens and grow fruit trees. But he would always say, 'Margie, I can't do that. Folks depend on me.' After Da was killed, Grandpa took over until I grew up and decided I wanted the job. Now folks depend on *me*, and I wish I knew half of what my father did." Delia let out a sigh. "Grandpa never bothered to look below the surface. He moved away last year to Montana to stay with my aunt. But he walked softly after my father was killed, and he tried to talk me into doing the same."

I didn't remember her grandfather—but then, even though I had been coming over to Bedlam since the 1950s for coven activities, I hadn't ever had much cause to talk to the law.

"Delia, what happened to your father? Who killed him?" While I'd had plenty of chances to talk to her, I really didn't know her all that well.

Delia paused, then said, "Da was out on a call, checking out reports of suspicious activity on the south side of the island. He radioed in that he was on the trail of something that—in his words—'looks mighty suspect.' That was the last they heard from him. When a couple of the detectives went out to check on why he wasn't answering the radio, they found him dead. No signs of struggle, but it wasn't of natural causes, either."

"Did they ever ascertain the cause of his death?"

"Yes, but that led to its own cascade of unsolved questions. The medical examiner discovered that he was poisoned. But even though the doc went over his body with a fine-tooth comb, he couldn't find any marks to indicate a bug bite or snake bite. The venom was still in his system but didn't match anything on record. Whatever it was, was highly toxic and would have killed him within seconds of being administered. Da...was just...dead. There was nothing to indicate suicide, and the case is still open and deemed suspicious, but nobody ever found out what happened."

I wanted to ask if that was why she decided to run for sheriff—to find her father's killer—but that seemed like prying. If she wanted me to know, she'd tell me.

"Anyway, the reason I'm telling you about all this is so that you're aware there are undertones to this island. I know you have been coming out here for over sixty years, but Maddy, don't make the mistake of thinking Bedlam is what it seems on the surface. It's a wonderful town, and magical and full of friendly people, but there's always a shadow side."

"Just like there is to magic," I murmured. "All right. Find out what you can about Essie and Thornton, and then get back to me. Meanwhile, I'm going to check on Bubba again tonight and start looking through my house for whatever it is that brought the hex in with it. Jordan Farrows said it has to be an object—Dirt Magic needs an anchor."

As I hung up, my mind was churning. I already knew about undertones and shadow sides, but Delia's story about her father stuck with me. What could he have found that got him killed?

"Penny for your thoughts," Sandy said.

"Just musing over something Delia told me. She's going to do some background checks on Thornton for me, as well as seeing if Essie might be up to anything. Meanwhile, I was thinking. We might want to go down and buy a bug finder—the electronic kind."

"We might also want to check with Krenshaw's Magic Supplies. They might have something to find magical bugs as well."

I stood and stretched. "I'll grab my keys and we'll head out. Then let's take a sweep through the house to see if we can find any eavesdroppers, and maybe—if we're lucky—whatever is anchoring the hex."

And with that, we got busy.

Chapter 10

BY THE TIME we had both a wireless bug detector and a magical bug finder, it was almost five-thirty. Of course, we had stopped for a late lunch—and by lunch, I mean shakes and fries. We arrived home to find that Thornton was out. He left a note saying he was on a date and would be home late.

"I'm glad he's gone," I mouthed to Sandy as we began our sweep. We silently went through every room, opened every closet, poked under every bed and in every cupboard. An hour later, we were back in the living room.

"Nothing. The house isn't bugged. That's one relief. Now I just need to figure out what the anchor is—"

"Anchors work when they're triggered. Which means whatever it was had to have a point that set it off. Which means either you, or someone in the house, had to have done something that released the magic." Sandy sat down. "My feet hurt. You sure have a lot of house. I thought mine was big, but the Bewitching Bedlam? Huge."

My mansion had two stories, not including the attic and basement, and fifteen rooms, not including the bathrooms, the basement, or the attic. Five bedrooms, a maid's room, the kitchen, butler's pantry, dining room, living room, laundry, parlor, grand ballroom, office, and the library. The basement had an additional three rooms for storage.

My phone rang and I glanced at the Caller ID. Delia. I answered it as I sat down at the dining room table. "Hello?"

"Maddy? I found out a few things. Brace yourself."

That didn't sound good. "What's up?"

"Thornton was Essie's favorite boy toy until two weeks ago. He was with her for almost five years. I'm not sure what happened, but he stormed out on her. If she found out that he's working for you..."

"Yeah." My stomach roiled. Essie would consider this an act of war, especially if she hadn't given him the go-ahead to leave. "Crap. Do you know why he left?"

"No, but I do know that once you're mixed up with Essie, you don't just walk away. Be careful, Maddy. This isn't going to go down easy." She hung up.

I sat back, contemplating my options.

"What is it?" Sandy tapped me on the knee.

"I know where Thornton spent the last five years."

"Where?"

"Under Essie Vanderbilt's rule. He was her boy toy until about two weeks ago when, apparently, he stormed out. And *bingo*, look who hired him and took him in." I rubbed my forehead, trying to decide whether to throw myself at Essie's mercy, or maybe just knock Thornton a good one over the head and drop him off in front of her house. "This is a delicate situation."

"Delicate situation? This is material for a full-blown war. You've hired the vampire queen's favorite. It won't matter that he stormed out on her. Nobody who pledges themselves to Essie ever leaves. Nobody gets out alive, anyway—not anyone who volunteers for her. You've got to fire him, or Essie's going to have your head."

"She *had* to be the one who set the hex on me. And in doing so, she's hurt my sweet Bubba and bilked me out of fifty-four grand. I don't care that I got the money back. The fact is she's a menace." I was getting angrier by the minute. "I agree, Thornton was an idiot for staying around Bedlam, but I won't throw him to the wolves. Or rather, to the bats." I paused, trying to think my way through the situation. "Essie Vanderbilt is not going to chase me out and she's not getting away with this bullshit."

"Let's find the anchor and destroy it, then we can concentrate on turning the tables on her, then. But what are you going to do about Thornton?"

"First, he and I need to have a long talk. He can't just put my household in danger without taking responsibility. He has to know Essie would come after him." I pushed myself away from the table. "I've brought a lot of things into the house, but now I know it has to have arrived after Thornton started working for me." I paused, then turned to Sandy. "*That pin.* The one that came the night that you and Max were here—the heart-shaped pin with the ruby? I put it on because I thought a friend had sent it."

"Crap. Where is it now?" She hustled me to the stairs. "In your room?"

"Yeah. Let's go." We raced upstairs and I sorted through the jewelry lying loose on my vanity table. There was the pin, and as I picked it up, in the pit of my stomach I knew this was the culprit. "This is it."

She held out her hand. "Let me see. I'm not quite so biased, given that I'm not the target."

I cautiously placed the heart in her hand and she closed her fingers over it, focusing on the pin. After a few minutes, she let out a slow breath. "The energy is cloudy and makes me cringe. Did you try to cleanse it after you got it?"

"I didn't think it would be magical. I thought it was new." I stared at the heart, wanting to tear the thing to shreds. "The good thing is, if I destroy this, Bubba will be all right, I think. Let me call Dr. Farrows."

Farrows answered within three rings.

"I found the anchor. What do I do with it? Can we help Bubba with it?"

He sounded pleased. "Definitely. But you should know that with a hex like this one—that probably bounced off of you—destroying the anchor will not remove the entire curse. If you want to break the curse on Bubba, bring it over and I can destroy it here and take care of the hex on him."

"Will it right everything else?"

"Not necessarily. For a hex as strong as this one, you really need a hex-breaker to take care of the entire muddle."

I paused, thinking. Other things had gone wrong, but nothing as serious as Bubba. At least nothing as serious for me. "Will having the anchor intact make it easier to create a hex-breaker?"

"Not necessarily. Not for a powerful-enough Dirt Witch."

That sealed it. I wasn't leaving Bubba in distress any longer than I had to. If needed, I'd take a plane down South to find me a Dirt Witch.

"All right, be right over." I hung up, scribbled a note for Aegis—who would be waking up in about half an hour—and then Sandy and I hightailed it out to my CR-V. We were at the doctor's office within fifteen minutes.

He examined the brooch, dunking it into some sort of solution. It turned a bright red for a moment. "Yes, this has Dirt Magic permeating all through it. I'm going to be destroying the brooch, the ruby and all. You do realize that?"

"Go right ahead. Be my guest. If I never see it again, it will be too soon." Sandy and I backed away as he placed it into a large stone container. I wasn't sure what he was planning on doing with it, but another moment answered my question as he poured a vile-smelling concoction over the brooch, just barely covering it. The pin instantly began to bubble and disintegrate.

"What the hell is that stuff?" Sandy tried to get a closer peek, but neither she nor I really had any interest in getting too close.

"Oh, I have a number of acids at hand that can destroy bone, metal, you name it." He laughed his best villain laugh. "Mwahaha!"

"Dude, if you want to play mad scientist, now's not the time. Not to be a buzzkill, but...Bubba..." I bit my lip, trying not to cry.

Farrows sobered immediately. "I get it. Sorry, Maddy." He moved to the table, where he gave Bubba a shot of something. Another moment, and the heart was totally gone. Bubba began to stir, and Jordan picked him up and carried him out of the magic-free room, with Sandy and me following.

We went into an exam room and waited. Bubba blinked, shaking his head, and woozily tried to get to his feet. He was still in cat form.

"Looks like it worked. Bubba won't be changing back into his human form."

"Oh, thank gods. Bubba—you're okay." I leaned down and kissed his head.

"Murrow?" Bubba hiccupped as he mewed.

"I know you don't understand exactly what's going on, but I'll do my best to explain later."

Jordan gave him a thorough examination. "Good news. The hex is gone—at least from Bubba. This doesn't guarantee that you and your house are clear, though. But, on the plus side, the moment the anchor was destroyed, it should have put a stop to anything new coming in. As for everyone who's been affected? You'll have to have a professional lift the curse, because it can still work on those who were touched by it."

"What about me?" I wasn't entirely clear on how this worked. "Is there a way to tell if I'm still being affected by the hex?"

"Chances are, you are. I can examine you and find out, now that I know what to look for." He glanced at Sandy's hand. "How did you get that?"

I answered for her. "Would you mind examining her, too? I'm thinking she ended up with that injury as a result of being near me. She was there the night the heart brooch arrived and I activated it—I assume just by pinning it on."

Jordan had us line up on the examination table. He checked our vitals, then proceeded to draw a vial of blood from each of us, carefully labeling the glass tubes. As we watched, he dropped three drops of a clear reagent into each vial.

"If it turns bright pink, you're under the curse. If not, then you're clear, at least from this hex. I had to go through twenty different tests with Bubba to find out just what kind of magic was affecting him." Jordan sat down on a stool, spinning to face us. "This will take about twenty minutes, so you might as well get comfortable."

I put in a call to Aegis, but nobody answered. "He's probably in the shower." It occurred to me that we needed some test like this for the Bewitching Bedlam. "Can you use this reagent on a house to figure out if it's under attack?"

"No, but I can compound a powder. Once you get home, you can set the container in any room, open it, and twenty minutes later, if it's turned bright pink, you'll know the whole house needs to be cleansed." He set to work on that while Sandy and I waited. I scooped Bubba into my arms and he began to purr and knead against my shoulder.

"Will Bubba be in danger again if the house is under a general hex?"

"No. By destroying the anchor for his curse, it will prevent him from being re-infected, so to speak. It's like...think of it as though he's been immunized to this particular spell. But, Maddy, once you do have your house cleared, you need to take precautions and beef up your wards every few weeks. You obviously have pissed off somebody. This hex wasn't a teenage joyride, so to speak. This was serious business. Dirt Magic is dangerous." He poured a white crystalline powder into a plastic petri dish, then covered it and taped it shut. "Here. When you get home, do as I told you."

"So things still could happen, then? Just not to Bubba."

"Right, though nothing that hasn't already been set into motion. But you know how hexes like this are. Some effects have a long brew time, others are quick. You could wake up covered in spots tomorrow, because the hex is working on you even now." He glanced at the clock. "Five more minutes."

"Yeah, I know."

He was right. Hexes like this one played out long term. Even though we had destroyed the anchor, if something had been triggered but not yet manifested, it would still go through the cycle until the hex was lifted. And it sounded like this was a doozy. If it hadn't been so strong, I could have used the heart pin to destroy the entire hex, but apparently it was powerful enough that I needed a hex-breaker.

"Okay, we have our results. Maddy—you're infected." He held up both vials. They were both bright magenta. "Sandy, you are, too. My guess is that everybody who was present that night, or who came into the house within twenty-four hours, has a good chance of having been slapped with the hex."

I turned to Sandy. "How has Max been doing?"

She groaned. "He was there, wasn't he? He's had one hell of a week. Two big malls where he was going to sell franchises to his clothing store pulled out of their deals. I dread telling him the most likely cause."

"Nothing seems to be going on with Aegis. I wonder if the hex works on vampires."

"If Essie cast it, maybe not since she *is* a vamp."

I shook my head. "That guarantees nothing. Her loyalty doesn't extend to anybody she thinks crossed her, and Aegis works with me. All right, we need to find a hex-breaker. I'm hoping that it won't have infected the actual house. If it's only us, it will be a lot easier to eradicate."

"What about Thornton? He was there," Sandy said. "And Mr. Mosswood and Mrs. Periwinkle?"

I paused. "Crap. I'll call the latter two and see how they're doing. Thornton's the one Essie is really pissed at. I wonder if he received anything—" I paused as my phone rang. It was Delia. Holding my breath, I answered. "Hey, what's up?"

She paused for a moment, then said, "Maddy, I hate to tell you this, but we just found Thornton. He's dead. His car skidded off the road and hit a tree."

And just like that, we had our answer.

I TOLD DELIA I'd be coming over to the station the next morning. There wasn't anything anybody could do to help Thornton tonight.

"Listen, Sandy, if my house is infected, can Bubba stay with you? Even though he can't be hit again by the spell, that doesn't mean he can't be hurt by collateral damage, like if the house burns down or gets hit by a fucking meteor."

"Of course." She regarded her hand. "The salve Dr. Farrows put on my burn really helped. He promised it would heal faster than what the paramedics used."

Before we had left, Jordan had examined both our hands. Mine, he had cast a little healing spell over and I could tell the sprain was already relaxing a bit. He had changed Sandy's bandages and pasted her burns with a thick, gooey salve that stunk, but that had immediately gone to work, bubbling up over the burns.

We arrived back at the house. The lights were off. Thornton wasn't at home, obviously, because Thornton was dead. But Aegis should be around. Cautiously, we approached the kitchen. The door was locked, and there was no sign of any problems.

I set down Bubba's carrier down right outside the door. "Give me twenty, Bubs, until I know whether it's safe to leave you here by yourself, or if you have to go spend time at Sandy's."

"Mrow." He didn't sound happy.

"I know you're hungry, but just be glad you're back in your own form."

"Purp," was the immediate response. Which meant, *Yeah, I'm happy.*

As we entered the kitchen, I flipped on the lights. Nothing looked out of place, but there was no note. "I wonder where Aegis is," I said. "Can you set up the powder on the kitchen table? I'm going to check the basement."

"Sure." Sandy took the petri dish from me and began to arrange it according to Jordan's instructions.

I headed to the basement. The door was over to the side of the kitchen, and it was closed but not locked. I was starting to get worried. Aegis was always up right at sunset, though he sometimes took a shower, which meant he might be upstairs in my bathroom. I opened the door and flipped on the switch. We had finally gotten the railing fixed and the basement level mostly cleared out. At least it didn't resemble the Munsters' home anymore.

We had also been through a number of the old trunks and furniture that had come with the house, and donated a good share of what we found to thrift shops. We had even sold a few pieces to antique dealers. But there were several pieces we had yet to touch.

The basement had three rooms. The main one

was quite large, with the furnace in the far corner. The second was a pantry, though I wasn't about to use it for that. I was thinking of converting it into a suite for vampires looking for a room, but hadn't decided yet whether that was the best course of action.

The third room was Aegis's lair. We had painted the long, narrow chamber sky blue with a white ceiling. The room held his coffin, a reading nook, and a small refrigerator filled with bottled blood. He also had a craft table that held his jigsaw puzzles. He was a fiend for the large, sprawling ones, and down here, Bubba wouldn't be likely to knock it over. Plus, if Aegis had spare time before going to sleep for the day, he could sit and work on the puzzle and not just twiddle his thumbs, waiting for the sunrise to drag him to sleep.

I tapped on the door. There was a soft squeak from the other side. What the hell? It didn't sound like a dragging shoe or anything like that. I cautiously opened the door and ducked as a bat swept out and over my head. A very large, black bat. The bat circled me, then hovered in front of my face. He didn't look very happy or friendly.

I started to shoo him away, but then stopped. *Oh, hell.*

"You *aren't*..."

Again, a loud squeak.

"Aegis?"

The bat let out another series of squeaks, very high pitched and almost out of my hearing range.

"Oh, crap. Aegis, is that you?"

He flew around the room quickly, clearly agitated, and then once again hovered in front of my face.

I wanted to ask what had happened but I didn't speak "bat" and Aegis was obviously in the midst of some sort of crisis. I cleared my throat.

"If you can't turn back into your human form, fly over to the puzzle and back."

Bingo. The bat flew over to the puzzle and then returned.

"Can you turn into any other form?" I knew that Aegis could turn into a rat if he chose, and sometimes, he could turn into a wolf, though he seldom did. "If you can, fly over to the puzzle. If not, over to the fridge."

He flew over to the fridge and back. Cripes on a platter.

"Okay, you can obviously understand me, so listen. Sandy and I found out what's going on. Fly upstairs and we'll find a place for you to hang out. Then I'll explain what we learned." I turned and dashed up the steps, grimacing as I jammed my thumb on the railing.

Sandy was staring at the powder. "We still have fifteen minutes to go. Where's Aegis?" she asked as I appeared at the basement door.

I stood aside, waiting for him to fly through.

"Right here."

He flew into the room, flipped upside down, and took hold of the curtain rod, hanging there.

"Uh-oh." Sandy glanced at Aegis, then back at me. "Stuck in that form?"

"Twenty points to the woman with the burned hand." I sat down, staring at Aegis. Slowly, I began to explain everything that had happened. "So, Thornton's dead. Sandy and I are both hurt. But Bubba's okay. I'm going to leave him over at Sandy's if the house itself was cursed."

Aegis let out a loud screech, then a series of chattering noises. He spread his wings a couple times, flapping them loudly. Obviously, he wasn't thrilled about the situation.

We waited, staring at the dish of powder, until twenty minutes passed. The powder remained white. Another five minutes and I let out a loud sigh of relief.

"Okay, the house itself is all right. The hex must have been aimed at me, and unfortunately it sideswiped everybody else who was here that night. It's probably been radiating out from me to affect others." At least one thing had gone right today, which—given the extent of things that had gone wrong—was actually a relief.

"Now what?" Sandy asked as I brought Bubba in and let him out of his carrier. He scampered around, then raced over to his food dish, letting out a plaintive yowl.

"Thank gods for electric can openers," I said, managing to position the can properly so that I could open it without hurting my thumb. As I shook out the food into a dish and put it down for Bubba, along with clean water, I ran over various options in my mind.

"We have to find someone who can reverse Dirt Magic hexes, which means we either find a very powerful multi-elemental witch, or we find a Dirt Witch. I still think Auntie Tautau is the best one to ask."

"You know, there's somebody else who might know how to deal with this. Remember Garret James? He's a snakeshifter and I think he has a background in Dirt Magic."

"It's too late to call him now, but tomorrow, I'll contact him. Since the house is clear, but we're both infected, it won't matter if Bubba stays here or goes with you. I guess I'll just keep him here tonight."

"All right," Sandy said. "But be careful. We know that Essie's on the warpath. Don't trigger her into trying anything worse. I love you, woman, but sometimes you can really pull stupid stunts. It's that impetuous, fiery nature of yours."

I gave her a long look. "Oh, really?" But my bark had no bite. I knew she was right.

She snorted. "I know you. And I know what I'd be tempted to do. Together, we've gotten ourselves in more trouble than a pack of hyenas in a room full of laughing gas." With that pithy advice ringing in my ears, she headed out for home, and I turned to face my boyfriend the bat.

Chapter 11

THE NIGHT PASSED fairly quietly. Having a bat hang over my bed watching me was a weird experience, but Aegis seemed intent on keeping an eye on me. Come early morning, I made sure he was back downstairs in the basement. He didn't want to go into his coffin, and given that, in bat form, he wouldn't be able to open it when he woke up, I understood. He settled down on top of it and fell asleep as soon as sunrise hit. Given there were no windows in his lair, I figured it would be safe to leave him there.

I slowly returned upstairs, thinking about the coming day.

By eight A.M., I stood at the door of my closet, wondering how the hell I was going to make it through the day. Today was Ostara, so tonight I'd be leading the town ritual. That meant making sure the Moonrise Coven had everything covered.

With Thornton dead, I was out another house-keeper, which entailed taking out another classified ad and explaining to prospective applicants why my turnover rate was sky high.

And I needed to find a Dirt Witch to break the hex. I also decided I should draw up a detailed plan so that my house and land weren't ever this vulnerable again, and that meant scheduling regular sessions to ward the house and everyone in it.

I finally shimmied into a pair of jeans and a tank top and brushed my hair back into a high ponytail. I slapped on some makeup and then dashed downstairs.

Damn it. No Thornton meant no coffee. Aegis in bat form meant no breakfast. I grumbled my way over to the refrigerator and pulled out ham and bread and mayo, slapping together a quick ham sandwich. I didn't bother wrestling with the espresso machine. I'd pick up a mocha on my way to the sheriff's office. Finally, I warned Bubba to keep an eye on things and hide if anything bad happened, and then once again, I headed out the door, on my way to see Delia.

AFTER A QUICK stop at Bouncing Goats Espresso Shack, where Gillymack greeted me again, I had my quint-shot mocha. I hightailed it over to Bedlam Town Hall.

The sheriff's office was part of a large building on the other side of Bedlam. The massive brick structure housed not only Delia's department, but the county clerk, the courthouse, the fire department, the utilities office, the mayor's office, and the library. Over a hundred years old, the Bedlam City Hall had been a mammoth undertaking of stonework and masonry. Outside, the building looked like a grave, stern structure, but inside, everything was all updated and calm. The halls might as well have formed a labyrinth, but signs directing visitors to where they wanted to go were clear and unmistakable.

As I strode past the library and City Hall, I realized that the hallways were so empty because most of the offices were closed for Ostara, which was a government holiday in Bedlam. The library was still open, but it looked like most people were out enjoying the sudden bout of balmy weather that had greeted me when I left the house. It was already in the low sixties, and while the sky was overcast, rain wasn't predicted for another twenty-four hours.

I continued through the hallways until I reached the back wing, which housed the fire department, courthouse, and the sheriff's office. As I pushed through the swinging doors, Bernice, the receptionist who was also the dispatcher, waved at me. She was talking into her headset, and she held up a finger, pointing me toward the waiting area. I nodded, taking a seat, listening as she attempted to field the caller.

"I'm sorry that you have an infestation of snails in your garden, Mrs. Chumalug, but we can't arrest your neighbor for cursing your garden. Snails are common around here. Might I suggest you set out bowls of beer for them? ... No, I am not being facetious. You set out the bowl, let them get in, then throw the slugs and snails away with the beer.... Yes, I understand you don't approve of alcohol, but—all right then, why don't you... No, I am not being flippant."

Delia peeked out into the waiting room, saw me, and motioned me back. Silently wishing Beatrice the best in dealing with Mrs. Chumalug, I followed the sheriff down the hall, through a maze of desks, into her office. She closed the door behind me and motioned for me to sit down. I was nursing the last of my mocha. The surge of caffeine had done a world of good in waking me up.

"So...Thornton's dead." I spilled out the story about the hex and Bubba and everything else that had happened, ending with, "I have a bunch of Thornton's things at my place. Should I wait for his family, or do you want me to bag them up and bring them in?"

She shrugged. "We looked for family but couldn't find anybody. You can keep them, if you want, or bring them here, I guess."

I glanced around her office and finally asked what was on both of our minds. "Given he was Essie's boy toy, are you certain this was an accident? Could it have been murder?"

"We've found no evidence, but who knows at this point?" Delia opened a file folder and shoved a couple pictures across the desk.

I picked up the photos, studying them. The car was a crumpled mass of metal. At least I didn't see

Thornton in the picture. I had seen a lot of people die over the years, but I really wasn't feeling up to seeing such a sunny, helpful man crushed by two tons of metal crashing into a tree. The other picture was of skid marks. He had suddenly veered off the road, so quickly there were scraps of tire on the asphalt.

"Tire blowout?"

"No, we checked for that. He skidded so quickly that it actually ripped some of the tread off the wheel. He must have been driving like a bat out of hell. See how wide of a swing the skid marks make? As totaled as the car is, he must have hit the tree at around seventy miles per hour."

"That doesn't sound like Thornton." My stomach lurched. "There must not have been much left."

"No, there really wasn't. I'm afraid that what's left of him is probably better off at the crematorium."

I was about to ask who was responsible for taking charge of his remains when Delia's phone rang. She answered, her expression changing from somber to guarded.

"No, really? All right, put her on." A pause, then she continued. "Good morning, Shar-Shar. To what do I owe the pleasure of this call?" Another pause, then Delia let out an exasperated sigh. "Really? Are you fucking kidding me?"

I leaned forward. I knew the name from somewhere, but couldn't place it.

"I can't do much about it if she has a POA. Yes, tell the morgue to prepare the body for you—or what's left of it. His things? Yes, I'll tell her. No, *I said* I'll tell her. She can bring them here and leave them for you. No, I am *not* going to accompany you to her door to get them. Deal with it and tell your mistress to suck it up." Delia slammed down the phone. "I probably shouldn't have said that."

"Who were you talking to?" I had the horrible feeling I had been included in the conversation in a way that I really didn't want to be.

"Shar-Shar. Essie's human lapdog. Sharlene is Essie's secretary who deals with all her business affairs during the day. Shar-Shar is more than a secretary, actually. The woman is a bloodhound. If there's something Essie wants, she makes sure Essie gets it."

I had had it up to my eyebrows with Essie.

"Essie can kiss my ass. She's behind all of this. I know it. And any fucking vampire who hurts me or my loved ones can take a ride on my broomstick." Exasperated, I flailed and a sudden flame caught hold in my hand. I stared at it, frowning.

"Maddy, put that out. *Right now*, before you set off the sprinkler system." Delia wasn't angry, she just gave me a warning look.

Frustrated, I pulled the fire back. But that didn't stop my fingers from itching. When I had snuffed out the flame, all I could think about was taking my long silver spike that I had recently dug out of the keepsake chest and driving it through Essie's chest. I had learned over the years that there were good vampires. But vamps like Essie gave the entire set a freakshow bad name.

"You will *not* go attack Essie. I can read you loud and clear. Listen, if she's guilty of hexing you, we'll figure out what to do about it. But if you dust her, that leaves her throne open to every wannabe in the area. And Maddy, you know as well as I do that there are bigger and badder vamps out there than Essie. A lot worse." Delia held my gaze for a moment.

I reined in my anger, but I was still seething. "All right. You make a good point." I debated telling her that she didn't know just how big or how bad some of them were, but I wasn't sure how secure her office was. "Delia, how well protected do you keep this office?" I brought out a notebook and scribbled, *Bugs, cameras?* I showed it to her.

She blinked. "That's a good question, and one I wish I had the answer to. We do a sweep every so often, but there's never any guarantee. How about if I walk you out after we're done here? I want to get that recipe for cornbread from you."

I stared at her like she was crazy. I didn't cook. But then I realized that she was giving me a chance to talk to her privately. "Oh, right. It's Aegis's recipe, but man, it's good. Anyway, what did Shar-Shar want?"

"Shar-Shar wanted to tell me that Essie will be claiming Thornton's body. And they want you to return his possessions. Apparently—" she shook her head as I was about to protest. "*Apparently,* Essie has a signed power of attorney giving her the right to collect his worldly goods. He signed it when he went to work for her five years ago. *There's nothing we can do.*"

For some reason, my heart ached when I heard that. Thornton had probably signed his soul over to her—metaphorically speaking, of course. Vamps didn't collect souls. But they collected lives.

"I'll bring everything to the station," I said with a quiet shrug.

"They wanted to come to your house to make certain..."

"That I didn't keep anything? They can fuck the hell off. I said I'll bring his things to the station. If Essie doesn't like it, she can fu—forget about it." I let out a long sigh, deflating like a popped balloon. The buzz from my mocha had died down and I felt exhausted.

"That will be fine. I told Shar-Shar that." Delia nodded toward the door. "Come on, walk me out to the parking lot. I need to get something from my truck, anyway."

As we headed out the door, all I could think about was the happy man who had just wanted to get away from a bad relationship, who had brightened my life for just a little while.

OUTSIDE, I MOTIONED for Delia to walk over to my CR-V. "Here's the deal. I wasn't going to bring you into this, but I think you should know. But do not tell anybody else without asking me, or your life could be in danger. Mine already is." I paused. "Actually, do you want to know? What I have to say could affect your life and your job at some point in the future."

"I make it my habit to keep informed," Delia

said. "What did you manage to dig up?"

"You remember when I was on vacation in January? Aegis and I went up to the Astra Alpine Chalet?" I shivered. The chalet had been beautiful. What had happened there had not been so lovely.

"You were caught in that avalanche, right?"

"Correct. I won't want to go into everything that happened, but I discovered that there's a secret society of ancient vampires called the Arcānus Nocturni. We're talking older than Aegis and definitely older than Essie. A number of vampires probably don't even know they exist."

"I don't like where this is going," Delia said.

"You'll like it a whole lot less when I tell you their biggest secret." There was no way to ease into the matter. "Delia, these vampires can walk under the sun."

She stared at me. "No. You're joking, right?" But the look on her face told me she knew I was serious.

"They're immune to the sunlight. They can walk among us and we'd never know by looking or talking to them that they were vampires. Unless you happen to notice they aren't breathing or you touch them and feel their cold skin. Delia, they have long memories, and I'm pretty sure they have an agenda that doesn't include our welfare on it. I'll tell you all about the trip some day, once I stop having nightmares. But trust me, when you say there are worse vampires than Essie, you're not kidding."

"Are you sure Essie isn't part of this society?" Delia asked.

"Not entirely, but I really doubt she has anything to do with them. Essie likes her power too much to accept anybody else's rules. But you and I both know the vampires are trying to dig a toehold in Bedlam. Even without the Arcānus Nocturni behind them, that's scary enough."

"True. So now we have both Essie to contend with and the possibility of this secret society trying to wedge their way in. Just what I wanted to hear. What are your thoughts on the matter?"

I thought about it for a moment, then shrugged. "I'm not certain. All I know is that I need to find someone who can break a Dirt Magic hex, because Aegis really needs to turn back into himself instead of hanging around as a bat. Not to mention, I'm tired of feeling like Typhoid Mary. Hey, do you know somebody named Garret James? Sandy mentioned he might know how to break a curse."

"Cripes, she really gets around, doesn't she? I *do* know Garret. He's basically a good-hearted person, but I wouldn't want to be on his bad side. And I'm not sure if he has any ties to Essie, so walk softly, Maddy."

"I will." I hadn't thought about the possibility that he might be in cahoots with the vampire queen. "All right, I'm heading out. I'll drop off Thornton's possessions tomorrow. If Essie complains—"

"I know, she can suck your ass." Delia laughed. "But I'll find a better way of wording it. Meanwhile," she sobered, her laugh disappearing, "you be careful. Given what you've told me, you need to watch your step, Maddy. Vampires who can walk in the sunlight... None of us would be safe at any time."

"Trust me, I've thought about that." As I drove off, watching her in my rearview mirror, it occurred to me that Delia had to walk a very tricky tightrope as the sheriff. I could never pull it off.

I WAS HUNGRY, so pulled into the drive-thru window at Piper's Chicken. While I was in line waiting for my order, I called Sandy for Garret's information and she texted me his address.

"Thanks. Say, how are things going with the arrangements for Bart's funeral?" With the focus mainly on my problems, she hadn't had much of a chance to talk through her pain.

Sandy let out a soft sigh. "It's going. It's hard because his ex—the waiter—is sticking his nose in. He's all out of joint because he thinks Bart should have left him a big wad of money. But they weren't married, and Bart broke up with him some time ago. I helped build the diners to the success they are today, and that little bitch can keep his fingers out of the pie."

She paused. Then, "Oh, Maddy. I didn't think this would hit me so hard. I was so angry when Bart first told me he was leaving—and it somehow made it worse that it was for a man. I never forgave him for not telling me when he first realized he was gay. He broke our vows, he broke my trust. But over the years, he's done what he could to rebuild it. I know he was sorry. I never stopped loving him, though that love changed over the years. When he stopped trying to be a good husband, he actually became a good friend."

The pain in her voice was palpable. I wasn't sure what to say. If I had been over at her house, I could have rubbed her back, or hugged her, or just held her hand while she talked, but the phone felt so freaking impersonal.

"Bart knew that you cared about him, and he cared about you. You two had the best post-break-up relationship I've ever seen. We'll do a Cord Cutting ceremony that would make him proud, but only when you're ready. And I'll be there for the service. I promise, I'll walk you through it."

She cried for a little longer, then hiccupped and sniffed away the tears. "Thanks. That means so much to me."

My chicken was ready. "I have to hang up now, but I'll call you in a while. Love you."

She let out a soft, "Love you too."

The driver behind me honked and I thought about flipping him off, but decided there was too much anger in the world already without creating more ill will. I pulled forward, paid for my order, and then eased back onto the street. Garret's house was on the other side of the island, so I headed toward Rosewood Road—the main road that encircled the island. I flipped on some classical music to calm my mood and tried to push away my worries.

GARRET LIVED IN the shady section of Bedlam. It wasn't exactly the wrong side of the tracks, but it didn't pay to walk through the streets in his neighborhood unless you either had a big, nasty dog, or a big, nasty stick. Or if you were recognized as having a big, nasty reputation.

I pulled up in front of his house and turned off the engine, staring up at the dilapidated shack that passed for a one-story cottage. Once, it may have been beautiful and cozy, but now it just looked like a weathered box that was falling apart. The color was an unappealing mustard, like baby shit, and the paint was peeling off in long flakes. I could sense the ghosts hanging around the house. There were numerous spirits hanging out. Next door gave an explanation for at least some of the spiritual activity. Garret's neighbor happened to be a graveyard, old enough to have lost its luster and even its somber dignity. It just looked like one of the sets from *Plan 9 From Outer Space*.

The house was built on a high slope, so there were two sets of steps leading up to the door—the first led to a wide yard, then another led to a smaller yard surrounding the house. I forced myself to get out of the car and cautiously navigate the broken concrete steps leading to the first sub-yard. The steps were so much rubble, and weeds were thick, growing through the cracks.

But as I approached the walkway directly in front of the porch, something felt off. I frowned, squinting, as wavy lines shimmered in the air.

Damn it—I knew it. There was a glamour over

the property. Pausing, I breathed out slowly, opening my third eye as I whispered a charm for clear sight.

When I opened my eyes, the grunge and grime were gone. In place of the shack stood a charming cottage, with a line of daffodils and tulips surrounding the foundation. I glanced back at the steps—they weren't broken, nor did the yard look overgrown. Instead, the grass was tended, the paint on the cottage was a warm golden color, and the roof didn't look like it was about to collapse.

So that was the way Garret kept people from thinking he might be good pickings. Realizing he probably wouldn't realize I had seen through his illusion, I ascended the porch steps and looked for the doorbell. There didn't seem to be one, so I knocked on the screen door. Another moment and I knocked again. Finally, I heard a shuffling noise and the door opened.

A man stood there. He was dark skinned with silver hair, and he was wearing a turtleneck and a pair of jeans. His hair was long, in thin dreads, and he had clear, hazel eyes. There was something about the way he moved that made him seem incredibly graceful and sinuous. Yep, he was a snake-shifter, all right.

"Garret James?" I eyed him carefully, trying to keep in mind there might be a chance he was mixed up with Essie.

"Who wants to know?"

I cleared my throat. "I'm Maudlin Gallow-glass—"

"Oh, the new leader of the Moonrise Coven." He

let out a soft snort. "What do you want? You here to make me move on? To get me to rethink my ways?"

I frowned, not sure what the hell he was talking about. "I have no clue what you're going on about, but this is a personal matter and I'm hoping you might have some advice for me."

That brought a look of surprise to his face. He paused, tilting his head, then he opened the door. "Come on in, if you like."

I followed him in to find myself in a neat, tidy room. The cottage was as small as it looked on the outside. I could see a kitchenette from where I stood, and two other doors, which I figured probably led to the bathroom and the bedroom. The living room was fairly generous, with one side given over to a small table and chairs, a sofa, TV, and a desk. The other side held what I recognized as a magical workbench and an altar. A wall of books stretched halfway around the room. Everything was neat, everything was orderly.

"You keep a tight ship, Mr. James." I motioned to the table. "May I sit down?"

He nodded, taking the opposite chair at the small table. "What do you want?"

"I heard rumors you may be fluent in Dirt Magic. I thought I'd come ask you myself."

"You may have heard correctly. I work roots and dirt. I know the Moonrise Coven doesn't take kindly to that, but it's what I learned from my grandma and it's what I'll practice till the day I die." His words practically flowed out in song, and I found myself mesmerized by the tone of his voice. Then another veil lifted and I caught a glimpse of his eyes. The pupils were slits, running vertically, dark against a flame-colored background.

"Snake-shifter."

"So you do have full use of the sight. Not many can tell at first, though I know rumors run the town." He eased back in his chair, grinning at me. "I know my kind aren't always welcome."

I laughed at that. "Garret—over the years I've found over that most of us are unwelcome at one point or another. I'm really not here to complain. If Linda had a beef with you, well...until I see a problem, I'm not looking for one."

"What do you need, Mad Maudlin?" He leaned forward, his eyes bright. "You see, I've heard a little about *you*, too."

There was no way to ease into it. If he was working with Essie, she'd know I was on to her after this, but that wouldn't be the first time I had to play a hand at face value.

"Somebody cast a hex on me and I need to know how to break it. It's a Dirt Magic curse. They didn't hit my house with it, but they managed to tag a few of my friends and it's caused a lot of heartbreak and difficulty. And you know as well as I do that to break certain hexes, you have to go to the core of the magic involved."

He held my gaze for a moment, then tapped the table three times with his knuckles. A faint light appeared in the air, like a wispy veil, and it floated over to surround me. The moment the light met my aura, it began to glow a faint red. Red as blood.

"You certainly know how to piss off people, don't

you? You've been hexed by a Dirt Witch, all right. A queen, it looks like. If you don't break this curse, I can tell you that it will kill you and your friends."

Chapter 12

A DIRT WITCH? A *queen*?

"I hear tell the local queen of the vampires was a Voudou priestess before she was turned." There was no way to pussyfoot around it.

Garret raised his eyebrows. "I hear so, too, but it's best to steer clear of the undead unless you have some control over them. And nobody has control over Essie Vanderbilt." He motioned for me to stand up. "I hope you don't mind, but I want to make sure you aren't being spied on."

I nodded and stood, holding out my arms. He ran his hands around my aura. I could see the energy flare here and there, but no holes, no telltale voids to indicate that somebody had a psychic phone line jacked into me.

"That good enough for you?"

He nodded. "Yeah, that's fine. Come over to my station." He led me over to his magical worktable and motioned for me to take a seat on the bench next to it. "So yes, there's a Dirt Witch Queen somewhere around. That much I can read from the hex cast on you. I'm not sure if Essie knows Dirt Magic as well as Voudou, but I wouldn't put it past her. Whoever did this to you is a powerful woman. The most powerful workers of roots and twigs are always women." He paused. "So, what *do* you know about Dirt Magic? I mean *really know*. Not what you've been spoon-fed about it."

I shrugged. "It's shadow magic. Heavy in nature."

"That's because it's tied to the soil, to the Earth. Of course it's heavy. But seriously, Dirt Magic can be a harsh mistress when she wants to be. She's not clean and neat, like the magic you work. I can smell the singe of fire wafting off your aura just like I can smell your perfume. You reek of smoke and bonfires and autumn, Maddy. And it's a good scent—I love that time of year. But you're steeped in just as much of a shadow as I am."

I nodded. "True. There isn't a power alive that can't be misused if the wrong person gets hold of it."

"Yes. The main thing is, Dirt Magic can turn really nasty, really fast. I can work up a set of roots that can destroy the average person without blinking. But I don't. Because Dirt Magic, like every type of magic, can be abused and misused, or it can be useful. My grandma used to whip me when I was a boy, when she caught me working roots for my own gain. She'd beat my backside till I couldn't sit down." His eyes were twinkling now.

"Where did you grow up?" I was quickly growing to like Garret James, despite all the warnings. He was honest and direct, and I'd take that any day over somebody who might be more "acceptable" but also more glib.

"Why, down in the Blue Ridge Mountains of Kentucky. But that was a long time ago. My clan— the Blue Diamond Copperheads—were nomadic. People feared us because of our magic. They knew nothing about our abilities to shape-shift. If they had, they would have killed every one of us they could." He paused, then shook his head. "I don't like to talk about my past with strangers, though, so that's all I'll say about that."

I glanced over at his workbench. At least fifty bottles lined the shelf behind it, each holding some sort of herb or twig or root. They were all labeled but I couldn't read the language.

"What you need to break the hex for you and your friends is a good dose of whompwater smoke." He shook out several roots, then closed his eyes and tossed them on the bench. After they landed, he opened his eyes and began to examine the pattern in which they had fallen.

"Whompwater?"

"Yeah, it whomps anything it touches, so to speak. The roots tell me I can break this spell, but it's going to take me at least two days to prepare the formula. This isn't something I can rush. I'll be at your place, Thursday evening, shortly before sunset. I'll have what you need."

I took out my purse. "I assume payment in advance?"

He stared at my bag, then at me. "I could easily charge up to a thousand for a hex-breaker of this magnitude, but I won't. I'd rather just say, you owe me a favor, Maddy Gallowglass. One I'll collect later, when I need it."

And with that, he stood, motioning to the door. "Now get moving. I fully believe you can take care of yourself, but it's still not a good idea to hang around here as the day wanes. Besides, if I'm going to have this ready for you, I need to start on it now."

I headed for the door, wanting to stick around and talk to him some more. The man fascinated me. But I also needed the hex-breaker and I didn't have any other alternative at this point. I waved at him as he turned back to his workbench and began sorting through his arsenal of herbs.

I WAS ON the way home when a call came through from Delia, but I was driving and didn't have my headset on, so I ignored it. I'd call her when I arrived home. The house seemed terribly quiet as I approached. Not being able to talk to Aegis had really put a damper on things.

A glance at the clock told me it was three P.M. Crap. The ritual was only a couple hours off and I was in no way ready.

"Oh, hell. I can't believe I'm running so late," I muttered to myself. I raced into the house and dashed up the stairs to take a quick shower. I grabbed my ritual soap and lathered up, trying to relax. The ceremony wasn't so much actual magic as it was ritual theater, but that didn't matter. It had to be real and sincere. We had practiced over the past couple weeks, so I knew the drill down pat, but as I put in a quick call to Sandy while toweling off, I realized that I had no heart for it. Too much had happened the past few days.

"Thank gods you remembered. I was going to mention it before I got off on my crying jag over Bart, but then it just slipped away. I'll meet you downtown at four. Don't be late." She hung up before I could ask her if she had been in touch with the rest of the coven.

I dried my hair, then groaned when I realized my main ritual robe was still at the dry cleaner's. Thank gods I had a backup. I sorted through my closet till I found the deep V-necked dress. It was open down to my navel, with a fastener at the waist, and was that royal blue that slid into purple. I contorted my way into my strapless bra—a long-line version with a deep plunge so that it didn't show—then pulled on my dress.

After brushing my hair and redoing my makeup, I fastened on my circlet. Both silver and bronze, the headdress was a beautiful Celtic knotwork of vines and leaves, meeting in the front to support a crescent moon with a moonstone in the center. I slipped on my ritual rings and my pentacle, and finally, I fastened a thin leather belt around my waist before I attached the sheath for my ritual dagger on one side and a ritual flail on the other.

Giving myself a once-over in the mirror, I

stepped into a pair of ballet flats and swung my blue cape over my shoulders, closing it at the neck with a beautiful gold brooch that Aegis had bought for me.

I let out a long sigh as Bubba peeked into the bedroom. He bounced up onto the dresser and pawed at me. I ruffled his fur, scratching him behind the ears.

"*M-row.*"

"I'll be careful, Bubs. You too. I'll be home as soon as I can. The ritual won't last more than an hour, and the rest of the coven's setting it up now, so I should be home by eight at the latest." I leaned down and kissed him on the forehead. "I'm just glad we broke the spell on you, babe. I love you. Be good and watch over things."

He let out another concerned meow before bouncing off to his food dish.

"Franny! Franny?"

Franny appeared as I dashed down the stairs. She was waiting at the bottom for me.

"I'm heading out. Keep an eye on things. Come into the library with me."

She followed me as I tapped quickly on the keyboard of her computer. I brought up a text messaging program. "You can use the voice commands to text me if anything happens. If it's an emergency— and only if it's an emergency—say 'Emergency Code Red' and it will set my phone off even if I'm in the middle of ritual. Otherwise, I'll check for messages every chance I get. You understand?"

She nodded. "I do. I won't let you down."

"Thanks. You and Bubba have fun." As I grabbed

my keys, I hoped to hell that nothing else went wrong before I got home.

THE TOWN WAS jumping, with everybody gearing up for the celebration. The BCU—the Bedlam Star Credit Union—had cordoned off a section of its parking lot for those of us in the Moonrise Coven, given we were leading the ritual. It was directly across from Turnwheel Park—a large city park that was used for holiday events. During the rest of the year, the city sold licenses to various vendors and events coordinators to hold large-scale productions.

During the spring and summer, the farmers' market ran almost every weekend, and the park was filled with Renaissance fairs. In autumn, the Bedlam County Fair held competitions, including a jam & jelly competition, a pickling competition, and the best baker's competition. Neverfall Academy held its annual spelling bee in the park, along with dances and other events. Thanksgiving saw the community dinner, where all were welcome. The Winter Carnival was a yearly event. And through the year, the Moonrise Coven led rituals for the four of the eight High Holy days. We guided the city through the equinoxes and solstices.

I found the rest of the coven and made sure to put on a good face for them. Tonight was about new beginnings and renewal and a balance of energies between light and dark. I forced myself to focus and leave everything else outside as we discussed the final preparations for the magical ritual we'd be leading.

Sandy and I checked over the altar to make certain everything was there—the ritual sword, with which I would cast the Circle, the chalice and cakes, the incense, and the spell components I'd need to conjure up the butterflies for the end of the ritual.

Finally, satisfied that all was in order, I motioned to the coven and we retreated into a small tent to the side. Everyone was there who was supposed to be: Sandy and me, Tristan, Angus, Terrance, and Tanith. Members of the current Inner Court Council, we would lead the ritual. The other members of the coven—sixteen in all—would take their places throughout the crowds, guiding the townsfolk through the ritual.

An auxiliary group, the Moonrise Drummers—a group of witches who found their magic through music—were there to play for us. Thirteen in number, together they possessed an amazing array of talents. They stationed themselves at the four directional markers and as we neared five P.M., they began to beat out a tattoo, calling the village to ceremony.

We waited until the precise moment, and then I led the other ritualists to the main altar.

The rest of the coven led the townsfolk who had gathered—there must have been a thousand people who showed up for the ritual—into a series of concentric circles around the main altar. The drummers built the tempo and then, when everyone was in place, I lifted the sword high into the air and the drumbeat fell to a hush.

"Welcome to Bedlam's Ostara ritual. We're grateful so many of you could turn out today to help us turn the wheel and celebrate the equinox."

I had a wireless mic clipped to me, and my voice rang out to fill the park, startling even me. This was the first public ritual I had led. Winter Solstice had been spent in transferring the power of the coven to me, and the city had made do with the Winter Carnival.

As I led the ritual, casting the circle with the sword, leading the others as we called in the elements, then guiding a thousand disparate people through the synchronized event, I forgot about my problems. I was able to let go and channel the energy of spring, welcoming it into the town, welcoming it into our community.

By the time we finished, ending in a massive spiral dance, people were singing together, dancing to the drummers, and setting up for the community potluck. The kids were playing games like "Pin the tail on the centaur," and the ever-old favorite, "Crack the whip."

Exhausted by how much energy I had channeled, I let out a long breath and forded through the crowds over to our private tent. Most of the coven was mingling with the public but Sandy, Angus, Terrance, Tanith, and I had all retreated. The entire ritual had rested on our shoulders and now, we just wanted a little time to relax.

Shauna and Kase, members of the Inner Court, brought in plates for us, stacked high with roast beef and macaroni and cheese and other assorted goodies. They returned with glasses of sparkling cider and water, then retreated once again, giving us our space.

"That was a good ritual," Angus said. "Linda was always a little hesitant on leading the community rituals, even though she was more than capable. At least we're done with this till Litha." He glanced at his watch. "I need to go home soon. My wife's pregnant and I don't think it's going to be much longer. I'll see you at the coven meeting next Monday, on the new moon." He found a to-go box and arranged his food in it, then headed out of the tent.

"I should go, too," I told Sandy. "I want to make sure that everything's okay at home. Aegis is still stuck as a bat, and Bubba's alone with just Franny." At least I knew there hadn't been any emergencies, given no texts from Franny.

She stood and reached out, helping me to my feet. I had barely touched my dinner, so Terrance scooped it all into a to-go dish for me, and I gratefully took it, linking arms with Sandy as we headed across the street to the parking lot.

"It's been one hell of a week," I said, as we stopped by our cars. "How's your hand?"

"Doing better. Whatever Jordan did to it, it worked. How's your thumb?"

"Sprained, but on the mend. Oh, I didn't get a chance to tell you. I stopped by Garret's today. I actually really like the guy. He's cagey, but he's smart and he's direct. He's working up some roots to break the hex for us. Told me he'd come by on Thursday, shortly before sunset."

"Thank gods you found a way to break this damned curse." She glanced over at her car. "At least Max was able to save his accounts. So maybe that wasn't from the curse, after all." With a sigh, she turned back to me. "I think I'll go home, too. Jenna's here at the celebration but she's with her class and I don't need to stay since she'll be headed back to school for the rest of the week."

"You really enjoy having her around, don't you?" I grinned. Sandy had far more of a maternal streak than I did, even if she didn't realize it.

"I guess I do. Okay, talk to you tomorrow." She gave me a quick hug and headed toward her car as I gratefully slid behind the wheel of my CR-V. I was more than ready to steer my life back toward normal.

I ARRIVED HOME to find the lights out. The fact that I had probably just forgot to leave them on didn't set well, and as I headed inside I decided I would find some sort of system where I could turn them on with an app from my phone. But as I approached the door, I realized something was wrong. The door was unlocked.

Crap, crap, crap. I was *sure* I locked it, but then again, I wasn't so sure of anything anymore. Had Aegis managed to break the spell? But if he had, why weren't the lights on?

Pausing, I thought about putting in a call to Delia. But then I thought about the crowd control down at the park. Every officer had been on duty tonight and I dreaded pulling them away for what could easily just be my oversight.

Finally, I decided to bite the bullet. I opened the door. I fumbled for the light switch and squinted as light flooded the room. Another moment, and I let out my breath as I looked around. Nothing looked out of place, nothing looked askew.

"Bubba? Bubba, where are you?" I peeked in the living room, flipping on the lights there. Nothing. But as I headed up the stairs, Franny appeared.

"Run, Maddy. Get out now!" She looked frantic. "Bubba's all right, but you have to get out of here—"

"What the hell is going on?" I turned even as I spoke. I had learned the hard way to run when someone said to run. But as I raced down the steps, aiming for the kitchen door, a shadowy figure lurched out from the pantry. It was Thornton, and he stepped between me and the exit.

"Thornton, but...oh crap, you're dead." I began to back up. The staircase leading upstairs was between the kitchen and the dining room, with the door to the basement to their left, at the edge of the kitchen. I began to edge toward the basement. If I could get to the door and slam it, I could lock it from the inside.

Thornton looked a lot worse for the wear. He was back in one piece, but he looked a little akimbo, with some of his parts not quite in all the right places, though it was hard to pinpoint just exactly what was out of joint. At first I thought he might be a zombie—Essie had been a Voudou priestess, after all. But then Thornton smiled at me and I saw the fangs.

"She turned you," I whispered. "I can't believe— how did she do it? You died in the accident."

"I drank her blood before I ever came to work for you. Three times. That's the magic number, Maddy. Drink three times and then, when you die, you end up a vampire." He sauntered my way, or rather—lurched. Again, his limbs didn't seem to be working quite right. But he was moving fast enough to send a chill down my spine.

"Thornton, why are you coming after me? I didn't have anything to do with your death."

"Oh, Maddy, you're delicious and I've heard all about witch's blood." His eyes gleamed as he moved toward me.

Oh shit, that's right. Witch's blood and vampires were a fatal mix—for the witch. But since Essie was his sire, he should be attending her, not chasing me.

"Go home to Essie! She's your maker." I couldn't dodge him and into the basement. He was too fast, even if he was clumsy.

"I'll never give her that satisfaction. I refuse to heed her call."

Even in death, he was trying to run from her.

And then I remembered two things: I could rescind my invitation to get him out of the house, but that wouldn't stop him from waiting for me. Or I could rely on old instincts.

Feeling trapped and not willing to give him a second chance to come for me, I fumbled with the dagger still strapped to my waist. As he lumbered forward, I drew the blade and lunged at him. Just like the dagger I used when I had hunted down vamps, my ritual dagger was silver plated, and like my hunting dagger, the blade was razor sharp.

My aim was still true, and though I might have been out of form, I still managed to thrust hard enough to impale Thornton in the heart. As the blade slid through his flesh, he shrieked once, a loud, angry cry. He reached for me, but then froze as the silver blade fed on the energy of his heart. With a sudden *pop*, he broke into a thousand pieces of dust and ash, slowly scattering to the ground in a pile.

Weakened, I sank to my knees, crouching beside the ashes. A loud "*M-row*" echoed from the basement and I crawled over to open the door, slumping on the floor beside the steps. Bubba came racing out, followed by Aegis, who was still in bat form.

Bubba bounced on my lap as Franny appeared.

"You're all right?" she said.

"Thanks to your warning. You saved my life, Franny. I never would have been prepared for the attack if you hadn't warned me to run." I stared up at her as Aegis landed on the top of my head. It was an annoying feeling to have a bat in my hair, but he wasn't stuck and he knew very well what he was doing, rather than being snarled in the strands.

She glanced over at the pile of ashes. "He let himself in a few minutes before you came home. I tried to text you."

"I had my phone silenced due to the ritual.

Damn it, I forgot to turn it back on."

"I thought so. Bubba used the secret cat door to get into the basement."

We had created a secret cat door that couldn't be seen, so Bubba could escape into the basement if need be. I hadn't told Thornton about it because it was a potential danger for Aegis if someone figured out how to get into the basement during the day while he slept.

"Well, I owe you a debt, that's for certain." I let out a soft sigh, thinking that once again I had better call Delia to let her know what was going on. But I was tired of calling the cops. I was tired of things going wrong. Two days and the hex would be broken and everything would return to normal.

But even as I texted Sandy about what had just happened and then fetched the broom and dustpan to sweep up what had been the remains of Thornton, I couldn't help but think that it wasn't over just yet, and until it was, I would sleep with one eye open.

Chapter 13

NEEDLESS TO SAY, I didn't sleep very well. By the time I woke up, the house was feeling very empty and a little scary. Two days in a row, I woke up without a love note on my pillow, and I realized just how much I missed that. Aegis as a bat had hung out with me till I calmed down, but I had made him return to the basement before I went to bed.

Bubba was stretched on the foot of the bed, waiting patiently. I blinked as I sat up, yawning. My body felt slow. Too much adrenaline the night before after running a public ritual like that had left me cramping and slightly sick to my stomach.

"Hey, Bubs. I don't like what's been happening," I said as he bounced up to crawl into my lap. I leaned over, kissing the top of his ears. "You think I should start working out? If I'm going to be fighting vampires again, it makes sense for me to get back into shape."

The thought of reentering that life was daunting. It had left me feeling scorched, like a dry husk in the wind. But maybe it wouldn't be as bad now. It wasn't like I was planning to cross the country, hunting down vampires like I had before. It simply meant being alert and prepared. And Thornton had taught me how far I had slipped on those factors.

Bubba let out a *"Purp"* as I scratched his ears. "Yeah, I guess I'll hunt for a gym today."

I showered quickly, then dressed in a skirt and tank top. Bubba bounced down the steps in front of me. I fed him, then stared into the fridge. Nothing looked appetizing. The phone rang and I let out a sigh as I answered it. It was the business line.

"Bewitching Bedlam, Maudlin Gallowglass speaking."

"Hi, I'd like to book two rooms for next week. Three days, for four people total. Two couples. My twin sister and I share an anniversary, and the four of us want to explore Bedlam." Her voice was pleasant enough.

"Hold one moment, please. I'll be right with you." I pressed the hold button and headed for my office, leaving Bubba happily chowing down.

As I settled into my office chair and opened my planner, I already knew that the days were clear. I'd canceled the guests for this week and there wasn't anybody booked again until the second week in April. I picked up the phone again.

"All right, when did you want to book a room for?"

"Can you accommodate us for the nights of April fifth, sixth, and seventh?"

"Sure can. I require half the amount up front, and you have forty-eight hours to cancel. I charge a nonrefundable twenty-five-dollar processing fee, though. If *I* have to cancel for any reason, I refund all your money regardless of the date."

I took her name, the names of the other guests, and her credit card information and charged her for three hundred seventy-five dollars. I gave her a confirmation number and sent her an email receipt. As I hung up, I sat back, relieved. At least *something* felt like it was getting back to normal, and by then, the hex would be broken.

Returning to the kitchen, I pulled out the bread and cheese and made myself a grilled cheese sandwich for breakfast. I also made myself a quint-shot espresso and poured chocolate milk into it along with marshmallows and popped it in the microwave. Sixty seconds later and I had a frothy marshmallow mocha.

Sitting down at the table, I called out, "Franny? Are you around?"

She appeared in the doorway. "Is something wrong, Maddy? Are you all right after last night?"

"Yeah, I'm okay." I flashed her a sheepish grin. "I'm just lonely, I guess. Life's been so fucked up lately that I'm feeling a little isolated."

She floated over and did her best to sit down at the table, although she was sitting through one of the chairs rather than against the back of it. I jumped up and motioned for her to move, then pulled the chair out for her to a normal distance so at least she gave the illusion of sitting on it.

As I ate my sandwich and drank my mocha, she watched me. "It's been so long since I ate that I can't remember what it's like."

"What did you used to like when you were alive?"

She tilted her head, a little more to the side than was natural, but then she straightened up, beaming. "Our cook made—I remember now—the cook made the most marvelous rolls. They were some sort of Danish pastry, I don't know their name. But they were sweet buns with a custard filling. I loved those so much. She also made a flourless cake using hazelnut meal. I remember that she used to have one of the men who helped on the estate grind the nut flour for her. And her fudge..."

Franny paused, looking wistful. "Life then seemed so much simpler than life does today. But it wasn't always easy. My best friend married young, four years before I died. She seemed to grow up so fast when the children came. She had three babies by the time I fell down the stairs. Once she confided in me that she wished she hadn't been in such a hurry to marry. She said she was tired and that the children, even with a nanny, were a handful."

I finished my sandwich. "You were engaged, weren't you?"

"Oh no, my mother was trying to make me accept an engagement, but that's what triggered the whole...well...that's partly why I ended up with a broken neck. I ran back to my room because we were arguing, and got absorbed in a book. You know the rest of the story." She gave me one of those *What-else-is-there-to-say* looks.

"Why didn't you want to marry him?"

"He was stupid. He was pig-headed and stubborn and didn't appreciate a woman with a brain. My mother thought I should just marry him and be done with it. But I refused. I wasn't about to let some fool run my life." She narrowed her eyes. "Sometimes, as I watch you and your friends, I think I would have fit in much better during this time period than my own."

"I think you probably would have, too, Franny. Again, I'm doing what research I can in order to free you from this house. You wouldn't believe what it's like out there now." I wanted to free her, and yet I had become used to her and it was comfortable having her around. But I didn't want to see her remain trapped.

"I have an idea of what it's like. Whenever you turn on the TV, I watch. I have a clue what the outer world must be like now. It's amazing, really. Things we never would have dreamed of are happening—both brilliant and horrific." She leaned forward, and her torso cut through the table. At my wince, she pulled back to look like she was resting her elbows on the surface. "Maddy, who do you think hexed you?"

"I'm pretty sure it was Essie. Now, I have no clue what she'll do given the fact I dusted Thornton. She wanted him back." I finished my mocha. "Well, there's not much I can do about it now. She'll have to find herself another boy toy. Part of me wants to know what she used him for, and part of me really,

really doesn't want to know."

I glanced at the clock. "I think I'll go down to the bank and make certain my money is still where it's supposed to be."

She vanished as I stood. I arched my back, and then remembered I was supposed to gather Thornton's things for Essie. After the attack last night, I wasn't quite so eager to do so, but finally I headed toward the maid's quarters where he was staying.

The butler's pantry was off the dining room, and behind that, the maid's quarters. I stared at the door, feeling an overwhelming reluctance to go in. I hated intruding on other people's private lives. But Thornton was gone, dust to dust, and his life was now fair game. Taking a deep breath, I opened the door and pushed through.

The room was neat, that was no surprise, and everything seemed organized in a particular way. I wouldn't have been surprised if I discovered that Thornton had suffered from some sort of OCD. But it was too late to ask.

I walked over to the closet and opened the doors. There, hanging in a neat formation, were three suits, six pair of trousers, and six button-down shirts. Two suitcases were in the corner and I pulled them out, peeking inside. They were both empty. I folded the suits and neatly tucked them in. If Essie wanted them, she'd get them. I was tempted to jam everything into a garbage bag, but that didn't feel like it would have been respectful to Thornton, and until he had turned into a vampire, he had been a likable man.

I found three pair of shoes—two pair of sneakers

and one pair of dress shoes—and added them to the suitcase. At the dresser, I opened the drawers one by one. Underwear, socks, and six polo shirts, all neatly folded. A box of condoms. I packed those away, then opened the bottom drawer. There in the back was a small black vinyl case. I set it down on the bed, and then added two manila envelopes, which were full of pictures, and all of his grooming supplies that were on the top of the dresser. As I stared at the barely full suitcases, it occurred to me that it wasn't much to show for a man's life.

Curious, I sat down on the bed and opened the black case. Inside, I found an odd array of items, including three bottles of spell oil—though they weren't labeled, I could feel the energy wafting off of them—and two scroll tubes, each bearing one scroll. I tapped them out and unrolled them, cautious not to set off any exploding runes or hex work. But neither were trapped, and I examined the writing on them.

It was an old runic script that I had learned when I was young. The first one appeared to be a scroll to create an illusion. The second stopped me cold. It was a protection from vampire glamour. What was the boy toy of a vampire queen doing with a scroll like that? A *human* boy toy, at that? Wondering if Essie knew about the scroll, I dug deeper in the case, but found nothing.

The room still felt like it was hiding something, so I looked around. I poked around the nightstand, finding nothing in particular, and on the closet shelf. Then I glanced at the bed. There was something there—I could feel it. I knelt and peeked under the bed.

Nothing. Not even dust bunnies. Thornton had been a good housekeeper. Then, as I started to get up, I paused, staring at the mattress. *Bingo*. I began feeling my way between the mattress and the box spring and finally, near the foot of the bed, found what I was looking for. It was a thin journal, about the size of a hardback book. I carried it over to the desk in the corner and began to flip through the pages, slowing down as I realized just how old the paper was.

The first dozen or so pages were diary entries with no dates, and I could barely read the script, the hand was so spidery. Then I came to what looked like a spell.

"What's this?" I murmured.

As I puzzled my way through it, I realized that the spell was meant to increase the strength of vampires, but it wasn't any spell I had ever heard of. As I read through it, it dawned on me that the witchery was a form that I didn't recognize, but I could tell that the spell was so complex, if it wasn't cast correctly, it would backlash horribly on the witch.

"This isn't good. I wonder just how powerful Essie aims to become?" I flipped through the remaining pages, finding two more spells.

One involved how to use a witch's blood to make the vampire glamour stronger. That one gave me the creeps because it required seven pints of witch's blood, enough to kill the average-sized witch. Given the blood needed to be fresh and not stored, it was pretty much *Drain her down to cast the spell.*

The third spell was four pages long. I could barely make out the handwriting. Some of the words were familiar, but it felt like it had been written by someone a long, long time ago, long before even my birth.

After a while, my sight began to blur as I tried to puzzle what it was. Then I came to one line and everything became clear:

Follow these instructions, and your vampire will be able to walk under the sun.

Holy fuck. I sat back, staring at the words. This couldn't belong to Essie. In fact, I was pretty sure the spell had to be from someone in the Arcānus Nocturni. Both age and power emanated off of it. So did this mean they found a way to transfer their abilities to other vampires who weren't as old, who hadn't developed the immunity to sunlight?

And *that* thought opened up a horrifying vista of possibilities. What was even scarier was that Thornton had somehow come across the journal and stolen it.

I froze.

Essie was so insistent on getting his effects back. Thornton must have stolen this journal from her, and...in turn...where had *she* come across it? Either she had come across a member of the Arcānus Nocturni who gave it to her, or chances were good she had stolen it from them.

It wasn't Thornton she had wanted back, but the journal. And if she didn't get it, I'd be in big trouble. But if I gave it back to her, I'd be enabling her in ways that could put Bedlam at risk.

I wished I could talk to Aegis—and that he could talk back. I needed some counsel and having a vampire's take on it would be helpful. A vampire that I trusted.

Slowly, I pulled out my phone and called Sandy. She answered on the third ring.

"I have a problem and I need to talk about it, but I don't want to talk on the phone. Can you come over?"

"I have to run errands. How about I pick you up and you can tell me while we're out and about? I'm close to your house. I can be there in five minutes."

I didn't know what to do with the book. I didn't want Essie or her cronies getting their hands on it till I figured out what the next step was. Essie couldn't visit—it was only around ten-thirty, and she couldn't walk in the sun yet. At least I didn't think so. Plus, I had never invited her in. But she could have someone break in. That I could take care of, at least for now.

"Can you give me ten?"

"Sure. I'll see you in ten."

I hung up, then quickly slapped the suitcases closed and zipped them up. I carried the book downstairs to the basement, where I hid it in an old dresser that was beneath a couple of outside picnic chairs. If somebody decided to go through the whole house, they'd have to search for quite a while to find it.

Once upstairs, I locked the basement door and pocketed the key. Then I slipped into the parlor, to the cabinet where I kept my magical supplies. One of these days I was planning on turning part of the parlor into a full-fledged ritual room, but for now, I just kept one side of it free for when I needed to work magic.

I sorted through my prepared spells and found a scroll I had written a month or so ago when I had an afternoon to spare. I unrolled it and began to read the words that would activate the magic locked within the paper.

Circle round this house and land,
Warriors stand and take command.
Let nothing fell cross boundary line,
Let nothing touch this house of mine.
Let nothing harm those within,
Let peace and quiet hereby reign.
By the powers of three times three,
As I Will, So Mote It Be.

There was an immediate hush as the day's energies fell away. Then, one by one, shadow warriors appeared, blending into the walls. Some of them headed out into the cloudy day. I could barely see them, quicksilver flickers against the light. They encircled the house.

I let out a slow breath. The house would be protected until I returned, and so would Bubba, Aegis, and Franny. My magic was strong, and it would take a powerful witch in return to try to break through my barriers. Essie, with her Voudou, might be able to, but she was in her lair for the day. And I doubted if anybody in her employ was as powerful as I was. Essie didn't like competition.

Feeling calmer, I grabbed my purse and threw on a light jacket. As I made sure I had my keys, I once again thought about the journal hidden in my basement. Thornton had balls, that was for sure. To steal something like that from a vampire queen and then stay in the community where she lived? That took guts, especially for a human. But in the end, he had paid for it. And thanks to him, we were all paying for it.

I hurried down the steps as Sandy pulled up. This time, I had double-checked both doors and made certain everything was secure, as well as the windows. Along with the shadow warriors, I had done all I could to protect my home, and sometimes, that had to be enough.

SANDY STARED AT me as I told her everything I had found.

"You're fucking kidding me. Thornton tried to steal something that powerful from Essie? Was he a fool? And by the way, are you all right from last night's little fiasco?"

"Yes, he was a fool. And yes, I'm all right. But I've decided that I should join a gym. Or at least buy some exercise equipment. If we're facing a growing menace from the vampires, I want to be in shape for whatever comes our way."

"I can work out with you—why don't you join my hot yoga class?"

I stared at her, snorting. "Listen, Sandy, you've been doing yoga for what...thirty years? Longer? I mean, you *live* in yoga pants. And you go to aerobics classes. I'd faint dead away if I tried to keep up with you. Consider me a remedial student when it comes to physical education. I don't think I'm going to be disciplined to follow through on my own so while we're out, let's find me a gym and get me signed up."

Sandy gave me the side-eye. "You do realize you're going to have to quit eating so much junk food. I mean, I love my junk food, but I only eat it when we're hanging out. Well, sometimes for breakfast. Moderation, Maddy. You can't live on cupcakes and hot dogs."

"I made a cheese sandwich for breakfast," I protested, but gave it up. Who was I kidding? I had the worst eating habits of anybody I knew, and it was only through the grace of the gods that my body hadn't converted all the carbs to extra weight. I liked my shape—curvy, busty, a nice amount of padding on the hips and thighs, but I knew that my stamina was pretty much on permanent holiday, and my muscle tone had taken a nosedive long, long ago.

"All right, damn it. I'll eat healthier, but I don't like salad."

"You don't have to eat salad. Just add more vegetables and meat, cut down on the starches and sugar, and watch the level of caffeine in your blood."

"You're *not* taking away my caffeine. Or my booze."

She laughed. "No, we'll still party. But maybe we should curtail the once-a-week bashes."

It sounded like a prison sentence, but maybe she did have a point. And it wouldn't hurt for a while to see what happened. "All right. We keep our parties a little less boozy, I'll eat better and maybe even have Aegis teach me how to make something besides a sandwich, and I'll start working out. But I'm not budging on the caffeine. Not yet."

"Well, you can't just throw everything away at once," Sandy conceded. She motioned to a large building up ahead. "That's a good gym and it's close to your house. Why don't we go in and have them show us around?"

And just like that, I found myself in the clutches of a werewolf trainer named Wilson.

Chapter 14

WILSON FAIRHAUL PUT me through a short but gritty set of tests to assess my state. Mortified, I had to acknowledge just how out of shape I was. By the time I left, he had signed me up for personal weight-training sessions twice a week, a low-impact aerobics class, and a yoga class.

He also gave me instructions on what to make for breakfast—a smoothie that had at least a dozen ingredients in it, most of which I had never heard of, and instructions to quit the caffeine by two P.M. each day. He had wanted me to stop drinking it by noon, but I had given him a look that had cowed him into silence.

Sandy stood there laughing the entire time. After that was done, we swept out of the gym, which was one of those Spandex wonder gyms, sans the incessant Euro-tech music that made me grit my teeth. My checkbook had taken a beating and so had my ego.

After the gym, Sandy took care of several of her errands. She dropped off her dry cleaning, and I took the opportunity to pick up mine. She stopped at the health food store, on the pretext of needing a few supplements. But I knew she was giving me the chance to get what I needed. I stared at the list Wilson had prepared for me and finally just shoved it at the clerk.

"Apparently, I'm now a fixer-upper," I said, already mourning the loss of my morning doughnuts and pastries.

"You are nothing of the sort. You'll be surprised by how quickly you respond. The Mad Maudlin I knew back in the day was strong enough to take down ten vampires before breakfast, which—if I remember right—was usually bread and cheese, and maybe an apple if we were lucky." Sandy narrowed her eyes. "We aren't anywhere near old, so don't use that as an excuse. Modern living has made us soft."

"It hasn't made *you* that soft," I muttered as the clerk handed me a package and I swiped my credit card to the tune of two hundred and fifteen dollars.

"That's because I happen to love exercise. But cheer up, at least you have a cute trainer." She winked at me.

I snorted. "Right. That's more of a distraction than a help. But he did seem nice, and as much as I hate to admit it, last night's encounter with Thornton convinced me that I really need a good, solid tune-up, so to speak. Okay, now what?" I was actually happy to be out running errands with her.

It took my mind off what I had hidden down in my basement.

"Well, we can't break the hex until tomorrow night, if what Garret told you is correct. I have to make a stop at Neverfall, so want to come along?"

I had actually never been out to the school, and it seemed like as good a use of the rest of the morning as anything else. "Sure. I called the bank and made sure that everything was set, so I'm good. Will Jenna be there?"

She nodded. "Derry asked if I could pay for Jenna's summer term. She sent me the money and I told her I'd be glad to."

Derry Knight was one of Sandy's socialite friends. The *air-kiss, hug-hug, ladies-who-lunch* crew. Shortly before Winter Solstice, Derry had asked Sandy if she would take over as her daughter's guardian while she went on a worldwide jaunt that was scheduled to last two years. That way, if anything happened to Jenna, there would be somebody who could be reached immediately. Sandy had agreed, and she seemed to be getting into the spirit of pseudo-motherhood. Jenna only came home on select weekends from the academy, and she was old enough to where she really didn't want constant mothering.

Sandy headed for the other side of the island, stopping at an espresso drive-thru. "I know how traumatizing this morning was to you. Go for it. Caffeine is your comfort food now, but don't overdo it."

I stuck my tongue out at her but ordered a triple-shot latte and was about to add a brownie on top of it when Sandy shook her head. I changed my order from a brownie to a banana.

As we pulled onto Rosewood Road, the traffic seemed brisk. The water was choppy today, and in the distance, clouds were rolling in, black and laden with rain. As we zipped along in that comfortable silence of friends who didn't need to talk, I nursed my latte, realizing it would be the last of the day. The banana tasted surprisingly good, and I decided that maybe this wouldn't be such a bad change after all.

"I wish I had had a school like Neverfall when I was young," I said after a while.

"I know. Instead, we had the witch hunters after us." Sandy shook her head. "At least now, even though there's plenty of hate against the PretCom, it's not as prevalent as it was and we can counter it more."

"If humans find out that some vampires can walk during the day, that may change."

"But are vamps really part of the preternatural community?" Sandy flashed me a quick look. "I mean, seriously, I want to know. That's never been fully decided, and who—if anybody—is the one who gets to make that decision? Do humans get to decide who belongs to our ranks? Or do we, as a whole, define the meaning of what it means to belong to the PretCom? And what about humans with psychic and magical abilities? They do exist. Are they part of the PretCom?"

I let out a long sigh. "It's too early for philosophical arguments. But if you want my answer? Yes, vamps do have a right to claim PretCom status. As far as humans with magical abilities, there's a vast difference between being a psychic human, and being born a witch. Our DNA is different—that's been proven. Just like a shifter's DNA is different, and so are the Fae."

"What would that make Franny?"

"She's a ghost. A spirit. She was once human. Ghosts aren't exactly PretCom, because you can be any race and end up as a spirit."

"What about vampires? Most of them were human before they died and were turned."

Sandy grinned as she steered the car around a slow-moving tractor puttering along. The road was long and winding, hugging the outside of the island as it made the entire circuit. It started at the ferry terminal, going around the entire island, and numerous businesses and beaches had sprung up along it.

To our right, the water stretched toward the horizon as the scent of brine and kelp filled the air. The tide was going out, leaving stretches of beach littered with seaweed and shells. They washed up on the quarter-sized rocks that formed much of the region's shores. The rocky beaches were filled in with gravel, and seaweed draped over the driftwood logs that came thundering in on the stormy waves of autumn and winter. The giant logs rolled across the shore, lodging on the beach as reminders of just how dangerous the waters in this area could be.

It amazed me that the Meré could survive in the riptide and the currents that lashed at the edge of the islands, but they did.

Here and there a stray patch of beachgrass sprouted up, shifting the structure of the dunes. The Bedlam Horticultural Society had taken to weeding it out because beachgrass displaced the nests of shorebirds and native foliage. Unfortunately, it was a tenacious plant. The fight against the patches of tall windblown grass seemed to be entrenched for the long run.

I watched the stretch of mudflats, exposed as the tide rolled out. "Makes me think of Fata, you know."

"I know," Sandy said. "You miss her, don't you?"

I pressed my lips together, turning over her question in my mind. Fata had been a force of nature. "I think at times, I do. But she was so chaotic, and so hard to control..."

"You can't control a water spirit. You just can't. Just like you can't control the ocean. She'll do as she wants, and her moods shift on a dime. But...I miss her too."

I shivered as she spoke. "I wonder if she thinks about us."

"I don't know whether I hope she does or I hope she's forgotten us." Sandy shook her head, as if to drive the thought away. "Let's talk about something else, all right?"

I knew why she wanted to change the subject. Fata had been our third—completing our triad of power. And she had also nearly been our downfall. When we last saw her, she was racing out to sea on a wave, her fury bringing up such a gale that more than one ship in the area had capsized. Sandy and I had had to let her go. We had to let her run free without trying to make her fit into our world. And yet…Fata could so easily be like cool rain on a thirsty morning, the comforting embrace of rising mist on a cold autumn day.

Pushing my thoughts of her away, I cleared my throat. "You said Max solved the problem with the clients who were backing away from their deal?"

The frown on Sandy's face vanished. "Yes, and what a relief. It would have been a nasty battle in court because they had signed contracts and he had gone ahead and put in orders based on those contracts. The orders were already under way, so he would have lost a tidy sum of money and been stuck with too much stock. But he worked it out with them to everybody's advantage. I never realized running a clothing business could be so complicated."

I paused, then blurted out, "What the hell am I going to do about Essie and that damned book? I can't give it back to her, Sandy—not with those spells in it. And if I tear them out and give it back to her, she's going to know I've seen it. The minute she gets those suitcases and finds out that Thornton's journal's not there, she'll either figure out I know what's going on, or she'll think he hid it in my house and send somebody to try to find it. Either way, I'm facing one hell of a mess. Times like these, I wish Linda was still here and I could take my problems to her. But now, I'm the High Priestess and I have to make the call."

"You talk to Auntie Tautau yet? She'd be the one I'd turn to."

"I tried, but she was out. On the way home can

we stop at her place and I'll give it another try?"

"Sure. Look—we're almost to Neverfall. It's out on that arm of the island."

Bedlam Island had several stretches of high land that reached out into the strait, long fingers well above the waters so that—unless a tsunami rolled in—they were safe from most of the storms and the high tides. Neverfall Academy for Gifted Students was a set of stone buildings that sat on a thousand-acre campus on the northeastern side of Bedlam Island.

The campus stretched out along the cliffs looking over the water, and a large retaining wall kept students from falling off. There were two branches, one for younger students and one for the students in their teens. The gray stone buildings were paired with the dormitories, also of stone make, that rose like towers behind the main buildings. While there were day classes for some of the pupils living on Bedlam, most of the students lived in the dorms and went home only for vacations.

As we pulled in through the main gates, we could see some of the students were outside practicing soccer. A younger class looked to be having a nature walk around campus. We drove slowly through the winding road leading up to the main administrative building. As we pulled into the lot, parking in the visitors' section, Sandy leaned back and took off her sunglasses.

"You know, we should become more active with the academy. The coven, I mean. We have a lot we could teach them," she said.

I thought about it for a moment. "You're right.

We're living history. We have a lot of first-hand knowledge that today's generation can never experience. Textbooks are one thing, but you cannot begin to impart what life was really like until you've lived through it."

"I'll have a talk with the principal and see if we can work something out. Meanwhile, let's go. It won't take long."

NEVERFALL WAS AS imposing on the inside as it looked on the outside. A labyrinth of staircases and hallways, the interior of the main building, with its hustle and bustle, actually perked me up. The atmosphere felt industrious, and the sight of so many kids hurrying from one class to another made me smile.

I had learned one-to-one. My grandmother had taught my mother as much as she could and then quit bothering until I came along. My mother had been more interested in how she could use a love charm to get somebody to support her. But Granny had seen a spark in me—literally. She told me that when I was still in diapers, I had gotten angry. I held out my hand, crying, and a flame had flickered for a few seconds over my fingers.

Luckily, she had been there to see it, and from the beginning, she had taught me, bringing me into the local coven before I was barely able to toddle around. The high priestess had mentored me herself, and as long as I was home to do my chores, my mother didn't care what I did. In fact, the less she had to deal with me, the better. I had been taught to read and write—illegal in our area, for anyone not of the nobility—and by the time I was ten, I was a whiz at counting sums.

A group of girls passed by, giving us a wide-eyed look. One of them stopped and, in what looked like a spontaneous burst of courage, asked, "Are you Mad Maudlin? We heard she lives on the island, and..."

I blushed. "Yes, I am."

"We're learning about you in history class—about the vampire hunts."

I decided then and there that if Neverfall was teaching stories about me, I should be there to make sure they were correct. "Well, maybe I can visit your class someday."

She blushed again. "That would be waysome!"

Waysome? Deciding to take it as a compliment, I waved as she hurried to catch up with her friends. I followed Sandy into the billing department and watched as she wrote out a check that made me cough when I saw the amount. Apparently, quality magical education didn't come cheap. Another five minutes and, clutching a receipt, we headed back to the car.

As we exited the building, I caught a whiff of some floral scent. It was too early for most flowers, but then we saw that a teacher was showing a class how to make a patch of daffodils bloom. There must have been a hundred flowers in the patch, and as they all opened up at once, the fragrance wafted past us.

"Talk to the headmaster. They're teaching classes about us, so I think we should be there to make certain that whoever wrote the history books got the info correct." I slid in and fastened my seat belt.

Sandy laughed. "I just hope they don't tell the kids about our hundred-year after-party."

Snorting, I agreed. "That would have to be sex-ed class, I guess. Anyway, so everything taken care of?"

She started the ignition and eased back down the driveway. "Yeah, tuition's paid and all is well. Where to next?"

I couldn't think of anything else that was pressing. "Let's drop in on Auntie Tautau. Maybe she'll have some advice for us. The gods know I could use it."

As we headed back to the other side of Bedlam, my thoughts strayed back home. Even with the shadow warriors protecting my property, I wouldn't be comfortable until I had figured out how the hell to deal with Essie and that damned book.

THE AUNTIES WERE a phenomenon onto themselves. They had always been, as far as we knew. They were power incarnate, beyond any witch known, and yet they belonged to no coven, no circle, no group. Ancient—we had never heard of a young Auntie—their origins were a mystery.

Most of them went about in the guise of old women who were seen as no more than the eccentric neighbor down the street, or the crazy cat lady who lived on the edge of the forest. But one mistake, one misstep over the line and the Aunties could twist you up and dice you into hash for breakfast. They protected and guarded those who were necessary to the web of fate, and while they weren't able to intervene when someone upset the balance, they were able to remove people from the path of danger if it was deemed necessary.

Auntie Tautau worked with the Witches' Protection Program, which was much like the human Witness Protection Program—only it protected its members more thoroughly. Once the witches in question were removed from their current life and sent into the tumble of changes that the WPP enacted, nobody would ever find the witch again. In fact, our former high priestess and her daughter had been sent into the program, and all we knew was that they were happy and safe. We would never see them again.

We pulled up in front of Auntie Tautau's house. A cozy cottage, it was nestled in the folds of tangled huckleberry and ferns, rose bushes and vine maple, all surrounded by fir and cedar. A single birch tree grew in the front yard, which was also overgrown.

As we stepped out of the car, Auntie Tautau appeared on the wraparound porch.

The first time I met her, she had been wearing a muumuu, but today she was in a tidy rose-print dress with a wide white bib apron over the front.

She was squat and short, sturdier than anybody I knew, with long gray hair that hung to her waist. Today it was in a ponytail rather than a braid, and she was wearing a straw hat with a pink ribbon. A crow sat on the bow. It blinked at me and I realized that it was alive. The first time I had seen it, I had thought it was stuffed. I was wrong.

"Come, come. I found your note the other day and wondered when you would return." The Irish accent was the same as I had remembered, a thick brogue that rolled off her tongue. She motioned to the door. "Fat raindrops are on the way. Hurry or you're likely to get drenched."

Sure enough, as we hustled toward her door, they began to fall—huge fat raindrops that splattered when they hit the sidewalk. We entered the cottage, and once again, the tidiness of the cottage belied the tangle outside.

"Sit. I have tea on the stove." She vanished through the door to the kitchen.

I glanced over at the fireplace. It was warm and inviting, and the flames crackled along, shifting color as they burned. The room was a kaleidoscope of curios, but each felt secure in its place, like part of a puzzle, and the clutter fell together so seamlessly that it seemed quite organized.

When Auntie Tautau returned, she was carrying a tray with a teapot and three cups. She eased it down onto the coffee table and poured the tea, handing it round. A creamer and sugar bowl, as well as a bowl of sliced lemon wedges, took up the rest of the tray. I added a dollop of cream and then stirred my cup, inhaling the fresh hints of black currant.

"So, you came to me about a problem, and I take it the problem has not been solved?"

"That's right." I frowned. "I'm sorry, I realize that it seems rude. I haven't come to visit since the last time I was facing a crisis." Suddenly, I felt bad, and glanced over at Sandy, who blushed.

But Auntie Tautau laughed. "I'm not offended. We Aunties deliberately keep a low profile. We come to mind when we need to come to mind. As for company, trust me, I have my share and they aren't all seeking my aid. No foul, girl. No foul. Now tell me, what seems to be the problem?"

A sudden wave of relief swept over me. Telling an Auntie about a problem might not solve it, but it felt then like the issue was off my shoulders— that I wasn't the only one bearing the burden. I told her about the Arcānus Nocturni Society, and about Essie, Thornton, and the hex. And then I told her about the book I had found.

"So, you do have a problem indeed. And not one easily compartmentalized. What I *can* do is to take that book from you and keep it for you. I cannot destroy it, but no one will find it here until you decide to give it away, and no one will be able to forcibly evict the knowledge of where it is from your tongue."

I looked over at Sandy. "That means if they try to force the knowledge out of me..."

"You would die before telling," Auntie Tautau said.

"That's a terrifying thought, but also oddly comforting." I could see no other way. It didn't solve my problem with Essie, but it would make certain those spells didn't reach her grubby fingers. But could she find copies of them again without a problem? At first I dithered, but then it occurred to me that if she *did* have easy access to other copies, she wouldn't be so anxious to gain control over Thornton's journal.

"I'll bring it to you this afternoon, before she has a chance to wake up. I'd feel better with it out of my house and in safe hands." I glanced at the clock. "I should go home and get it now."

Auntie Tautau nodded. "A good move. And Maddy, be aware, Essie is no more looking for the spotlight to be turned on her than you are. Her agendas run deep and long, and while she is a problem, she is by far one of the least that you will face in the coming years. There's a tightrope to be walked, and you are firmly on that path."

Great. Just what I wanted to hear. But I thanked her and we headed for Sandy's car. My phone beeped and I glanced at the reminder.

"Crap, I forgot. There's a city council meeting tonight I have to be at. We're endorsing Delia as the mayor officially, rather than as a stand-in." Linda, the former leader of our coven, had also been the mayor of Bedlam. I had no desire to take over that part of her job. By now, Delia had proven herself more than capable.

"Let's go. We'll get the book, drop it off, then I'll take you back home. I don't want you riding alone with that thing until it's safely under Auntie Tautau's roof." Sandy glanced at her watch. "It's well past lunch time. We'll stop on the way back for a sandwich."

My mouth watered. "I want chicken. Fried chicken and don't you tell me it's not good for me. I'm under a lot of stress. I'll forgo a shake, though."

Sandy laughed. "One step at a time, I guess. Chicken it is."

Chapter 15

AFTER STOPPING AT Chicken-Chicken, we hurried back to my house. The shadow warriors were in place, and everything seemed fine. Bubba perked up when I came in, and I realized that with all the commotion lately, he was lonely and still nervous.

I turned to Maddy. "Can Bubba visit Mr. Peabody this afternoon? I hate leaving him here in this colossal house with nobody for company. Franny can't exactly pet him and she seems to think he's more of a piece of furniture than family. I could pick him up after the meeting tonight."

"Sure, I think Mr. Peabody would like that." She glanced down at Bubba. "You want to go hang out with my skunk?"

Bubba let out a chirp, then he said, *"Mrow,"* which pretty much meant *"You betcha, I need love and fun."*

I found his carrier and he willingly jumped inside. If I didn't lie to him about where he was going—no "We're going out for some fun" when I was actually taking him to the doctor—then Bubba was pretty good about the whole transportation issue.

As I darted down to the basement to grab the book, I glanced again at Aegis's door. Once again, a feeling of loneliness swept over me and I realized that I hadn't called the boys in the band to tell them what was going on. They must have been ringing his phone off the hook the night before and I hadn't heard it, since it would be with his clothes in his lair.

I hurried back up the steps and made certain the door was barred. While it meant he couldn't get out unless he figured out how to open Bubba's secret entrance, it also meant nobody could get in. The thought of leaving a bat-door open for him to get outside was tempting, but too scary, given the number of vampire hunters on the loose.

I quickly showed Sandy the book. "That script is ancient. And I'll bet you if you have the paper analyzed, that's going to be at least five hundred years."

"I don't think this is Essie's handwriting," she said.

"It can't be. She's not that old. She was born in 1844 in New Orleans. She had to have ripped off some member of the Arcānus Nocturni. She won't dare let them find out. If one of *those* vampires found out she stole something from them? It would be good-bye, Essie."

"Yeah, well, that would be one way to be rid of

her." Sandy laughed. "I know it's mean to say, but it would be handy to have somebody else take her off our hands."

"You don't want anybody from the Arcānus Nocturni to take her place. Think about it for a moment. A vampire king or queen walking around in daylight, and us being unable to tell who they are? We still don't know what agenda the vamps are brewing in their lairs—or even if there is a general, vampire-worldwide agenda. But even if it's only a local issue, it's bad enough."

"Come on, let's go. I'll bring you back as soon as we drop off the book and Bubba."

Grateful for her company—I didn't want to be driving around with that journal alone, either—I slid into her car again after depositing the carrier in the back seat, along with the suitcases full of Thornton's things. Bubba had curled up and was sleeping peacefully.

We drove back to Auntie Tautau's, where she took the journal from me and shooed me on my way again. Another stop to drop off Thornton's effects at the sheriff's office—where I had hoped to talk to Delia, but she was out—and we headed over to Sandy's.

As we entered the kitchen, Alex came bustling out from the kitchen. Her personal assistant, he was as necessary to her life as air. Alex had been, for a short while, her lover, but they both realized it wasn't going to work and they played together better as boss/employee, and as friends. They hadn't been immersed enough in the relationship for it to color their friendship and so things had returned to normal between them and Alex watched over her like an old mother hen. He was the perfect example of a metrosexual—and was pretty much the gayest straight man I had ever met.

"Maddy, love, you look wonderful," he said, breezing past me. He stopped long enough for a kiss-kiss on the cheek, and a wink, and then immediately was back in motion, a whirlwind of efficiency.

"Max called, he wants you to call him back as soon as possible. I told him to try your cell but he said that he was in the middle of a meeting. The funeral home called—they want to know if you have Bart's obituary ready for the paper. I told them I'd fax it to them by tomorrow. They also asked again if you would consider burial and I told them that if they didn't stop hounding you about it, they'd be left with no client whatsoever. They're as bad as ambulance chasers. Burials are big business, you know, where cremation, not so much. Anyway, I took care of them, and then I also rescheduled your meeting with the board of Sand Witch Delights. I figured you wouldn't have time tomorrow morning because Bart's parents are coming into town for the service." He let out a long breath, suddenly out of words.

"Thanks, Alex. Can you bring Mr. Peabody in? We brought Bubba home for the evening."

Alex suppressed a smile, but solemnly carted in the skunk, cradling him like a baby. He set Mr. Peabody down on the ottoman and I opened Bubba's carrier. Bubba leaped out, alert and ready to play. Sandy and I had arranged several play dates for the pair, and they seemed happy enough together, so we assumed that everything was going fine.

Mr. Peabody waddled up to Bubba and sniffed him, then let out a series of happy-sounding squeaks. Bubba brightened up, reached out, bopped him on the nose, and then bounded away with Mr. Peabody struggling to keep up.

"I guess all is well. I still have a bad feeling that one day Bubba's going to offer Mr. Peabody a wish and...well...we have no clue what kind of mayhem could ensue." I shook my head. "I'm not sure I want to find out, either, but it's all good." Feeling relieved, I headed for the door. "I'd better get home and prepare for the meeting. You're coming, aren't you? As my second in command, you should be there."

"Can I beg off tonight? I have so much to do with the funeral."

"Oh, that's right. I'm sorry. Okay, but I'm calling you after to tell you how it went. Unless you and Max are going to be knocking bits. If you don't answer, I'll leave a text."

She laughed at that. "I wish we were, but tonight is all about preparing for Bart's parents. You'll be at the service, right?" She was smiling but the pain in her voice was raw, and I knew that the moment she was alone, she'd be crying again.

"Of course. I wouldn't miss it, hon. I'll be there to support you. I just wish I could do more."

And on that note, she drove me home.

RELIEVED THAT THE journal was out of the house, I took a quick shower and foraged through the cupboards till I found a can of stew. Figuring it was healthy enough, I nuked it and ate standing up by the sink.

I wanted to go check on Aegis, but it wasn't sunset yet, and he would still be asleep. Deciding that I'd make sure he was okay, anyway, I darted down into the basement. His coffin was secure and he was sleeping on top of it in his bat form. The sun couldn't reach this room, so no matter whether he slept in the coffin or out of it, he'd be okay down here. In human form, he didn't mind. I could see how it would be terrifying—he wasn't strong enough as a bat to lift the lid and get out of it.

I went over to the white board on the wall and wrote a note in huge letters—bats weren't that good with their sight. I wasn't even sure if he could read while in bat form, but it couldn't hurt. I wrote that I had gone to the city council meeting, that Bubba was over at Sandy's, and for him to use the secret cat door into the basement if he wanted to fly around the house. I'd leave it ajar just enough so he could get through. I added "I love you" and a note about tomorrow I'd be picking up the hex-breaker, and that was all the room there was on the board.

Standing back, I knew I had done all I could. Resigned to yet another night of this mess, I left the lights on, returned to the kitchen, grabbed my purse, and headed out for the meeting.

THE BEDLAM TOWN council was made up of the mayor and a number of representatives from the various PretCom races. Leonard Wolfbrane was leader of the Alpha Pack. Brentwood, a rabbit shifter, was the representative from the rodentia shifters. Two members of the Fae Courts—Naia from Summer, and Atcria from Winter—were here. Ralph Greyhoof represented the satyrs. I glared at him and he glared back. Elsa Liftwing spoke for the avian shifters. There were also reps from the werepumas, weretigers, werebears, elk shifters, a member of the Woodland Fae, and a human. I represented the witches as High Priestess of the Moonrise Coven.

Goblins, ogres, and their ilk weren't allowed to sit on the council. While vampires were allowed to live in Bedlam, they were under the rules imposed by the coven and weren't allowed to speak at council. Other more nefarious creatures were deported whenever they were found on the island. They were generally up to no good, and couldn't be trusted to keep to a treaty.

As I entered the room, it looked like everybody else was already there.

"Sorry I'm late. I've been having a lot of trouble lately. Somebody hexed my household." I wasn't feeling in the mood to gloss over matters.

"I heard you paid a visit to Garret James," Leonard said. "Be cautious. He's not all that friendly."

"He seemed fine to me, and what matters most is that he thinks he can break the hex." I slapped the agenda that someone handed me on the table. "Let's take care of the important matters first, all right? Delia? Do you mind? I'd like to call for a vote on keeping Delia as mayor. I'm happy with her. I think we're all happy with her. Delia, are you willing to continue with the job?"

She tugged at her collar. "Well, it's a lot of work, but I can do it. However, I'm going to need to hire another deputy to take up some of the slack over at the sheriff's office."

"That's fine, don't you think?" I looked around. Just about everybody nodded. "Bedlam's budget is pretty healthy. So I motion to make Delia's temporary position as mayor permanent. Next election is in three years." We all knew that the elections were only a matter of formality here on Bedlam, at least as far as the position of mayor went.

"Second the motion," Elsa said, raising her hand.

"Show of hands, please," Naia said.

Everybody but Ralph raised their hands. When the rest of us stared at him, he hesitantly joined us.

"Motion carried. Delia, congratulations, the job is yours for the next three years at least." I reached over, picked up her gavel, and banged it.

She grabbed the wooden gavel away from me, grinning. "Gee, thanks. All right, so that's taken care of. Next on the agenda, we have a request from the neighborhood around Fourth and Yew Streets for a stoplight. Apparently some of the teens like to use the street for racing at night and there are a lot of kids on the block. I recommend we assign someone to conduct a feasibility study on Bedlam as a whole. We've grown by about five hundred over the past couple years, and it might be time to start beefing up our infrastructure. Until then, we can always put in a three-way stop sign at the intersection. Yew ends at Fourth."

As the debate spilled over into stop sign discussions and from there into requests for business licenses and so forth, I lost track of the conversation. By the time the evening ended, I had no clue of what we had discussed, except for the fact that we had voted Delia into office, and also agreed that we needed a three-way stop sign on one intersection, and a roundabout on another.

I didn't stick around for the after-meeting cake and coffee, but headed for the door.

"Maddy? Are you all right?" Ateria caught up with me before I exited the room.

"Not really. I mean, I'm fine, but we've had one hell of a week over at my house and frankly, I can't wait until tomorrow. Leonard's right—I consulted Garret James, and he's making me up a hex-breaker. Until then, I'm just holding my breath and trying to get through this." I paused. One thing I had learned about Ateria over the past couple months was that she was nobody's fool and she didn't cave to popular opinion. "Do you think I'm making a mistake by dealing with Garret?"

She considered the question, then let out a soft laugh. "Maddy, Garret might frighten a number of people around the area, but he's got nothing on the

Winter Fae. We make him look like a cuddly baby and you know it. I think you have to do what you need to in order to protect your loved ones. If hiring Garret brings you peace, don't let anybody stop you. We're all in this life with a limited amount of time and resources—even the Fae, though it may not seem like it. You can't make everybody happy, so you make those happy who mean the most to you."

She wrinkled her nose, then turned away. Naia glanced at her retreating form, then walked over to me. "I know Summer and Winter are always at odds, but I heard what she said and I agree. Garret's not so bad. I met him some time back and while his root magic is rudimentary compared to what we work with, it's effective enough when it needs to be. He makes no pretenses to be anything other than he is. I like his honesty."

I paused, then headed over to congratulate Delia before I left. She was just finishing a sweet bun, and was already on a second cup of coffee. Werewolves seemed to have an uncanny nature for assimilating caffeine. I drank a lot of it, but she swam in it.

"So Garret's helping you?" She glanced at me, a question in her eyes.

I nodded. "Dirt Magic, yes." I debated telling her what I had found out about Thornton's journal. And then, I realized I hadn't even told her about Thornton. I motioned for her to join me in the corner where we wouldn't be overheard. "Last night, Thornton showed up."

"What? But..." Delia stiffened. "Vampire?"

"Vampire, yes. And now, dust. Delia, I know why Essie's so damned insistent on getting his things back. I dropped them off earlier today, but she's not going to be happy." I was struggling with the decision what to tell her about the journal. It wasn't information to be passed out lightly, and yet, she was both the sheriff and the mayor. She deserved to know what was going on in Bedlam. And I had already warned her about the Arcānus Nocturni.

"You look like you're about to throw up," she said.

"That's because...listen. There are two suitcases. When you give them to Essie or her lapdog Shar-Shar, tell her that's *all* I found in his room. That I scoured it, and that's *all that was there*."

Delia regarded me. "What aren't you telling me?"

I shook my head. "All you need to know for now is that I made certain everything Thornton left at my house is in those bags. And if they ask, all we know is that Thornton is dead, that he died in the crash, and that's it. *Get it?*"

"In other words, the last we saw of him was on the morgue table before Essie came to claim the body."

"Exactly. There are things that I need to talk to Aegis about, but I can't till after tomorrow when I get the hex-breaker and can release him from being stuck in his bat form. After that, I'll tell you what's going on and we'll talk about what we can do about it. I've already talked to Auntie Tautau." I paused, shrugging. "I've done what she suggested.

I hope it's enough."

She froze. "Whatever it is, was important enough to talk to Auntie Tautau? Are you *sure* that you're all right, Maddy?"

"Yes...no. I don't know. That all depends on what happens over the next twenty-four hours. If the hex-breaker works, then I can figure out what to do next. If not, then I'll have to start looking into another avenue to handle matters." I gave her a mirthless smile. "I'm glad we voted you in. At least I feel secure in the fact that you are running the show in Bedlam. I'm going home, Delia. I have a headache and I think I just want to crawl into bed."

"All right. Text me when you get home, all right? I just have...I just want to make certain you get there all right."

I promised her and headed out to my car.

THE NIGHT WAS cool, the scent of rain heavy on the incoming clouds. I let out a slow breath as I walked across the parking lot. A number of cars were there still—not only had the town council had its meeting tonight, but as I had passed by the library, I saw that there was some sort of talk or presentation going on there.

I approached my car slowly, not wanting to hurry. I was tired, and the thought of the lonely house with just Aegis in bat form waiting for me wasn't at all beckoning. Franny was fine to talk to for a while, but I missed my sweetie's voice and touch. But then, I kicked myself for the thought. He had it worse, stuck in that form, unable to communicate. He also needed to drink, so I would have to let him out because in bat form, he needed fresh blood and would have to visit one of the nearby farms and drink off a cow or something.

A black van was parked next to my CR-V on the driver's side, and on the other, a large sedan. I would have to squeeze through in order to open my door unless I crawled in through the back. As I stared at the space between the van and my SUV, a sudden noise from behind startled me. I turned to see who was there, and the next thing I knew, my arm stung and I realized that somebody had jabbed a needle into me.

Crap! What the hell is going on?

I thought about yelling, but everything suddenly began to swim. As I opened my mouth, only a few scattered words came slurring out. Apparently, my tongue had forgotten how to form complete sentences, and I couldn't muster enough breath to try to shout.

I staggered forward, trying to open my SUV, thinking if I could just get in and lock it, I could call for help. My purse strap slid off my shoulder and I distantly felt it fall to the ground. The next moment, whoever had stabbed me with the needle was trying to support me.

"He...hel...yo...need..." I realized I sounded drunk. I knew what I wanted to say, but the words wouldn't come out. Everything was becoming blurry, and I squinted as the van next to me started pulling out. Maybe they could help me?

But as the van eased out of the parking spot, the side door opened and I was stumbling toward it, pushed along by whoever had hold of me. I tried to resist, my legs noodling under me. I started to sink toward the ground when another pair of arms swept me up. I found myself staring at a broad chest, clad in a dark shirt and denim jacket. I tried to look up, to see the face of whoever was holding me, but he was wearing sunglasses and some sort of a hat. Hazily, I wanted to tell him that it was nighttime, he didn't need the glasses, but that seemed like it wasn't the right thing to say.

Confused, I rested my head against his chest. He smelled like cigarettes and brandy, and I winced, the stench of smoke making me gag. As he lifted me into the van, I saw three others there, though I couldn't make out any of their features. And then, I was resting on a blanket on the floor, and as I drifted off, I felt someone tying my hands and feet. The last thing I remembered thinking was who was going to tell Aegis where I went, and that it was a damned good thing Bubba was staying the night with Mr. Peabody.

Chapter 16

HOW LONG IT was before I woke up, I don't know. All I knew was that I began to come to, and my arms and legs felt like lead weights, unable to move. I was sitting up in the chair, and my neck ached from my head drooping. I moaned as I lifted my head, longing to stretch. I tried to open my eyes, but they seemed to be stuck shut by goo. My lashes were welded together. I blinked rapidly, trying to pry them open. After a few attempts, my left eye opened, feeling gritty and sore, and then my right one followed suit.

"She's coming around." A woman's voice echoed somewhere behind me.

"I'll tell Essie." Another voice nearby, then the sound of footsteps on what sounded like a stone floor.

Essie. Oh, lovely. Well, at least I knew who had decided to kidnap me. I cracked open my lips, tentatively. "Water?"

I didn't like that the first thing I asked was for a drink instead of demanding to know where I was or that they let me go. Then again, I already knew who had hold of me, and I knew full well they wouldn't just merrily trip along to my side, untie me and say, "Sure, go ahead! Sorry for the kidnapping gig." Asking for water seemed a safe bet.

"Here. Drink slow at first or you'll throw up." The woman who was standing in front of me was wearing a pair of jeans and a turtleneck. She also looked remarkably pale and by the color of her eyes, I knew she was a vampire.

She held a cup to my lips, slowly dribbling the water in. I knew enough to accept that what she was telling me was good advice. So many of the drugs that could knock out a witch were harsh on the system, especially the stomach, and my gut was gnarled in knots. I took a slow sip, let it trickle down my throat, and then another. A third and fourth helped clear the tickle from my throat, and a fifth was just enough to ease the dryness that had formed in my mouth. I knew better than to take a sixth—my stomach wasn't thrilled with the first five.

"So...Essie...?"

"You're at Essie's house, yes. She has some questions for you."

"She has a lousy way of getting my attention."

The vampire gave me a wry look. "Just so you know, Essie has a definite style when it comes to finding out what she needs to know. She told us not to hurt you, though."

The fact that she warned them not to hurt me was either a very good thing—or a very bad thing. She either was concerned enough that she didn't want to piss me off too badly, or she wanted to save the joy of inflicting pain on me for herself.

"What's your name?" I figured I might as well find out what I could, in case I got out of this scrape. I knew what Essie wanted to know, and I wasn't sure just how I was going to convince her that I didn't know. Auntie Tautau had made it so I couldn't be forced to tell, but how far could Essie push me before I gave up the info? And yet, was it really willing when torture was involved?

"Ruby. Why?"

"No reason," I said. "Can I have some more water, Ruby?"

Ruby held the cup to my lips again and I took a few more sips. Finally, I leaned back to look around the room. We were in a small space, but the walls were painted a *lovely* shade of dull charcoal gray, matching the atmosphere. The wainscoting was an off-white. At least it wasn't all blood red and black, but somehow, the muted tones seemed more striking than if it had been a garish-goth. A table and chairs sat to one side, and next to me was a sofa. To my right was a grand arch, leading out of the room. If I leaned forward, I could probably just see what was beyond it.

I was in one of the chairs from the table, from what I could tell, and my arms were tied straight down to my sides, and my ankles were bound. The rope was irritating against my legs—given I was wearing a skirt, and it was chilly enough that

I was rapidly starting to shiver. There weren't any windows in the room, which led me to think it was either an inner room or in the basement. Without any art on the walls and with no real decor, the room felt stark and more like a concrete cell rather than a tastefully done parlor.

"So...Ruby...how long have I been here? How long was I unconscious?"

"You've been here about two hours, and you were unconscious for about twenty minutes before that."

Then I was right—I was in Essie's house. Or someplace close to it. Unless the vamps had developed the power of flight, I was still on the island.

"What did you give me? That stuff's rough on the system."

My chatty nature seemed to have run its course with Ruby. She frowned, shaking her head.

"Rutillite. Now, how about you just be quiet till Essie gets here? Want any more water?"

Rutillite. That was one hell of a powerful drug. Like Novocain, it left the system in a wave. Unlike Novocain, when it suddenly drained out after several hours, the result was a crash and burn that beat any hangover or migraine.

I shook my head. By now, Aegis would be worried—I had left the time on the note when I should be home. But Bubba wasn't there, and how Aegis could contact Sandy or Delia was beyond me.

We waited another ten minutes before I heard the sound of heels on wood. By straining forward, I could see that, beyond the grand arch, was a set of stairs leading up. The footsteps were coming from there. I quickly pulled back. I didn't want to appear too eager, or too concerned. It was probably a stupid ego thing, but I wanted Essie to respect me. Thornton might have been her boy toy but I certainly wasn't going to suck up to her, in restraints or out of them.

Another moment and Essie Vanderbilt entered the room. Essie might not have decked out her hidden parlor with much pomp, but she made up for it. She entered the room in a long dress that swept the floor. It reminded me of a Victorian ball gown, in a shiny champagne satin with black lace overlay that ran up the front. The dress cinched in at the waist, then flowed out over what looked to be a huge hoop skirt. The neck was square-cut, with black lace lining the collar and top of the bodice, and the sleeves were bound at the elbows with the same lace, as well as a poof of lace flowing from the bottom of the sleeves.

Essie's burgundy hair was coiffed into an elaborate chignon, with the sides braided back over loose tendrils that curled down by the sides of her face. The bun was held in place by a cloisonné comb, and her hair seemed frozen so that when she moved, even the dangling curls remained still.

"Maddy, welcome to my house," she said, but there was no welcome in her voice. Her eyes were a neutral brown, ringed with crimson, and she whispered effortlessly between crimson-stained lips. "So nice of you to be able to come."

I stared at her, struck by the absurdity of the words. "You'll pardon me if I dispense with the chitchat, but I don't think being drugged and kidnapped constitutes accepting an invitation."

"Ah, well, a simple matter of semantics."

Trying to suppress a snort, I couldn't help but blurt out, "No, I *don't* think so. If that were the case, every date-rape suspect in the world would be at your door begging you to defend them." I stopped, realizing that I was arguing about the wrong thing. "Essie, why did you have me brought here?"

She leaned down, resting her hands on the arms of my chair, her face inches away from mine. "Oh, darling, I have my reasons."

"Such as?"

Essie arched her eyebrows. She paused, then looked over at Ruby. "Give us a moment."

Ruby nodded, vanishing out the door. Essie waited until she was gone and knelt beside me, her skirts billowing out the sides. Her voice a bare whisper, she said, "Maudlin, listen to me. You must play along for both our sakes. Play the part and follow my lead and perhaps, we both shall manage to stay alive. Cross me, and I'll throw you to the wolves."

I STARED AT her, silent, as I let what she said settle into my thoughts.

Obviously, I was in a lot of trouble, but it seemed to be catching. What the hell was Essie afraid of and what did I have to do with it? It also struck me that nobody knew where I was, so it was going to be up to me to get myself out of this. I quickly ran through my resources. I couldn't text anybody—my phone was somewhere on the ground near my car, along with my purse. That much I remembered.

I couldn't fight Essie while I was tied to a chair. And if I killed her, I'd be facing the rest of her brood. My best bet was to somehow get loose and sneak out. The steps to how I was going to accomplish this were still up in the air. The stairs led up, which meant they were potentially the only portal to freedom, unless there was an underground entrance to this level. Given Aegis had a secret underground entrance, I wasn't discounting the possibility, but frankly, I didn't have the time to find out.

Essie had walked over to the table and she was sorting through a sheath of papers. She glanced at me every now and then, but her attention seemed to be elsewhere. Obviously someone was listening in, considering she had whispered her warning to me, and I didn't have a clue what was going on, so decided the best plan was to keep my mouth shut.

Another moment and she motioned to Ruby, who started untying my ropes. She was carrying a pair of handcuffs and the moment she freed my hands and feet, she wrenched me out of the chair. I thought about trying to fight and run, but I had been sitting so long that my joints and muscles had stiffened to the point of where I could barely move. Before I could stretch, she had my hands behind my back and the handcuffs on.

I shrieked as my sprained thumb took the brunt of her force. "Be careful, you fucking idiot. My thumb's sprained." I caught myself, hoping that wouldn't be enough to set them off.

But all Essie said was, "Maudlin, I expect you to behave, or we'll have to taste some of that delightful nectar that runs through your veins." And with that, she swept out of the room.

Ruby was about my height, and she stared into my face as though she knew what I was thinking. With a faint grin that showed the tips of her fangs, she shook her head as she touched my lips with one finger.

"Remember, no chants, no invocations. Nothing to make me decide that you could use a good spanking." She sounded like she'd very much enjoy it if I did.

I cleared my throat. "Fine. I'll behave."

"Good girl." She grabbed me by the elbow. "Come on, buttercup, let's move."

My legs protested—they had been tied up so long that my left foot had gone to sleep. I let out a groan as I stumbled. Ruby gave me a disgusted look, then with an air of exasperation, she swept me up in her arms. I blinked, but said nothing. Vampires had superhuman strength regardless of their gender. Ruby could knock down a linebacker with her little finger.

I squirmed but she pinched my thigh. The pain was quick and sharp, and I settled down. At first I thought we were headed toward the staircase and my heart jumped. Get me up those stairs and I'd figure out something. But then, I saw that opposite to the stairs going up was a staircase leading down. We turned to the left and I realized that we were indeed heading deeper into the bowels of the house.

By the time we reached the bottom, my mood was sinking as fast as our descent. We were now crossing through what appeared to be a cellblock built of concrete, with a dirt wall at the end. There were cells on either side of the walkway, and some of them had bars that looked to be silver plated. That told me right there, Essie definitely punished her own kind.

We stopped in front of one of the cells and Ruby set me down. I stumbled, but she steadied me until I caught my balance.

"You able to stand now?"

"Yeah."

"You see this cell?"

I nodded.

"That's where Thornton spent the last six months, before he escaped. Essie wasn't very happy with him, you see. He wanted to run off and start a new life, after he had pledged his life to her. He had begged her to turn him and she bit him, then let him drink from her three times. But even the promise of life eternal wasn't enough to make him behave."

I snorted. "Some people are just never grateful, are they?"

"I know you're being sarcastic, but it's truth enough." She shrugged. "Thornton wanted to be king. He wanted Essie's job, as well as Essie herself. In fact, most of us felt that he just wanted her crown. He was a sweet talker, though, polite and so talented, and so eager to help. So she gave him the first part of what he wanted. That's when she found out that he was messing with some of her bloodwhores. One of them showed up pregnant."

Bingo. Thornton had *really* fucked up. Essie was Queen Bee and she wasn't about to put up with her favorite boinking anybody else, especially when he got the woman pregnant.

"Really, now? That certainly answers a few questions." I tried to spur on Ruby to tell me more—the more I knew the better.

She seemed to be warming up to the fact that I wasn't trying to run off. I also had the feeling she was bored and dying to talk to somebody. She pointed to the fourth cell on the left. I counted ten on each side, which meant Essie was either running a much bigger show than we had figured, or she had bought the house from a pervert.

A woman sat on the single bunk in the cell. She was human, I was pretty certain of that, and she was about seven months gone by the size of her belly. She was wearing a tattered dress, very loose, and she was staring at the floor, with a blanket wrapped around her shoulders. I felt incredibly sorry for her, even though I never had understood the desire to be some vampire's bloodwhore. As much as I loved Aegis, the thought of anybody drinking my blood still gave me the creeps.

Speaking of creepy, Ruby was standing at my back. She took a long whiff and I quickly shifted to one side, not running, but putting another step between us. I knew she was smelling my witch's blood. I hoped to hell she'd remember that Essie had said "hands off."

Ruby's fangs were down, but after a moment, she seemed to regain her composure and gave a little shrug, as though she didn't care. "Anyway, that's her. She's carrying Thornton's spawn. I have no clue what Essie has planned for them."

Right now, I wasn't so sure I wanted to know, either. To keep a pregnant woman down in conditions like these seemed appalling, but vampires weren't the best of hosts even when they were in a good mood. Piss one off and you got what you asked for. I wondered why Ruby had brought me here, but when she steered me toward one of the cells, I thought she was about to lock me in.

"Oh no, I'm claustrophobic!" I didn't want to be stuck in a cell. Chances were she'd lock me in an anti-magic zone.

"Oh, stop whining. I'm not locking you up, so don't get your panties in a wad. Not yet." And with that, she pushed me through to the door beyond.

I HADN'T NOTICED the door on the end before, but now Ruby stepped through it, dragging me behind her. I glanced around. We were in a good-size chamber and by my best calculation, we were underground, well away from Essie's house. In fact, I'd bet we were somewhere in the woods. Which meant that if I escaped down here, I'd have to race all the way back to the staircase, then up the *next* staircase, and somehow make it to the front door without being caught.

The room into which we had entered was set up as a throne room, which made sense, given Essie was a vampire queen. I guess I had never thought before about whether the vamp royalty actually held any sort of court. Apparently, they did.

The throne against the back wall was uphol-stered in a rich gold velvet, and to either side, tapestries covered the walls. Here, the light was brighter, coming from a huge crystal chandelier overhead, and I squinted at the wall behind the throne. Beneath one tapestry, I thought I could make out the outline of the bottom of a door.

In front of the throne was a low bench with railings on both sides. "That's where you kneel in front of the queen," Ruby said.

"I don't kneel in front of anybody," I grumbled.

"You will if I say you do."

To either side of the chamber was the gallery, with rows of chairs behind thick red velvet ropes. The ropes were attached to brass poles, like at a movie premiere, and the chairs were set at a kitty-corner angle to have full view of the throne. Tapes-tries covered most of the walls. They were old, but well taken care of, but all in all, the throne room felt sparse—not at all like Essie.

Ruby hauled me front and center toward the bench and I was prepared to protest, but then she dragged me beyond it, toward the throne. I tripped over a fold in the carpet and fell against her, knocking both of us down. As we faceplanted on the red velvet that covered the concrete floor, I was grateful for the cushion of carpet. Still, I reached for my nose, which felt bruised.

Ruby sputtered. "You're really pathetic, aren't you?" She dragged me back up on my feet. "If I untie your arms, will you stop being such a klutz?"

"I'll do my best. It's not easy walking with my hands behind my back." I glared back at her.

"You try any funny stuff and I'll hogtie you and carry you over my shoulder. Got it?"

I nodded. I'd behave, at least until I had a good opportunity to escape.

Ruby started to poke me in the chest, then stopped. I was wearing my silver pentacle. She frowned at it. "You witches and your silver."

"I like it." I smiled a big old smile at her.

Sputtering, Ruby unlocked the handcuffs.

I behaved. I wasn't quite ready to run yet—I had to get my bearings first. She motioned for me to bypass the bench and we headed toward the throne itself, veering off to the left. I now had a good view and the chandelier showered enough light in the room that I could definitely see the outline of a door.

Wherever it went, we appeared to be heading there. If it went further into the underground labyrinth, escape was going to be a problem.

"Straighten up." Ruby prodded me in the back as we approached the tapestry. From close proximity I could see the cloth was hanging from the ceiling, not against the wall, and there was a wide-enough space behind it to allow easy access to the door.

Ruby cleared her throat as she opened the door. "Kneel before the Queen of the Pacific Northwest Vampire Nation!" She went down on one knee, dragging me with her, as we entered the room.

WE WERE IN a private chamber, in front of a wide table. There were chairs around the table, and standing behind one of them was Essie, with a spindly vampire on one side of her and a dark stranger on the other. I realized he was a vampire as well, but there was something different about him. Spindly vamp reminded me of a tall, thin Charlie Chaplin—sans the humor. The other man was dressed in a black suit, and he carried a bowler hat. His look could freeze hot water.

Essie was in her champagne dress still, but now she wore a crown, and carried a large fan that matched her dress. She motioned for us to stand and enter. "Sit."

Ruby pushed me toward a chair and I hesitantly sat down as I kept my eyes on the vampires across from me. Ruby was seeming safer by the moment. But as I caught Essie's gaze, she gave me a long warning look. What the hell was going on? There was definitely something rumbling below the surface.

The strange vampire's gaze fixated on Essie. He looked haughty, far more than I knew Essie would allow from her subjects. He was about average height, with jet black hair plaited in a braid down to his lower back, and when he spoke, his words held some sort of a faded accent though I couldn't place it.

"I trust we will get to the bottom of this matter

now?"

A veiled look of anger flashed through her eyes, but she nodded. "Now that Maudlin has the energy to join us, yes, we will. She's sorry it took her so long, but she's been laid up with some sort of malady."

What the hell? I stared at Essie, getting ready to say that I wasn't exactly here under my own volition, but beside me, Ruby tensed. She still had her hand on my shoulder and now she dug in her nails and I swear, she drew blood. I tried to shrug her hand off, but she ignored the attempt.

"Good," the vamp said. "Because, if we don't, you do realize I will be forced to drag the both of you in front of..." His voice trailed off, but the warning in it was all too apparent.

What was this? So Essie really was in trouble? And whatever it was, I was apparently her comrade in arms.

"For now, Kayo, I expect you to accord me the privilege of holding this meeting in the manner in which I see fit. In the process, I trust you will see that I've told you everything that both Maudlin and I know about the matter." Essie's cool demeanor vanished, and she lowered her voice. "I will brook no threats in my own kingdom, do you understand?"

Kayo, whoever he was, let out a soft chuckle. "Very well. Carry on."

And with that, Essie Vanderbilt nodded at me. "Maudlin can fill in the blanks. She'll verify that not only did Thornton deceive her, but that he was in possession of the journal you seek, and that he, not I, was the one who stole it."

And with that, my stomach hit the ground and I promptly vomited onto the table.

Chapter 17

KAYO LET OUT a grunt of disgust. Ruby jumped up and, in a blur, was back with a cloth to wash up the table, as well as a glass of water for me, and a mint.

Essie smiled softly. I was surprised she wasn't upset but then she said, "See, I told you Maudlin was feeling under the weather."

Not sure whether to laugh at her ability to turn on a dime, or to cry because I knew what was going on and who Kayo was, I let Ruby clean me up and then drank the water and ate the mint. The last of the sedative—or whatever it was they had used to knock me out—felt like it was trying to work its way out of my system.

Kayo rolled his eyes. "Whatever the case, let's get on with it."

I cleared my throat, then finished off the water. Essie was up shit creek without a paddle, and so was I, if he decided he didn't believe us.

"Very well. Maudlin, will you verify that you hired Thornton, and when?"

Apparently, the ball was in my court. I thought fast. "I hired him, yes. It was on October eleventh, I believe. I had no clue he was part of your stable at the time. He answered my advertisement for a housekeeper." I tried to choose my words carefully. If this was what I thought it was, I could easily slide the noose around both our necks.

Essie paused, then nodded. "Did he ever tell you he had been part of my entourage?"

I snorted. "I don't keep track of your love life, nor of your comings and goings, Essie. Thornton never mentioned it to me." I figured I had to make my answers realistic, even if I was trying to lie through my teeth.

Essie arched her eyebrows. "Yes, well...perhaps you'll tell us what happened when he arrived. I *assume* you helped him unpack?" She put a stress on the words and I hoped to hell I was reading her correctly.

"Um, yeah, I did." At her nod, I continued. "He only had a couple suitcases with him." I paused, then decided to run with my intuition. "Well, he mostly unpacked. But he had one box that he set to the side, and he asked if I owned a safe. I don't, so he said he'd find someplace else to keep it. I don't know what was in the box, but he seemed to be protective of it."

"Did he ever tell you what was in the box?"

Kayo stiffened, focused on me. I tried to remain unreadable. Luckily I could see both of them because I knew that if I so much as flickered over to Essie to look for a cue, he'd be on me. She shifted, just slightly enough to tell me that this was a make-or-break point.

"No. I didn't ask, either. I don't pry into people's personal affairs."

One beat. Two, and Kayo leaned back just enough to indicate that he was buying it.

Essie paused, then asked, "After he died, when you packed up his things to return them to me, was that box still in the room?" Her gaze was unnerving.

I froze, scrambling over the potential responses. Both Kayo and Essie were poised, waiting for my answer. I shook my head.

"No, I didn't see it anywhere. But then, I didn't expect to."

"Oh?" Kayo asked.

"No, because the day he died, he went out to run some errands and he was carrying the box with him. I assumed that he either gave it to someone or that it was destroyed during the crash that ended his life."

Essie visibly relaxed, deflating as a relieved look flashed through her eyes. "When did you find out he had been working for me?"

I licked my lips. "Shortly before he died. I swear, if I knew he was still in your employ, I never would have hired him." And that was the truth.

Essie turned to the strange vamp. "You see? It's as I told you. Thornton accompanied me to the castle the weekend before he ran off. Your records will show that. During the day, he must have bro-

ken into your study and relieved you of the journal.
We had so much luggage that I never noticed it
and when we arrived home, he unpacked. The next
evening, I woke to find he was gone. I thought he
was out running errands. It didn't occur to me that
he had run off till the next night, when he didn't
appear and we found his closet cleaned out."

This went against everything Ruby had told me
about Thornton being stuck in a cell, but I wasn't
about to bring that little fact up just now.

Kayo leaned back in his chair, crossing his arms.
"So the man is dead and no longer available to
answer my questions. I thought you would have
already started the process of turning him into a
vampire? Favorites are usually accorded the status."

Essie frowned, but inclined her head. "As I did,
but he turned while in the morgue. He escaped,
showed up at Maudlin's house in search of witch's
blood, and she staked him."

"That's true. I had just returned from the Ostara
ritual and I had my dagger with me. He attacked
me and I dusted him." I shrugged. "If you want his
ashes, they're in my trashcan. You can probably do
some sort of spell to figure out it was him."

Kayo rubbed his temples, looking pained. "I see.
Then I suppose I'll have to take your word for it
that he left your house with the journal?"

I bit my lip and played a bold move. "You can
come over and search for it if you like. I very much
doubt you'll find anything."

Apparently, that was a good-enough play to put
it to rest.

"No, I trust that you're telling me the truth when you say it's no longer in your house." He regarded me closely, then turned to Essie. "As for you, the next time you're asked to one of my affairs, you'll kindly leave your bloodwhores and sex slaves at home. I have more than enough to share. Very well," he said, suddenly straightening up and sounding all official. "We're done. For now. But both of you, watch yourselves."

And with that, he swept out of the room without saying good-bye.

Essie leaned back against her chair, shaken. I had never seen her look anything but pulled together and the fact that he could send her into such a spiral of fear worried me. I decided I'd have to look him up later on.

"Ruby, Joseph, please leave us until I summon you."

The skinny vamp and Ruby left the room. Essie reached into the folds of her skirt and brought out what I immediately recognized as a mandrake root. I had one at home. Any witch worth her salt did. She set it on the table and ran her fingers over it, chanting:

Silence be, silence will be.
No ears to hear, no eyes to see.

Another moment and it felt like a dampening field had closed down over us. She was skilled, all right. She regarded me quietly for a moment.

"You have saved our lives...for now."

"You stole that book from him. I can't believe

you'd pull something like that on the Arcānus Nocturni. Don't you realize just how dangerous they are?" Before I realized what I was doing, I had launched into her. "How did Thornton escape? Ruby showed me your prison block and pointed out his baby mama, whom you have locked up in there."

Essie waited until I finished. "Are you quite done?"

"Well...yes, for the moment. No, actually, I'm not. You kidnapped me off the street for this? Why didn't you just come ask me yourself?"

"First, it was a time-sensitive matter. I had no notice Kayo was arriving until I woke up and found the note. I didn't have time to go round and round with you, so I sent someone over to the meeting, where I knew you would be. Consider that my official invitation."

"Your official invitation could get your minions staked." I rubbed my head. "I'm really pissed at you about this, but for now, we'll let it go. You stole that book from the Arcānus Nocturni? What the hell were you going to do with it? Go gallivanting around in the daylight and make yourself the target of every wannabe Buffy in town?"

Essie *tsk*ed away my concern. "Why would I worry about them when I have the real hunter under my nose? You're far more dangerous than any two-bit vampire hunter out there. I know your past, I know what you did to my kind." She leaned forward, her eyes glowing. "But the fact is, no, I did not intend to use those spells for myself. I was planning on destroying it."

I froze. Had she just said what I thought she said? "You were going to destroy it? Why?"

"For precisely the reasons you mention. If vampires gain a foothold during the day, we'll be hunted down and exterminated. At least the human world has some feeling of superiority, given our inability to walk under the sun. But if vampires start showing up in daylight, then we're suddenly a much bigger threat than we were before. I've heard rumors, girl. I've heard rumors that several members of the Arcānus Nocturni were planning to use the magic on a number of vampires, to bring them into the fold. Usually, it takes thousands of years to reach the state of walking in the sun and few vamps ever get to that point. And by then, most of them keep to the shadows and themselves. But the society wants to expand the control we have over the world."

I pressed my lips together. So Essie wasn't all that thrilled with them either. I tried to reason it out. She was on point about becoming greater targets, but there was something more. She seemed almost...*afraid.*

"What are you afraid of, Essie? What's out there that I don't know about?"

Essie held up one finger. "A moment." She crossed to a bookshelf on the other side of the room and sorted through the books until she found what she was looking for. When she returned, she opened the book and slid it across the table.

I pulled it over. The book looked to be a who's who of the vampire world. I was staring at the sketch of a woman, tall and thin, with an angular face so sharp it could have cut diamond. She was holding two leashes, and on the end of those leashes were what looked like twin boys, around three years old. They were on all fours, with crazed expressions on their faces. The entry was in a language I didn't recognize.

"It's heresy for me to show you this. You are, after all, a mortal enemy of my people, even though you claim to love one of them—"

"I *do* love him. He's taught me not all vampires are—"

"Are what...deadly? Oh, he's deadly. Dangerous? Trust me, Aegis is plenty dangerous."

"Fine, so he's just as dangerous as you are. But... he's not as selfish. He doesn't have the same mindset." I cocked my head to the left. "Who is this?"

"I think you'll find that all vampires, in the long run, live by ulterior motives. But suit yourself. The woman you're staring at is the queen mother of all vampires. I won't tell you her name—it's better you don't know. But she's growing antsy. She's growing bored. She wants change, and she's willing to stir up trouble to get it. And she's quite mad."

I still wasn't putting it all together. Maybe my head was still foggy thanks to the drugs, or maybe I was just running on empty today, but I wasn't clear what was going on.

"Spell it out for me, would you?"

"She's bored. She wants a change of the status quo. She's ordered the spells to be used. Trouble is, when a vamp becomes able to walk abroad at all times, they lose the downtime that gives us a chance to pause and contemplate. Sleep for us is very much like sleep for you, it's just dictated more strongly. And then, there's the problem with mortals finding out. And there's another issue." Essie paused.

"That being?"

"Young vampires are like young men with a full testosterone load. They are immersed in their newly found sense of power. They want to prove themselves the strongest, most dangerous, most deadly." She leaned forward, the cool smile dropping away. "All vampires are deadly, but young vamps are quite often...killers."

"And young vampires who don't have the restrictions of only being able to come out at night..."

"Precisely. Their already bloated egos will be uncontrollable. They'll challenge the older vampires like myself. Most would lose, but right now, the vampire nation works mostly in harmony. The Arcānus Nocturni have always kept to themselves, only nominally participating. But an event recently changed that. Their morning star was struck down."

I felt the blood drain out of my face. "Oh fuck. You don't mean..."

"Precisely. What you did at the chalet? The ramifications are still rippling through the society. Rumors that you're walking with your silver stake again are spreading. *She's back*, they're whispering. *Mad Maudlin's back in action*, they're saying."

"That was self-defense." I realized just how this was going to play out. No matter what the truth was, I had set into motion a revolution among the vampires.

"I know it was, Maddy. I know what happened. I'm not blaming you, but the fact is, your actions had a butterfly effect on the eldest vampires. They remember the days when they had more freedom to do as they wanted. The days before the treaties and before the PretCom came out of the closet. They long for those days."

"What about *you*, Essie? Do you wish we still lived in that time?"

She laughed, but there was no mirth behind that voice. "Do I long for days I don't fully remember? I was a Voudou priestess. I had more power then than I do now. Do you understand that when you become a vampire, when you're turned, if you're a witch your powers diminish as the vampirism takes hold. Oh, you can still play petty magical games, but Maudlin, right now? You're far more powerful when it comes to magic than any vampire."

"Then just how did you curse me? And why, if you were so worried about Thornton, why didn't you just come to me and tell me what happened? Why go through all the trouble of throwing a Dirt Magic curse on my household? Aegis is still in bat form and I'm having to deal with Garret James in order to break the hex you placed on my home. On *me*!"

Essie froze. "You were cursed by a Dirt Witch?"

"Yes, and it's well known that Voudou and Dirt Magic often go hand in hand."

"Trust me, Maddy, I didn't cast any spell on your household." She looked worried as she took the book back from me and put it back on the shelf.

"You're sure it's Dirt Magic?"

"I'm sure. The doctor verified it. And we had to destroy the brooch to lift the curse off Bubba." I stopped, suddenly aware that she was telling the truth. Vampires were good at lying, but I was good at telling when I was being lied to. And unless Essie herself was under a curse, she couldn't fake the expression that had slid across her face.

"Crap."

It was the first time I had heard an obscenity fall from her lips. I almost snorted. "You're really telling me the truth. If you weren't the one who cursed me, who was?"

"That's something you very much need to find out. Dirt Witches are more vengeful than vampires." She played with the mandrake root. "Now, before we wrap this up, let me ask you an equally awkward question. Where did you put the book?"

I stood, quite ready to get the hell out of here. "I don't know what book you're talking about."

"Check, and mate, then."

"Tit for tat?"

"Colder than a witch's tit," Essie said, laughing. "One last bit of advice. Don't ever think I'm your worst enemy. I'm no fan of yours, but I can stand as a liaison between an uneasy truce and all-out war. As long as I hold my throne, no one will take it from me. At least, no one I won't fight tooth and nail against."

I understood the nuances. I couldn't let Essie lose her throne. Feeling trapped the same way Linda had been trapped, though with very different circumstances, I nodded.

"Heard and noted. But also note this: the Moonrise Coven is the backbone of this island and will always be. If you want to be part of the makeup of Bedlam, you need to play by our rules. Then, perhaps, we can find a way to work together. I'm not Linda. Never forget that."

"As well, heard and noted." Essie held up the mandrake root and blew on it. A wisp of mist ran through the air and once again, it felt like time moved, and like we were part of the outer world again. "I'll have Ruby escort you back to your vehicle. Thank you for accepting my invitation." She pressed her lips together but I could tell she was smiling.

Ruby returned as Essie called for her. The vampire motioned for me to follow her. We walked back the way we had come. As we neared the stairs, Ruby tapped me on the shoulder.

"Listen...I want to apologize. I hope you aren't still sore at us."

I blinked. "You knock me out, kidnap me, and tie me up and you expect me to just shrug it off as though we were just meeting for coffee?"

"Look, I did what I was told. But I kind of like you. I know you're a big-time vampire hunter and all, but I was thinking, if Essie doesn't mind, maybe we could get together and go shopping? Or even get coffee? I don't have many friends here."

I was done and over with Essie and her minions, but Ruby sounded sincere and she had such a plaintive look on her face that I felt like a heel for being ticked that she'd even ask.

"We'll see. Give me some time to cool off."

"I get it."

We drove back to my car. My bag was nowhere in sight. Great. I not only lost my purse, but my phone. Then it occurred to me maybe somebody had found it and turned it in. I motioned for Ruby to head out, and I went into the sheriff's office, feeling decidedly worse for wear.

I glanced at the nearest clock. It was almost five A.M. Lovely. Aegis was probably worried sick. As I rounded the corner, Delia came barreling down the hallway, in full SWAT gear with several cops behind her. She skidded to a stop in front of me.

"Where the hell were you? We were just headed over to Essie's to break down the joint in an attempt to find you. A couple people saw you being abducted into a black van and the license plate was traced back to someone at her house."

I let out a long breath. This was going to be a long night and a long explanation, and given what Essie had warned me we were up against, I was going to have to convince Delia that we were better off with her in Bedlam than we were with her out of the city.

With the wistful thought of bed and sleep, I followed her into the office to give her the rundown on what had happened.

Chapter 18

SANDY DIDN'T APPRECIATE the early morning call, but she needed to hear what I had to say, and I really didn't want to repeat it again. I was tired, hungry, and still feeling clobbered by the after-effects of the damned drug they had used on me. But she agreed to meet us and within twenty minutes, she showed up. Her hair was caught in a makeshift ponytail, she had no makeup on, and she was clutching two mega-sized lattes, but she was there.

By the time I finished, I had finally talked Delia out of staking Essie. And I had talked Sandy out of trying to pour massive amounts of coffee into me.

"I haven't even been to bed yet. If I drink caffeine now I'll be a nervous wreck. The Rutillite is just finally starting to fully leave my system."

"You slept while you were drugged," Delia said.

"That's not the same thing!" I sighed, then shook

my head. "So, what this comes down to is that if we try to evict Essie from the town, somebody bigger and badder will take her place. Somebody who might be in league with the Arcānus Nocturni."

"Did she tell you where this vampire queen lives?"

"No. Nor did she tell me her name, but the picture...the picture was scary." I stared at the doughnuts on Delia's desk. I wanted a maple bar or three, and I wanted it *now*, but I also knew that sugar on top of the drug and all the adrenaline wouldn't exactly make me feel my best.

"Who the hell cursed you, if Essie didn't? And do you believe her?" Sandy slumped in her chair, nursing her drink.

"That's what I'm wondering. Who the hell could have it in for me? Besides Essie and the Arcānus Nocturni, who have I pissed off in the past couple of months?"

"Ralph. You were in here three times complaining about him, twice which resulted in me serving him with a ticket. Once for the fireworks, and don't forget the speeding." Delia shrugged. "Granted, he deserved those, and I would have gone after him about Snow White, but I don't think he's feeling all that friendly toward you."

I thought about it. Ralph and I were definitely rivals, but I took it in stride. Usually. Then again... something struck a bell. "Wait. I remember something." I ran through when I had chewed him out about Snow—there was... "Honey. Honey! I wonder if she could be a Dirt Witch."

"Who's Honey?"

"A Daisy Duke impersonator. No, seriously, she's one heck of a pinup girl who was at Ralph's when I went over there to bitch at him. She's his cousin, apparently. She was carrying a plant and a trowel, and something about her made me stop. I remember something about her energy set off my alarms, but I was too pissed to really pay any attention."

"If he does have a cousin who's a Dirt Witch, then she might have some wood nymph in her as well. They can be nasty when crossed and if she has any sense of family loyalty, he might have prevailed on her to cast a hex on your house." Sandy shook her head. "What's her name again?"

"Honey. I don't know her last name. But I'm going to find out." I jumped up. "I'm exhausted, but I'm not going home till I find out what the hell kind of games Ralph and Honey have been playing at my expense."

Sandy stopped me as I headed toward the door. "You are going home and you're going to sleep on it first. You know as well as I do that you're about due for an energy crash. Rutillite is fucking hard on your body. You said it's not completely out of your system yet, and you know full well that if you aren't near your bed when it is, you're going to be hurting mighty bad."

I grumbled, but Sandy was right. And I could feel the last bits of the drug starting to dislodge themselves. Like Novocain, when suddenly you started to feel your jaw again and then—in one big rush—it was gone and you suddenly felt the after-ache of the appointment. Only Rutillite's after-ache was more like a sledgehammer to the head.

"Fine. Then you'd better take me home. But the minute I get up, I'm heading to Ralph's." I glanced at Delia. "Don't you dare go over there without me."

"Hey, hexing a neighbor or a business rival is against the law, but it's so hard to prove that I'm not sure I want to bother. But I can have a little talk with him if you want me to. I can tell him that I'm going to watch the both of you from now on, to make nice and quit shitting in the sandbox." Delia arched her eyebrows, smiling.

"Oh, lovely thought. Satyrs are so crude and lewd that I can actually see him doing just that. Taking a poop in my garden as an act of defiance."

"Well, stop badgering him and maybe he'll get bored and stop badgering you."

"He started it." I stopped, suddenly feeling the last of the drug wash out. "Cripes. There it goes. And...right on cue." I rubbed my temples as they started to ache. "Headache incoming. I need to get home and get to bed."

"I'll take her," Sandy said. She gathered my purse and phone from Delia, then looped my arm around her shoulders and helped me out to her car. "Don't even protest. You won't be able to drive in a few minutes. We'll come get your car later. It's early enough that I'll be able to explain to Aegis what happened—he'll understand, even though he's in bat form."

I nodded, feeling queasy again. I needed gentle, bland food and I needed a bed, and I needed them now. Sandy drove me home, checking on me every few minutes.

Feeling like I had been hit by a truck, I finally whispered, "How's Bubba doing with Mr. Peabody?"

"Bubba and Mr. Peabody have developed a brand-new game, and I was going to talk to you about it later but I might as well tell you now. Thanks to Bubba rolling over and Mr. Peabody taking the time to groom Bubba's belly, Mr. Peabody apparently got his wish. He has scent glands again. Alex has been spending the last few hours trying to de-scent the house. Mr. Peabody is going to have to undergo a new operation, which isn't a lot of fun, and Bubba stinks to high heaven."

I groaned. "So not what I needed to hear right now."

"Hey, you asked. I just gave you the 4-1-1 on it. Now, when I get you home, you promise you aren't going to call a cab or do anything stupid and go holler at Ralph? At least until you're feeling better? You need a solid morning of sleep."

"Yeah, yeah, I'll save that for when I really wake up. Maybe Garret will have the hex-breaker ready by then." By then, my head was throbbing to the point of where I couldn't have even stumbled to Ralph's door.

Sandy again helped me inside, where we found a frantic Aegis flying round and round the house, screeching like a banshee. Sandy shushed him as she tried to get me upstairs, but there was no way I could manage the steps and she wasn't strong enough to carry me. So she helped me into the parlor and laid me down on the sofa, drawing the afghan over me. Then, bringing me water, she settled down in the rocking chair by the fireplace as Aegis hovered over me, anxious.

I stared up at him. He was hanging upside down from the lamp that overlooked the sofa, stretching his wings and flapping to punctuate whatever it was he was saying.

"You do realize you're making me dizzy." I squinted, trying to make out the rest of the room, which looked like a badly focused movie that kept moving around. Real Blair Witch stuff.

Aegis squeaked again.

Sandy reached out her finger and he smelled it, settling down. "Listen, dude, Maddy's really fucked up because of the Rutillite, so maybe you could lay off the kvetching until Garret gets here with the hex-breaker."

I groaned, rolling into a ball on my side, huddling against the pillows. "Can you go ask him if he's by any chance finished early?" I couldn't even put in a phone call.

"Yeah, I will, but not till you're sound asleep. It's six-fifteen, so he's probably not going to be up yet."

"How do you know?"

"I don't, but before I go out running any errands for you, I'm going home, taking a shower, and then getting dressed in something a little less frumpy. These are my pajamas, you know." She leaned forward, rubbing my back. "Now go to sleep."

"I can't," I whined. "I'm too tired."

"All right. You wait here." Sandy stood. "Aegis, you...well, if she tries to get up, you fly in the kitchen to tell me. I know what will knock her out."

She headed out of the room.

I tried to doze, but I couldn't get out of my head. I was overexhausted and my body had taken a rough hit from the drug. I coasted, floating on a dizzying sea, until Sandy returned. She was carrying a bowl of instant mashed potatoes.

"Eat this."

I didn't want to eat, but the potatoes smelled good, and my stomach lurched with hunger. She slid her arms around me and helped me sit up enough so I wouldn't choke, then fed me, spoon by spoon, until I had eaten it all.

A blissful warmth began to spread through me, cushioning my nerves, easing the raw, frayed feeling. A few minutes later, my eyes were beginning to close.

"What'd you put in those?" I asked, barely conscious enough to form the words.

"Honey, I had a bottle of Valerio in my purse. I figured it might come in handy."

Valerio was a compound that Andy McGee made at his pharmacy and it rivaled the strongest sleep aids out there. I usually slept just fine so I didn't keep it around, but now, I decided, I was damned well going to. And with that last thought, my breathing eased, and I let myself slink into blessed, dreamless sleep.

THE FIRST SOUND I heard was a woman's voice. Then I heard Sandy answer her. As I blinked, trying to pull out of the fog-shrouded sleep, I picked up bits and pieces of the conversation.

"Please, you know that Maddy would let us stay here if she knew what was going on."

The voice sounded familiar, and then it registered—it was Snow White.

"I know, but she's had a lot of problems lately and I don't want to make a promise without her approval. Can't you find another hotel or something?"

"Ralph cut off my money and took my car keys. It's not even my car—we don't have them in Storybook Land. Since I refused to finish the movie, he told me and the boys to find our own way home."

"How the hell did he manage to conjure you out of the book, anyway? That kind of magic isn't always looked on too highly." Sandy didn't sound all that pleased.

"Ralph's cousin did it. She's some sort of dust queen...dust witch..." Snow paused. "I'm not sure of the technical term, but I didn't even know about her till the other day when I found her in the back yard."

"So, she *is* a Dirt Witch."

"That's right! Apparently she knows all sorts of tricks—"

I stopped listening, staying very still on the sofa. I didn't want Sandy to know I had heard her and Snow White talking. For one thing, I was pretty sure Sandy wouldn't like it if I got up and ran over to Ralph's and had a little talk with Honey. For another, my muscles felt frozen into place, and I needed to get up very slowly and stretch.

"Tell you what. Let me call my assistant and have him take you all out for a drink. Maddy should be waking up soon, and when she does, I'll see what she says. But for now, don't mention the Dirt Witch to her. She's been through a rough patch and really doesn't need to hear that."

Snow agreed, and the next thing, I heard Sandy calling Alex, and then a taxi. She shooed Snow and the boys outside to wait for the cab and, in another five minutes, I heard her heading back toward the parlor. I slowly shuffled around, making noise, and yawned loudly.

"Sandy? Sandy, are you still here?" I sounded like a bullfrog, my voice was still a bit tenuous.

"Right here, Maddy. Are you all right? Do you need help?" She rounded the sofa, and I blinked, rubbing my eyes, and let her help me sit up.

"I'm a little foggy, but overall, a lot better than... what time is it? How long have I been asleep?" I glanced at the clock. It was three-thirty. "Aegis! Did he—"

"Don't worry. I put him to bed in his lair for you. Good thing he trusts me," Sandy said. She rubbed my back and shoulders for a moment. "So, is the Rutillite out of your system?"

I closed my eyes. Stomach—check. Head—a little foggy, but check. Blood felt fine. Everything checked out except for the ache in my muscles, and that would work itself out as I moved around. Finally, I took a deep breath and my lungs felt fine.

"I'm good." I opened my eyes again. "What happened while I was asleep?"

Sandy paused, then slowly said, "Snow showed

up, looking for a room. Ralph apparently kicked her and the boys out when they refused to finish the movie."

I shrugged. "They can stay the night, I suppose." I thought about pushing Sandy into telling me what I had overheard, but decided why bother. I had confirmation of who the Dirt Witch was, and that was the most important thing. "Did you call Garret?"

"Yep, and he's on his way over right now. He told me he'd be here around three-forty-five." Right on cue, the doorbell rang. Sandy motioned for me to sit still. "I'll get it. You just get used to being awake again."

I winced as I stretched my arms over my head. Then I stood and bent over, balancing myself on the edge of the sofa. The back of my legs ached, but the stretching began to ease the tight muscles and by the time Sandy re-entered the room, I was able to stand without pain. I looked a wrinkled mess, but with everything that had happened, I really didn't give a damn.

Garret nodded as he sat down on the sofa next to me. I motioned for him to wait a moment.

"I'll be right back. I had a rough night and just woke up. Excuse me." I turned and hightailed it out of the room, heading for the downstairs bath. I needed to pee, and pee bad. Afterward, I washed my hands and splashed cold water on my face, blinking as it woke me up. I found a brush and tugged the snarls out of my hair, then took a wash-cloth to my underarms, given I didn't have time to run upstairs and take a bath.

Next stop was to pop into the laundry room, where I found a pair of clean jeans and a pair of panties in the dryer, along with a tank top. One of my bras was hanging up on the drying rack, and I quickly slipped out of my wrinkled clothes and into the clean ones. Feeling halfway presentable, I hurried back to the parlor.

Garret was drinking a glass of wine, which Sandy had poured him. She held up the bottle. "Want one, Maddy?"

"No, but I need caffeine, stat. Could you be a love and make me a latte?"

She nodded, setting the wine on the sideboard. "How many shots?"

"Four, and add in a couple shots of chocolate syrup, if you would." I waited till she left, then turned to Garret. "I'm sorry I took so long. I had a run-in with somebody last night, and it left me knocked for a loop today." I wasn't about to explain any further to Garret, given I knew next to nothing about him, and to my relief, he didn't ask.

"No problem. Well, I have your hex-breaker for you." He pulled out a paper bag and brought out a complex series of twigs and roots that had been intertwined in an intricate design. The wood practically glowed and I could feel the magic emanating off of it from where I sat.

"What do I do with it?"

"You burn it and breathe in the smoke. Anybody who got hit by the hex should do so as well. And the smoke will filter around your house and seek out any hidden elements of the hex and counter it."

Sandy reentered at that moment, handing me a large mug. "I heard the last of that. Does that mean that both Max and I should be here?"

"Yes, and Bubba, even though we already broke the spell on him. I want him here just in case there's any residue hiding in that little furbrain of his."

"I'll call Max and have him pick up Bubba and head on over." Sandy moved to one side.

"Will this work on somebody who's asleep?" I was thinking of Aegis. I really didn't want to have to wait another moment to break the spell on any of us.

"Yes ma'am, it will do that. And it's simple enough. There are no incantations or anything else that you need to do to trigger it. The fire will be enough." Garret leaned back with a satisfied smile. "It's rare I get asked to make these anymore. At least around here. When I was younger, I helped my grandma make a lot of them. I guess back then, working roots was a pretty common way to get revenge on someone you were pissed at."

"What do I owe you for this?" I asked. I had asked before, but I wanted to make sure. I wasn't sure where my purse was, but Sandy would know.

But Garret surprised me again by shaking his head. "No charge. One thing I promised my grandma when I moved away was that I would help folks in need. She never worked roots against people—well, maybe a few, but they were always on the wrong end of a deal. She only went after those who took advantage of others. She made me promise when she passed on the power to me that I would use it wisely, and that when someone in real need asked, I would help. And I continue to keep that tradition. I make my money through the spells that shore people up, that nourish their lives." He paused, then laughed and added, "And I grow a mighty fine strain of marijuana, should you ever feel the urge."

With that, he glanced at his watch. "I have to go. I have an appointment with my acupuncturist."

I stared at the hex-breaker. It was alive with energy, practically jumping in my hands. This would do the trick, that much I knew. I walked him to the front door and, when we were on the steps, out of earshot of Sandy, I said, "I found out who the Dirt Witch is. She's new to town, and frankly, I'd like to send her packing. She hexed me for a relative of hers, someone with whom I have a rather fractious relationship."

Garret's eyes twinkled. "Let me guess, a certain inn owner?" At my look, he shrugged. "I keep up on the local news."

"Ralph's cousin...her name is Honey. I didn't even think about her being the one. She's probably part wood nymph, though I can't be a hundred percent sure."

"If one wanted to drive out a Dirt Witch, one might want to find her grounding root. Sprinkle salt on it and it will wilt just like a snail or slug, and the Dirt Witch will leave."

"Grounding root? What's that?"

"Dirt Witches carry pots of soil from their home base with them—a lot like a vampire bringing his coffin with him. If you disrupt the soil, the Dirt

Witch will have to leave because otherwise, they'll lose their anchor to their center of power. And most Dirt Witches only carry one grounding root with them at a time. Otherwise, they're too obvious."

I thought about the pot of soil Honey had been carrying earlier. Maybe it had been just dirt in a pot, or maybe... "How do I find it? Where would she keep it?"

"Somewhere in the room she sleeps in. There's no other way to protect it from either a stray animal chewing on it, or somebody coming along and dislodging it or trampling it. When you find the root," Garret said, lowering his voice, "don't wait. Just tip it over, find the root buried beneath the soil—there will be no plant growing off of it—and salt it with sea salt. Use a good cup at least, for a small pot. Mix the salt into the earth and rub the root with it. The root will look a lot like a scrawny, ghostly white potato. It's usually twisted, as well."

He motioned to the sky. "Really, I have to leave now. But be careful. Even though she won't have time to make another long-term hex—not if you confront her right away—that doesn't mean this Dirt Witch won't be able to attack you. Most are sweet on the surface and hard as nails beneath the veneer. Don't let her throw you off guard or you could easily end up dead."

And with that, Garret headed down the steps to his car. I waved as he drove out of sight. First, I was going to break the curse on my household, and then, I was going after Honey. And if I could, I'd spank Ralph's butt in the process.

Chapter 19

ON THE WAY back inside, I debated whether to tell Sandy what I was planning. But at least Garret had given me some useful information, and I planned to sneak over to Ralph's after dark and deal with Honey. But first, I'd need to break the hex.

Sandy was waiting for me as I entered the kitchen and sat down, nursing my latte. I glanced over at the clock. It was four-thirty.

"How long till Max gets here?"

"He said he'd be here by five. He'll bring Bubba, though I warn you, Mr. Peabody's wish is going to be with all of us for a while. I'm looking for a scent-removal spell, because most of the cleaning products don't work worth a damn." She laughed. "You should have seen it, Maddy. Mr. Peabody was grooming Bubba's belly and then...there was this look. I happened to catch it. Bubba looked like the cjinn that ate the canary and then, *boom*. Mr. Peabody started racing around like he was high on X, and then he started scenting every which way. I think more out of excitement rather than anything else."

"I don't smell much skunk on you."

"That's because I managed to dart out of the way before I got hit too bad, and I used a spell to drive the air the other direction. I blew out two windows with that gust, but it drove the scent out into the yard. Unfortunately, Alex and Bubba were in the way and both got showered."

I decided right there that until Bubba and I had a little talk, that would be the last play date he had with Mr. Peabody. Some people—and creatures—just shouldn't be handed their heart's desire, especially when the answer to the wish came from anybody in the efreeti world, be it an efreet, djinn, cjinn, or any other variant.

I stared at my drink, thinking through what we needed to do. "We have to bring Aegis out of his lair, into the main room of the basement. There aren't any windows in the primary room, so if we shut off the third door, we should be safe enough. I need to burn this hex-breaker and we all need to cloak ourselves in the smoke. I think I'll put it in a wok, light it on fire, cover it briefly to build up the smoke, and then we can all gather around it and take off the lid. That way the smoke should billow up over us all."

Sandy laughed. "Wok this way?"

I stuck my tongue out at her. "Dream on."

"Oh, let's not get started," she said. We could

play the song title game for hours when we were drunk. "So tell me, just when are you going to sneak over to Ralph's to take care of his cousin?"

I blinked. She was on to me. "How did you know?"

"Oh, give me a break. I knew you heard me talking to Snow White. I was just waiting for you to ask me to help you out. Honey's a Dirt Witch and she's a nasty one, at that." Sandy shrugged. "Since we can't really prove anything so that Delia can kick her out, we take care of the matter ourselves."

"Right, but..." I paused, then laughed. "Okay, we need a distraction for Ralph while I search for Honey's pot."

Sandy sniggered. "Oh, I'm sure she'll like that."

I swatted her. "No, really," I said, laughing. "Garret told me how to deal with a Dirt Witch. She's got a pot with her root in there..."

"Oh, sugar, this is sounding better and better." By now, Sandy was leaning back, cackling loud enough that I thought she might have laid an egg. Her laughter was infectious, and by the time we managed to get hold of ourselves, Max was knocking at the back door, Bubba's carrier gingerly in hand.

I let him in, wiping my eyes. I had needed that laugh. The moment I opened the door, a waft of fetid sickly scent washed in, thanks to Bubba, and I groaned, taking the carrier from the weretiger.

"Dude, I'm sorry. I had no idea Bubba was going to be so strongly...scented."

"Yeah, well next time he and Mr. Peabody have a party, maybe they could leave the party favors at home?" Max shook his head. "Sandy said something about a hex-breaker?"

"Right. Come on, let's head down in the basement now that we're all here. Sandy, can you grab the wok?" I picked up the bag with the root charm in it in one hand, and Bubba's carrier with the other. "Come on, twerp. We're heading for the basement."

Bubba stared at me through the carrier, trying to appear blasé. But he let out a little "*Mrrr*" and I realized he knew he had gone too far.

"Yeah, that's right. Always apologize after the fact, just like most men. Can you just once restrain that ticklish tummy of yours? You don't have to go offering everybody the chance to—" I stopped at Bubba's wide-eyed look. I knew full well that he had been entirely aware of what he was doing, yet he looked so hangdog that I felt sorry for him. "Okay, you win. I trust that you're sorry. But buddy, if you want to play with Mr. Peabody, you can't do that again. Promise?"

Bubba regarded me for a moment, then said, "*Purp.*"

"All right. I am taking your word on this." I flipped on the light switch leading to the basement and cautiously descended, making certain that both Bubba and the hex-breaker reached the bottom step without incident. This was the one part of the house that I still wasn't comfortable with, and I never felt entirely secure down here. Neither Aegis nor I could figure out why—he felt secure as far as having his lair here, but there was an odd feel to the basement and I always had the sensation that I was being watched.

It suddenly struck me that Franny might have been affected by the hex, though it seemed like a long shot. "Franny? Franny!"

"Yes?" She appeared at the bottom of the steps. We had already had the talk about not showing up right behind me when I was descending a steep staircase.

"I want you to stick around, if you would. Just in case. I want to make certain that, on the off chance you were affected by the hex, that we clear your aura as well."

She actually smiled at me. "Thank you, Maudlin. I appreciate you thinking about me, given I'm just a ghost." It was both so self-deprecatory but so genuine that I had no clue how to answer.

"Yes, well..." I trailed off as I reached the bottom and she pulled back. We had also already had the *I don't want to walk through you* talk, and she had stopped darting through people.

Max and Sandy followed, brushing a few stray cobwebs out of the way. No matter how hard I tried, I never seemed to be able to keep the basement fully clean. If we finished it and cleared out all the rest of the clutter from years gone by, I supposed it would be another matter. And if we put in a decent ceiling that covered some of the beams...

Shaking my head, I returned my focus to the matter at hand. I set Bubba's carrier down on one of the tables. "Listen, you stay put, all right? I'll let you out in a few minutes."

Bubba ignored me, licking one of his paws. He looked rather disgusted.

"That's what you get for giving Mr. Peabody back his scent glands. I hope you remember your promise in the future." I pointed toward another table that was out in the open, away from anything flammable. "Go ahead and put the wok there."

Sandy did. "What do you want to use as a fire starter?"

"I'm fire starter enough. Max, can you open up one of the folding tables and arrange it near the wok? We have to have something big enough to hold Aegis when he returns to his natural form."

While Max did as I asked, I headed into Aegis's lair and gently picked up the sleeping bat. He was pretty much dead to the world. I carried him gently into the main room and arranged him on the table. Then, motioning for Sandy and Max to stand next to him, I shook the hex-breaker out of the sack and placed it in the wok. It fit just fine. The roots were so intricately woven and so pretty that, for just a moment, I felt sad that I had to burn it. But *only* for a moment. The second I glanced over at Aegis and remembered just how much havoc Honey and Ralph had caused, I was ready to burn the hell out of it.

I was going to have to do something about that damned satyr, but it would take a while to figure out just how to put a stop to the stupid feud. I had been willing to let it rest after the Rachel incident, but he just couldn't let go of the rivalry and jealousy that the Bewitching Bedlam was doing a good clip of business.

"Are we ready? Garret said I don't need to do anything except light the thing on fire and let the smoke seep into the timbers of the house and over those directly affected. Thornton was also a victim—and here I thought Essie had killed him—but he's so much dust now."

"Ready," Sandy said. Max nodded and Bubba, well, Bubba just stared at me. I opened the carrier and he primly stepped out and sat by the door.

I held out my hand and conjured a small orb of fire, the size of a golf ball. The flames tickled my fingers and I grinned as I aimed it toward the hex breaker and let it fly. The glowing white ball hit the roots and instantly ignited them into a quick blaze. The roots caught immediately, flaring up to turn the wok into a blazing cauldron for a few seconds before dying back into a steady burn. I covered the burning hex quickly, leaving just enough space open to draw air into the pan, then after a moment, pulled away the lid.

A billowing cloud of smoke roiled out.

Sandy held out her hands and caused a stir in the air, sending the smoke over me, over Max and herself, over Bubba, and Franny, and Aegis. She closed her eyes, concentrating as she pushed the billowing clouds up toward the ceiling and into the walls. The wood absorbed the smoke like a sponge absorbing water and I could almost hear the house let out a sigh of relief.

I closed my eyes. The smoke was tingling in my aura and it felt like it was eating up a scritchy energy that I hadn't even realized was there. A few moments later, I opened my eyes to see the last of the hex-breaker fall into ashes. I glanced over to the table and there, lying peacefully asleep, was

Aegis in vampire form.

"Aegis!" I knew he couldn't hear me or respond, but I raced forward and leaned down to kiss his forehead.

Bubba let out a *"Purp"* and bounced onto the table, too, licking Aegis's face before rolling around on his back and showing his belly.

"I guess that takes care of that." I turned back to Sandy and Max. "That felt...good. I never expected Dirt Magic to ever feel like that."

"It was like a shower of feathers. It almost tickled." Sandy looked as delighted as I felt. "I can tell that something sloughed off."

"Just like dead skin," Max said, laughing.

"Ewww," both Sandy and I managed to say in stereo.

"I guess that takes care of that. What next?" Max asked. "You want me to help you get Aegis back into his coffin?"

"Yeah, I'd really appreciate that." I slipped into his lair and lifted the lid, raising it back on its hinges. Then Max slid his arms under Aegis's arms and knees and carried him into the room, laying him in the coffin with no sign of effort. Weretigers weren't as strong as vampires, but they were no slouches in the muscle department.

"Thanks," I said, lowering the lid after we straightened Aegis out. "I bet he's going to be one happy vampire when he wakes up."

"Now that that's settled, what are you going to do?"

"Oh, relax, I guess." I didn't want Max worrying about Sandy, and there was no need to tell him what we were planning.

He gave me a skeptical look. "Yeah, right. That's why Sandy asked me to go back to her place and help Alex get Mr. Peabody under control. By the way, have you had a talk with Bubba?"

"Oh yes, trust me. Bubba and I had a discussion about his behavior. I won't promise that it will never happen again, but I do know that Bubba's not happy about smelling like skunk, either." I winked at Max. "So, don't you worry. If you would do as Sandy asked, she'll be home later on in the evening. Oh, and can you take the wok back up-stairs?"

Max let out a "Hmmm" but said nothing more as we returned to the main room in the basement. Sandy was carrying Bubba's carrier and was half-way up the stairs, Bubba following her, playing the sad-kitty-cat-eyes game. Franny was zipping around the basement, looking at the furniture.

"Maddy? Come look at what I found! I forgot this was here." She was standing by a small chest of drawers. It was old, that much was apparent, but the wood was a rich warm cherry and as I knelt to look at it, I saw that it was hand carved, built without nails or glue. The craftsmanship was superb.

"I never noticed this piece. We're still working our way through the labyrinth of antiques down here." I ran my hand over it, wiping the dust off with a nearby cloth.

"This was in my bedroom," Franny said shyly. "I always loved it. My father made it."

I glanced at her. The look on her face was wistful, almost longing. Slowly, I opened the drawers. There were several scarves, some handkerchiefs, and a faded picture. As I picked up the oval painting—it was about the size of a greeting card—I saw that it was a painting of Franny.

"Look, this is you, isn't it? When was this painted?" I held the painting up to the light. It depicted the golden-haired young woman Franny had been at what looked to be a happy moment. She was sitting beneath a tree, a book in one hand, her bonnet in the other, and she was smiling.

Franny pressed her fingers to her lips, studying the picture. "That was painted when I was eighteen. My father asked a local painter to sketch me. He did a remarkable job. I remember that day—I was quite taken by him, but there was no chance of anything ever happening. My mother wanted me to marry for money, and he was French...which would never do. Besides, when he was sketching me, all he could talk about was his home and how much he missed it, and how pretty the women there were compared to American women."

The wistful look vanished. "So I wrote him out of my thoughts and focused on my books, and did my best to avoid the stuffy matches my mother tried to make for me."

I dusted the frame off. "Would you mind if I hung this upstairs? And brought up the chest of drawers? The dresser would be a lovely addition to the parlor."

She blinked. "You would do that?"

"Of course."

"Thanks, Maddy," she said. "Just...thank you."

And with that, she began to get all flustered and quickly vanished from sight.

Carrying the painting with me, I headed back up the steps. I was ready to go dust a Dirt Witch.

I HUNG THE painting in the parlor first thing so I wouldn't forget it. If Franny had to be trapped, at least she could feel like this was still her home. Afterward, Max headed back to Sandy's place, grumbling all the way out the door about how he knew we weren't going to just sit around eating cookies.

Sandy laughed after he closed the door behind him. "He's protective, I'll say that. We're still finding our rhythm. I'm not used to being in a real relationship and he's still coming to grips with the fact that I'm not Gracie."

"That must be hard." I opened a cupboard, feeling peckish. My gaze immediately fell on the cookies, but I decided we needed a bit more sustenance. I opened a box of crackers and pulled a block of cheddar out of the fridge, setting them on the kitchen table along with two bread-and-butter plates and a knife. I added a bowl of green grapes, and motioned to Sandy to sit down. She slid in opposite, taking one of the grapes off the stem and popping it in her mouth.

"It is, sometimes, but he loved her and that's a good thing. I think it would be harder if he hated her, or if she had deserted him or something. As it is, I encourage him to talk about her and he knows

I'm not jealous of what he had with her, and that helps." She paused for a moment to slice off a piece of cheese and put it on a cracker. "And he's been so helpful with the memorial for Bart. That's tomorrow, remember."

I nodded. "Didn't his parents come in today?"

"Yeah, I was supposed to meet them at the airport but sent Alex instead—I wasn't about to leave you alone after what happened at Essie's."

That made me feel awful. "Oh, no—"

"Not a problem. His parents are a handful, anyway. They liked me so much, but when Bart came out to them, they blamed me for it. At least at first. His father was convinced I must have done something horrible to drive Bart into the arms of a man. It took a couple years of Bart working on him before Sal decided that it wasn't my fault and that I had been...well...collateral damage. Then Sal started taking my side in every argument. He even apologized to me once for Bart's 'behavior.' It's complicated." She handed me a slice of cheese.

I sandwiched the cheese between two crackers and ate it. "I'm glad Aegis has no mother for me to deal with, to be honest. Have you met Max's parents yet?"

"Oh, hell no. You'll be the first to know when I do. Now, what the hell are we going to do about Honey?"

I grinned. "I want you to keep Ralph's attention while I sneak around and find Honey's room. She was carrying a pot of dirt. That has to be her grounding root. Once I find it, I'm going to salt it heavily and that should send her home. I'll ask

Delia to have a little talk with Ralph about how, if Honey should appear in Bedlam again, she just might not be entirely welcomed. Maybe I can't prove that she did it, but I know she and Ralph are behind this whole mess. And Thornton lost his life because of it. We can throw in the threat of starting a murder investigation and that should make Ralph back off big time."

"All right. Now, what can I do to get Ralph's attention? And what if he's not working the desk?"

I pointed to her phone. "Call and see who answers."

Sandy held up one finger. "Got something better. My name would come up on Caller ID." She whistled. "Lihi! I need you!" A moment later, Lihi appeared. The size of a Barbie doll, Lihi was a homunculus. Cute as a button, she looked like a tiny woman with bat wings and ears, but she had a rat-like tail. Today, she was wearing a pair of denim cutoffs and a green halter top, and her hair was pulled back in a long ponytail. She was bound to Sandy by a seven-year contract. They were four years in and both enjoying the perks that their agreement brought them.

"Lihi, pop over to the Greyhoofs' inn and find out who's manning the desk. Don't let them see you. Also, while you're at it, do a little snooping. There's a woman named Honey there. She's a Dirt Witch, so be careful. Find out which room she's staying in, if you would."

Lihi nodded. "On it, boss." She blinked out the next moment.

"The more I'm around that girl, the better I like

her." Sandy laughed. "We talked about it last week and agreed to extend the contract, even though we're only a little more than halfway through it. Lihi says this is a better gig than any of her friends have, and she didn't want to take the chance on losing it to another homunculus." After a pause, she asked, "Have you ever thought of engaging one?"

I shook my head. "I've got a Bubba. I don't think I could handle a homunculus as well."

"Point taken."

We were just finished the last of the crackers and cheese when Lihi returned. She sat down on the edge of the butter dish.

"Ralph's on duty. His brothers are locked up again. Both of them. I heard him arguing with one of them on the phone. I guess George and William managed to get drunk a few nights ago and they went careening around a parking lot on Lars's back. They ended up damaging a few cars, so the sheriff locked them up." Lihi shook her head. "Ralph was really mad that he was left to do all the work."

"Poor baby. I'm sure he'll manage to return the favor when they get out. Idiots. And who is Lars?" I asked.

Sandy snorted. "Didn't you know? The dryads up at Durholm Hall invited a group of centaurs to join them there. So we now have several hunky centaurs running around, along with at least two gorgeous topless females. They're high spirited, but I didn't think they'd get involved with the likes of Ralph and his brothers."

I rolled my eyes. "Wonderful. *Just* what we need. Okay, then. So Ralph's the only brother at home right now. That's helpful. What about Honey? Did you find her room?"

"Yes, she's staying on the second floor in the third room right off the stairs. I don't know where she is right now. I looked around to see if I could find her, but she wasn't in sight. I didn't look all the way through the inn, though. I figured it would be better to just get the info back to you." Lihi let out a long breath. "Need me for anything else?"

Sandy held out her hand and Lihi sat on it, swinging her feet over the side. "I might, so don't go far and keep an ear out."

Lihi nodded, then vanished.

"Well, we know where to go, and what to look for." I crossed to one of the cupboards and brought out a box of sea salt. "This should be enough to do the trick. Are you ready to go catch ourselves a Dirt Witch?"

Sandy snorted. "Hey, at least we don't have to stake her." And with that cheery thought, we gathered our things and headed to the Heart's Desire Inn.

Chapter 20

AS WE STARED up at the inn, it occurred to me that Ralph and I were getting dangerously close to starting a feud that could filter down through the ages. The Gallowglasses and the Greyhoofs could easily end up rivaling the Hatfields and the McCoys, and that wasn't exactly the legacy I wanted to leave. But Honey had to go, and then, maybe we could talk some sense into the satyrs and get them calmed down. By *we* I meant Aegis and me, with Delia for backup.

"All right, you ask Lihi to tell me when you have Ralph's attention. He needs to *not* see me sneaking in." I hid behind one of the baby cedars that hadn't had a chance to grow up nice and tall yet. It was six feet high and wide enough so that nobody should notice me from inside the house. If I was lucky, Honey wouldn't come along on the outside to give me away.

Sandy nodded. "Heading in. Leave it to me."

I didn't know how she was going to distract him, and I wasn't sure I wanted to know. Satyrs were horny buggers, and flirting was probably the most expedient route, but somehow, I really didn't think Sandy had any interest in playing that game. We had caroused with satyrs for a long stretch after burning the vampire village, but those days were over and gone.

She headed into the inn and I leaned back against the tree, waiting. It was chilly, and it smelled like rain was coming, but I just ignored the weather, focusing instead on what I needed to do. I had my salt. I had the directions. All I had to do was climb the stairs, find the third room on the right, and then find Honey's grounding root. She couldn't very well carry a planter around with her all the time—it would look too weird.

A few minutes later, Lihi popped onto my shoulder.

I jumped. "Damn, girl, you startled me!"

She giggled. "Sorry, but it just kind of works that way. My mistress has distracted the satyr and it's safe for you to go in now. You might want to be cautious. I think the stairs squeak."

I nodded. "Thanks. Okay, go back and keep an eye on Sandy, if you would. I want to make certain she's safe."

As Lihi vanished, I darted across the lawn and softly took the porch steps two at a time. The screen door also squeaked—I remembered that from before, so I opened it slowly, easing it back so it wouldn't make any noise.

The front door was ajar—Sandy must have left it that way for me and I blessed her heart. I slid inside and, seeing no one at the front desk, quickly crossed the foyer to the staircase leading up to the second floor. I began tiptoeing up the stairs, freezing as a faint squeak echoed on the third step. But nothing happened, and nobody appeared, so I continued up till I was standing in the hall. Now, all I had to do was find Honey's room and we'd be done with this mess.

"Third door on the right." I counted the doors and found myself in front of door number 205. "Okay, Miss Honey, we're going to have ourselves a li'l bit of fun here," I muttered as I took hold of the handle and turned. Except the door didn't open. It was locked.

Hell, now what should I do? I could pick locks but I didn't want to spend the time at it. I could melt the lock but that would be a little obvious and a stray spark might accidentally torch the inn and that wasn't what I was after.

I paused, staring at the handle. Then, before I could figure out what to do, Lihi appeared again. "Sandy sent me back up to you. Ralph's getting bored, but she still has his attention."

A wave of relief flooded through me. "Lihi, can you get in there and open the door? Is there a deadbolt or something you can unlock?"

"Back in a flash." She vanished and a moment later, I heard a soft *click*, and she reappeared. "Try it now."

Once again, I turned the knob and this time it opened. I slipped inside, closing the door behind me. One look around told me this was Honey's room. There were short shorts on the floor, along with a couple tank tops and what I figured were dirty underwear. A half-eaten sandwich sat on the nightstand, and a glass that had probably contained milk, though now just emanated a sour scent. Wrinkling my nose, I pressed forward, looking around for anything that might contain her grounding root.

"Looking for this?" The voice came from behind me.

I whirled to see Honey entering the room. She was carrying the same planter she had been when I saw her a couple days back, and the look on her face was no longer either charming or wide-eyed naive. In fact, she was about as naive as my lecherous cousin Kenny.

"So, you just couldn't leave well enough alone? Ralph's right. You're a nuisance." She moved into the room, her gaze fastened on me.

"And Ralph's an asshole, as are you. We don't care for Dirt Witches much around here. I'll give you one chance. Gather your things and leave." Hands on my hips, I decided that the best defense was a good offense, and I knew how to put up a good offense. "I'm the High Priestess of the Moonrise Coven, and we run this island. Your kind? Not welcome. At least not if they're like you. I know you cast that spell on me."

She moved into the room, holding the planter by her side. I backed away, quickly running over the things I could do. I needed to incapacitate her—hopefully without hurting her—and salt that damned root.

Honey set the planter down on the desk near the door. Her eyes narrowed, she took a step toward me, reaching in her pocket to bring out three roots. Crap. She was going to cast some sort of spell on me.

"I know you're supposed to be leader of the coven and all that, but back home we deal with things a little differently. You messed with my cousin, and I thought you'd learn your lesson with the hex, but no, you're not that smart." The twang in her voice made me wince.

"Honey, your ego's getting away from you." I straightened my shoulders. "Do you have a clue what I can do, sweetheart? Did Ralph tell you *who* I am?"

"Some booze-soaked, washed-up witch, that's all I know." Honey began to braid the roots together, muttering under her breath.

"Put down the roots. All I want to do is send you home, Honey. I don't want to hurt you." I held out my hand, coaxing a flicker out of my fingers. The flames burned steadily and I thought if I could just get the right shot at her, I could knock out her roots without catching her clothes aflame.

But Honey wasn't listening. She kept braiding away and I felt the edge of a shadow push into the room. It was thick and heavy, like smog, and felt dirty in a way that soil never should. It was the shadow of slugs and maggots, and the scent of a fetid earth that had turned sour from decaying flesh. It was reaching out for me, the tendrils of energy looking for something to latch onto. Honey's eyes glowed with a dangerous light, and a snarl of a grin appeared on her face, cunning and foxy.

I condensed the flames into a ball of burning light. "Don't make me use this."

"Go ahead and try," she whispered, almost done braiding the roots. Whatever she was conjuring was almost in the room. At that moment, the door slammed open and Ralph stood there, along with Sandy.

"Ralph, restrain your cousin or I'm going to hurt her." I looked straight at the satyr. "You already sicced her on my household and now one person's dead because of it. Thornton was killed by her hex. Do you really want to be party to that?"

A look of surprise washed across Ralph's face. "Dead? Somebody died?"

"What do you think?" Honey said, not even glancing at him. "I don't play games. You told me somebody was messing with you, I went after them." She went back to whispering her incantation and she came to the end of the roots.

"Stop—don't do it—you don't want this." I increased the size of the ball of flames, holding it up so that Ralph could see. "Stop her."

He began to twitch a little. "Honey, she'll use it."

"She'll have to get through my shadow poppet first!" Honey finished braiding the roots and blew on the poppet. The shadow in the room increased and solidified into a hulking creature that promptly stepped on the bed, breaking it. The beast looked like a tall, narrow dinosaur with a serpentine neck. It was a muddled mass of smoke and shadow, with glistening scales that shimmered through the immediate darkness. Its eyes glowed with a pale amethyst light and its face reminded me of an odd bird—feathered with fur, with a sharply curved beak that had a piercing tip to it. It twisted its head, curving down toward me in one blur of movement.

I let loose with the fire, aiming it not at the creature, but at Honey. She was controlling it, and I was pretty sure that I'd need to knock her off her guard before we could dissipate the shadow poppet.

Sandy let out a string of curses and a sudden gust of wind knocked me out of the way as the creature struck. Its beak shattered the floor where I had been standing.

Ralph cried out, racing forward to drag Honey back but before he could grab hold of her arm, the fire hit her, blazing so bright that the shadow poppet screamed and withdrew. Honey let out a piercing shriek as the flames clung to her, beginning to eat at her clothes.

Sandy body-slammed her, knocking her to the ground and sitting on top of her. The braided roots slid across the floor toward me and I grabbed them up, ripping them apart. The shadow poppet began to flop and flounce as I did so, and I realized I was tearing it to pieces.

Ralph stared at the scene with a look of horror on his face. He grabbed Honey's planter and I tossed him the salt. With a look of mingled sadness and fear, he poured a handful into the dirt and began working it through.

Sandy managed to put out the flames on Honey's shirt, but I got a look at her face and could tell that the Dirt Witch was going to have some nasty blisters. The next moment, Honey jerked away, turning to Ralph.

"How could you? I helped you fight this bitch and you're..." She was beginning to fade, and was almost translucent by now.

Ralph set the pot down. "I never meant for you to kill anybody. I don't...that's not what I do." He sounded heartsick.

"Coward." Honey let out one last snort and, holding her hands to her blistered face, she faded completely away. The last of the shadow poppet vanished with her.

Sandy was putting out stray fires that had started from my spell. I quickly moved to help her, tossing salt on top of the flames. We managed to corral them all before they became a bigger problem. Ralph stared at us, his mouth hanging open. For the first time in a long while, he looked contrite.

I walked over to him. "Listen, Ralph, enough. Just enough of the fighting and the arguing. Because of our bickering, a man is dead. There's no proof that our fight played a part, but you and I both know that Honey's spell was dangerous. And that doesn't even begin to cover the rest of the damage you did. I think it's time we put our feud to rest, don't you? And this time, I mean it."

His shoulders slumped and he hung his head. "I didn't mean for anybody to really get hurt. She said...never mind what she said. I shouldn't have asked her to help." He held out his hand. "Truce?

For real this time?"

I honestly wanted to just stand here and bitch him the fuck out, but I decided that we already had too much collateral damage. "Truce. But see that you abide by it. And don't you ever invite her here again. You want to see her? Go visit where she lives."

"All right." He turned, starting to shuffle away, then stopped. "Maddy? What say we do a joint promotion? Maybe we can entice more tourists if we go in on something together?"

I was about to say, "You've got to be kidding," but stopped myself. "On one condition. You send Snow and the boys home right away."

He squirmed. "There's a little problem with that. I can't. It was Honey's spell and I can't undo it. I don't even know if another Dirt Witch could."

"Great...just great. All right, then—*new* condition. You stop making cheesy porn flicks, you pay for Snow White and her boys to find a place to live and you help them find jobs. Good jobs that they *want* to do." I leaned toward him, hands on my hips. "Do that, and we'll figure out some joint advertising venture, as long as it's tasteful."

Ralph shifted from hoof to hoof, but then just shrugged. "Fine. I'll help them, and until they find a place to stay, I'll make room for them here."

I looked at Sandy. "Are we done?"

She thought for a moment, then nodded. "I think we are."

"Well, I'm not." The voice from the door was one I hadn't heard in a couple of days and had been longing for. I whirled as Aegis came slamming into the room, and before I could say a word, he decked Ralph with a right hook that sent the satyr careening onto the already broken bed.

Ralph groaned, pushing himself up as he rubbed his jaw. "I suppose I deserve that."

"Oh, I'm not done yet," Aegis said, his hair flowing over his shoulders. He wasn't wearing a shirt, and in his leather pants, he looked entirely yummy as his eyes blazed crimson.

"Stop, love. I already had a long talk with Ralph. And we sent his cousin home to where she came from." I stepped between the two men.

Aegis glared at Ralph, but then he paused, staring at me, before he swept me up into his arms. "Maddy, I've missed you," he whispered as he covered my face with kisses. And then his lips met mine, and the feeling of his kiss was all I could think about.

Relieved and grateful that he was all right, I whispered, "I love you."

And Aegis whispered it back.

Chapter 21

THE NEXT EVENING, I entered the Memoriam, which was next to Wyers Undertakers, my arm wrapped around Aegis's. Sandy and Max were there, near the front, and a number of people were milling around looking for a seat. The urn sat on a podium, and I saw what had to be Bart's parents sitting in the front row.

"How's Sandy taking this?" Aegis whispered to me.

"Hard, but Max is helping her through it, and she has me, too. Bart was really a good guy, but his parents wanted him to be the all-American son, and because of that, a lot of people got caught in his deception, and hurt." I leaned on his arm, my head resting against his shoulder. "Aegis, will you come visit Essie with me? She called last night and left a message asking to see me. I know she wants to discuss the situation with the Arcānus Nocturni, and I don't know what to do or say around her. I'd feel better if you were there."

"I'd be happy to, love." He kissed the top of my head. "I wish we could have stayed home tonight. I really didn't enjoy being stuck in bat form, and it's put me behind on rehearsals and a number of things. But most of all, it took me away from you for a couple of days."

We found our seats and settled in. The hall filled up, and Sandy took over, introducing various people who knew Bart and were slated to speak about him. We listened quietly, the mood solemn and melancholy, as people allowed their grief to have its reign. When Sandy was ready for the Cord Cutting, I would lead the ritual, but for now, we were all just a group of people saying good-bye to someone who had been a part of our lives.

I thought about all the people I had left behind, all the people I had lost in my life, and I found myself wondering: what drew us together? Why did we instantly click with some people who became a part of our lives forever, while with others, we moved on and left them behind?

Sandy was in my life from near to day one. We were best friends. Soulmates, of a sort. I couldn't imagine her *not* being part of my life. Bubba, too, was here to stay. And Aegis—he was quickly becoming a fixture in my life. The thought of being without him made me want to cry.

There were others who passed through, and then, like a glimmer of sunshine on a cloudy day, vanished. Tom, my sweet Tom, who was stolen by vampires and roamed in a realm of shadow and fire, forever taken from me.

And then...there were some who walked in twilight, appearing and vanishing at will. We loved them, and yet, we dreaded the thought of seeing them again because when they entered our lives it was on a whirlwind of chaos, and they left a trail of debris and love in their wake. Fata had been one of those.

As the service progressed, I found myself thanking the gods for my life, for Bubba and Sandy, for Aegis and Max and even Delia. As much as I loved playing with fire and power, and as much as I loved the parties and mayhem and exploits that I had lived through, what mattered most were my friends. The family of friends that I had gathered around me. Because when it came down to it, when you stripped away the glamour and glitz, in the end, we had only our deeds to be known by, and the love in our hearts, to walk us through the veil.

~End~

If you enjoyed this story and haven't read the earlier books in my Bewitching Bedlam Series, hop on over and pick up the prequel, BLOOD MUSIC, and the first novel—BEWITCHING BEDLAM. A novelette—BLOOD VENGEANCE—is available for preorder, and the third book—SIREN'S SONG—will be available in October 2017.

If you like dystopian paranormal romance, check out my Fury Unbound Series! FURY RISING (available for $2.99), FURY'S MAGIC, FURY AWAKENED are available now, and the final release in the first story arc—FURY CALLING—will be available soon.

Book 19 of my Otherworld Series—MOON SHIMMERS—is available, and KNIGHT MAGIC, a novelette, will be available in September 2017.

Be sure to sign up for my newsletter to ensure you always get updated on new releases! You can find out more about ALL my books on my web site at Galenorn. com, and in the Biography/Bibliography at the end of this book.

Upcoming Releases
(Subject to Change)

August—December 2017
Fury Calling (Fury Unbound—Book 4)
Blood Vengeance (Bewitching Bedlam—Novelette)
Knight Magic (Otherworld—Novelette)
Siren's Song (Bewitching Bedlam—Book 3)
Witches Wild (Bewitching Bedlam—Book 4)
Tiger Tails (Bewitching Bedlam—Novelette)
Silent Night (Otherworld—Novelette)

Playlist

I often write to music, and here's the playlist I used for this book.

AC/DC: Back in Black; Rock and Roll Ain't Noise Pollution
Amanda Blank: Make It Take It; Something Bigger, Something Better
The Asteroids Galaxy Tour: Zombies; X; Sunshine Coolin'; Heart Attack
AWOLNATION: Sail
Beck: Qué Onda Guero
The Black Angels: Don't Play With Guns; Always Maybe; You're Mine; Phosphene Dream
Black Mountain: Wucan; Queens Will Play; The Way to Gone
Blind Melon: No Rain
Boom! Bap! Pow!: Suit
Cake: Short Skirt/Long Jacket; The Distance
The Clash: Should I Stay or Should I Go
Cobra Verde: Play with Fire
Crazy Town: Butterfly
Creedence Clearwater Revival: Susie-Q; Green River; Run Through the Jungle: Born on the Bayou
David Bowie: Diamond Dogs; China Girl; Cat People
The Doors: Alabama Song (Whiskey Bar); Hello, I Love You; Hyacinth House; Moonlight Drive; My Wild Love; We Could Be So Good Together
Elektrisk Gonner: Uknowhatiwant
Eurythmics: Sweet Dreams (Are Made of This)
The Hollies: Long Cool Woman (In a Black Dress)
Jefferson Airplane: White Rabbit; Plastic Fantastic Lover
The Kills: Nail In My Coffin; You Don't Own The Road; U.R.A. Fever; Sour Cherry; No Wow

Ladytron: Paco!; Ghosts
Lord of the Lost: Sex On Legs
Men Without Hats: The Safety Dance
Nilsson: Coconut
Nirvana: Heart Shaped Box; Come as You Are; Plateau; Lake of Fire
Oingo Boingo: Dead Man's Party; Elevator Man
People In Planes: Vampire
Rob Zombie: American Witch; Living Dead Girl
The Rolling Stones: The Spider and the Fly; Mother's Little Helper; Lady Jane
Shriekback: Underwaterboys; Over the Wire; Big Fun; Dust and a Shadow; This Big Hush; Nemesis; Now These Days Are Gone; The King in the Tree
Simple Minds: Don't You (Forget About Me)
Tom Petty: Mary Jane's Last Dance
Warrant: Cherry Pie

Biography

New York Times, Publishers Weekly, and *USA Today* bestselling author Yasmine Galenorn writes urban fantasy and paranormal romance, and is the author of over fifty books, including the Otherworld Series, the Fury Unbound Series, the Bewitching Bedlam Series, and many more. She's also written nonfiction metaphysical books. She is the 2011 Career Achievement Award Winner in Urban Fantasy, given by RT Magazine.

Yasmine has been in the Craft since 1980, is a shamanic witch and High Priestess. She describes her life as a blend of teacups and tattoos. She lives in Kirkland WA with her husband Samwise and their cats. Yasmine can be reached via her website at Galenorn.com.

Yasmine's Currently Available Indie Books:

Bewitching Bedlam Series:
Blood Music (Prequel novelette)
Bewitching Bedlam
Maudlin's Mayhem
Blood Vengeance

Fury Unbound Series:
Fury Rising
Fury's Magic
Fury Awakened

Otherworld Series:
Moon Shimmers
Earthbound
Otherworld Tales: Volume One
Tales From Otherworld: Collection One

Men of Otherworld: Collection One
Men of Otherworld: Collection Two
Moon Swept: Otherworld Tales of First Love
For the rest of the Otherworld Series, see Website

Chintz 'n China Series:
Ghost of a Chance
Legend of the Jade Dragon
Murder Under a Mystic Moon
A Harvest of Bones
One Hex of a Wedding
Holiday Spirits

Bath and Body Series (originally under the name India Ink):
Scent to Her Grave
A Blush With Death
Glossed and Found

Misc. Short Stories/Anthologies:
Mist and Shadows: Short Tales From Dark Haunts
Once Upon a Kiss (short story: Princess Charming)
Silver Belles (short story: The Longest Night)
Once Upon a Curse (short story: Bones)
Night Shivers (an Indigo Court novella)

Magickal Nonfiction:
Embracing the Moon
Tarot Journeys

For other and upcoming work, see Galenorn.com

Made in the USA
Lexington, KY
13 September 2017